WITHDRAWN

D0459672

DEATH'S HEAD

DEATH'S HEAD

DAVID GUNN

DEL REY

BALLANTINE BOOKS

NEW YORK

Published in the United States by Del Rey Books, an imprint of
The Random House Publishing Group, a division of Random House, Inc., New York.
Published in Great Britain by Bantam Press, a division of Transworld Publishers,
a member of The Random Group Ltd.

DEL REY is a registered trademark and the Del Rey colophon
is a trademark of Random House, Inc.

ISBN 978-0-345-49827-4

Printed in the United States of America

Book design by Jo Anne Metsch

This is my only vow:
However it comes, I will look death in the eye.

—SVEN TVESKOEG

DEATH'S HEAD

PROLOGUE

INDIGO JAXX, general of the Death's Head, wipes sweat from his forehead and straightens the sleeve of his silver-and-black uniform. He hates himself for doing so and knows that he will make someone suffer for his moment of weakness. He's a Death's Head general, after all.

"You understand?"

Raising his head, General Jaxx meets the eyes burning into his own.

"Oh yes," he says. "I understand."

"You find him," says the voice.

The general nods.

"He is nobody. It is important you remember that." The voice has said this before. It is obviously significant. And a response is obviously required.

"Nobodies can be difficult to find—"

"But you will find him?"

"Yes, sir."

Other functionaries give OctoV a wide range of titles. *Great leader, victorious emperor, all-seeing mind . . .* General Jaxx calls him *sir.* So far, OctoV has not complained. In fact, the general is pretty sure he likes it.

"And when I find him, sir?"

"You bring him to me."

"Alive or dead?"

The boy standing in front of General Jaxx smiles and a cold wind blows through the general's mind, eviscerating the last fragments of his self-control. Every meeting is like this. The general has known officers to kill themselves because they cannot bear to come into his presence.

"Alive, obviously," says the voice. "You will test his loyalty, his stamina, his ability to obey orders . . ."

"And if he fails the tests, sir?"

"You will have failed me."

"I will not—" begins General Jaxx.

But it's too late.

The general finds himself standing alone. The last flicker of OctoV's mind offers General Jaxx a sixteen-digit set of coordinates. As the general checks these against a database in his own mind, he discovers the planet in question is a worthless piece of rock at the outer edge of the spiral.

He didn't even know it was inhabited.

PART I

CHAPTER 1

THE CAGE opens at the front, a double loop of chain hinging its door at the bottom. At the top a thicker chain and a fist-sized padlock keep the cage safely shut.

It sits against a dirt-colored wall, a position chosen so the desert sun can broil its occupant. Occasionally a trooper will give the cage a quick glance as he marches across the parade ground, but most men are careful to look away.

Bad luck is catching.

"Drag him out then." The sergeant's voice is raw, almost triumphant. Nodding to his corporals, he points at the cage. As if there can be any doubt about what Sergeant Fitz means.

He tosses the larger of the two corporals his key.

Behind Sergeant Fitz stands a blond boy in a neat uniform. He's our new lieutenant, fresh off a troop carrier and quite obviously terrified by what is about to happen.

As the smaller corporal jacks his rifle, the larger one fumbles catching the key. Close up, I can see that he's sweating, his fingers trembling as he reaches for the lock on my cage.

Everyone holds their breath.

Yanking at the door, he jumps to one side as the door hits dirt, raising dust. I could make them wait, but why bother? Instead I erupt from the cage with my good hand already lunging for his throat.

The man steps back, instinct kicking in.

He's too late.

I have his larynx between my thumb and curled first finger, and it's the work of a moment to crush his windpipe. For good measure, I slam my forehead into his face, breaking his nose. The corporal's already dead, he's just too stupid to realize that fact.

"Shoot the man . . ."

That's our new lieutenant. As expected, everyone ignores him. Does he really think Sergeant Fitz will allow me that easy an exit from life?

"Take him down," says Sergeant Fitz.

Reversing his rifle, to use as a club, the other corporal advances toward me. I'm naked, I've been in the cage for fifteen days, and Fitz severed half the wires on my prosthetic arm before locking me away. I'm so thirsty, I'd probably drink this man's blood if I could get him close enough . . .

He thinks he can take me.

I grin.

And that's enough to make him falter.

Dropping to a squat, I kick out the corporal's leg, roll myself up his falling body, and reach his throat as his skull hits the dirt. My elbow does for this one what my thumb and first finger did for the other. He dies gasping, and I'm back on my feet and smiling at Sergeant Fitz before the lieutenant can get his pistol from its holster.

"No, sir . . . Let me." The words are a hairbreadth away from being a direct order.

The lieutenant takes his hand from his side.

For a glorious second it looks as if Sergeant Fitz is going to challenge me himself. Unfortunately that's too much of a dream to be true, and he signals to a couple of recent recruits instead, then a couple more.

Can I take all four?

It's barely worth asking the question. They're children in uniform, cropped hair doing little to hide the softness of their faces and the fear in their eyes. *Is the sergeant that clever?* I ask myself as I watch the recruits ready themselves for an attack. One of them has wet his pants, the stain a dark shame on his sand-colored trousers.

"Get on with it," the sergeant growls.

The boys glance at one another.

As they advance, I let the anger drain from my body. It's one thing to kill NCOs, and I know enough about those two corporals to see them hanged. It's quite another thing to kill children and I don't intend to start now.

A BULLHIDE WHIP tears skin on its first blow, rips muscle within five, and opens a victim's back to the bone before reaching double figures. Men begin to die when the number rises above fifteen, and no man has lived beyond fifty.

This is a fact.

In the legion fifty lashes is a sentence of death, and any decent officer will give permission for the victim to kill himself before whipping begins. But Sergeant Fitz is not a decent officer. Mind you, he's not an officer at all. He is an NCO and they're the worst. I should know, I used to be one.

"Three minute break."

Being broiled in the cage is a bad way to die. I'm fifteen lashes into a far worse one, tied naked to a whipping post, with the flesh on my back peeling away like torn paper, and the man who put me here has just given his whip master a water break.

"Want some?" asks Fitz, holding the flask in front of my face.

Of course I do. Not that I'm going to tell him that.

"Too bad."

I'm a big man, built with physical exertion and kept lean by the demands of frontier life. Like all the soldiers in the forts south of Karbonne, I've burned away my body hair with quick swipes of a firebrand.

We are not ferox. We will not share even secondary characteristics with them.

Above me, on top of the whipping post, is a trophy; it's probably going to be the last thing I ever see. It has fangs and narrow eye sockets, because ferox need to shield their eyes from the harsh light of the desert, and few stretches of desert come harsher or brighter than the dunes around Fort Libidad.

The skull is taken from an adult male.

If the heavy jaw does not tell you this, the bony ridge running like a helmet crest from its forehead to the back of its neck undoubtedly will.

A dozen stories revolve around this skull. Apparently I killed its owner in hand-to-hand combat and dragged his head back to Fort Libidad as proof. This is bullshit; what's more, it is dangerous bullshit. No one goes hand-to-hand with a ferox and lives. I found the skull eighteen miles away. This was how far I tracked a deserter on the old lieutenant's orders.

"Track him for a day," he told me. "After that, return."

We both knew what went unspoken. If a man is not found inside a day, then he is dead anyway, killed by the temperature drop that hits this planet in the hours before dawn . . .

Out of my sight, the whip master picks up his whip. I know this from the crack it makes as dried blood is flicked from the lash. "And again," says Sergeant Fitz, and I tense myself against the next fifteen blows.

Sixteen.

Seventeen.

Eighteen.

I'm not sure how much more of this I can take. And then the skull grins. Bone twists like flesh, rotten teeth bare, and the slitted eyes narrow further, in obvious amusement.

I'm going to die . . .

My thought comes as a shock.

Aren't I?

The ferox grins some more. Jaws curve upward in a way that defies physics and all logic. *Not yet*, it says. *And not here.*

CHAPTER 2

THE FIRST I know of a raid is when an explosion shocks the air. Our gate guard goes down with a spear in his throat. A short spear, thrown using a sinew wrapped around its notched shaft. There's a good chance that sinew came from a human leg; most of them do.

"To arms," shouts the lieutenant.

Sergeant Fitz is more pragmatic. "Free fire," he yells, my execution already forgotten.

The skull above me says nothing. It merely grins.

Able to move at speed and deadly with bow, blade, or throwing spears, the ferox fight silently and to a preagreed plan. Speed and silence are a deadly mix in the desert, where sounds can carry for miles and a guard with good hearing is more valuable than one with good eyes.

The ferox pour through our gate in a wave.

And we get slaughtered, that's the only way to describe it. Most of the legion are new and barely know one end of a pulse rifle from another.

I watch a boy, little older than me when I first joined, drop to his knees and raise his gun to take careful aim. He even takes a breath and lets it out slowly, holding his fire until his heartbeat is steady. His first shot should blow a bull ferox apart and kill the beast behind, but he's forgotten to flick his precharge lever to load the coil.

The kid pulls his trigger repeatedly, shaking his head. Safety catches were abolished because new recruits kept forgetting to toggle them, but there's no future for a recruit so raw he forgets to precharge his weapon.

He dies with irritation on his face. Still unsure why his rifle won't fire. I'd tell him, but the gag in my mouth prevents it.

"Fall back," cries a voice.

It's our lieutenant, aged all of seventeen and still so new that few of us have bothered to learn his name. There's no need now. As a ferox drops from a roof behind him, the boy turns and the ferox flicks out one claw, opening a second mouth in the lieutenant's throat.

He dies in silence.

"Riddle's down!" someone screams.

And so I learn the boy's name after all.

"Fall back, fall back."

Stand, I want to shout. *Hold steady and die well.*

The ferox are cruel to soldiers who run, as unforgiving as our own dear leader, and troopers are dying around me in the dozens as they try to fall back toward an inner wall, which simply provides a backdrop for their slaughter. The air is hot with shit and guts, the stink of angry ferox and human blood on boiling sand. Flies settle quickly on the broken bodies.

Eggs will be laid, larvae hatched, and the desert will take back what should never have been here in the first place. *The XVth Brigade, Legion Etranger.* A ferox goes down, a youngster, half its armor burned away.

The only beast to be wounded so far.

It feels like hours before the last boy dies. In reality it's probably a handful of minutes and the ferox are kind, in a way rumor says is not in their nature. They kill quickly and cleanly, forcing each cadet to his knees, dragging back his head, and cutting his throat before moving on.

Anyone who says these beasts are mindless knows nothing.

Seven years ago when we first built Fort Libidad the beasts would no more have cut a man's throat than open his belly; ferox have plating across their throats and over their guts and believed we must have the same.

They've obviously discovered this is untrue, because I'm looking at the proof. A hundred dead teenagers with their throats and bellies ripped open.

Their chieftain is huge.

A bull standing nine feet tall, four feet across the shoulders, his mottled armor is chipped and cracked, and age has grayed his fur and dimmed his eyes, but when he moves toward me the others fall back to give him space.

Claws grip my jaw and turn me to face him.

This is it, I think, but his claws never close.

Instead dark eyes glare into mine and my head is twisted farther, to allow him a better view. Releasing my jaw, he taps my metal arm, considering the sound it makes. The prosthetic is crude, all pistons and rewelds and braided steel hoses that are past their safety date, but it looks better than the broken stump beneath.

"You did that," I mumble.

Dark eyes watch me.

"Well, not you exactly." I nod to the trophy above me. "Him."

The ferox follows my glance. Then his other hand moves to the broken flesh of my back as he dips his fingers into my blood and carries it to his mouth.

Seconds later, he spits and keeps spitting.

I could have told him.

Bad blood, my father always said.

As the others watch, the old bull considers his options. I have no doubt my death is at the top of that list. Every other human in Fort Libidad is dead, their blood staining the sand of the parade ground, the stink of their voided bowels so strong it fights with the scent of my executioner.

I wait, keeping my eyes on his.

This is my only vow.

Everyone makes and breaks promises and we all carry our share of those. Vows are different. Well, they are where I come from, which is a backwater so distant our dear leader barely bothers to include it in his list of glorious conquests.

My vow is simple.

However it comes, I will look death in the eyes. I will forgive myself every broken promise and debt still to be repaid, but if I break this vow, God will never forgive me.

So we lock eyes, a tribal chief standing over nine feet tall, and me, an ex-Etranger-sergeant, aged twenty-eight, standing as upright as pain allows.

What? it asks.

I blink, despite myself.

My world suddenly reduced to a pair of dark eyes and a voice in my head. *Maybe it's the pain,* I tell myself.

As I said, fifteen lashes can kill.

If not for my unnatural ability to heal, my corpse could have been waiting to greet the ferox when they arrived. The pain is extreme, so extreme I have trouble concentrating on the beast's question.

What? Its demand is louder this time.

The gag used for a whipping post is crude. It's the victim's own belt, fastened tight enough to make speech impossible, but not so tight that groans are stifled, because that defeats the object of the exercise.

Free me, I think.

After a moment's consideration the beast cuts my gag with a single flick of one claw. It is an object lesson in precision and reinforces why a hundred boys barely old enough to leave home lie dead in the dirt behind me.

"Soldier," I say, wanting to answer its question while the beast is still interested.

The beast looks blank.

"Human."

It thinks about this, head turned slightly to one side. When it grins, the beast reminds me of the trophy nailed above me. And once again I see the bull ferox flick its gaze upward. I have no idea how much of my thoughts it can read, but it obviously catches enough.

Not human, it says.

I shrug, which is stupid.

Catching my wince, it grins some more.

"Ugly bastard," I say.

Claws tighten around my jaw, closing slowly. Too much of that and something will break; in a man less thick-boned it would probably have broken already.

What? it demands.

Lashed to a post, surrounded by bodies, and in the grip of a beast that wants to ask existential questions is not a great place to be. As the claws keep closing, I feel the bones in my jaw stress to cracking point, and think *What have I got to lose . . . ?*

"I don't understand your question." When in doubt, fall back on stupidity, because it works every time.

As its grip loosens and gaze becomes less fierce, the bull turns to another ferox, younger and half its size. I'd think it female but for its skull ridge and a row of tribal markings daubed onto its breastplate.

The two beasts stare at each other.

And then the chieftain steps back, waving one hand as if to say, *All yours.*

Terrific, I think, *slaughtered by the tribal runt.*

But the youngster doesn't strike. Instead it grips my face and twists my head from side to side, and then up and down, as if checking the articulation. Finally, the beast turns my skull beyond what the bones can stand and I wince. At which the beast steps back, obviously puzzled.

"My neck doesn't bend that far," I say. "You dumb fuck."

Grinning, the youngster bares its fangs in obvious amusement.

What? it says.

"Human."

The amusement vanishes and into my mind comes the picture of a creature bound naked to a post, blood drying like a cloak across his back and buttocks. Splintered bone is already mending, and the gashes on his back have begun to close. He's shat himself, which I don't remember, and he looks smaller than I would expect, less than significant among the half a dozen ferox who . . .

Two thoughts stop me in my tracks.

One, that fewer than a dozen beasts can destroy a whole fort and, two, that for the first time ever, I'm thinking of the beasts as . . .

"*Who,*" I say.

The youngster looks at me.

Into my mind it replays its picture of the bound soldier.

"Me," I say, then remember the ferox have no sense of personal identity. Apparently the beasts think of themselves in the third person, as *him.* Although how any man can claim to have discovered this or had time to write it down before being ripped to bloody shreds, God knows.

"Sven," I say. "I'm Sven."

The beast appears to taste the word in its head. After a moment it nods, and the others nod also. As one, they turn and lope away toward a break in the wall I've barely noticed before.

"Come back.

"Don't go . . ."

When pleading fails I fall back on curses, calling the brutes everything from fuckwits to freaks and gutless cowards. And still they amble away from me and the slaughter they've left behind. A silent file of shambling ferox, already beginning to blend perfectly with the sands beyond the breach in the fort wall.

"Kill me," I shout.

The beast at the back turns and for a second my heart stops, but then my heartbeat kicks in again and the smallest of the beasts turns and hurries after the others.

CHAPTER 3

THE FEROX COME back before midnight.

Well, the smallest one does. He slouches into the fort through that hole in the wall and moves like a shadow across the parade ground, picking his way almost daintily among the piles of dead. Ignoring me, he reaches for the skull on the post above my head and tries to pry it free.

"I can help."

My words startle the youngster and that tells me ferox can hear, unless he's simply surprised to find me still alive. Twisting my head to the double moon, he stares deep into my eyes.

After a second he lets his claws drop, obviously disappointed.

A question has been asked and I've failed to answer. More worryingly, I've failed even to hear his question.

Why? I ask myself. *Why could you hear last time?*

Because fear provided a key? Possible, but fear is controlled by the limbic system and my body is now too frozen with cold to feel much more than resignation.

Glaring at the ferox, I see he's gone back to ignoring me. Without the others to be matched against, he looks huge, his teeth recently formed and razor-sharp, his armor shiny with the bloom of youth. And his claws are cruel but clumsy as he struggles with the trophy still nailed to the pole.

He can kill you, I remind myself. *Gut you and strew your insides across the sand.* But they're just words, insufficient to create the fear their truth demands.

"Free me," I say.

Again that flicker of interest. Only this time it vanishes as quickly as it arrives. I need a way to remake the bridge between us.

If not fear . . . then pain?

As he reaches for the skull, I stretch up with my hands, not to help him but to snag the base of my thumb on his lower claw. Before the beast can react, I drag down my wrist and feel flesh tear and a single word comes into my mind.

Why?

"Must talk," I tell him. "Only way."

He looks at me with interest. *What?* he asks.

I try not to sigh.

"Sven," I say.

The beast jerks his head at the bodies strewn across the parade ground around us. Ugly in the moonlight, they're already beginning to freeze as the night strips what little heat they have left. *Sven?*

I shake my own head, realize how ridiculous that is, and say *No,* loudly, inside my own skull.

Not Sven?

"No," I say. "Not Sven."

He considers this for a moment and says nothing when I reach up again and snag my wrist, harder this time. The thought of words vanishing before this conversation is finished is more than I can bear.

Captive, he says.

Am I? Does that mean he's taking me prisoner?

Enemies capture Sven. He says this as a statement, one allowing no argument. And as soon as I realize what he means I laugh.

"Yes," I agree. "Enemy capture Sven."

And God knows, in the twenty-eight years of my short and so far brutal life few enemies have been worse than Sergeant Fitz, who now lies faceup to the stars with a throwing spear through his heart.

"Let me help," I suggest.

The youngster's eyes flick from the trophy to my hands, and he breaks the ropes as simply as a child might snap cotton. With little to lose, I hold out my wrists and wait while he hooks his claws into my metal cuffs and pulls until they split at the hinge.

Help, he insists as I begin to walk away.

"Need something first."

He follows me all the way to the armory door. It's as well he does, because the door is made from some aerated ceramic that weighs little more than foam but is far stronger than it looks.

"Can you break this?"

Dark eyes catch mine, amusement replacing anger. *Of course I can,* says the voice in my head, except it's not quite a voice, more a wisp of thought that tatters into silence; and the amusement is not really in his eyes, it's more . . .

God, I think. *I've begun to match feelings to the ugly fuck's smell.* The youngster turns at that, looking quizzical, and I decide to watch my thoughts.

"Door," I suggest.

Putting his hands against the door, he pushes. When nothing happens, he pushes again. Then he draws his lips into a snarl and barges into the door with his shoulder. Something creaks, and I have a nasty feeling it might have been his bones.

In the end he sinks his claws into the door near the hinges, which is a good guess. The lock is flashy and semi-intelligent, certainly too bright to be bluffed by claiming an emergency. The hinges, however, are priced down to a spec just high enough to avoid the contractor getting killed.

It's harder work than he expects. A good five minutes wasted while I stand shivering and barely conscious and he digs his claws slowly through the shiny surface of the door, chipping his way toward the soft material beneath.

Help, he says.

And as I prepare to protest that I'll be no help at all, I realize he's reached into the door and is prying away one hinge. Great gasps come from his throat, and I know that whatever we find has to be worth his effort.

Swords, by the hundreds.

What is it with crazed dictators and cavalry? We have no mounts and the dunes are totally unsuitable for heavy horses, but we still have sabers by the thousands. Also, we have enough new-model pulse rifles to turn a whole desert's worth of sand to glass. These are locked down, without barrels or power packs, and a chain runs through each trigger guard. From the way the youngster's glance sweeps over them he doesn't recognize them as weaponry.

Just as well.

Of course, with the barrels in place, the guns would still need charging and unchaining. The more I think about it, the more obvious it seems to me that the new lieutenant was destined to die—deserved it even. He just didn't need to take a bunch of half-trained boys with him, but since that was what he was himself . . .

In one corner is an old box covered with dust, fixed to the wall with an explosion of spiderweb containing everything from mummified flies to the desiccated corpse of the spider itself. MEDICAL SUPPLIES says the side of the box. EMPTY, announces a red sticker slapped across its top.

The blade is where I left it five years before.

"We don't want this falling into anyone's hands," the old lieutenant told me, in that way of his that left me uncertain whether he meant what he said or intended the direct opposite. Maybe he was saying, *Make sure this gets into unsuitable hands.*

He'd be capable of it.

Other officers succumb to wounds taken in battle or self-inflicted. Lieutenant Bonafont suffered terminal ennui. So terminal that one day his heart simply stopped beating.

Maybe a laser blade in the hands of a homesick recruit would have provided entertainment enough to keep him alive. In which case I failed, but then the old bastard failed us all by shuffling off his mortal coil and leaving us in the care of some child doing a six-month tour of duty.

"Got it," I say.

The whipping post comes apart like fat melting in the sun. I cut from below, slicing away at the wood until a steel spike is revealed. After that, removing the skull is simple: A couple more cuts, a flick of the wrist, and the trophy comes free. I'm armed again, of course. I wonder if the ferox realizes that.

"Here."

The skull has a nail hole in the top but still looks pretty good for something that's been scoured by desert winds for the best part of five years. I treat the object with respect. For all I know the ferox indulges in some form of ancestor worship. I really don't want to blow my survival at this point.

No, he says faintly.

Flicking on my weapon, I touch its blade to the back of my hand and hear his voice grow louder.

You carry it.

CHAPTER 4

THREE DAYS and a hundred miles later I meet the first woman I've seen in five years. I'd like to think I'd be impressed even if she wasn't naked, although it's hard to put an age to her to begin with, because she's smeared with dirt and her hair is so long it falls around her shoulders and hides her upper body.

And I'm not being disingenuous. When I first see her, it's dark and I'm tired and she's running across a cave floor on all fours, her breasts hanging low like the teats on a sand wolf.

Human? The young ferox is intrigued by my interest.

I nod.

We've been thrown into each other's company during the desert crossing. I've come to learn the meaning of at least five basic smells, while the youngster now realizes that the way I articulate my head carries the meaning of two of these.

He points at me. *Not human.*

I'm not inclined to argue, since the youngster's certainty that I'm something other than her seems to be one of the things keeping me alive.

"Sven," I agree.

Pointing to the girl, who has frozen under his gaze, the ferox tells me she's mine, but first I have to meet the elders. This is inevitable, I suppose. Everything about the ferox is tribal, and tradition for them seems to be interchangeable with law. In fact, both concepts come from the youngster as a single thought.

The very idea of elders suggests a solemn gathering, probably around a fire. Well, that's what it suggests to me. The reality is simpler and much more boring. The youngster drags me through a huge warren of tunnels and caves, stopping only to tell every male he meets, *Not human.*

Not, they agree.

And then one of the pups, so young that his armor is still soft, brings me the girl. *Human,* he says, and I begin to understand the problem.

The girl is fifteen, maybe a few years older. From the way old whip scars cross her ribs it looks as if she's moved on all fours her entire life. She can stand and climb and fit sideways through cracks in the rock that would stop me at the shoulder, but she can't talk and when I lift dark hair from her face, there is nothing in her eyes but wariness and the sullen anger one expects from any caged animal.

I ask her name.

I ask her age.

I ask how she ended up living with ferox deep in the desert.

After a while, in disappointment and tiredness, I begin to demand answers to the impossible. Why is our beloved leader such a prick? What keeps the stars apart? Is God hardwired into our minds? If so, who did the hardwiring? The stuff that passes for serious thought in legion bars across the empire.

In a sweating tunnel hacked into a cliff face by a long-dead river, a hundred miles farther into the desert than any human is meant to have gone, I lose myself for a week in questions and thoughts of death.

She sits, she watches, after a while she brings me water.

"Thank you," I say.

Nothing in her face suggests she distinguishes these words from the noises I make as I rage and weep and mourn for a hundred children whose names I've never bothered to learn.

In my defense I offer their slaughter, a desert hike that has reduced my feet to bloody pulp, and the fact that the first woman I meet in five years—and quite possibly the last person I will ever see—is little more than a ghost of what I believe humans to be.

Questions about her tribe, her mother and brothers bring no answers. A legionnaire quickly learns patois; how can we not? We take the sweepings of a fifth of the spiral arm and provide immunity from all crimes that have gone before, except treason, in return for certain death, the time and place to be the legion's choosing.

Common tongue, city tongue, outlying worlds . . .

I even toss the girl words from traveler speech and machine cult but she recognizes none of them, and I am a man who can order a whore or a drink in fifteen different languages.

I began to agree with the ferox. If she is human then I am not.

Nor were the boys now dead at the fort, though the ferox have no way of knowing this. Nor were the women I knew in Karbonne. Nor my sister, who holds a family together in my memory, relying on sheer determination and guts when the money goes and an entire planet falls into poverty and chaos.

However, the girl is beautiful beneath her dirt. So I give her a name, though I'm uncertain she understands that *Anna* refers to her. Still, she quickly comes to recognize the tone. Anna shares my food, follows me like a shadow, and no longer flinches when I come within striking distance.

It's not much, but it's enough.

Things will improve, I tell myself. *She'll learn to speak.* And in the meantime, if I want proper conversation I seek out the youngster and talk to him about the tribe and the desert and what went before. The tribe is old, a thousand chiefs if the youngster is to be believed; old, venerable, and very certain of their right to this land. They have only ever lived in caves, and their laws state—quite clearly—that nothing must change.

But Sven is change.

He asks me about my tribe, then retreats and sulks for days at my answers. We fly, I tell him, among the stars and between the moons. A whole people are out there, their history written in those flickering lights that cross the sky each night.

Many Sven, he says.

I sigh.

He understands sighing now, along with tears and nods and shakes of the head. In turn I can identify seven separate smells and a handful of his gestures. The laser knife has stopped being a weapon and become the means by which I communicate. A strange Sven ritual, which involves touching light to the back of my hand until my words become clear enough for a ferox to hear.

We return to Fort Libidad before the onset of high summer. The youngster doesn't bother to tell me why, but I know my presence is required. It is nearing the middle of the year and the winds have begun to rise; food is already scarce. Animals die when the heat comes, and the ferox refuse to eat carrion.

Next dawn, he says.

So next dawn sees us ready.

Even the chieftain makes the journey, his face wrapped against the wind and a hundred miles of sifting sand. We walk in single file, following in his steps. Mostly the wind blows our footprints away, but crossing the dried edge of an oasis I look back and see that we leave only one set of prints, albeit deep ones and made strange by the fact that I cannot always match the chieftain's stride.

The fort is abandoned.

And the stench inside is vicious. Flesh has fallen from bones and rotted to matted spoor beneath half-visible skeletons. In time the heat will rot what remains completely, or desiccate it, but that time is not yet.

Door, says the youngster.

So I nod.

Walls, he adds. We speak almost effortlessly.

"What about the walls?"

Like doors? he asks.

"Are walls like doors?" The heat, the winds, and being near enough to the only one of my kind are beginning to get to me.

Door, he repeats, more intently. A dozen ferox stand around us in a circle, watching closely. That's twice the number of beasts needed for the original attack, so this has to be important. Also, the chief is growing impatient, his head swinging slowly from side to side.

"Which door?" I ask.

It is the right question.

The youngster can only remember the armory door. Since nothing was able to stand in his way, nothing else counts. So we walk to the armory, followed by a silent procession of the others.

The pulse rifles are in place, broken down to lock, stock, and barrel and still chained through their trigger guards. Enough weapons to launch a revolution. A wall of cavalry sabers looks as gratuitous as it ever did.

We take, he says.

"What?"

Everything.

For a moment I feel panic. Unarmed, these beasts are deadly enough. The thought of a tribe of ferox armed with pulse weapons is beyond horrific. On the very edge of doing something stupid, I realize my mistake. To Youngster the broken-down rifles are simply clutter.

He wants the armory itself. At least, he wants its door and walls. It takes us three days to cut the building into cartable pieces. When I suggest that smaller pieces are easier to carry, the youngster just smiles. A quick baring of his fangs makes him look as if he might slip into laughter or outright savagery, had the first not been impossible for a ferox, and the second their default position on almost everything.

Work, he says.

I work.

And when the cutting is done we carry the pieces away among us. Well, I carry a door, which is lightest of the pieces into which the armory has been hacked. We carry our booty a hundred miles and it takes seven days, using up what little reserves of energy we all have left.

I sweat, drag my feet, and fail to follow in the leader's footsteps. The ferox slow down, letting me grab ragged breath from the hot desert air. When I've finished vomiting a thin sour stream, which is all that fills my stomach, the youngster hauls me to my feet and the march begins again.

"Tell me why," I say to one after another.

Their answers are strange, oblique.

I cut myself harder, and burn myself more sharply, but their words still hover on the edge of meaning.

Flamefire, says Youngster, but it means nothing to me.

Those pieces, which looked ragged when we ripped them from the walls of the armory, fit perfectly into the entrance of the main warren, across a turn of tunnel behind this, and into a gap where the walls narrow a hundred paces after that.

Not fit close enough to jam into place: They fit perfectly, every bulge in the wall matched by a curve in a slab of ceramic. No mortar is needed, because every tunnel narrows at exactly the point chosen. The ferox simply haul the ceramic slabs upright and use brute force and that natural narrowing to fix each slab into place.

Only seeing it prevents me from believing it impossible. And even then, while describing what is happening to Anna, I find myself wondering if what I'm saying is really true.

Done, says the youngster.

He seems happier than I've seen him in weeks.

Eat, sleep, get strong. Now we wait.

The youngster trundles away, and when I next see him he's curled up on the edge of a rock pool, letting a thin trickle of water wash across his fur. He's snoring, loudly.

CHAPTER 5

A HOT WIND seeps into the cave system at dusk, finding its way through faults in the rock and up the slanting chimneys that climb toward the cliff tops above. For all its heat, the wind is a blessing. Our caves are beginning to stink of closeted ferox, dung, and too many beasts scrabbling a living in too small a space.

As the temperatures rise the males claim their own areas, only returning to the females for sex.

I find a small cave of my own. Since none of the adults disputes this, and most have become friendly since I first arrived at their camp dragging the skull of a long-dead chief, my landgrab is obviously acceptable. After all, I live in the warren and I eat what they eat, which some weeks is precious little . . .

There was a boy, they tell me, a man, and an older woman. All found wandering in the desert. Ferocious, almost as fierce as the ferox, Anna is what's left. The others are gone, but no one seems willing to tell me where.

Anna = Human, they say. *Human = Anna.*

I think it's a statement. After a while I realize it's a question.

Looking into the girl's eyes shows me nothing. I believe she is feral, a human like me, but run wild or maybe just wilder. Now I'm beginning to wonder if we're even the same species. Strange things happened in the very early days of colonization, when people were still being changed to match planets, rather than planets being changed to match people.

Still, I feed scraps to the wild girl, who grows friendlier and begins to curl herself around me whenever I appear.

What happens next is inevitable.

One morning Anna arrives early, a dead lizard in her hand. She's obviously really pleased with herself, understandably enough. She smiles when I say her name. It might be my tone of voice, although I pretend to myself that it isn't. She looks up, and she smiles.

My own smile ignites a grin on her face.

We eat the lizard together, sucking it down to bones and mangled shreds of silver skin, and then I say, "Let's clean you up."

She keeps smiling and I keep talking, my voice low and soothing as I cut her hair with my laser blade, leaving her standing in a tangle of filthy curls. Her underarm hair goes the same way. A sweep of blade above her skin and an acrid smell of burning keratin and it's done.

We are not ferox.

Only, some days, it seems we are.

In the deepest recesses of the cave system I show Anna a stream that slides down a gray wall and fills a pool that looks almost as old as this planet. I've been coming here for weeks, cooling myself against the wind and washing away the worst of the cave system's stink.

"Come on," I say.

She screams at the shock of the water, but not seriously, and anyway I'm in there first and it isn't really that cold. After washing away my own filth, I attack what looks like a lifetime's dirt on the girl in front of me. Her skin is pink, unquestionably paler than mine is.

When I splash the girl to rinse her, she splashes back. We laugh, fight in a lazy fashion, and then I scrub grit from her scalp. Most of the dirt in her hair is too ingrained to come free, but by then Anna's probably cleaner than she's ever been, and finishing the job is the last thing on my mind.

From the speed with which Anna grapples me, one of her knees still dragging in the water of the pool, she must have been wondering what took me so long.

Most people who talk about animal sex haven't tried it; or if they have, they're probably locked up where they belong. This is different. Anna looks human but behaves like an animal, and right up to the point where she sinks her teeth into my neck and rides herself to real screams, I'm uncertain which she really is.

So loud are her shouts as they echo off the cave walls that I expect Youngster to appear, anxious to discover the cause of the fuss. Only he probably already knows, because the ferox are open about sex, which is entirely hierarchical for them and mostly to do with power and prestige.

I'm talking about the males, obviously. I doubt if anyone asks the tribe's females for their preferences. Anna and I rut endlessly over the next few weeks and keep rutting as the cave system grows hotter and food becomes ever rarer.

The ferox grow sluggish and bad-tempered. A young bull is killed. Youngster says it was a challenge fight to an elder, but everybody knows the battle was about food. I gut any prey the hunt finds, using my laser blade to hack fresh kills into crude joints. No one worries about cuts of meat; they just want food quickly.

As the heat rises, the food situation gets worse. The chief takes most, the females eat scraps, and the pups grub in the dirt for insects. I should have seen what was coming, we both should . . .

Come now.

"Me?" I ask, surprised.

Youngster nods.

When he tells me I'm needed on a hunting trip, I'm more than puzzled. For a start, I'm slower than he is and less able to move silently, and

I'm already weak with the bubble shits; but five groups are going out that evening, and if Youngster wants me to hunt with him, then hunt with him I will.

We eat well that night. And it's only later, with my hands full of scraps for Anna, that I realize she's gone. The others are restless around me, unwilling to help me find her, so I track down Youngster.

"Where is Anna?" I demand, already fearing his answer.

Gone, he says.

"Where?"

It is a fairly stupid conversation.

We ate, he says. *You ate. Now she is gone. If the hunting does not improve, we begin to eat the pups.*

I land only one punch before his backhand throws me against a cave wall. When I roll to my feet with the laser blade in my hand, two other ferox are standing beside him.

Challenge? asks one.

"No challenge," I reply.

The ferox avoid me after that. They watch from the corner of their eyes, tensing as I turn corners in a tunnel to meet them. I've gone from being a member of the tribe to being a problem. I can smell hesitation on their fur, a restrained fury that sees them turn away from me.

My anger is more open, less wise.

The pool where we first bathed is almost gone, but I use what water is left to wash out my mouth, then take grit and scrub the fingers that picked crudely roasted chunks of flesh from that evening's cooking fire. And I sleep curled around a dark void that is my anger, until someone shakes me awake in the early hours of the morning. It is the youngster, the mixture of scents rolling off him too complicated for me to translate.

He picks me up. *Human?* he asks.

Behind him, ferox shuffle in a passageway.

"Not human," I reply.

The youngster allows himself to look doubtful and my guts churn, not from what I have eaten but from what may come next. His paw is holding my face, and a yellow sickle of claw is visible at the edge of my sight, ragged with use.

We talk later, he says.

I nod.

A hundred miles beyond the frontier, trapped in an underground cave system with ferox, in the middle of a summer so hot that the water in the deepest cave pool will eventually be reduced to dampness and nothing . . . I am in the wrong place, at the wrong time, and that has to be the history of my twenty-eight years to date.

I sleep alone, I eat alone.

In so doing I reduce my food intake to scraps and sacrifice the company others might bring me. It is the only way to keep my anger in check.

The laser blade stays in my pocket.

Pups who once regarded me as an object of interest start to bristle if I come near, as if what is thought by their elders filters down. Still-soft armor strains to flex, heads are raised, and half-grown fangs are bared, so I nod and smile and begin to count the days until high summer comes to an end, because this heat can't last much longer.

After all, how long can it take some scuzzy little planet to negotiate the shallow bend of its solar orbit?

CHAPTER 6

F*LAMEFIRE* IS RIGHT . . .

When the attack comes it's not against me, and comes not from the tribe but from outside. I still wonder how Youngster knew it would happen. Can ferox read the future? Or is the answer simpler, with rumor running through his world as swiftly as our own?

"Death's Head."

The cry is amplified.

A human voice stretched by electronics into a weapon itself. Its source might be a hundred or more paces away, but my head still hurts from the sudden blast of noise.

"Surrender Now."

The words are said for form only. No quarter is asked or given.

Above and below, from the sides, through fissures in the rock, tunnels, and natural chimneys, the attack appears to come from every direction at once.

The Death's Head clear the cave system with flamethrowers, using the lower vents to flood the main camp with gas, which they then ignite. And flamefire pours in from above, sticky and stinking, igniting everything it touches and flowing relentlessly downhill toward the caverns where the females and the cubs hide.

What had been hot became an inferno.

Fire curls against rock, and the darkness of the caves becomes an unholy half-light, with ferox in flames like moving candles. They die fighting, because that's the way it goes.

Instinct tumbles me into the last of my pool of water, and common sense holds me there, my face barely above the surface as oxygen burns out of the air and my lungs begin to choke. Anybody who tells you they don't feel fear in battle is a liar. Fear keeps you alive, by focusing the mind so you know that what you're about to do is not some childish game.

This is my own side; these are my own people. Maybe that's why I'm so terrified.

Youngster dies as he lived, in silence; but I hear his death inside my head, even without a knife to summon his thoughts, and his screams are no less terrifying for being silent.

I'm huddled in my pool at the end of a deep tunnel, crouching in the water when a Death's Head appears. Raising his pulse rifle, the man sights along its barrel and begins to tighten his finger on the trigger.

It's instinct alone that saves me.

Throwing myself to one side, I scream at the top of my lungs before he has time to take a second shot. *"Human."*

The man hesitates, and that hesitation saves my life. Up goes his visor, his lips already moving as he relates the news to his commander or someone else on the surface. "Human," I hear him say.

A crackle of static.

"Name?" he demands.

It takes me a second or so to remember.

Whoever is on the other end obviously gets impatient, because the soldier in front of me opens his mouth just as I remember.

"Sven," I tell him. "Ex-sergeant, Legion Etranger."

The law of the legion requires me to tell him I was once a sergeant. It's a way of identifying troublemakers early.

"Where did you serve?"

The name of Fort Libidad comes growling off my tongue. I'm beginning to regret quite how loudly when he raises his rifle for a second time; but it's unconscious and nothing suggests he feels anything other than shock.

He relates my name and last posting to his unseen superior, who promptly comes back with another question. "How did you get here?"

How indeed?

I walked for days beside a ferox who decided to keep me for a pet . . . Somehow, it seems the wrong answer, so I decide on another.

"Captured."

"And they let you live?" The question obviously comes from him, because there's not time enough for it to come from the surface.

I nod.

"Just you," asks the man. "You were the only one captured?"

"The only one from the fort," I say. "But there was a girl here when I first arrived."

"She died?"

"The ferox ate her," I tell him.

I ate her.

And I find myself on my knees, vomiting again.

"Can you walk?" he demands.

I look at him. Something keeps me from saying, *Of course I can walk.*

Instead I limit my reaction to a nod. And when he turns, I crawl naked from my pool of water and follow him toward a wire ladder that seems to hang in space. It disappears into speckled darkness above, and I realize it's still night out there and I can see stars inside the circle of the chimney's distant top.

A tiny lift motor runs up the edge of the ladder, and he makes a loop from his own belt, hooks it under my shoulders, and fixes the buckle to a hook. I'm being drawn upward before I realize he's activated the machine.

"What the fuck's that?" he demands as we crawl past sections of ceramic jammed across tunnel entrances halfway up. He has his helmet light playing across the sides of the chimney. I guess he didn't see the makeshift barricades on his way down.

"Armored ceramic," I tell him.

The light when he turns blinds my eyes.

Muttering something, the man tilts his head. And then repeats whatever he originally said.

"Ceramic?" he checks, looking at me.

"Yes," I say. "Stolen from the fort."

The man mutters into his throat mike. "Will do," he says finally. "We're on our way out now."

HANDS HELP ME over the rim and I stare at the starlit sky. A sight I haven't seen since the hunting trip, when Youngster tricked me away from the caves so the others could kill Anna—from a ferox that is almost compassion.

"Can you stand?"

What is it about officers and idiot questions?

Of course I can stand, I start to say, then discover I can't and swallow the rest of my sentence anyway. The boots in front of me belong to a Death's Head colonel. Small, intense looking, with wire-framed spectacles, he wears one of the empire's most easily identifiable uniforms.

You know the one. It's black, with silver piping to the shoulders, narrow silver epaulets, and silver bars on the collar. A skull stares from each button. A tiny dagger hangs on his left hip from a silver chain, as much an affectation as the spectacles, which have smoked-glass lenses.

Other cavalry regiments rely on gold braid, scarlet cloaks, crimson linings, and even cavalry knots in nauseating shades of green. They all look like doormen in overpriced knocking shops.

Not the Death's Head. No one who has ever seen that uniform could mistake it for anything else. And in the unlikely event you might mistake it, the men wrapped in its understated arrogance are usually happy enough to correct your error.

A sergeant hauls me from the ground and holds me upright in front of the officer. At a nod from the colonel, the sergeant drops me again.

"Ceramic?" says the colonel "Are you sure?"

"Yes, sir."

"Army-issue armored ceramic . . . ?"

I nod again, having nodded the first time as well as barked out my reply. "Yes, sir."

Is this man an idiot, his gaze says. *If not, then what am I dealing with here?* He does not look the type to take battle fatigue kindly.

"And where do ferox get ceramic?" he asks, his voice quiet.

"From Fort Libidad," I tell him.

"I see," he says. "And they carried it here? All the way across the desert?"

I'm bored with nodding. "Have you seen Fort Libidad?" I ask. Around me, half a dozen officers tense.

"What if I have?"

"It occurs to me," I say slowly, wondering how to finish a sentence I shouldn't have begun in the first place, "that perhaps you might have noticed the armory?"

"Might I?" says the colonel, turning to a major. The major looks nervous, as well he might. Other officers are discreetly backing away, obviously worried about being included in the question.

"You noticed the bodies, sir."

"Everyone noticed the bodies," says the colonel. "It would be hard not to, given how many there were. Tell me . . . what did I notice about the armory?"

"I'm sorry, sir," the major admits finally. "I'm not sure."

"There isn't one," I say.

Both officers turn to me, but only the colonel is smiling, and it's the smile of a cat that's seen a particularly interesting piece of prey.

"Isn't one?" His voice is quiet and sounds eminently reasonable, always a bad sign in a senior officer.

"They cut it up," I tell him, already bored with the conversation. Part of me knows I'm living dangerously, but the shock of getting away from the ferox has gone to my head, and my relief at being back among my own kind is giving me unrealistic expectations of how I can expect my own kind to behave.

"And then," I say, "they carried it across the desert. Not one bit, but the whole fucking thing. The reason you didn't see an armory is that there's no armory left to see. It's been patched into their tunnels and disguised with mud, rubble, and assorted shit . . ."

I'm rambling, but no one seems to mind.

"How do you know this?" the colonel demands.

"I was there."

The two officers glance at each other.

"You went with them back to the fort?"

It's a bad question. Yes, I'm a traitor. No, I'm a liar . . . "They took me," I say. "It wasn't like they told me why."

A hard stare, then the two officers glance again at each other. I've gone from being a traitor or a liar to being insane. Of the three options, it's probably the safest. So why do I have to blow it?

Some habits are difficult to break, I guess.

"I learned how to communicate with them."

That really gets their attention.

"It's true . . ." Pushing aside a medic, in my anxiety to sit up and make what I say sound true I scramble as far as my knees. A tube is already in my wrist and the medic seems to be trying to force another up my nose, for no reason that seems obvious.

"Leave us," demands the colonel, waving the medic away.

From the look the colonel gives the major, he's obviously wondering whether to send him away as well. In the end the senior officer shrugs and lets the major stay.

"You know as well as I do, ferox don't speak."

The major has obviously thought of something else. He's practically hopping from foot to foot. "This man made their barricades," he tells the colonel. "Ferox don't have that level of skill."

Helping the enemy is a capital crime. Around here, practically everything is.

"They cut it with their claws," I tell him. "A hundred miles from their camp, they shaped ballistic-strength ceramic from memory, with every single sheet proving a perfect fit."

Whatever the major is about to say gets chopped short by a single glance from the colonel. "You're saying they're intelligent?"

I think about this. "Maybe not in a sense we understand," I say. "But they're organized and they plan ahead."

"And you talked to them?"

"Yes, often."

The colonel shakes my hand, which is so unlike a senior officer that I'm immediately suspicious. He wishes me well and says he'll probably see me again. A few hours later the major comes back to tell me I've been tried in my absence, found guilty of desertion, and condemned to death. Since I'm to die at dawn, the major suggests I spend what remains of tonight making peace with whichever God the scum from my planet embrace.

CHAPTER 7

WITH MORNING come six soldiers in the combat dress of the Death's Head elite. They tote pulse rifles across their chests and wear dark glasses beneath their raised visors. An affectation, since we are still barely into half-light.

"You," they say. "Come with us." There must be a boot camp somewhere that teaches these people how to speak.

Two of the Death's Head drag me from my cell, which is actually the luggage hold of an air copter. It's an overhot, sticky, and deeply unpleasant place to spend the last few hours of my life.

The major waits at his chosen spot, stamping back and forward in irritation, as if my death is just another inconvenience keeping him from breakfast. "Stand him over there," he orders.

Death's Head troopers are far too professional to roll their eyes at the stupidity of a senior officer, but if they did, now would be the time to do it. A natural wall is formed by an outcrop of sandstone, so it's fairly obvious where I'm meant to stand.

When a trooper tries to blindfold me, I begin to struggle. God knows why I ever took that stupid vow, but promising to face death with my eyes open seemed like the right thing to do at the time.

"Leave it," says the major, sounding bored. "We've wasted long enough."

I stand where I'm told to stand.

As an unexpected mark of respect, the sergeant flicks off my cuffs to let me face death freestanding and unbound.

"Don't try to run," he tells me.

"The legion never run," I reply. "We stand and we die."

The look he gives me is almost sympathetic. And suddenly it seems more important than ever to die well.

So when they raise their rifles and sight along the barrels, I stare back. My head is high and my body locked so solid that my arms and legs refuse to shake.

"Load," says the major.

The sergeant nods, his response instinctive, and I watch his finger begin to tighten on the trigger. He will shoot first and the rest will fire in the split second that follows his shot. This is how the Death's Head work, the legion also . . .

Unless free fire is declared, firing before your NCO is a capital offense, much like lying under oath, treason, and hitting a senior officer. And if not for an eccentric interpretation of those rules by my old lieutenant, I'd be dead long before this anyway.

As it is, I was simply broken from sergeant to private for *wanting to hit a senior officer.* Actually, I had hit him, but the lieutenant decided it was the *wanting* he found offensive.

As the sergeant's finger reaches trigger pressure he locks his eyes on mine, which takes guts, because you need courage to look someone in the eyes as you take his life. That's why killing is a young man's job and it's old men who send them out there.

I nod, to signify I'm ready.

And he smiles.

It's a clean shot, a hit to the chest. I barely have time to register this fact before five other pulse rifles fire in unison and darkness takes me.

. . .

YOU DON'T WAKE . . . This is my first thought. *You don't wake after someone shoots you with a pulse rifle.* Largely because there isn't enough of you left to wake up again.

My second thought is, *God, that hurt.*

Even the memory of having my arm ripped off by a dying ferox has paled before an ache that locks tight my chest and forces my lungs to fight for each breath. Every nerve in my body feels on fire.

"Lowest setting," someone says.

When my eyes finally allow themselves to focus, I realize the voice belongs to the colonel, who is sitting on the end of my bed, cleaning a handgun that seems to be constructed mainly of glass.

Since I was shot in the middle of the desert, and beds out there are few and far between, I decide I must be somewhere else.

Lowest setting?

"Bullshit," I say.

Beyond the edge of my vision, someone laughs.

"We adjusted the power packs," says the colonel. "A small modification, but my own."

"Why?" I demand.

Again that laughter. "You were right," says the voice. If I didn't know better I'd say the colonel is relieved.

"You can go," the voice adds, and the colonel almost scurries from the room. I wait and the voice waits and after a while it sighs.

"A legionnaire?"

I nod, and then, in case that was not enough, add, "Sir."

My reasoning is that anyone who can send a Death's Head colonel from a room deserves all the respect he can get. I have no idea quite how right I am until the voice became a man at the edge of my vision, in simple black and silver. And the man turns out to be General Indigo Jaxx.

I know who he is. Everyone knows who he is. The general has single-handedly prevented an assassination attack on our dear leader, throwing himself in front of a crazed woman whose son was killed in the eastern spiral.

"You were a sergeant?"

"Yes, sir."

"Why were you broken?"

"I hit an officer."

He looks at me, considering. "I didn't hear that," he says. "Let's try again. Why were you broken?"

"Insubordination."

"What kind?"

I blink . . . Most officers aren't even aware there is more than one kind. "I refused an order," I tell him. "Then punched out my lieutenant before he could issue his order to anyone else."

General Jaxx sighs. "And what was this order?"

"Shoot the lieutenant, shoot everybody else, and then shoot myself."

"That never happened," says the general.

"No, sir."

"Why," asks General Jaxx, "would he have issued such an order? Had he, which he did not."

"He was drunk, sir. And bored."

"This was at Fort Libidad?"

"Yes, sir. The boredom killed him eventually."

"And then the ferox killed everybody else."

I nod.

"Except you," he says, holding my gaze.

We've come to the crux of the problem. We both understand that, and I'm the one who is surprised, because it has never occurred to me that I'm important enough to be a problem, at least not to anybody over the rank of lieutenant.

"Colonel Nuevo wants to kill you," says the general. "This would be the commonsense answer. Luckily for you, Major Silva sometimes has his own opinion on things."

Walking to the window, General Jaxx looks out at a landscape denied to me. I have no way of knowing if I am in Karbonne or even on the same planet. The temperature in this room is controlled, and walls of black glass keep me from whatever is outside. Also, I'm lashed to the bed with a woven band across my chest and another above my knees, but low enough to keep my legs from moving. I am, however, definitely still alive, and this is more than I have any right to expect.

"We can't send you back to the legion," he says. "You know how it is. One man left after an entire fort is slaughtered. No brigade would take you . . ." He hesitates, amends his words. "Well," he says, "no brigade would take you and let you live. So we have to think of something else. Do you have any thoughts on the matter?"

It doesn't occur to me to wonder why a general is taking the trouble to discuss matters with an ex-legion ex-sergeant.

"I don't care where I go," I say. "So long as it's not back to the desert."

"Had enough of the sun, have we?"

"Yes, sir."

"Right," he says. "Leave it with me. I'll see what we can do."

CHAPTER 8

"FALL IN," orders a corporal, so I do.

I wear a militia uniform at least ten years out of date and a size too small. Maybe it amuses the general to see me look so shabby beside his men's black-and-silver uniforms. And I travel in his entourage, although it's probably more honest to say I travel with the baggage.

We leave Karbonne in a sleek black fighter that takes far more passengers than it should, given its rapierlike profile. An hour later we rendezvous with a mother ship in high orbit above the planet. Why the mother ship bothers with high orbit is anyone's guess. There were precious few people left on the surface of this world with weapons to do more than bring down a simple kite.

I'm sent for again two days later. My meeting with the general is brief. He simply nods at the sergeant who led my execution party, and then nods at me. "Horse will look after you," he says.

The sergeant nods. "Yes, sir," he says. "We'll have a good time." He's quite obviously talking to the general.

"Dismissed," says General Jaxx.

And away we go.

"He's taken a liking to you," says the sergeant. "Just as well. If Colonel Nuevo had his way, you'd be dead."

"If I had my way," I growl back, "he'd be slop in the bottom of some bucket."

The sergeant smiles at me, a death's-head grin that goes with his silver buttons and the badge on his cap. "You ever been on a mother ship before?"

My snort is answer enough.

I've jumped planet in low-level troop carriers, surrounded by the kind of recruits who throw up if forced to cross a puddle, and I've dropped from a pod, years ago when we first took this system from the Enlightened, may their metal heads catch fire . . . Mother ships, battle cruisers, and high fighters are not usual forms of legion transport.

"Let me show you around."

As it happens, he doesn't show me very far. An elevator drops us eighteen levels and we exit into the bowels of the recreation area. If anything this clean can be so described. Black glass walls and black glass fountains. A row of tables outside a café, pushed tightly together, because the corridor down which we walk isn't that wide.

A smartly dressed woman with two small children sits at one of the tables. The man sitting opposite her is ridiculously elegant and drinking something cloudy and green from a tiny glass. An Obsidian Cross hangs from his collar, and silver braid waterfalls down one side of his chest. He wears the uniform of a Death's Head lieutenant as if it's a particularly amusing form of costume.

He glances idly at the sergeant beside me, and the sergeant comes to attention. A polite nod and we've obviously been given our orders to move on.

"Let's find a bar," I say.

Horse laughs. "Okay," he says. "The general wins."

I frown.

"He said this was about as far as you'd get . . ." As the sergeant looks around him, I wonder what he sees. To me it's a new world, one where Death's Head officers and NCOs slouch down corridors, black-and-silver jackets slung loosely over their shoulders. A world where barkeepers smile and whores are polite, instead of asking to be paid in advance.

As we move away from the main drag, with its awnings and pavement tables, the air changes slightly and officers become a rarity. There are no troopers here, but a wide variety of NCOs. Now the air smells of beer and sex and sweat, but only a little. Just enough to make the surroundings feel real.

"On the house," says Horse.

"What is?"

"All of it," he says, indicating bars on both sides of the passageway. "Anything. The general said charge it to his pad."

My eyes go wide.

"That's a joke," Horse says. "You think anybody in their right mind would . . ." He runs his words into the dirt, obviously appalled that he needs to explain anything quite so obvious. "What do you want first?"

Get laid, get paralytic.

The obvious answers. Only I want more than that, or maybe it's that I want less. Whatever, it definitely involves remaining sober enough to remember everything when I wake tomorrow.

"I want a beer," I say. "A cold beer . . . And then I want a whore for the night, in a bed, maybe in a place with its own bathroom."

Horse smiles. "I've known men," he says, "who'd want ten whores and the general's finest champagne."

"And I've known men," I tell him, "who'd swap this entire ship for a glass of clean water."

"It was tough?"

I nod. "Yeah," I agree. "Even before the ferox attacked. We're legion. If the meat is cheap, we'll eat it. If the beer is watered, we'll drink it. And if the weapons are outdated and the power packs are faulty, we'll fight with them anyway . . ."

A couple of corporals have stopped to listen, but a glance from Horse sends them on their way. I'm out of place on this ship. My prosthetic arm is rusty and I've had to tear the cuff to make my shirt fit. My boots are so worn that one heel slopes. It's hard not to believe that my being here is some kind of joke.

"We're cannon fodder," I say, bitterly. "We make no pretense to be anything else."

"And you think we do?"

"No," I say. "That's not what I mean. You're elite, we're grunts. No one in their right mind would expect high command to treat us the same . . ." Shrugging, I look around me and nod at the nearest bar. I've changed my mind about getting drunk.

"That will do."

"I know a better one."

We walk for another ten minutes along a corridor, then turn right and drop a level, walking for the same length of time again. As we walk, I count my footsteps and try to work out the width of the ship from the distance traveled.

It's big; anything that lets you walk a thousand paces in the same direction is big. And when we walk a thousand paces again, more or less in the same direction, I realize this is not a ship as I know it.

I did this in the caves; that's how I learned the ranking of the ferox. All bull ferox claim territory, and the more senior the male, the larger the stamping ground he claims. And the weirdest thing I discovered was that the youngster was second in command, which confirmed their intelligence for me. No one looking at their chief could doubt he was the strongest and deadliest, but the youngster? He'd have lost a fight to any of the others, and yet the space he claimed was larger than theirs was.

"What are you thinking?"

"About the ferox."

Horse hesitates, glances around, and hesitates again. It's not the behavior you expect from a Death's Head sergeant, particularly not one who's been awarded the Obsidian Cross. I hadn't noticed it before, but he's wearing the tiny silk ribbon folded into the buttonhole of his jacket.

"Say it," I tell him.

"What really happened?"

"The ferox came," I say. "They slaughtered everybody except me."

There's doubt in his face. As if he knows I'm not telling him the entire truth.

"Maybe it's their idea of a joke," I add. "Maybe they were just having a good day. I asked once, but I couldn't understand the answer."

"You asked . . . ?"

"The ferox talk . . . I know the general doesn't believe me, but it's true."

"Who knows what the general believes," says Horse, and that's the end of our conversation.

At a small door set into a shiny black wall, he stops. Almost inevitably the door knocker, the handle, the hinges, and the mask embossed into the center of the obsidian door are all death's heads.

The woman who answers his knock takes one look at me and opens her mouth to object.

"General's orders," says Horse.

So she shuts her mouth and moves aside. A narrow corridor leads to a bar. The counter is cut from a single block of black marble, black leather lines the wall, and black tiles cover the floor. Looking around, I wonder if this is irony and realize, as a dozen serious faces turn to greet us, that it is anything but.

"Welcome to the NCO club," says Horse.

"Is he a noncom?" The question comes from a man with half his face replaced by metal, and eyes that are all ice. Horse slides him a glance before I have time to answer.

The man looks away.

My beer is cold and so far removed from any other I've ever tasted that I find it hard to believe it's the same drink. This is sweet and smooth, where the others were sour and bitter. It bites at the back of my throat and trickles into my stomach, filling my guts with a slow warmth.

Someone laughs.

"Where did you find him?" another asks, his meaning plain. *Who is this peasant and why is he in our bar?*

"I didn't," says Horse. "The general found him."

They leave us alone after that. When my beer was done, Horse offers me another. But I've changed my mind again. One beer is what I'm allowing myself.

"If you're sure?"

I nod.

"The girls are upstairs," he tells me, nodding toward a spiral staircase that vanishes through a hole in the ceiling. "I'll wait for you here."

"Don't you want . . . ?"

He smiles. "This is new for you. I've been here for thirteen months." And then he catches himself, shrugs, and obviously remembers my words about the difference between the Death's Head and the legion. In that moment I almost like the man. Although I know he will kill me at a single word from one of his superiors.

"Enjoy yourself," he says.

CHAPTER 9

A DOZEN GIRLS line up according to height. They wear very little apart from smiles and enough body hair to prove that no one worries too much about being like ferox up here. In age they range from late teens to early thirties, and in looks from the acceptably attractive to so beautiful it makes me want to cry.

I ignore the most beautiful. We'll have nothing to say to each other and she looks delicate, the kind of girl to be scared by the scars she'll find on my back. I ignore the oldest and youngest as a matter of principle. One will be bitter, the other sullen, and I can do without the fuss.

In the end I choose the one in the middle, quite literally.

In the middle of the line, middling in looks and size and age. Her name is Caliente; at least that's the one she gives me.

"I'm Sven," I tell her. "Do we need to find a room?"

She looks embarrassed that I can ask so stupid a question in front of the other girls. "We have rooms," she says. "Perhaps you'd like to make a choice?"

As she leads the way, I'm happy to follow, not least because Caliente's hips are wide and her buttocks curved, and I can see enough light between her thighs as she climbs the steps to let me know what I'm getting.

Who knew beds came in so many shapes and sizes?

The room we choose is smaller than the others, less ornate. It is the final one on offer and she seems both surprised and reassured by my choice.

"You can read a man by the room he chooses?"

She shrugs away my question, and when I return to it decides to give me an honest answer. "Most of the time."

"And this room says what?"

"That you ask too many questions."

I smile and let the matter drop. Every profession has its secrets. Why should hers be any different? I want to ask how Caliente comes to be in this job, whether it's from choice, how long she's been aboard the ship. But my ignorance about not needing to buy a room has made me cautious.

"What do you want?"

"What can I have?"

Caliente smiles sadly. "Anything," she says, as if that should have been obvious. I guess that answers my question about choice.

"I want a bath," I tell her. "And time to talk and sleep and do the other stuff in between."

And so it happens.

She doesn't bite or howl and we don't fight each other for scraps of food when it's all over, and for that I'm grateful. Instead Caliente sits astride me, with her breasts overflowing my fingers and her nipples hard beneath my hands, and she talks about nothing very much, until the slow movement of her hips takes away my need for conversation.

"Take what you want," she says later.

It's dark in the room. A single clap of my hands will summon light and a click of my fingers will dim it again. Caliente has a trick that involves flicking her fingers and tapping her index finger against her thumb that somehow microadjusts the lighting so that each change is almost imperceptible.

She has many tricks, although only one to do with adjusting the lights. So many tricks, in fact, that I'm rapidly beginning to discover how much I don't know about sex and what makes women happy.

"I'm serious."

A clap of my hands summons lights and she nurses them down to a gentler level, smiling to show she knows I didn't intend to make them that bright.

"What?" I say, seeing something in her eyes.

Her face goes blank, and remains blank as I sit up on the bed and reach down to stroke her face with my good hand. Despite herself, she looks at me and I recognize pity.

"When's your mission?" she asks.

What mission?

I fall back on the traditional excuse, and she's apologizing and I'm trying to wave away her apology before I've even finished telling Caliente that it's confidential and I'm not allowed to talk about it.

We stroke the lights back to near-darkness and I go down on her. Spreading her thighs to bury my face between her legs and force my tongue deep into her. Caliente tastes of salt and soap and something else, which I realize is me.

She breathes deeply and her body begins to tense, her thighs tight around my skull. And then her hand reaches down and grips my head as she forces my mouth hard against her. She has her fingers wrapped into my hair and her sex grinding under my tongue. I can taste blood from my lips where they're bruising against bone.

"Don't stop."

Her demand is urgent.

So I do what I'm told, swallowing blood and salt and myself, and remain that way until her fingers twist in my hair, her hips rise one final time, and she pushes herself against me, whimpering.

It's a first, both going down and having a woman come for real, but I'm careful not to tell Caliente that. And I was told by my old lieutenant—although I don't know if it's true—that in the minutes following release the muscles around a woman's anus relax. So if a man's tastes run that way . . . He told me many things. Not all of them suitable for the twelve-year-old boy I was.

Caliente says nothing when I roll her over and merely smiles in the near-darkness when I tuck a pillow under her hips to raise them slightly. It's as if she always knew this is how we'd end up. Sweat slicks her spine and beads between her shoulder blades.

When I lick it, she shivers.

"I'm sorry about my arm," I say.

"It's okay."

"I can take it off," I tell her. "But that would probably look worse."

"Really," she says. "It's fine."

So I spit on my hand, having supported myself on my arm, and carry my fingers to her buttocks, sliding one finger inside.

"In the drawer," she says. "The pink sachet."

It's lubricant of some sort, so I use that instead, slopping it around her and on me until she tells me it's enough. And then I ease myself inside her and stay like that, for a count of a thousand, until Caliente asks if I'm okay.

"Fine," I say.

Sometimes need is more complicated than it should be.

The girl lets me stay until morning, shares her breakfast when she realizes no plans have been made for me, and helps me shower, watching as I struggle back into my too-small uniform with its cutaway badges. If she has any more questions of her own, she keeps them to herself.

CHAPTER 10

PARADISE IS FOUND at the end of the southern spiral. Don't ask me how astronomers decided which arm of the spiral is north and which south. It was done years before I was born or it occurred to people how many habitable systems there are in a single galaxy. Several hundred years ago, in fact: long before our resident lunatics began arguing about who owns what.

Of course, back then the idea of simply shifting an uninhabitable planet into an orbit that made it habitable was still new and no one really had their heads around the physics, which are quite simple.

Writing to his cousin, a prince called Archimedes once boasted he could move whole worlds given the right tools. He was correct, just a few thousand years too early. Like most of my barroom facts, I have my old lieutenant to thank for that particular gem.

Below me a planet turns slowly, a ghostly white sphere with a sickly-looking sun in the far distance. I'm watching it through the window of a troop carrier that has been converted to a convict ship. This mostly seems to involve taking out all the walls and removing anything that might create an air of comfort.

We're sitting in a long metal hold on metal benches. And the filters on the windows look like they gave up screening light for radioactive particles years ago.

"Paradise?"

The woman next to me nods.

I seem cursed by officers who pride themselves on having a sense of humor. As the convict ship gets closer, I can see a great expanse of cloud stretching from both poles and meeting in the middle. We are too high still for the sight of towns or cities.

Turning to the woman, I ask the obvious question. "Storms?"

She shakes her head. "Sheet ice," she says. "Miles of it."

"*Shithead,*" I say.

A dozen exiles turn to glare at me.

"Not you," I tell the woman. "The general."

"Which general?" asks a man.

And the woman shakes her head in warning.

"Jaxx," I say. "General Indigo Fucking Jaxx."

A hush falls along the row, and I realize that others have been listening in. "Know him personally, do you?" asks a man several seats along. He has one of those ratlike smiles you find on the faces of pimps just before they try to hand you the wrong change.

I flick him a scowl, and he's the one who looks away. When I check again, his face is red and he's chewing his bottom lip. I've made an enemy and we haven't even landed.

"What's the wildlife here?" I ask.

The rat-faced man laughs, nastily. "Wildlife?" he says. "This is Paradise, final destination for everybody on this ship." He laughs again, then stares down at his feet, and I realize he's doing his best not to cry.

"Well," he adds, moments later. "Final destination for anyone traveling in the cheap seats."

"It's an ice planet," the woman tells me. "Everything has to be freighted across. In the early days that included oxygen. Now they crack it from the ice. Use the spare hydrogen for fuel . . . And there are rumors that the dead end up as source material for the protein slabs."

A man swears.

And she shrugs. "Just telling you what I've heard."

The woman is old enough to be my sister. A good fifteen years older than me, with a tired face and bitter eyes and a flatness to her voice that speaks of someone on the edge of despair. She could even be my sister, with her belief in facts to keep life at bay, but her upscale accent betrays her. She shares it with the pretty-boy lieutenant who died in that attack on the fort.

"You're not a common criminal," I say.

She looks at me, almost amused despite her surroundings.

"Are you?" she asks.

Several of the others smile, and for a moment the atmosphere lightens.

"We're exiles," she adds. "Paradise is an exile planet. No one here is a common criminal."

A thought occurs to her. *How could I not know this?*

"And you?" she asks. Several people seem to be waiting on my answer.

"Oh, I'm common enough," I tell them. "And a criminal."

"So what are you doing here?"

"Wrong place, wrong time . . ."

"Which means what?" demands a man across the aisle. He's been friendly enough until now.

"I survived a massacre," I say, my words matter-of-fact. "A tribe of ferox attacked us and slaughtered everybody but me. I don't really know why . . ."

"Except you do."

It's uncanny. The woman even nags like my sister.

"I was lashed to a whipping post," I tell her. "Naked, with most of my back laid open. I guess the ferox figured the legion were my enemies, too."

"You are in the legion?"

I nod. "Yes," I say. "Fifteen years."

She turns away. "The legion killed her parents," says the blond man who sits beside her.

"Mine, too," I tell him.

The woman turns back. So I answer her question before she has time to ask it. "I'm twelve, homeless, without a family. A lieutenant offers me food, clothes, and somewhere to sleep. All I have to do in return is—"

"Kill people," says the woman.

We make the rest of our descent in silence.

As I glance around, I can tell that the others are wondering what kind of monster they have in their midst. This creature, with his metal arm and ragged clothes, a scar on his face, and a wrist so thick that the shackle bites into flesh.

In my turn I wonder how long it will take each of them to turn into somebody else. The convicts down there might have begun as exiles, polite and well spoken. But circumstances change everybody, circumstances and hunger and poverty and necessity . . .

You can put a dozen fancy words to that most basic of needs.

"Welcome to Paradise," announces the rat-faced man when our ship finally reaches the surface and guards begin to walk up the line, undoing shackles as they go. "That includes you." He smiles sourly in my direction.

I don't answer or look away or do anything that might draw attention to myself. I just watch, as one of the guards punches the man in the mouth, half drags him from his seat, and slams him back again so hard that when his skull hits the wall behind him, everyone in the hold hears the sound of bone on metal.

Opening her mouth to scream, the woman next to me halts when I put my hand across her mouth and hold it there, receiving a nod of grudging respect from one of the guards.

Speak only when you are spoken to. None of this lot has the faintest clue.

"Keep quiet," I say.

Very slowly, she lifts my hand from her mouth, and though she wipes her lips with the back of her own hand and looks like she's about to be sick, she does what I suggest and stays silent.

"And you," I tell her friend.

They stay close to me after that. My monstrousness, my knowledge of how this world works has become an asset. *Typical liberals*, I tell myself. Even Rat Face trails along behind us, blood trickling from his broken mouth. Whatever he's carrying wrapped in a cloth is kept close to his chest.

"If you can eat that," I say, "eat it. And if not, and it's small enough, then swallow it while you still have time."

Narrow eyes watch me.

"Stuffing it up your arse isn't enough," I tell him. "They're going to search us. And if we get lucky it'll be limited to a cavity search."

"And if you get unlucky?" asks the woman, her voice acid.

"A fuck-off body scan. Maybe random surgery, to make the point. Anything you've got hidden under chest muscles or sewn into your guts will get found."

It's obvious from her expression that she didn't know you could hide objects beneath layers of muscle or inside the upper gut. They're amateurs. My personal opinion is that no one should attempt to start a revolution unless they've got some chance of success. This lot, forget it.

"Line up."

We do, and I notice most of the others doing whatever the woman does. And since she follows my example, I find myself leading a row of puppets whose ham-fisted movements reflect my own.

Having made us strip, the guards stand us by our clothes while we wait to be cavity-searched. It's done in the open, with sexes mixed to ensure the maximum humiliation and make sure the prisoners realize their place.

There are sixteen of us in our group. Twelve men and four women. The men are younger than the women, mostly my age or a little less. One of the women is our age, the rest a good fifteen years older. This has to say something about revolutionaries.

"It says women die more willingly," a voice beside me announces.

I turn to find the woman from the ship.

"Given how they're treated after capture," she says, "it's a sensible

choice . . ." She smiles at my shock. "I read people's faces. It's one of the things I do."

"And you?" I ask, wondering how to phrase my question.

"Was I raped? Did OctoV let a group of his little fuckwit teenagers practice their torture routines on me?" She shakes her head. "I was bailed almost before I was arrested. My family refused to let me go anywhere without guards. They hired the best lawyers money could buy . . ."

"And the judges still found you guilty."

"Oh no." She smiles, sourly. "I was found innocent. But I got jailed just the same."

She's the first to be cavity-searched, in front of one friend and fourteen strangers. And she takes it because she has no option. Something is already hardening behind her eyes. I'm second, her friend third. It looks like a hierarchy is being established.

A thin man is standing naked in the middle of jeering guards. At an order from their corporal he squats until his buttocks almost touch the cold tiles, and then thrusts his arse into the air and kisses the ground as ordered. Fingers force their way inside him and he screams. When they let him climb to his feet he's crying.

"It's barbaric," says the woman.

"Intentionally."

She stares at me, crossly. As if to say, *I realize that.*

"I'm Sven."

"The mercenary."

"The ex-legion-sergeant . . ."

For a moment she's about to argue. And then she shrugs. "You're right," she tells me. "This isn't the place for semantics."

The question must show in my eyes.

"What words really mean." She holds out her hand. "I'm Debro Wildeside."

"Sven," I repeat.

"What's your second name?"

I stare at her. It's a good question. To the best of my knowledge, I don't have one.

"Do you know the story of Sven Tveskoeg?"

We weren't keen on stories in my family. So I shake my head, wondering what this has to do with me. This woman is odd. Mind you, looking around the holding pen, where a good half of us are scrabbling back into our clothes and the rest stand naked awaiting their turn, I realize that we're all a little odd.

Ungainly, occasionally ugly. We're almost normal in how odd we are.

"He was a king," Debro says when she sees she's got my attention back. "In the old days."

"Which planet?"

Most of the known galaxy is ruled by the United Free. Our dear leader holds much of the rest, or so we're told. The Enlightened and the Uplifted reckon they hold more, but repeating that is treason. The only worlds that still have kings are the worthless ones. Princes of rubble and rock, my sister used to call them. She had firm opinions on those people, which didn't stop one of them hiring a legion for six months and reducing three planets in our system to cinder.

"Which planet?" says Debro. "The original . . ."

"Farlight?"

She sighs. "Earth," she says, fastening her top.

I don't mean to laugh. "Earth's a myth," I tell her. "Fairy tales." I know nothing, and even I know that.

She shakes her head. "It was real. A lot more real than most of the crap that passes for history these days . . ."

"Debro." The word is a warning.

"You know it's true."

"I'm Anton," says her friend. He's been dressing with his back to her. Unless she was the one who had her back to him.

We shake.

"My ex-husband," she says, almost fondly.

In his rags he looks like a stick insect wrapped in cheap plastic. Since he doesn't seem the type to dress like that, someone has obviously stolen his real clothes farther up the line.

"You were condemned as well?"

The glance he gives Debro is strange. It's as if he is asking her permission for something. "We have a daughter," he says. "Under the age of majority. You know the law."

Obviously enough, I don't.

"She's legally still bound to her mother. Since her mother is here Aptitude should also be here . . ." He hesitates. "My family made overtures to OctoV. The emperor agreed to let me take her place. For old times' sake."

Anton talks of OctoV as if he's just another man.

"You've met him?"

"My father and his grandfather were friends."

It explains why Debro is still alive. Although, I realize, it could equally well explain why she was dead had that been the case. "Who is looking after your girl?"

Again that glance.

"My cousin," says Debro finally. "Thomassi was the only one who offered."

A story is obviously hidden in the looks they give each other and under the silence Debro lets hang at the end of her words.

"You've quarreled with the others?"

"Hardly," Anton says. "My mother would have offered. As would my brother. They were too afraid to upset the senator . . ."

Who has to be the cousin, I guess. Anything else Anton might say is lost as the last of the new prisoners climbs up from her squat, head held high despite the tears in her eyes. She's the youngest of the women, and the guards have saved her until last. As she passes the corporal, she mutters something.

It's a bad mistake.

A baton to her gut, an upsweep between her legs, and she's on the floor again, rolling from side to side in her own piss.

"You," the corporal says. "Pick up her clothes."

Anton does as he's ordered.

"And you," I'm told. "Take her with you."

I come to attention. "Yes, sir."

His response is a sour smile. “Strip,” he orders.

It seems best to do it without question.

“Turn around.”

Waiting for the blow, I wait some more, but the man is reexamining the scars on my back.

“A sjambok?”

“Yes, sir.”

“I’m surprised you lived.”

“Yes, sir. Me, too.”

“Dress,” he tells me. Walking over to the girl, he hooks his boot under her rib cage and rolls her over, scowling at the mess. “And take your garbage with you.”

CHAPTER 11

THE ICE is five miles thick, it is ten . . . it is so thick, no one will ever be able to drill that deep. In fact, ice is all there is, and anyone who imagines real rock somewhere beneath all this frozen water understands nothing about space. Because Paradise is a vast comet trapped by the gravity well of an inconveniently placed star.

There are as many different opinions as there are prisoners in our group. The guards undoubtedly have their own theories, but they're hardly about to share them with us.

Apart from the landing field, which undomes to allow entry to visiting craft, the whole of the complex is underground. This makes it easier to conserve what little warmth there is. Exiles are held on the lowest level, guards on the level above, and the governor above that. The theory is the heat generated by the exiles will rise to heat the guards, who will heat the governor and his family.

At some point everything probably worked. But the fact that the prison is now run by its inmates means new tunnels are dug and resources diverted, so now the lowest level is like a giant starfish expanding forever.

Guards and governor still have their quarters above the starfish's body.

Unfortunately its legs are now so far under the sheet ice, the center cannot hold; private kingdoms are created, passing from generation to generation. At the same time, little principalities are built, often hacked directly out of the ice. These tend not to appear on any of the existing maps.

Debro's done her research. I wonder if knowing what she does makes things worse or better.

"Okay, boys . . . We'll take it from here." The words are arrogant, an open challenge to the guards, who scowl but bite their tongues.

The man facing them laughs.

Tall and missing one eye, he wears his beard braided and twisted about with copper wire. "I'm Ladro," he announces. "I run this section. You'll need to remember that . . . What happened to her?"

He's looking at me.

"Spoke out of turn."

"And him?"

"The same," says the rat-faced man, who wears dried blood like a beard of his own.

"You'll learn."

"I have," he says.

Ladro smiles. It's not a kind smile, and I wonder if the new prisoner realizes he's just spoken out of turn again. But the rat-faced man's correct: He does learn. Because whatever he's been clutching so tightly to his chest is gone and both of his hands are now empty and hanging loosely at his sides.

"Your ring," I say to Debro. "Swallow it."

She looks shocked.

"Now," I hiss. "We're about to be taxed. You'll lose it if you don't."

Reluctantly she pulls the signet from her little finger.

"Do it."

While she's still hesitating, I grab the ring from her hand and swallow it as discreetly as I can. When I glance across, Anton is grinning.

"Turn out your pockets," orders the man. "Put your open hands in front of you. I won't bother strip-searching, because the guards will have done that already."

We do what we're told.

"Here's how it's going to work. You're going to give me anything you've got left. If you refuse, I'll break the arms of the people standing on either side of you."

"You can't—" one man tries to say; he doesn't get to finish his sentence.

"Pick him up."

Someone does.

"All right," says Ladro. "Turn out your pockets and offer up your hands."

Walking down the line, he stops occasionally to thrust his hands into a woman's jacket or check that the out-turned pockets of a man really are turned out far enough.

Roughly every third person has something. Wedding rings are plentiful, and one man has a neat little watch that looks like it does an awful lot more than simply tell the time. Ladro stops when he gets to me and gapes at what rests in the palm of my broad hand.

I think I've overdone it, but his amazement stops him from thinking too hard about why I haven't tried to keep it hidden for longer.

"Where the fuck did you get that?"

"Stole it."

He picks up the little Death's Head dagger and turns it over in his hands. It's short, double-edged, a blade made for slicing rather than stabbing deep. Being Death's Head, its decoration is minimal and the scabbard almost bare.

It belongs to Horse, whose real name is Sergeant Hito, my minder back on General Jaxx's mother ship. I imagine he knows to the second when I took it. He'd put it on the side in a bar, turned away to look at something, and seemed not to notice it was gone when he turned back.

"You stole this?"

I nod.

"Where?"

"In a bar from a Death's Head sergeant."

Ladro considers that, decides it's plausible. "And how did you get it past the guards?"

"Swallowed it." I look at him. "Just threw it up a little too early."

He grins. "Too bad," he says, pocketing the blade. "You can't win them all."

You should see what else I swallowed.

And I don't mean Debro's ring, either . . . But I keep my silence and wait for him to pass down the line. When we're done, he jerks his thumb toward a corridor. "Keep going until you can't go any farther and you've arrived."

We're about to discover where we are going to be living. From the look on the faces of most of the new arrivals they're shattered enough already at where they find themselves; I doubt if any of them is ready for what will come next.

"Wait," says Ladro, suddenly magnanimous. "Anyone stops you, tell them you've already been taxed, *by me.*" It's obvious he feels this is the clincher. No contraband has been overlooked. We can safely be left in peace.

"How far?" Debro whispers.

"A mile," I say. "Two miles."

It could be more, a lot more. I wonder how she expects me to know. A hundred paces beyond Ladro's turnoff, I make them stop and have two of the women dress the girl, who's almost in a fit state to walk by now. Debro supervises and puts herself between the girl and a handful of the men who just want a better view.

"Debro's going to get herself in trouble," Anton says.

He sounds worried.

"It's possible." Debro could be adopted as pack mother or she could be cast out. It's too early yet to have any sense of which way it's going to go.

"Can you protect her?"

My smile makes him look away.

"I can pay you," he says flatly.

"With what?"

"Gold," says Anton. "Furs, dried bush meat, illegal crystals, real estate. You want it, we trade it. You get the reward as soon as we get out of here."

"No one gets out of here," I tell him. "This isn't the kind of place people leave." I hold up one hand, stilling him. The injured girl is now dressed and Debro is stroking her face, saying something encouraging. I want to get this said before Debro comes back and we move off again.

"Looking after her is your job," I warn Anton. "But I'll do what I can." We shake hands on this and when I glance up it's to find Debro watching us, a strange smile on her face.

"Come on," I say. "Keep moving."

The tunnel is low and lined with ceramic; it's cracked in places, and on at least three occasions a hole has been hacked into the lining and a smaller tunnel vanishes into darkness.

"It's warmer than I expected," says Debro.

"Won't last," I tell her, then smile, trying to take the sting from my words. None of them yet understands a word they've been told.

"Keep up with me," I tell Anton and Debro, and somehow that means I inherit the girl and Rat Face, whose name turns out to be Phibs. He owns a printing press on a planet so primitive, it isn't even networked. He claims to have produced samizdat pamphlets to order, for money. And doesn't see why he should end up on Paradise.

"You're lucky," I say.

He glares at me.

"Do you have posh contacts, like Debro or Anton?" I ask him. "No, you're here because the authorities couldn't be arsed to kill you. And the reason they couldn't be bothered is you were in it for the money. Being a moneygrubbing little fuck saved your life."

"You know," Phibs says, "you're not as thick as you look."

I punch him, but not very hard.

The tunnel gets colder and narrower as we push on into the gloom. Strange luminescent strings hang from the ceiling. They look as if they're fungal, although Debro's trying to remember if fungus can work at this temperature. She's also shivering. Probably because she's given her coat to the girl who walks behind us. Anton keeps darting back to check if she's okay, but his interest seems fatherly.

"Here," I say, giving Debro my own coat.

She glances at Anton, who smiles.

"He's only being kind," Anton says.

Debro looks doubtful. "I should probably tell you," she says. "I've been celibate for fifteen years."

So loud is my laughter that a boy sticks his head through one of those holes in the tunnel wall to see what the noise is about. He takes one look into my face and disappears.

"What?" demands Debro, sounding almost offended.

"It would be like fucking my sister," I tell her. "And you need to meet my sister to know how bloody scary an idea that would be. She's more my type . . ." My nod takes in the girl, all long black hair and features so fine she looks like she'd crumple in the first decent wind.

"She's everyone's type," says Anton, earning himself a glare from Debro.

"I mean it," he says. "She's going to be trouble."

Debro looks at him.

"You saw the way Ladro looked at her. You've seen Sven's interest. There isn't a man in this group who hasn't checked her out with his eyes. It's going to get worse."

"What do you suggest we do?" asks Debro.

"I don't know," Anton says. "What can we do?"

"Trade her," I suggest. "Now, while her value's high."

Debro shakes her head. "We . . . Are . . . Not . . . Trading . . . Anybody." She is so upset she can barely bring herself to look in my direction.

"And if people die?"

She does face me then.

I sigh, think about what words I want to use.

Anton and Debro have had people listen to them for their entire lives. If anyone ever listened to me it was because I had stripes on my arm, and when those went I fell back on silence.

"People will die trying to protect her," I say. "And those left will resent her and want what they're protecting her from. I've seen it happen."

"All the same." Anton shrugs. "We can't just give her up."

"We can get food," I tell him. "Maybe blankets and medicines."

"No," Debro says. "She stays."

"Why?"

"Because," says Debro. "That's the right thing."

I think about Debro's words as we wander deeper into the tunnel. The rough-cut holes in the walls are becoming more frequent, the light fungus rarer. The temperature drops a degree or so every few hundred paces, and already our breath hangs around our faces like smoke. We have no food, few possessions, and little enough to keep us warm.

In the legion you protect your own. Debro's demand is a version of that, but she's widened the group to include everyone in need of help, including people she's only just met.

It is a really dumb idea. I just can't work out how to tell her so.

As it gets colder the group behind us become quieter. People are beginning to wonder how much worse the situation can become. They have no idea. Although when the tunnel does change, the change is so spectacular that even Phibs forgets to be miserable. The ceramic wall just stops and we step into a tube of frozen white gauze, with a thousand translucent ribs where bracing struts should be. A primitive backbone skims into the darkness above our heads.

"Impossible," says Debro.

Anton shakes his head. "It's here," he says, touching his hand to one of the frozen ribs and wincing, as he has to peel it free.

"So Paradise does have wildlife," I say.

"It would seem so." Anton's voice is matter-of-fact, and he begins to walk on before the rest of us have finished staring. He's a strange man, and it's hard to tell if he likes Debro or hates her.

"What is it?" Debro asks.

"It's a worm."

"Worms don't have ribs."

I take a look around us. "This one does," I tell her.

CHAPTER 12

A HUNDRED, maybe two hundred paces beyond the beginning of the worm a man in a side tunnel has a fire burning. The smoke is sour, and whatever he's cooking smells rancid. I'm interested in what he's found to burn; Anton is more interested in his source of food.

"Hi," says Anton, ducking his head to fit into the burrow. "I'm new here."

Hard eyes stare at him, and then flick to where I stand in the doorway. The man is bearded, dressed in a dozen different layers of rags, and his hand starts moving toward his boot the moment Anton enters his world. A knife, I guess. Probably homemade and crude, like his shelter.

He's a loner. We've all seen them before.

"No," Anton says, shaking his head. "I'm not here to cause trouble. I just want to know where you found the food."

The old-timer's grin shows broken teeth.

"Well?" My patience is not up to Anton's standards.

"Wall," the man says before going back to prodding his fire. Most of the ashes seem mixed with bone. I have my answer.

"We eat the worm," I tell Debro.

Phibs looks sick.

"I'm serious . . . It's frozen and vast. There's got to be some kind of goodness in the bones, and the flesh can probably be dried for use later." The girl is looking at me with horror. Debro's expression isn't much better. So I leave them to tell the others and push ahead. When I can go no farther and the worm gives way to a wall of sheer ice, I know we've arrived.

"We're going to die," announces Phibs when he catches up with me. He's looking at our new quarters, which used to be somebody's old quarters until that person obviously moved up in the world. A cave has been hacked directly into the ice, and a mound of frozen shit and yellow ice decorate one corner. All you can say for the arrangement is that at least the subzero temperatures mean the shit doesn't smell.

A ragged piece of canvas is bundled into one corner. It's ripped and filthy, but it's better than nothing, and some of the men are wearing more than one layer of clothes. At least one of the older women has a cloak. Debro herself is wearing my jacket.

"I need that back," I tell her.

Beside me, Anton bridles.

Phibs already understands. "We must make a doorway," he says. "Keep in what heat we can, right?"

Debro slides herself out of my jacket, and I notice the expensive black suit beneath. No one has stolen Debro's clothes anywhere up the line. I find that interesting in itself.

"And your jacket," I tell another woman.

She glares at me.

"And yours."

The man next to her clutches his arms across the front of his jacket. "Or what?" he demands.

"I'll break your skull against the wall and take it anyway."

Behind me, Debro sighs. "I think you'll find he means it," she says, looking at the man, who climbs out of his coat in sullen silence. A second later the woman does the same.

We collect up spare clothes among us—Debro, Anton, Phibs, the girl, and I. Her name is Rebecca, but I only discover that when we've finished sorting the jackets and coats by size. She's nervous around me, maybe because she heard me suggest swapping her for food.

And then, once Debro has found something to go across the door, which turns out to be the rag we found at the start, I leave her redistributing clothing according to need and wander over to the pile of frozen shit, making myself vomit and catching the laser blade before it hits the floor.

A quick flick of its handle and my blade appears. The m3x has a default set to cobalt blue, which lets the user see what he's doing. At its purest setting the blade is entirely invisible and all the more frightening for being so.

"Holy fuck," someone says.

But by then I'm working.

Sandstone, ice, or carbon, there's little difference among them as building materials and they're all better than piss-stinking adobe. I cut block after block from the ice until I have enough bricks to build a wall. The ragged curtain provides camouflage, hiding my work from anyone outside.

Waving the others back, I slash the cave entrance into a square, giving myself a surface to which the ice bricks will bond. And then I carry my blocks, three at a time, and lay them in place. It's quicker than having to show someone else how to do it.

When this is finished we have a doorway narrow enough to be guarded by one or two people, if they keep their nerve.

"We'll be attacked tonight."

"By whom?" asks Debro.

I shrug. "Whoever gets here first."

The new walls keep in the heat and the cloth across the narrow entrance keeps out the worst of the cold and within an hour we have a temperature in which humans can live. My laser blade, jammed handle-first into one wall, provides light.

"You and you stand guard." I choose two people at random. "Then you two. You take the next watch."

"And you?" asks Anton.

"I'll stay awake the whole night."

"Because tonight is the most dangerous?"

I nod.

"Then I'll stand with you." He catches my look and smiles. "I can fight," he tells me. "I used to do it for a living."

"Militia?"

"Palace guard. Believe me, the training was tough. And before you ask what happened, I met Debro . . . Her family were furious."

Yeah, I think. *I bet.*

In the early hours of the morning Phibs raises his head, like a rat questing. "Outside," he whispers, "a lot of people." Before Anton or I can reply, Phibs puts up his hand, stilling us and the two of our group currently standing guard.

"A dozen," he announces finally. "Two groups, different captains."

He must have seen my doubt.

"Aural augmentation," he says. "Very useful in my business."

Printing? I want to say, but have other things to worry about. "I'll go," I say, moving toward the curtain.

"Take your blade," suggests Phibs.

"No." Anton shakes his head. "It's too early to show our hand."

"Then take mine," says Phibs, handing over a crude blade with rounded handle and rounded sheath, ideal for swallowing or shitting. "Not as impressive as yours," he adds, glancing toward where my blade still burns in the wall. "But still effective."

It's Ladro, with four others, all wearing warm-looking jackets. Half a dozen hangers-on crowd behind, dressed in rags.

"Impressive," he says, nodding at my knife. "Although I'd have bluffed with that and kept the other. It's got real balance." He's holding my stolen Death's Head knife, lightly and very professionally, between his first finger and thumb. Ladro's right about the sweet point. He's got it exactly, from the look of things.

"Glad you like it," I say.

"And I'll take the girl while I'm at it," Ladro says. "Hand her over and

you can walk away from here unhurt." He's very sure of himself, a man so used to getting what he wants that it's obviously never occurred to him things can change.

"Afraid not," I say. "We're keeping her."

Someone sniggers.

So I move out from the doorway and feel Anton and Phibs slide out behind me. With the two guards inside we should be able to hold out for quite a while.

"I'm going to take her anyway," says Ladro. "Give her up now and we'll treat her well."

Again, that snigger.

"Hold out," he says, "and we'll make her pay."

"You don't get it," I tell him. "We're not giving her up."

He comes in then, fast and dirty. The knife in his hand, my knife, slicks toward my throat and I spin away. It's a feint and he goes for his real move, which involves trying to kick out my right knee. There are a dozen ways the outcome can go and each offers a slightly different outcome for our group.

I decide on quick and dirty myself—knowing, as I make my choice, that Debro will not approve and wondering why I care.

Twisting, I let his kick go past me and take his blade in my shoulder. As Ladro grins, I spin my own knife—well, Phibs's knife—so my blade juts to the right of my fist and tear its edge hard and fast across Ladro's throat.

He jerks back, and I rotate my blade, dragging upward from scrotum to breastbone, releasing his guts. The hot stink of shit fills our corridor.

I take down two others. A vicious slash at one severs his jugular. The other I kill by grabbing his head and twisting until bones break. Both of them are from the ragged brigade. We store up less long-term trouble for ourselves that way.

"Go," I tell the rest.

Hostile eyes watch us. A flaming torch is held high, as if someone i trying to get a better view.

"They're dead," says Anton. "And so will you be if you don't fuck of

His voice is raw, his customary politeness discarded. This is the Anton that Debro must have met, the one who worked for the palace guard.

"We'll be back."

"And we'll be waiting," Anton tells the voice.

They leave with threats and curses, dragging Ladro's body and the bodies of the ragged behind them.

"Was that necessary?" Debro asks.

No, I want to say. *It wasn't . . . We could have given the girl up as I suggested.*

"We made our choice," says Anton. "Now we live with it." Which is his version of the same.

Debro wants to say something but turns away. The next time I see her she's comforting Rebecca, who is in tears and protesting that it's all her fault.

"No," I hear Debro say. "It's men."

Anton sighs.

"We've lost Phibs," he says, about five minutes later; something I've already noticed.

"Give him time," I say. "He'll be back."

And he is, dragging food and flammable rubbish wrapped in a stolen blanket. "I thought," he tells us, "while they were busy I'd see what I could find."

"Who?" asks Anton.

"The next lot in." He glances at me. "They're already talking about another attack. Revenge for their dead."

"What's their camp like?" I ask.

He smiles. "Warmer than this," he says. "It's inside the worm. Well, it joins the worm through a hole in the skin. Maybe twice this size. They've even got a mattress."

"We take it tomorrow night."

Anton scowls at me.

"It's warmer, that's one. And if we don't attack them, they'll attack us, that's two. As for three," I say, "we started this and they'll slaughter us if we back down now."

CHAPTER 13

IN THE EVENT we take two days to prepare and attack the moment we're ready. I've spent the previous forty-eight hours laboriously hacking away blocks of ice to run a corridor around the outside of the worm to the back of their camp.

It isn't the cutting that's laborious, but the carrying away of the blocks in utter silence. Phibs helps, although he draws the line at joining me in the attack. This isn't really a problem, because I want him and all the others in the corridor, where the ragged camp exits into the body of the worm.

It's time to get them bloodied.

"You know what you're doing?" I ask Anton.

He nods.

"Good, give me three minutes."

He smiles, then starts counting, adding thousands to the end of each second to make the time stretch correctly. Sixty seconds from now he's going to lead everyone out into the corridor, move a couple of hundred paces as silently as possible, and arrange them in a half circle around the entrance to the next camp. I'm going to use that time to navigate the corridor and slice out one last section of ice bricks.

"One hundred and seventy-eight . . . one hundred and seventy-nine . . . one hundred and eighty . . ."

Kicking in the wall, I stab my Death's Head blade toward the first person I see, slitting his face from eye to neck and adding a fresh wound to his collection. It's a man from the earlier attack.

He falls back, so I open the guts of the idiot who grabs his place. My attacker is tired and hungry, his fighting as ragged as his death. The corpses from our previous scuffle are piled in one corner, mostly eviscerated and reduced to bones and a bucket of innards.

My first thought is that these people are no better than ferox. And then I realize they're not eating their dead, merely rendering the bodies for tallow and fat. The oily lights on the walls indicate their success.

A woman slashes at me so I twist away. When she slashes again, I block her blade with my arm and stop her with a single jab to the throat, shaking her free from my own blade. She opens her mouth to scream and dies without saying a word. As the others retreat into the corridor, a sudden explosion of noise makes it obvious that Phibs, Anton, and the others are ready and waiting.

The fight is brutal, but then it's meant to be.

In the space of five seconds Anton breaks the legs from under three men using the same sideways kick, then takes a fourth by surprise, grabbing his wrist and using the man's own momentum to swing him into a wall, dislocating his arm at the shoulder. A kick to the skull kills him.

"Practice," says Anton, seeing me nod.

As for Phibs, he's everywhere, ducking under blows and sliding in from the blind side. A punch to the throat, a kick to the balls, if possible an attack from behind. He fights dirty, as if taking a special pride in it. And he stops, every time, to rifle pockets or steal some object that catches his interest. Within ten minutes we own their camp and everything in it, although Phibs mutters darkly about having to drag back the booty he stole from them only a couple of days before.

"Cut blocks of ice," I tell Anton, tossing him my laser blade. "Seal the tunnel we made in case the survivors try to use it to do the same."

He nods, obviously amused to be taking orders.

"And you?" asks Debro.

"I'm going to talk to the next camp along."

"Make nice now," says Phibs.

Debro scowls.

My warning to the next camp is stark. We've killed Ladro, and we've just claimed the camp that helped his men. If they leave us alone we will leave them alone. If not, we won't be held responsible.

It's an arrogant speech.

As I walk back along that bizarre corridor and wonder what exactly feeds the light strings that grow beneath the great worm's spine, I calculate it will take those I've just insulted a week or more to get angry enough to attack us. I'm wrong; it takes them less than three days.

"Outside," says Phibs. "People."

Anton's on his feet and I'm reaching for my laser blade before Debro and Rebecca have even woken.

"Keep her safe," says Anton.

His ex-wife nods.

Like it or not—and it seems she does—Rebecca's been adopted by two adults looking to fill a hole in their own lives. If I were the kind of man to have a daughter on Farlight, I'd probably be adopting the kid, too.

"Ready?" I ask.

Everyone nods.

This is politics, I realize, finally understanding something that has eluded me. This is what OctoV does. Says one thing and means another. He does something that looks intended to get one result and what it actually achieves is something else altogether. It's not as complicated as I thought.

Almost to the hour, three days after I return from warning them to leave us alone, the next camp in launches its attack. They are better armed, better dressed, and better fed than the last group we fought. But we are new arrivals, we're organized, and the physical strength we brought with us has yet to dissipate.

Also, they're nervous. Not good in soldiers.

We kill fewer than in our previous battle. There's no need for extremes. Ladro's death and our reputation go before us. We lose three men to their five, gain a child they apparently stole from another camp only days earlier, and establish our right to live within the ceramic tunnel itself.

The next camp surrenders without a fight. The camp after that offers to swap places before we even begin to make warlike noises. We have moved five times in less than nineteen days, gathered a dozen people to us, lost half a dozen of our own, and picked up clothes, weapons, kindling, and food along the way.

People are beginning to pay us taxes.

The camp after this is Ladro's old base, and I decide to visit it by myself. Anton and Debro are all for staying where we are, and most of the others feel the same. But that's not how war works, at least not in my world. The legion has rules. You take ground and then you keep taking ground until casualties make farther advance impossible.

"Let it go," Debro suggests.

"I can't."

She sighs, glances at Anton. "You talk some sense into him."

Anton shakes his head. "Different rules," he says.

I go alone, the Death's Head dagger carried openly in one hand and my laser blade tucked into the back of my belt. Nobody outside our camp knows of its existence and nobody is to know, unless it's unavoidable.

And so I march up a corridor our group shuffled down only a few weeks before. Blankets move slightly as loners and families peer from their burrows. It's the camps that interest me, places built around a central fire, with inhabitants organized enough to keep guard and run shifts, even if the shift just says the weakest do all the work. For every such camp, the corridor has a dozen burrows, squatted by people who wrap themselves in rubbish and hope to be left alone to live out what remains of their lives.

I ignore them and in their gratitude they ignore me.

"Hello? It's Sven. I've come to talk."

Knocking at the door seems only polite. And since it's the first camp I've seen in Paradise to have a door, I enjoy doing so. Being in the legion makes for simple amusements.

Silence is all I get, utter silence.

So I knock again, and then keep knocking.

"Oh for God's sake," someone says. "Come in."

Knife in one hand and what I hope is a suitably deadly expression on my face, I push open the door and freeze . . .

"Afternoon," says a voice. "I was wondering what kept you."

It's the Death's Head colonel, sitting in an armchair in an otherwise utterly deserted ice cave. The armchair has undoubtedly been brought with him, as has the bottle of vodka and two shot glasses.

"That was a joke," says Colonel Nuevo.

I realize I'm already standing at attention.

"The general is impressed," he adds. "'Three weeks and you've already formed a team, taken half a dozen camps, killed one of the trustees, and begun to make people worried."

I nod.

"The least you could do," he says, "is look smug." Flicking open a silver cigarette case, he extracts a long black cigarette and ignites it with an ivory lighter, offering one to me as an afterthought.

"No thank you, sir."

"Why not?

"Bad for you," I say.

He looks at the knife in my hand and smiles. "You've lost me a month's wages," he says, sounding less than upset.

"Really, sir?"

"The general said you'd do it in three weeks. I told him five. Get your things," he says. "We're out of here."

CHAPTER 14

I'VE BEEN on Paradise for less than a month. And yet, leaving is harder than I ever imagined. Phibs will come out on top, or be trusted adviser to someone who does. He will collect his little pile of gold, or whatever it is Phibs is so busy collecting.

He will grow rich, establish power bases. People will come to him for medicines and knives and food, because there's always one man who has these available, for a price.

Anton and Debro are different.

They have only their ideals, and these crack, tarnish, and break. Some people are unable to live with the damage this does to them. I know. Lieutenant Bonafont lives in my memory as a brilliant tactician, natural teacher, and able handler of men. Which is probably why he ended up running a two-bit fort hundreds of miles south of a city that was a city only in name.

He began as somebody like Anton. I understand that now. His voice in my head is educated, polite, well brought up . . . all the things I will never be.

This sets me wondering. *Why did the man waste his time on me?* Because no officer in the legion, not even one reduced to commanding a fort in the middle of nowhere, need ever bother himself with a twelve-year-old refugee, an accident left over from an afternoon's casual slaughter.

Yet Lieutenant Bonafont did.

He taught me how to hold a knife and fire a pulse rifle. He taught me how to track and how to understand the weather. I learned to read skies and be able to tell from the grit beneath my feet whether someone had walked that route before me. And he taught me other things, which seemed pointless to me.

Not to eat with my fingers. How to hold my temper. Why I should always drink a glass of clean water before going to bed drunk.

Maybe it's the debt I owe Lieutenant Bonafont that makes me keep returning to the debt I owe Debro and Anton, because I'm worrying about them. Mostly I'm worrying that Debro will stop Anton from being sufficiently ruthless to keep the things we've gained. And as I walk back along the corridor, with a knife still hanging loose at my side, my thoughts should be on the shower I've been promised, the new clothes, and my meeting with the general . . .

I regret having failed to persuade Colonel Nuevo that the others should come with me, an essential part of my team.

He will not hear of it.

Although he is prepared to consider Phibs, which is a surprise in itself. He is prepared to consider Phibs, but not Debro or Anton. And so I condemn a man who doesn't even know he has a second chance to no chance at all, because I want Phibs to back up Anton, at least in the short run.

I'm coming to understand politics better than I expect.

"Well?" asks Debro.

She's sat in one corner of our newest camp, stroking the hair of the child we gained along the way and talking and talking to the small girl endlessly. I have no idea what she says, but Debro speaks incessantly and quietly and sweetly, in a way I've never seen her speak to an adult, not even Rebecca.

"What did they say?" asks Anton.

I glance around the camp, see Phibs watching from one corner, and nod to him. A second later I nod to Debro and Anton and wander outside. Phibs arrives first, Anton second, and finally Debro. Behind her I can hear the rising whine of a child.

"How old?" I ask.

"No idea," says Debro. "In this place it's almost impossible to say."

"Are you planning to keep her?"

"Of course I'm keeping her," she says crossly. Shaking her head as if there are subtleties I will never understand.

"What happened?" asks Phibs. "We got problems?"

I shake my head. "The camp's already deserted," I tell them. "Someone's even left you an armchair, a bottle of vodka, and two glasses."

Anton's eyes go wide.

"What is going on?" Debro says, her face suddenly serious. Out of all of them, she's always the one who can read the signs. One of life's natural trackers.

I take a deep breath, look around at the ceramic walls and the crudely cut door into what has briefly been my world. "I'm leaving," I say.

Phibs opens his mouth, but no words come out.

"No one leaves," says Anton.

"What do they want from you?" asks Debro.

Looking at the woman I've briefly borrowed as a sister, I have to admit that I don't know.

"Who came?" she asks.

"A colonel," I say. "From the Death's Head."

"And you know this man?" Debro's voice is matter-of-fact. As if the answer to this question is already obvious. Which, in a way, it is. People do not get dragged out of Paradise on a whim. Although it seems I've been sent here on exactly such a whim.

"This colonel," says Anton. "Would he work for General Jaxx?"

I nod.

"And where are you going now?"

Thoughts flicker across his face. A certain calculation can be seen. He's not cruel or conniving, just very intense and very very serious. As I consider how to answer, I realize that both he and Debro are waiting on my words.

Phibs, too, but in a different way.

He's just interested.

"Farlight City," I say, and catch it then. In that second I understand what they want and what I can do for them. I know it before Debro even opens her mouth to ask. *Makes few friends,* said my first and only psychological test on joining the legion. *Utterly faithful to those he does . . .*

I will protect their daughter. Whatever it is Debro and Anton want from me I will do . . . I tell them this and give them my word. It's a legion oath, binding until death, and for all Debro's professed hatred of the military she kisses me on both cheeks and tells me her prayers will hold me to it.

CHAPTER 15

"CAN YOU GET me a drink?" The naked girl glances up from her screen, on which an impossibly beautiful tribal woman is saying good-bye to a legionnaire who has the kind of rugged good looks and smoldering smile that would see him a target for everyone's spite in the real world.

I wonder which role Caliente is playing and why she doesn't just jack the feed straight into her mind like everybody else on this ship.

"Sure," I tell her. "Vodka okay?"

She smiles.

"What are you playing?"

"It's new," she says. "Really neat."

The vodka comes already chilled over ice. I love the drink machine in her room. Waiting while Caliente shifts on her chair to make room for me, I take another glance at her game; it all looks pretty ordinary to me. "What's good about it?"

"Thing's got rules."

I look at Caliente and remember why I chose her last time. Full breasts, but not too heavy, and hips that can be gripped. The chair is too small for both of us. So I pick her up and put her on my lap.

"All games have rules," I say.

She looks slightly disbelieving. As if she wants to contradict but isn't sure she dares. Instead she wriggles prettily. Which, if it doesn't get my uniform stained from inside, is going to get it stained from outside anyway.

"Wait."

I lift her again, just enough to unfasten my trousers.

"Now you can wriggle," I tell her.

It's day three of life aboard the general's mother ship and I've had my shower, a uniform has been found for me, and I've been camping in Caliente's room for the last fifty-six hours.

She wriggles. Mechanically at first, then with more interest as she realizes I'm getting aroused. "Those games," I prompt, because the lieutenant once told me you should always make conversation with girls in a brothel.

"Most don't have rules," she tells me.

"Really?"

"Well, not the ones I play."

"What happens?"

"You play until you get bored. Or things fuck up."

"And then?" I ask, steadying her speed slightly so her buttocks and inner thighs brush against me more slowly as she swivels her hips. If I'm not mistaken, she's begun to get wet.

Caliente hesitates.

"Don't stop," I tell her. "I just want to know what happens if you fuck up."

"You turn the game off and start again."

"Ah, right . . ." The games supplied to the legion are simpler. You go into battle, you die, along the way you collect brothel tokens and medals. You can even go for promotion, in the games world obviously, but I've never seen the point.

We shuffle in silence for a while, if heavy breathing counts as silence. Then I lift Caliente one final time and lower her onto me. She's tight, more involved than last time, unless the position just makes entry deeper.

"Is that augmented?" she asks.

I shake my head. "No," I say. "Everything's just in proportion."

She does it once for one of the tokens Sergeant Hito gave me, and once again for nothing, and is about to do it a third time when hammering on the door tells us both that the sergeant has lost patience for "babysitting a berserker," as he calls it.

He's wrong. I've seen berserkers. We have nothing in common at all. For a start, I'm not a fucking marsupial.

"You're wanted."

I'm wanted in here, I almost answer. Instead I lift Caliente off me, thwack her once on the buttocks, and smile when she yelps. The slap she aims back barely catches my face.

"Enough," says the sergeant. He sounds as if he means it. "She can go," he adds, his voice loud despite the door between us.

"She's already gone," Caliente says, flipping him an invisible finger before kissing me lightly on the lips and disappearing into her shower room in a wiggle of red ass, cheeky grin, and white towel.

"Oh for fuck's sake," says the sergeant.

"What?"

"You might at least put yourself away."

It takes me a moment to work out what he means. When I've fastened my zip, I look around for my coat. "Does this mean the general is ready to see me?"

It's been three days of doing nothing much but fuck Caliente and take showers. I've been expecting to be bustled in to meet the general for so long that I've begun to wonder if he even knows I'm on the ship. Except obviously he does, because it's dangerous for everybody if I'm on the ship and he doesn't know. Everyone is open about the general's ruthless nature and vicious anger. But then, everyone seems to regard this as a good thing.

I'm not so sure. My opinions are that anger has no place in battle, except on the part of the men. Officers are meant to be ice-cool. As I said, my old lieutenant was an idealist.

Obviously enough, I don't mention his theory. I just camp for three days in a room above the sergeants' mess. Most of the sergeants openly resent my presence anyway, and only accept it because Hito outranks them and the general is known to take an interest.

"What?" says Sergeant Hito. "See you? Looking like that?"

That's the other thing about the legion: We don't worry too much about dress regulations and personal standards. The Death's Head, on the other hand, all look like they come out of the same vat. Unless, of course, not caring about dress regulations only applies to the bits of the legion in which I've served. *Frontier forts. Suicide missions. The bits that die.*

"What are you thinking?"

I stare at Sergeant Hito. It's such an inappropriate question from a sergeant. A woman maybe . . . if she's making conversation.

"I mean it."

"How neat you all are."

"You can learn."

No reply is merited.

"I mean that, too. You can learn. The general may demand it . . . And that arm," he says. "Why?"

I don't understand the question.

After he repeats it and adds something about the prosthetic being fifty years out of date and mostly broken, I realize what he's saying. *Why don't I have a better one?*

"They cost," I tell him, voice cold. "This cost."

So he asks the price and I give it. And something in my eyes stops him from laughing, although he glances instinctively toward the door through which Caliente vanished.

"Okay," I say. "So she's expensive."

And beautiful, experienced, and intelligent. And there probably isn't a legionnaire in this part of the spiral who wouldn't give his real arm, never mind a crappy little prosthetic, to have her. But I'm not about to tell Horse that.

"Do you know what she costs?"

It's twice what my metal arm cost. I've had Caliente at least seven times in the last three days, not including freebies, which means I've put the cost of fourteen mechanical arms on the general's bill. I wonder if he'll mind and decide I don't care. How much money do these people have? And why do they get to fuck with the rest of us?

Except I'm not twelve and I had this conversation with my lieutenant. Only back then I was talking about the sergeants and didn't yet realize the lieutenant got to play God with their lives as well.

"We can fix you another arm," says Sergeant Hito.

"I don't want one," I say crossly.

His face hardens. "Don't play games," he says. "It's a bad move. People who play games around General Jaxx die early."

And there the conversation is meant to rest, except I can't let it go. "Don't you have a favorite weapon?" I ask him.

He looks up, eyes still hard, then realization catches him.

"That's your weapon?"

"It's one of them."

"We'll find you something better," he says. "Not just new, better . . ."

And we go down to the sergeants' mess, where a dozen hostile faces watch me as I cross the room and keep watching as the door shuts behind us and we head along a corridor toward an elevator.

"It wouldn't hurt you to say *good day.*"

"*They* don't," I say, and beside me I hear Horse take a deep breath.

"You're the stranger," he tells me. "It's their room, their club. No one gets access to the sergeants' mess except sergeants. Even officers have to be invited."

"So why am I allowed?"

"Because the general wants it."

"Why?"

Sergeant Hito is about to say *No one questions what the general wants.* One of those hardwired reflexes we all have instead of thought. But he doesn't. At my side, he hesitates, thinks about it.

"You lived among the ferox."

I nod.

"No one has done that before. And you claim to be able to talk to them."

"I can," I tell him. "Well, I could. Maybe it was only *those* ferox."

"And maybe you were insane with hunger and exhaustion, and had lost control of your thoughts and only imagined it. That's what Colonel Nuevo thinks."

"Youngster and I spoke," I say firmly. "Sometimes it was hard to understand him. When I was on the whipping post he had to cut me before he made sense."

"And then there's that," says the sergeant.

"The whipping post?"

"That, too. Medical scans show seventeen lashes in a single whipping. No one survives that level of abuse."

"I did."

"Apparently. But that also worries the colonel, I can say this because he's already said it, and has told me he's told the general."

I wait for Sergeant Hito to reach his point and wonder if he knows what this negation of personal responsibility says about him. Maybe it says something about the Death's Head as a whole.

Negation of personal responsibility. I'm proud of that. It sounds like something the old lieutenant might say; probably did, come to that.

"You cut yourself to stay sane? While you were a captive of the ferox. Have we got that right?"

"I did it to talk to them."

Stepping out of the elevator, the sergeant indicates that he is listening. Two men in lesser uniforms step aside. The uniforms are complicated. Sergeants look grander than lieutenants do, and the colonel's uniform is simpler than that. From what I can remember of General Jaxx, his uniform is almost entirely plain. Apart from the Obsidian Cross hanging from his neck and silver death's heads on the points of his jacket collar, nothing indicates that he outranks them all.

The men who step aside are probably corporals. One of them slides me a glance and then hurriedly looks away.

"You were saying . . . ?"

"Pain focuses my ability to hear the ferox."

"You insist that they *can* speak?"

"Only in here," I say, tapping the side of my head.

"They're telepaths," he says, adding . . . "They speak with thought?" In case the word is too strange.

"Yes, that's exactly right."

"And you can hear their thoughts?"

I shrug. "I could hear the speaking of one tribe. What if different tribes speak differently?"

"Thought is thought," he says.

CHAPTER 16

THE ROOM to which he leads me is small and dusty, which is surprising in itself, since most of the ship is spotlessly clean and seems to be kept that way by an unseen army of cleaners who are either invisible or so small that they work at levels below human sight.

There's uniformity to the mother ship's design. The walls are black and shiny, obsidian or glass. The floors are also black, made from what looks like marble. Lights are set into the floors to create pathways when the ship is in darkness, which it is for eight hours out of every twenty-four.

The air is clean, the temperature is pleasant, and everyone seems to know exactly what they are doing. If I were the general I'd never set foot on another planet again. When I say this to Horse, because that's how I still think of Sergeant Hito, he smiles and nods approvingly as if I've just passed some test.

"I've brought you a present," he says. His words are addressed to an old woman who sits behind a counter.

"What have we got here?" she demands.

"An ex-legionnaire."

"I didn't ask *who,*" she replies, more snippily than necessary. "I asked *what.*"

"He's human," says the sergeant, his voice amused. It looks like they've known each other for a long time. "You can run tests."

"We'll all human, darling," she says. "Or didn't our beloved leader tell you?"

"Madie . . ."

"I know. All beings in the empire are human, even the ones that aren't. It's the new rules."

"It's been a hundred years."

"Exactly," she says. "The next emperor will probably change it. And then there'll be no end of trouble . . ."

"Strip," says the sergeant, and it takes me a second to realize he means me.

"God," she says. "Couldn't you have showered him first?"

"He's been in the sergeants' brothel."

"You don't say . . . Use that," she orders, pointing to a cubicle door. It's an oval tube made from glass, with a touch pad set into a shiny black console. There's nothing to say what any of the buttons do. Choosing one at random, I tap it once; when that doesn't produce an effect I tap it again.

A few seconds later I'm sitting on the floor clutching my hands to my eyes, blinded by a light brighter than any I've ever seen in the deserts south of Karbonne, and the sergeant is standing over me, swearing.

"What happened?"

"I'm fucking blind," I tell him, trying to struggle upright and tripping over my own feet. Two sets of hands help me.

"Don't tell me," says the woman. "You looked at the light?"

"I didn't know there was going to be one. No one told me."

She sounds more serious when she speaks again.

"How long did you look?"

"A second."

"You sure?"

"If that," I say. I've been in enough deserts and enough battles to know that light blinds. Already I can see her silhouette peering hard into my face. My reflexes probably kicked in before any real damage could be done.

"I'm all right."

"No, you're not," says the sergeant. "We need to get you down to the medical bay immediately."

"I'm fine," I repeat. "Look, I can already see both of you."

Fingers grab my face and wrench it around. It's the woman, and she has a grip like steel. Her face gets closer to me and I can smell sour breath as she stares deep into my eyes, peering so hard it feels like she's trying to see through to the back.

"Fuck," she says. "He's a self-healer."

They disappear into a huddle and return looking determined. "We'd like to do some tests," says the woman.

"To tell you what you already know?"

Sergeant Hito grins.

I can see it already. She wants to be able to tell General Jaxx what she's discovered without having to reveal how she discovered it: by potentially blinding his new pet.

"Okay," I say, figuring I probably owe the sergeant. And the shower has killed the stink of living with the ferox, something even a spell in Paradise was unable to do.

As the woman sits me in front of a computer, Sergeant Hito begins to walk the length of a row of prosthetic arms, shaking his head every few paces. At the end of the row, he turns around and starts again.

"Nothing big enough."

"Grow him one," the woman says. "With this level of healing you'll have no trouble at all."

"He wants a metal one." The sergeant looks at me. "That's right, isn't it?"

"Tell him he can't."

"The problem," says the sergeant, "is that he probably can."

"Ah," she says. "Close personal interest, eh?"

For a second the sergeant looks as if he wishes this conversation hadn't started, but I'm not really listening, because I'm sitting in front of a computer that seems to be doing nothing but sticking needles in me and slicing blades lightly across my skin. And whatever the computer's finding out, it's making a lot of noise and flashing dozens of lights and whirring.

Unless it's just designed to behave like that.

"You're right," she says finally. "He's human."

"Plus?"

"One point eight percent something else."

The very blandness in her voice makes the sergeant look up.

"What?"

She shrugs, releasing my good arm from a row of unnecessary straps. A wipe of something that smells like alcohol and already my skin is beginning to heal. "It must be a useful adaptation," she says at last.

"That's one way of putting it."

Something in my tone makes them both turn.

"There's no cutoff," I tell her. "The body just keeps going. No pain is too much. Few wounds too extreme. The day I lost my arm to a ferox I walked thirty miles back to the fort."

"A ferox did that?"

"A child," I said. "Probably a baby."

"You were doing what?"

"Hacking the head off its father."

The woman glances at Sergeant Hito. It says, *What are you doing bringing this lunatic in here?* So I start to explain that the adult was already dead. Well, almost dead, and old age not weapons had taken him down. But it's too late. I can see in her eyes what I saw in the eyes of new recruits until I stopped bothering to speak to them. Something between fear and awe.

"Okay," she says. "I can see why the general might want him. Why do you like the arm you've got?"

"It's strong."

The woman sighs, and I get so bored with thinking of her as *the woman* that I ask her name and ask it politely.

"Madeleine," she says.

"That's a nice name," I say, at which the sergeant raises his eyebrows, but I mean it. I'm not making conversation with a whore. It's a nice name.

"Very old," she says. "From the Earth days."

I look at her. "You know," I say, "you're the second person to mention Earth recently."

"Who was the other?"

"A prisoner on Paradise."

"I don't want to know," she says to Sergeant Hito. "Do I?"

The sergeant shakes his head.

"Did Earth exist?"

"Why do you think it didn't?"

I shrug, trying to remember. "Something my sister said," I say at last. "About Earth being invented to explain why things in the galaxy were once simpler . . . She was always saying stuff like that and I didn't really pay much attention, but I always assumed it was true."

"That's heresy," Madeleine says quietly. "You might want to forget your theories about Earth while you're around the general."

I nod, smile to show that I've understood and am already taking her advice. She doesn't smile back.

"Bad times," she says. "A lot of people died."

"I know," I tell her. "Guess I was meant to be one of them."

The sergeant smiles and nudges Madeleine's attention back to the dusty row of prosthetic arms. But the life has gone out of her, so I guess she has some history of her own.

"We'll make him one," she says finally.

"What?"

"Just because no one's done it for decades . . ." She shrugs, her mind made up. "We've got the fabricators. Got more templates than anyone understands. Give me his false arm."

When my arm comes free, she actually looks away.

"You should have seen it before."

"Who did the surgery?"

"My old lieutenant."

"God," says Sergeant Hito. "You'd think he'd have had some battlefield modifiers."

I consider explaining that the battlefield medical supplies were empty when we got them, that few in the legion can read enough to understand written instructions anyway, and most good officers can do things with a heated knife that are beyond mere metal boxes. But I decide not to bother.

"He was drunk," I say. "But he still saved my life."

"You saved that yourself," says Madeleine. "When you picked up your arm and carried it thirty miles back to the fort."

I nod, because now doesn't seem a good time to mention I left the arm, knowing it was useless. Having tied off my wound, I decided to take the ferox head instead.

"We'll fix that first," she says.

And so she does, with a cold precision that impresses the hell out of me. Wherever she learned her stuff, she knows precisely what she's doing.

"What finish would you like?"

"For my new arm?"

"The stump."

In the end, because it takes me so long to understand her question, she gives me something that looks like golden tortoiseshell. It begins as flesh and slowly changes into something close to buffalo horn. With a flourish she produces a tiny laser dagger from her desk drawer and slashes a quick series of marks across its surface.

"You've signed it," says Horse, sounding surprised.

She nods. "First thing I've done in years I like . . . You know what the old man wants him for?"

The sergeant scowls, and she laughs.

"I don't mean the exact mission. Well, maybe the type."

He hesitates. My feeling is if I weren't in that room he'd be more open. "Infiltrate and extract," he says. "Only you can leave out the extraction bit."

"Likely to be in disguise?"

The lieutenant looks at her, and then stares pointedly at me. His look asks, *How would you expect me to disguise that?* And for the first time I wonder what it is about me that he keeps finding odd. In the legion you meet all sorts; that's the whole point. No one minds what language you speak, what color your eyes are, whether your skull shape differs slightly from the man alongside.

I'm tall and reasonably broad, but apart from the scars on my back and the fact that one arm is missing, I've never had cause to think of myself as different. A little stronger, maybe; a little more willing to hike the final mile. But that's only about having extra strength.

After the tortoiseshell decoration to the stump I'm not about to object to anything Madeleine suggests. Although, in the end, she skips the suggestion and just does what she wants anyway. This is fine, because I've seen blacksmiths and weapons repairmen at their best and neither comes close to the level of concentration she brings to making my new arm.

The old one is balanced on a stand, which somehow closes, and then the arm is scanned. She looks at a plate on her desk and tuts, walks over to the row of dusty arms and tuts some more, although she's already said she's not going to use those.

"Getting ideas," says the sergeant. "Let her be."

I nod.

In the end the arm she creates is impressive because it is so unexpected. My old arm, the one the lieutenant bought me, is hard-edged and obvious, all steel plates and pistons, with woven metal hoses leading to clumsy fingers.

The arm Madeleine constructs is exactly like my real one. Only made from black metal. At a distance it could be flesh, although closer up it becomes obvious the skin is not natural. I say *metal* because its surface rings when hit, but the elbow bends like a real arm without any need for overlapping plates and the wrist twists as if it had bones and sinew beneath.

"Like it?"

I nod. "You don't want to sign it?"

Madeleine smiles. "Made one before," she says. "Can't claim it's original. You want me to do something about your back?"

I shake my head.

"Why not?" asks Sergeant Hito.

"Some lessons are best remembered."

He glances at the woman. She smiles and sighs. An old woman in a strange job on a ship that is unlike any I've ever seen. It's as if I've wandered into another world without knowing I was invited. By now I'm getting nervous. I know this because a low ache like hunger has begun in my gut. The feeling I get just before battle.

"What are you doing about armor?"

"That's up to the general."

"But he will be in uniform?"

It's a game between these two. Somewhere between cards and chess. An alliance built on mocking each other. And I'm discovering more about the sergeant every minute and I've begun to wonder why he's letting me learn so much.

"I'll make him some," she says. "If the old man doesn't like it, we'll scrap it."

"Okay," says Hito. "Give him the basic black."

"Insignia, rank, company?"

Sergeant Hito shakes his head. "No identifiers," he says.

CHAPTER 17

I'M SEARCHED before being allowed to meet General Jaxx. A group of four officers close in on me and pat me down. Since I've already passed through a full-body scan I know this is tradition, part of a ritual to be undergone before being shown into the presence of a Death's Head general.

"Weapons?"

I shake my head.

"You'll have to remove that arm."

Behind me Sergeant Hito begins to object, very politely. All four men outrank him. "The general himself . . ." They retract the moment the sergeant explains that General Jaxx wants to see Colonel Madeleine's latest work.

"You stay here," one says.

The sergeant looks like he wants to object to that, too, but does what he is told and I enter the general's study alone. It is the same man. As tall as he ever was. Only now he's wearing a black smoking jacket with narrow trousers, both decorated with a single band of silver piping.

Out of uniform, the only sign he controls a regiment is the silver signet ring on his left hand. A grinning skull, mouth mocking and hollow eyes taunting the world.

"Sven," he says.

I wait; it's all I can do.

"We have a job for you. One ideally suited to your talents."

What talents? I want to ask, but I make myself stay silent.

"What do you know about Farlight?"

"Nothing, sir."

He nods. "Even better." Walking across to a sideboard, he pours two drinks from a decanter. He doesn't tell me what the drink is or ask if I want one, but since he sips from his first and then downs the rest in a single gulp, ending with an obvious sigh of satisfaction, I do the same.

"Single malt," he says. "An old Earth drink." He hesitates, smiling slightly. "You know about Earth?"

"Very little," I say.

"What about its end?"

It's one of those days for keeping my face blank. Whatever I know, or in this case don't know, it seems best to keep to myself.

"Slightly over six hundred years ago the singularity swallowed its own children . . ."

He pauses. "Or maybe it ate its own parents. Experts disagree . . . You don't have the faintest idea what I'm talking about, do you?"

I shake my head.

He smiles. "I can't tell you," he says, "how happy that makes me."

The job is simple. I'm to flip to Farlight, hunt out a traitor whose name I will be given on arrival, and kill him, his bodyguards, and his entire family. If his palace catches fire at the same time that will be even better.

"We will, of course, deny having even heard of you if you fail."

"And if I succeed?"

"You will be inducted into the Death's Head, undergo formal training, and fight the one campaign all new entrants must undertake. After which, you will work for me and only for me."

He waits.

Am I meant to thank him?

After a moment, he smiles. "I like you," he says. "People say you're an animal. They're wrong. Animals don't think. Well, not the way you do. I can see we're going to work well together."

I might think, but obviously not fast enough. It takes me a second or two to realize he's given me my cue to leave.

CHAPTER 18

FARLIGHT IS VAST. A sprawl of a city trapped in the bowl of a long-dead volcano. It's layered with history, like some exotic omelet. For a start, single streets have half a dozen different names, while boulevards end abruptly and grand squares have lost out to viral attacks that leave half their buildings looking like molten wax.

Palaces fill the center and slums crawl up the slopes of the volcano's caldera until the sides become too steep for normal building, and huts on stilts and hardfoam shacks become all that cling to the rock. After a few hundred paces even these peter out and the crater's sides can be recognized for what they are.

All this I see in the time it takes an old cargo freighter to overfly the city at a height I'm surprised the emperor allows. When I mention this a crew member grins.

"Upset someone, probably."

"Who did?"

"We're being paid to drop low over Boulevard Mazimo. So presumably we're ruining someone's posh lunch." He laughs. "I guess they left someone off their guest list."

Carl grins, slaps me on the shoulder, and offers me half of what remains of his sausage, which seems to be made from rancid meat mixed with enough garlic to bury the stink of one thing under the stink of another.

As good a description of Farlight politics as I'm likely to find.

I thank him, say I've just eaten.

He's the ship's cargo skipper. We originally met in a bar in high orbit. A joint I've never visited before, obviously enough, but recognize immediately. A row of stalls at the back speak of hasty blow jobs and up-against-the-wall fumbles. I get the same glance from a dozen different men, checking for the law, ex-wives, and debt chasers. And a barkeep comes out from behind his counter the moment I trip some scanner built into the door.

"No weapons," he says.

"I'm not carrying."

"You've been scanned."

"All right. I'm not intending to use."

He opens his mouth again.

"I could, however, change my mind."

The madam laughs. "Give him a drink," she says, and I'm in.

Carl wanders over to ask where I got my coat. I examine his question for double meanings and wonder if some other query is coded beneath its surface, but the man is serious. He prides himself on dressing well and wants one like it.

"Belonged to a Death's Head sergeant."

He looks startled.

"Don't worry," I say. "He won't want it back." This is true enough. Sergeant Hito took it from stores, the previous owner having no need of it. "You can have it," I say, "if you can get me to Farlight."

"There's a drop shuttle," he tells me. "Leaves every hour."

It's my turn to look at him.

"Ballistic silk lining," I say. "Half-chameleon outer layer, runs on sunlight and sodium glare. Infinitely more effective than full chameleon, which is much too obvious." I'm only repeating what Sergeant Hito told me, but it sounds convincing and I want to get rid of the coat. Call me suspicious, I can't help suspecting General Jaxx has a neat little transponder bug fixed in there somewhere.

Carl's sold, and I have my ride . . .

"You sure you aren't hungry?"

"Quite," I say, waving away his offer of rancid salami. So Carl wanders away to do whatever he does on *Trillion Two Zero Three*, which seems to be very little. A while after we land he looks around quickly, checks that the ramp exiting the cargo bay is clear, and nods meaningfully.

A quick shake of my hand and I'm out of his life, my coat still on his back and a half-chewed mouthful of salami still churning away in his mouth.

The landing area is one vast field of docked craft. A high steel fence surrounds it, and from the battered condition of some of the newly arrived ships my guess is the fence exists as much to keep the crews in as to keep the rest of the city out. No one stops me as I slide between two vast pod-shaped vessels and duck under the belly of a third. People come and go, a man laughs out of sight, and a small boy sits on an upturned box watching a five-legged spider bot make a clumsy repair to a runner.

Even out at Fort Libidad we saw runners. They're those tiny two-man hovers that barely rise above head height, but can handle any terrain. I wonder what use a runner is here and realize, as the boy's father appears, that the craft is used to navigate the landing area and the boy is a cargo worker's son.

"What are you doing here?"

"Watching," I say, which seems fair enough.

The boy's father scowls.

"Your spider bot's fucked," I tell him.

He scowls again, maybe at my language, maybe at my accent, or maybe he just objects to people pointing out the obvious.

"Which is more important," I ask him. "Getting that weld finished, or having the bot work properly?"

"No one can mend bots," he says, but I can see him thinking through my question. "Bot," he decides finally.

Stepping up to the fist-sized metal insect, I grab it while its attention is still on the weld, flip it over, and rip off another two of its legs before tossing the thing to the ground. As the man prepares to shout in outrage I hold up a hand for silence, grab a piece of scrap iron from a half-full skip, and crumble it into small pieces, using the fingers of my new prosthetic.

I drop the crumbs next to the stunned spider bot.

Nothing happens.

Counting down from ten, I hit zero and reach again for the bot when it decides it's damaged enough already, thank you, and starts eating like its little mechanical life depends on it.

"Three hours," I say. "Maybe four. Feed it extra for the next few days, until it settles down again." Already we can see that the bot is beginning to bud three new legs to replace the two I stole and the one that was already missing.

"Fuck," he says. "Where did you learn to do that?"

"Off world," I say. "From an engineer. That's an old combat bot, designed to keep going until it hits fifty percent damage, then instigate emergency repairs. Next time one gives you trouble, mess it up a bit. They usually respond."

The man looks at me, and then glances around him.

"Ex-army?"

I nod. "And you?"

He doesn't need to reply, it's already in his eyes. "Come off one of the ships?"

A glance toward *Trillion Two Zero Three* answers that one for him.

"Looking for a job?"

"Always."

The man smiles tiredly. "Yeah," he says. "Been there . . . Take the east gate and you'll find a row of flophouses. Ask for a room by the week and refuse to give a deposit, and don't pay more than two credits." His glance takes in the coat Carl found for me after agreeing to transport me for the price of my own.

"You do have two credits?"

"Yeah."

"Good," he says. "When you've got that sorted, come back and ask for Per Olson. I'm friends with the foreman. He may have something you can do."

"Thanks," I say, knowing I'll never see him again in my life.

CHAPTER 19

PROFESSIONALISM SAYS I should go back to kill both man and boy. But then, by the same token, I should kill Carl, and maybe those other guys in the first bar, because they might also identify me . . .

It's always struck me that leaving a trail of dead is a really bad way to remain inconspicuous. Far better for Per Olson to think I took his advice about flophouses but found myself a better job.

As I head east the cargo vessels grow ever scuzzier. I begin to wonder how such craft can be airworthy and quickly realize they're not. A host of spider bots are crawling across their broken carcasses. As the creatures go, they chew and strip, removing anything that looks usable, converting this into that. It's what spider bots do, what the bots have always done so far as anyone knows.

I keep walking until I hit five flophouses in a row, a bar, a cantina of sorts, and a brothel. All are made from fiberbloc, epoxy, and patched metal roofs. They look as if they were thrown up as temporary housing while the landing site was being constructed and never taken down again.

"Five credits," says the first.

Deciding to save myself the argument, I walk next door.

"Three."

"Two," I offer.

The girl behind the counter glances from under her bangs, which probably still works for about 50 percent of her customers, and shakes her head. "Two and a half," she tells me. "My best offer." She perks up. "Mind you," she adds, "that's everything included."

"Including you?"

She prepares to be insulted, then takes another look at me and bats her eyelids instead. "Absolutely not. But we can talk about that separately if you want."

Her name is Lisa. She lets me have the room for two credits.

There follow the worst three days of my life. Control for a soldier is everything. The world might be going to hell in a handcart and the battle lost long before it began, but you still need control over yourself and your fears and emotions.

Sergeant Hito has warned me what will happen. Even told me it will take seventy-two hours and I should keep that in mind when I decide I can't take any more. And he's right: It takes exactly that long, almost to the minute.

Nothing he says, however, comes close to describing how it actually feels.

Ripping open a foil packet, I extract a flimsy piece of skin and unroll it as instructed, dropping it into the basin that acts as the sole source of clean water in my new room. I sit down to wait the fifteen minutes I've been told to wait.

After five minutes the skin reveals itself as a hollow tube, and a tracery of blood lines begins to spread across its swelling surface. Another five minutes and tiny ripples began to roil across that surface, as it flexes like a caterpillar attempting to crawl.

I'm feeling sick already.

By the time my fifteen minutes are up my stomach is a hard knot and the slug is attempting to climb out of the basin.

This is *Aculeus accipio*.

They are illegal to own and breeding them is punishable by death anywhere within the empire. It is said—well, Sergeant Hito says—that on outer systems whole cities use them and see nothing odd about the fact. But his face displayed his own doubt as he said it.

If I'm going to do this, I have to do it quickly. Picking up the slug before it can escape, I open my jaw and swallow, feeling tiny hooks scrape my gullet before it is even halfway down.

I gag. The reflex is instinctive.

It fights the reflex, its hooks sinking deep into the sides of my throat. By now I'm on my knees, retching. Habit makes me crawl toward the toilet until my mouth is over the side. Clutching my gut, I heave the muscles under my hand, and my stomach finally loosens and lets go its contents.

The vomit rises up in my throat and passes through the slug on its way out of my mouth. The *Aculeus* kicks and strains, but that's excitement. This is what it's been waiting for. It's alive and has found itself a host.

Spitting, I feel the slug tense and the reflex throws me into a vomiting fit that empties my stomach, and then empties it again, until I no longer know or care where the liquid and already digested food is coming from. Within three bouts of vomiting, my stomach is empty, and within seven I've emptied my upper intestines and am spitting bile, which etches its way through the dirt lining the toilet bowl.

The diarrhea begins shortly afterward.

Waking to find I've soiled the sheets, I roll out of bed, dragging the sheets with me, and wash them in the basin until the shit is gone. The mattress is also stained, so I wipe it down, spreading the mess rather than actually cleaning it. This engages what is left of my brain and I scrape the cotton cover with my combat knife, not caring if the blade takes away cloth so long as it rids the mattress of the dirt.

Once I'm done scraping, I scrub the stain with a sodden pillowcase until the material looks no worse for wear than any other bit. Flipping the mattress over, I hang my sodden sheet up to dry from a light fitting and spread a huge and filthy towel across the mattress for my bedding. And then I fall unconscious for the next five hours.

The towel is dirty but the mattress is still clean.

So I wash the towel and feel too sick to do more than toss it back onto the bed and fall asleep again. A vomiting fit wakes me and I see blood in the toilet bowl. Music can be heard in my head; it's that weird stuff women play sometimes, waves and wind and natural noises. After a while I realize my body is playing itself back to me, but there's something extra.

A real music, odd and dissonant and weirdly seductive, with an unexpected echo. I can hear my own thoughts, but they're time-lagged by a split second. A waterfall of fears and memories that I have . . .

no way of turning off

My throat hurts, and as I cough the slug seethes slightly and then settles.

I vomit again, a sour stream little thicker than beer, but it's almost from habit now, and I know that next time I'll be able to swallow the reflex and the taste in my throat. Either the slug is thinner, it's dug itself deeper into my gullet, or I'm already getting . . .

used to this

The towel is clean for the first time in days.

My eyes are hollow and my cheeks stubbled, my gut sinks in toward my ribs where fever has stripped what fat I had from my frame. My muscles look like bundled wires beneath my sallow skin. I'm pretty sure my eyes have changed color but that has to be . . .

impossible

As my thoughts synchronize with themselves, I feel the music in my head fade and the sounds of my own body recede into the background. In their place is a great emptiness. I can see myself for what I am, some hick soldier out of his depth in a strange city on a mission still to be revealed.

It's a very scary thought.

Except it isn't.

Already I've noted my arm, the strength in my body, the mind that's barely been stretched to thought in the first twenty-eight years of its life. The potential is there, I can use that.

I will use it.

Staggering to the window, I look out on the edges of Farlight. Ahead of me I see the Bosworth Landing Field and beyond that the Emsworth Favelas, climbing the lower slopes of the caldera. Above is Calinda Gap, a gash cut by time and strange tides in the bowl's rocky edge.

How do I know these things?

I don't know, but accept that I do. And as I turn to look at a different section of this outer city, facts slip into place and history backs up behind physical objects. These are my thoughts and I can just about control them, but the information is being drawn from somewhere else.

This is definitely not how it is meant to work. The slug is meant to allow access to a low-level neural link to let me pass and receive messages, sliding them under even the most sophisticated surveillance devices. An agent of the general's should be making contact, mental contact, but I don't think he is this vast hollowness and intelligence that is filling my head.

You are mine now.

Are you listening?

Pushing away the emptiness, I stagger back to the mirror. How I look has never much interested me. I get the usual girls a legionnaire gets, which is mostly the ones other men don't want. It's a cruel fact but then it's a cruel world and I've forgotten how many times my sister told me that when I was a child; and everything I've heard and seen since suggests it's true.

Doesn't have to be.

"Who are you?" I demand finally.

The voice laughs. "Who do you think?" it says. "I'm OctoV, your *emperor.*" Something in the way the voice says this makes me swallow, and sourness immediately fills my throat.

"I don't understand."

"Few of you do."

"Of us?"

The voice nods, absurd as that sounds. I can hear the voice, but only in my head, and what I'm hearing is more thought than actual speech. I get the inflections, the nuances that a speaker might put into the words were they actually verbal, but it is more an intimation of how they should sound.

Inflections, nuances, intimations—where do these terms come from?

Don't underestimate yourself, says the voice. *Anyway, you heard them from your guardian as a child.*

"What am I meant to do?"

Your job.

"Are you going to tell me what that is?"

Someone else will. You must do the job the general sends you to do. Because if you don't he will have you killed, and that would be inconvenient. So do what you do and be who you are. We'll talk later.

"When?" I ask as the voice begins fading.

A day or so, a week, a month, a few years. It's hard to be exact. Necessity is so fluid at this level.

And then the voice is gone and I'm alone again. The urge to vomit is also gone, and in its place is a hunger to see this city and do my job. I examine those thoughts carefully, worried they might belong to someone else, but they genuinely seem to be mine.

A knock at my door spins me around and the laser knife is in my hand before I'm even aware of the fact. Lisa stands there, eyes wide and appalled. Maybe it's at my nakedness, at the knife in my hand, or at the fact that one of my arms is made from black metal. Maybe it's just the stink and the state of my room.

"There's someone here to see you."

"Someone?"

"A man," she says. "He's been waiting."

"How long?"

"About three hours."

"Why didn't you tell me earlier?"

This time her eyes definitely flick to the knife in my hand. "I did," she says. "You threatened to kill the first person who came into this room."

"Had my mind on other things," I say.

There's a fear in her face that looks ugly.

She's not as young as she'd like, but she's still a lot younger than I am and this is her life and where she lives, and where she'll probably always live. I need to learn to handle these things.

"Sorry," I say. "Battle fever. It's over now."

She looks around my room and her nose wrinkles.

"Yeah. It stinks. I'll get it cleaned up and get myself cleaned up and then I'll go have a beer. Maybe you could join me?"

"Battle fever?" she asks, neither accepting nor rejecting my invitation.

I nod, looking sheepish.

"You were a soldier. Where?"

Fort Karbonne, a wretched little planet in a wretched little solar system so far from here you won't even have heard of the nearest star.

I'm right, she hasn't.

"You're a long way from home."

"Yeah, a long way."

Something in my eyes makes her accept my earlier invitation to have a drink. "But you'll need to get yourself cleaned up." Her voice is hesitant, because she's anxious not to offend me, and I smile, realizing that I really must look dreadful if I'm not fit for some dive on the edge of a Farlight favela.

"Send the guy up," I tell her.

"I'M CHARLES DECHARGE," he says.

He's small and wiry, an underfed version of Phibs. When he hurries into my room his eyes are already flicking from corner to corner, as if searching for unexpected enemies.

"You're meant to have swallowed your kyp by now."

"My what?"

"*Aculeus accipio* . . . You were given one."

"It's fitted," I say, opening my mouth. "Want to take a look?"

He backs away, his face blanking as he concentrates frantically. The very faintest echo of a thought appears inside my head. It's a whisper to the roar I heard earlier. I have almost no sense of emotion and certainly nothing resembling nuance, but it's there.

"Got you," says deCharge.

"Yeah."

"Did you have a hard time of it?" He takes one look at my room, sees the drying sheets and sodden towels, and realizes the absurdity of his own question.

"Can you hear me?" he asks.

And his question is inside my own head, so I nod.

"Good," he says. "This is your mission."

He's talking quickly, anxious to get away from a face-to-face meeting, because such meetings are obviously a rarity for him.

"Five weeks ago Senator Debro Wildeside was disgraced in a plot instigated by her cousin, Senator Thomassi. She's in exile, as is her ex-husband Anton Urbana, who has taken the place of their daughter Aptitude . . .

"With me so far?"

I nod, trying to keep my face neutral.

"As tradition allows and Thomassi hoped, Debro Wildeside settled her whole fortune on Aptitude, who is now in Thomassi's care. The senator plans to marry the girl himself. Should that happen it will create the greatest trading house this empire has ever seen. Your job is to stop that."

"Senator Thomassi dies?"

"Of course," he tells me. "Begin with Thomassi and end with the girl. Spare no one and burn down the house. Do it tonight."

I finally understand why deCharge wants to do this meeting from a distance. He's been told I might be dangerous. And someone is playing with me, unless they're playing with Debro and Anton. Either way it stinks. Meet the family, kill their kid . . .

CHAPTER 20

MORNING COMES and the House of Thomassi is still standing, and a very elegant house it is, too. A five-story villa set in its own gardens, with steel gates and trees that look as if they grew from seed. The villa occupies the best position on Boulevard Mazimo, one of Farlight's more expensive streets, about a fifteen-minute walk west of the central palace complex.

But all this comes later, much later.

About twelve hours after I decide I need to clean myself up, buy some weapons, and take Lisa out for that drink . . .

MY SHOWER IS cold, which is what you'd expect from a dive on the edge of the Bosworth Landing Field in the shadow of Calinda Gap. I don't mind, because the city is hot and muggy, the night air thick with hydrocarbons and sharp with ozone from the cutting sheds that line the landing fields below.

By the time my shower's done, I'm too clean for my old clothes. So I shrug myself into the trousers, take the credit chip deCharge left on his way out, and go looking for a cheap clothing emporium. What I actually find is a stall about two streets back from Golden Memories, which turns out to be the name of the brothel where I'm staying.

"That's all you've got?"

She's looking at my credit chip.

I nod.

"How much is on it?"

My shrug says it all.

The old woman pulls a wry smile and tells me her best offer is sixty cents on each credit if I'm expecting her to launder a stolen chip as well as sell me clothes that don't announce I've just flown in from off planet, and probably broken my contract by wandering away from my ship.

"It's not stolen," I tell her.

Her eyebrows are white, like her hair. She reminds me of a ghost owl with her exaggerated expression of disbelief.

"I was given it."

She laughs. "Sure," she says. "How hard did you have to hit him first?"

We settle on seventy-five cents and she takes the whole card and promises to give me cash for what remains, after I buy what I need, provided what remains doesn't come to more than 25 percent of what is on there in the first place.

Something tells me she's done this before.

"What are people wearing?"

The woman looks at me. "What people?"

"People like me . . ."

I get a leather coat, too heavy for the hot night air. It's a cheap copy of the one Carl took as price for my passage aboard his ship. The two shirts she offers are black, their dye is poor quality, and both look ready to fall apart after a couple of washes. When I pull a face the old woman tells me to take a closer look.

They're ex-military, ballistic polymer mixed with spiderweb. The color is crap because polymer and web take dye badly, but the cloth is thick enough to slow blades and wind itself around incoming bullets, making them easier to extract.

She has me pegged as a mercenary, someone mugging rich kids to make ends meet between jobs. It's not a bad cover story for a man of my temperament. It also makes it easier to ask my final question, although I ask another one first.

"How much left on the chip?"

She debates lying. Decides against. "Three thousand and eight credits."

Seeing the shock in my eyes, the woman scowls. She could have lied anyway, because I obviously had no idea just how much was there.

"Must have been a good friend," she says bitterly.

I stare at her.

"To give you this."

We lock eyes and she glances away. "I can't give you anything like that much in cash," she tells me. "I said that up front."

"I need a gun," I say. "Something good. You can take another two five . . . I want the last five hundred in cash. Small notes." I wonder what I've said to make her laugh.

"This is Farlight," says the woman. "No one takes paper."

It seems inflation makes banknotes worthless, and OctoV keeps printing scrip to pay his troops, so now even credit chips have to be underwritten with gold from private banks, at least they do in Farlight. It's my ignorance of this that convinces the woman I'm from way off system.

And then she weighs the chances of someone that distant getting this far into the center without serious backing, and begins to wonder if she should be dealing with me at all. I've gone from being an out-of-work mercenary to something more dangerous.

"A gun," I tell her, making my voice hard.

She nods. Greed, and the thought of the credits she can take, overcoming her fear. "You wait here," she says. "I'll be back in five minutes."

It's more like an hour.

"I THOUGHT YOU'D forgotten . . ." Lisa is slouched behind the counter at Golden Memories, her hair carefully brushed and then messed up again where she's flicked it back in irritation at the heat and the length of time I've made her wait.

"Had to get this," I say, pulling back my coat.

Her eyes widen at the shoulder holster and the length of gun it carries. Something smaller would have been nice, but this is nearly new and came with enough clips to need a second holster on the other side, just to carry the ammo.

"You're not planning to go out wearing that?"

"Why? You think it's a bad idea?"

She does, but I wear it anyway. For a start, I want to know if the rig looks obvious under my coat—and then there's the excitement factor. For her, not me. I've been wearing concealed weapons most of my life.

We drink at a cantina two buildings along. A place that caters to men from the breaking yards and landing fields. For this part of the city it's practically a class joint. All the men look over and most of them know Lisa by name, if the litany of *heys* and *his* and *hellos* that hits her is anything to go by.

Eyes skim over me, note my clothes and the way I carry myself. If anyone registers the concealed weapon it doesn't show in his face. I'd say *his or her face,* but Lisa's the only woman in this cantina, apart from a girl who could be her twin, and she's serving beer behind the counter.

Carl's in a far corner with two men from *Trillion Two Zero Three.* His gaze skims across me a little faster than the rest.

"Who's your friend?" It's the girl who looks like Lisa.

"He's from off planet."

"Lisa," the girl says, smiling. "Everyone's from off planet."

"No." Lisa shakes her head. "He's, like, off off planet."

The girl behind the bar examines me with new interest. "You here looking for a job . . . ?"

"I've got one," I tell her.

Lisa looks at me with interest.

"You going to tell me what it is?" That's the bar girl again.

I give her my best smile. "Believe me," I say. "You really don't want to know."

When the girl opens her mouth, Lisa glares. So the girl shuts her mouth again.

"Meet my cousin," Lisa says. "Angelique."

Angelique shakes my hand, although she seems to find the gesture hilarious. "Where are you from?" And then before I can answer, she mock-scowls at Lisa. "I'm allowed to ask that, right?"

Somehow we all end up in bed roughly an hour after the bar closes. It's Angelique's bed, so maybe Lisa is nervous about taking me back to her room at Golden Memories, not that I care whose bed we use. Lisa and Angelique are young, they're blond, and both have obviously long since discarded their inhibitions, assuming they had any to begin with.

We fuck, we sleep, they drink cachaca and I nurse a beer until the cousins are sprawled in a tangle of naked limbs on a filthy mattress and I'm standing at the window watching the sun come up over the capital of my world.

Somewhere out there is a girl not that much younger than these two. She should be dead, because I should have killed her. The fact that this hasn't happened is obviously worrying deCharge, because I can feel his voice tugging at the edge of my mind.

What? I ask.

Voices break through, far too many voices, and I find myself on my knees. When I look around the girls are still sleeping, but the sun is a little higher in the sky. Mr. deCharge is in the mix inside my head, his voice more urgent than the others.

Where are you, he says.

Sick, I tell him.

His voice comes from a distance, bleached of its worry and anger. Only the length of time it's been demanding my attention lets me know he's upset.

What do you mean sick?

I feed him a memory of my vomiting, so real and vivid I can almost feel him lurch back to escape its full horror.

Shit, he says.

Yeah, I agree. And then I ask a question that's been troubling me. *How do I get rid of the kyp?*

You don't, he tells me, but in asking I've reassured him. Mr. deCharge thinks I'm worrying about the fact that my kyp is not working properly and is making me vomit . . . well, as far as he knows.

Where are you now?

Something stops me from telling him the truth. *Out for a walk. Where are you?*

Waiting for you.

I nod, slipping three fat silver coins from my pocket. One goes on Lisa's side of the bed, another goes on Angelique's side, and the last goes into Lisa's shoe. She'll know to keep quiet about that one.

"Buy a dress," I scrawl on a scrap of paper.

And then I'm out of there, eyes scanning the street to check if anyone's been waiting for me. Dogs and a hen, a cat on a high roof, and a broken-tailed skink chewing a fly halfway up a filthy wall. It's still early and I need to be somewhere else.

Can you hear me?

Just about, I say. *It's erratic. I can't believe it's meant to be like this.*

It isn't.

And I can't get it out?

No, he tells me, sounding reassured by my repeated questions. *You're just going to have to work with that one.* He listens to me swear and agrees that a faulty kyp is not ideal.

I'm on my way back, I tell him.

He hesitates.

Unless you want me to go straight there?

Where?

The Thomassis' villa.

I can almost hear him wrestle with the questions, and behind his anxiety lie other voices, a mix of direct questions and fragments of thought. It's like listening to a badly tuned military radio with everyone talking at the same time. Somehow that doesn't seem right to me.

The voices, I say to him before he's had time to answer my previous question. *Should I be able to hear them?*

And it's his turn to swear. *You can hear other voices?*

Hundreds, I say. *It's like a permanent headache. It's one of the things that's making me sick . . .* This is a lie obviously, but it's a good lie.

You can turn them off . . .

A wind almost sweeps me from my feet. When it's gone, I'm sagged against a wall being watched by a puzzled boy who's clutching a broken stick of bread. Seeing me stare back, the child makes off before I can steal his family's breakfast.

You there? deCharge asks. *I lost you for a moment.*

Yeah, I tell him. *Still here.*

I can turn it off?

Voices get louder in my head as I think about them and then fade, leaving silence and the voice of the little man who came to see me the night before. I turn him off completely, and then turn him back on again. A hundred voices, one voice, no voices. It's all possible. I can hear deCharge properly now, complete with nuances.

What happened? he asks.

Don't know. Although I do. OctoV's just taken time out of conquering some part of the known galaxy to show me how to turn down the volume on knobs and sliders I didn't even know existed.

Got you, says the man

Yeah . . .

How does it feel?

Clear, I tell him. *Like we're in the same room.*

His relief is obvious. *And the voices?*

Gone. All I can hear now is you.

Fuck, he says, then repeats it, and for the first time I understand how worried he's been, how scared for himself as well as for me. *First time that's ever happened,* he tells me. *Didn't even know kyp could glitch.* He thinks we're bound together by adversity, so I throw him another crumb, something to feed back up the line.

My biology's fucked, I tell him. *Self-repairing. I guess it's been fighting the kyp, that's probably why it glitched, but everything's cool now.*

That stuff about my biology is checkable, and I know for a fact someone will check; they'd better, because I'm not going to forgive the general my experience with the slug for some time, if ever . . .

You wait, he tells me, *while I check where we go from here.*

I shake my head, watched only by the black cat, which is busy necking what's left of that broken-tailed skink. As the skink's head disappears into the cat's gullet, I remember that deCharge can't see me, and realize he's probably still waiting for my answer.

No, I say, *I'm going in.*

Wait, he tells me, but I've already broken the connection.

History is like a sandstorm. I can't remember who told me that. But you need to choose carefully where you sit it out, because the silent center is often more dangerous than out on the noisy edge.

CHAPTER 21

I'M IN a bar on the far edge of Zabo Square when word comes in that a day's work is available, a bar favored by ex-soldiers.

A dozen men stand up as one.

The work is available because I've called ahead to warn Senator Thomassi that a rival faction intends to upset his wedding. He probably still has people trying to track my call.

We're to gather outside Villa Thomassi. The money will be good but only professionals need apply.

"Where have you worked?" asks a hard-faced man when I finally get to the front of the line. He's head of security for the Thomassis, an ex-legionnaire judging by the way he holds himself.

"That's confidential."

The head of security glares at me. "You'll need to do better than that."

The Death's Head dagger is in my hand before he has time to blink. In my other hand is the laser blade, although he doesn't realize what it is until I cut a chunk out of a sandstone gatepost beside him.

"Does it really matter?"

His eyes flick from blade to blade, widening. "Is that real?"

"Which one?"

"The dagger."

I nod, flip it over in my hand, and offer it to him hilt-first. He takes it gingerly, as if the handle might be poisoned.

"This really yours?" he asks, and then tells me the rate of pay before I've had time to answer.

Give terror a black uniform and a grinning logo, and let superstition do the rest. It's a neat trick if you can pull it off. Just suggesting I'm ex–Death's Head is enough to get me this gig.

So now I'm outside an ornate cathedral, trying not to melt in the heat as sweat trickles down my ribs inside my leather coat and a crowd of ragged children gather to watch the show. They're drawn by the decorated hover and the music from inside, and by the weapons in the hands of the hard-eyed men lined up around me.

I could do it here, as Thomassi and Aptitude come out of the cathedral, but I'd be cut down in seconds and the door is too narrow to let me get a clear shot at everyone else.

And then there's my other problem.

Sweet little Aptitude.

Thinking about her in clichés makes it no better. By the end of today I will have failed someone, and such is the training the legion enforces that I know whichever way it goes, I can't afford to fail myself. It's the worst failure, *the failure that makes you fail others*.

The old saying sits in the back of my head, all buffed up and shining, but it's no use because I still don't know where my real duty lies.

Aptitude Wildeside looks just like her mother.

The same dark eyes as Debro and the same intense gaze, her cheekbones high and her lips full; looking at her is like seeing Debro made young again. She's wearing white, as befits a bride, and her hair is up, braided and folded around her skull in a complicated pattern held in place with pins.

She's young, just not as young as her inexperience suggests.

And she's beautiful.

A perfect body and a perfect face, probably matched to a keen and inquiring mind. Her dress is expensive, her jewelry beyond price. There are diamonds the size of quail eggs in the handle of the fan she carries as she exits blinking into the sunlight and is led toward her wedding vehicle.

I'm not sure what kind of hover it is, because the thing is buried under frills and bows, but from what I can see the vehicle is new. And the driver keeps it completely still, so that it barely rocks as a step unfolds and Aptitude climbs into the backseat, doing her best to smile.

Her eyes flick across my face and I'm forgotten.

Just one of a dozen men called in at the last minute to provide security. *A precaution,* Senator Thomassi tells Aptitude, not specifying against what. I'm there when he says it, as invisible to him as I am to her.

We line up on both sides of the vehicle, which moves away at a speed that allows us to keep her safe. On its way here, the hover contained only Aptitude; now it contains both Aptitude and the senator, who holds her hand tightly. Aptitude has tears in her eyes, and they don't look like tears of happiness to me.

The veil is back from her face and her eyes are skimming the streets as if seeing them for the last time.

I should have done this last night.

It would have been cleaner and kinder to spare the kid the trauma of finding herself married to a man who's outlived three wives and is an cient enough to be her grandfather, if not far older than that. The high clans of Farlight live longer than normal people. Well, what I call normal people, who are probably not what the Thomassis call people at all . . .

"You want to take your pay or do another shift?"

I'm tempted to take the shift. It's a neat way to get into Villa Thomassi—maybe too neat, and something warns me to play it straight. So I pocket the cash, which comes to a handful of silver pieces, and walk back to the bar where I first got news that jobs were on offer. Most of the others follow.

A group of us order beers, and two of the men go upstairs with a dark-skinned girl. The others begin to drift away as darkness creeps across the huge square. Music comes from a café nearby. So the owner of our bar responds with some music of his own.

Obviously enough, the songs clash.

A thin woman is cooking lamb in the yard behind our bar, fat falling into the flames and turning the night air greasy with the smell of griddled meat.

I keep looking for Farlight's famed elegance and failing to find it. Zabo Square is vast. So vast, in fact, you could fit the whole of Fort Libidad into one corner and barely use a quarter of the space. I wouldn't be surprised if you could fit the whole city of Karbonne into Zabo Square as well.

"Something out there?"

It's one of the men. He's watching me watch the square.

"Just thinking how big it is."

"You new here?"

I listen for criticism in his words, but the question is exactly that, a simple question . . . So I nod, and he tells me his name is Pietro, and he's been in Farlight for five years, and it took him a while to get used to the noise and crowds. Pietro warns me against pickpockets and swindlers, and tells me to be careful of people who want to be my friend. He smiles as he says this, and offers to buy me another beer, leaving me wondering if he can see the incongruity in his own words.

Incongruity?

Stumbling over the term brings a scowl to my face. Explaining quickly that I was remembering an old sergeant, we both agree they're fuckers and best forgotten. Then I buy another round, although I haven't yet drunk the beer he bought me, and Pietro says he's going upstairs to see if his friends have finished with the dark-skinned girl.

He asks if I'm interested in taking a turn.

So I thank him for his offer, and tell him I have stuff to do.

CHAPTER 22

ZABO SQUARE is in darkness. An edging of light filters from the cafés and cantinas around its perimeter, while its black center stretches away beneath my feet. Villa Thomassi is on the far side, three streets back and hidden behind wrought-iron gates and a thick canopy of trees. I've memorized its position for this moment.

A man comes to the gate as I rattle it. He's one of the few who stayed on to take a second shift and I want to apologize and say it's nothing personal, but I'm already lowering him to the ground, and the edge of my laser has cauterized the wound to his throat, sealing its edges.

Dragging him close, I lift *keys* from his belt.

I ask you.

Heavy brass keys, with curiously cut end bits that turn out to be the Thomassi arms. I know this, because the same arms are carved into the gateposts and welded in steel to the wrought iron of the gate.

There's confidence and there's arrogance, and then there's blind stupidity, which is closer to the previous two than most people imagine. The Thomassis have computer security, but its eye is a single lenz discreetly positioned in a tree to one side of the entrance so as not to spoil the look of the gates.

By the time the lenz is on me I'm inside the gate, the dead man is in a bush, and I'm wearing his jacket and standing in his position. The lenz swings past me and then stops, locking on to something in the street beyond.

One gun, five clips, a dagger, and a laser blade, plus the pistol I've just taken from the man in the bush. Killing Thomassi's people is not going to be a problem; burning down his villa afterward might take a little more ingenuity.

I hear the crunch of feet on gravel behind me.

"Everything okay?"

The split second it takes the man to realize he doesn't recognize me is all the time I need to drive a spike under his chin and into his brain. Shock dies as the light goes out of his eyes, and I lower him gently to the ground.

These are ex-soldiers, men who are paid to face death. Essentially, they're me in another life. Maybe that's why I'm finding killing them unexpectedly hard.

Get over it, I tell myself.

Thomassi's head of security comes next and killing him proves no problem at all, nor does dumping his body into shadow beside the main steps. A lenz in the portico catches me, but no alarms trigger. The camera just reaches the end of its travel, then begins to swing back, sliding over me a second time. Either the software is useless or the family have a human on the other end, in which case their security is more useless still.

Three steps, a quick check behind me, and I'm through the front door.

A rich and sickly scent of flowers fills the hall. Huge tapestries line one wall. A heavy light fitting hangs above my head, supporting several dozen candles. It's held in place by a fat chain and worked by a rusty-looking winch in a far corner. If the winch is rusty, then it's meant to be rusty, because everything else in the hall is in perfect condition.

This is what money looks like.

A huge portrait of a heroic-looking officer stares down at me. His chest is bedecked with medals, and an Order of Merit hangs from a ribbon around his neck. It takes me a second to recognize the man as Senator Thomassi, and the silver ship behind him as an in-system battle cruiser. At which point irritation kicks in, because the man is no more a soldier than Aptitude is, and at least she doesn't pretend.

Anger and music carry me across the hall. An altogether different sort of music from that of Zabo Square. This is elegant and made mostly of silences between the notes. It fills my mind and I find my feet taking steps in time to its rhythm, my sudden halts and sideways flicks making me grin, anger forgotten.

A gun sits in my hand.

Fifty people wait for me beyond that door.

Twisting sideways, I slide myself into Senator Thomassi's dining room and scan the table. Thomassi dies before he has time to realize I'm not one of his men. Both his bodyguards go down, guns undrawn. The first dies with his brains redecorating a wall behind him, the second trying to scream through a hole in his throat.

Aptitude just stands there.

This is the moment that counts, understand that.

Everything I am or want to be comes together in a single shot, as the girl spins around and drops to the tiles.

"Murderer," screams a woman.

I nod.

Three of Thomassi's hired muscle die in the space of three bullets, the last one diving behind a wooden chair, only to be killed by a blizzard of splinters. Wherever the old woman found my gun, it packs a punch.

"Party's over," I shout.

When no one moves, I empty a clip into the ceiling. Stucco falls like snow and the dining room empties in its turn. A guard with a pistol pops his head around the door and loses half his skull while still looking for the source of the gunfire.

Ceramic over bonded core, with polymer tip and steel expansion ring: Can't beat it for punch. The slugs achieve 300 percent spread while retaining 97 percent of their weight at fifty paces, which has to be worth every credit of someone else's money.

A tiny velvet purse sits beside most table settings. A few have been taken by fleeing guests, the rest abandoned. When I check, each purse contains ten gold coins. Thanking whichever god the Thomassis believed in for establishing such sensible traditions, I pocket the lot, deciding it's worth carrying the extra weight.

This just leaves burning the villa.

Pouring brandy, vodka, and something sweet and sticky onto the table, I knock over an ornate silver candelabrum and watch blue flame run its way along a white linen cloth. For good luck, I splash vodka onto a brain-splattered tapestry, but there isn't really enough left to make a difference.

Another face, another dead body.

Grabbing Aptitude by the waist, I hoist her over my shoulder and head for the hall with its long flight of marble stairs. Every NCO in existence will tell you don't climb stairs in a fire, and don't ever retreat to the top of a house unless someone with a copter is waiting to collect you. But I skimmed the skyline on my way in, and at least three trees touch the villa's roof, with another five within jumping distance.

What comes next is nasty.

A woman stands at the top of the stairs. She has a gun and it's held in front of her, pointing squarely at my face. She's somewhere in her twenties, clear-eyed and determined. She might be biting her lips, but her hands are rock-steady and she looks like she's handled a weapon before.

Not a member of the family then.

"Stop where you are," she says.

I shake my head.

My coat's been discarded, I have guns in both hands, and my metal arm is glinting in the half-light from a chandelier above. Holsters hang under both arms, and my throwing spikes are visible. It's obvious what I am.

But the woman's brave. She just stands there, raises her gun a little more, and begins to tighten her finger on the trigger. As she does, I drop Aptitude and the woman loses her concentration as Aptitude's head hits a marble step.

She fires all the same.

And it's a good shot, just not good enough.

I might be on my knees, knocked back, and something cracked in my shoulder, but I'm still alive and the guard's eyes are on Aptitude. She's transfixed by the wound to the kid's skull and the black stickiness in Aptitude's elaborate braid. By the time she gets her attention back to me I'm on my feet, and my gun is locked on her head.

"Drop it," I tell her.

"No," she says, raising her own weapon.

"I'll kill you."

She shrugs, the most magnificent shrug. One that says, *I don't care*, and *Fuck off*, and *Why don't you die while you're at it.*

She goes down a second ahead of pulling her own trigger. Chunks fall from the roof as her final shot blows apart a stucco ceiling rose and exposes beams above. She has her clip loaded with alternate ballistic and explosive. I'm glad I didn't know that.

Picking up her gun, I realize it's a SIG diabolo, shaped for a hand far bigger than her own. It fits me perfectly.

"Lock and load," the SIG announces.

I look at it.

"Imprinting new information. Genotype human equivalent. Status DH class three, override . . ."

That's when I realize it wasn't my coat the general had chipped with a dinky little transponder, it was me; and I've got honorary Death's Head status, albeit at the lowest level. I'm still trying to work out how this fits with his threat to disown me if the mission goes wrong when splintering wall flicks my attention back to the present.

Two security guards are heading upstairs from the floor below.

"Missed," I tell them.

A second shot pinpoints the first guard for me, and he drops with a bullet through his head, fragments of bone half blinding the man behind. Wiping his face, the second man is just in time to see the SIG buck in my hand. Where he was standing becomes a fireball. My gun's just wasted an incendiary and I'm shocked, because you can hire a legion brigade for a week for what it costs to buy a box of those.

"Overkill," I say.

"He's dead, isn't he?" The SIG sounds crosser than I am.

For a moment I consider leaving it behind. But intelligent guns have to be valuable, and although I've heard of them before I half thought they were a myth. "Two men," it warns me. "Mounting the stairs."

I decide to keep the gun.

Having killed more men in the last half an hour than in the first twenty-eight years of my life, I add another couple to the list before hoisting Aptitude back onto my shoulder, and then hesitating. The woman at my feet is about Aptitude's size, older by a few years and harder-faced even in death, but similar in build.

She's the answer to a problem I didn't know I had.

Beneath her clothes lies body armor. It's slick and formfitting and looks expensive. For a second I'm tempted to take it, but the thought of stripping a corpse turns my stomach and the fastenings look complicated and I've talked myself into leaving the armor in place when I realize that doing so will defeat everything I'm trying to achieve.

The body armor unfastens at the back.

It's thin and seems to be made of spun silk that tenses according to how it's treated: Scrunch the stuff hard enough and it will probably cut your hands. The default coloring is whatever is underneath. As I strip the corpse her armor goes transparent and then takes on the white and black of the tiles.

I'm in the process of unbuttoning Aptitude's chemise when she opens her eyes. A split second later she opens her mouth to scream, and tries to bite my hand as it fastens across her face.

"Shut it," I tell Aptitude.

She's fighting so hard to roll herself away from me that I give up being nice and put a gun to her head.

"I'm trying to save you."

Aptitude spits.

"Strip," I tell her.

She knows a lot of bad words for someone so well brought up.

"Change into this." I toss her the body armor, then the clothes that the dead woman was wearing. Seeing them is enough to make Aptitude's face crumple. We're seconds away from a full-blown meltdown, and those are spare seconds that we don't have.

"Change," I tell her.

She looks at the dead woman, then the clothes in her own hands. My guns are taking half of Aptitude's attention, but there are too many questions and no obvious answers. Outside in the street there are sirens and a chopper is hovering overhead and that's not good, either. We need a clean getaway, no lenz and definitely no witnesses.

"Aptitude," I say.

She looks at me, wondering why I'm using her name.

"Your mother sent me . . ."

It's not true, but it's not quite a lie.

"Believe it or not," I tell her, "I'm trying to save your life."

Her eyes flick to the dead woman and I can tell the kid wants to say she doesn't believe me for a minute. But why is she alive if I want her dead? And why would I drag her mother into it anyway?

"Listen," I say.

She waits.

"I met your ma in Paradise, Anton, too . . ."

"You know Dad?"

"Tall man, used to be a soldier. Loves your mother, even if they're divorced and she drives him a bit nuts."

Aptitude's crying. "They're still alive?"

"Yeah," I say. "Both still alive. We need to get you out of here."

"But you killed Sophie."

My gaze flicks to the dead woman. "Your bodyguard?"

The kid nods. "Sophie."

"Sophie tried to kill me. She died doing her job." Maybe that means more to me than it means to Aptitude, because she doesn't seem to regard it as much consolation.

"Change your clothes," I tell Aptitude. "Please. Do it now."

"Turn your back," she orders.

"Already turned."

At the bottom of the stairs flames are already beginning to eat the portrait of Senator Thomassi. That's good in one way and bad in another. Fire locks us off from the hall and keeps us safe for the moment, but it also means we can't go back that way.

"You done?" I ask, glancing around to catch a flash of naked shoulder. Body armor rustles as it fits itself to its new owner and begins to adopt her skin coloring.

"Hey," says Aptitude. "You're not allowed to look."

"I'm not."

The kid glares at me.

"You done here?" I ask her.

She nods, struggling into a combat jacket that doesn't quite fit. The trousers are better.

"And the boots."

Aptitude does what she's told.

It takes longer than I'd like to get Sophie into Aptitude's wedding dress. Although first I have to get her into that silk chemise.

"Not my choice of clothing," says Aptitude.

"The senator?"

She nods, face carefully impassive. This is a girl who's gotten used to hiding her emotions.

"Turn your back," I tell her.

My shot takes the dead bodyguard through her head, blowing away half her skull and smearing sticky jelly across suddenly shattered tiles. As Aptitude tries to look back, I turn her roughly away and strip gold bracelets from Aptitude's wrists and a ring from her finger. It's a struggle to make the wedding ring fit the dead woman's hand, but the bracelets go on easily enough.

The fire is climbing the stairs now, helped by wall hangings, polished wooden banisters, and the sheer force of the flames.

"What's up there?" I ask Aptitude.

"Bedrooms."

"And beyond that?"

"Servants' quarters . . . the attics. Some storerooms."

We take the stairs in silence. All the while Aptitude's glance flicks between my face and the flames behind her. She's having a hard time working out where the danger really lies. When she looks at me again, I realize it's because I'm swearing.

"What?" she demands.

"Just thinking."

Mostly about how the fuck I'm meant to be getting the kid out of here. What have I got? A talking gun, a collection of dumb weapons, some weirdshit slug in my throat, and voices clamoring for answers at the edge of my mind.

Realization halts me midstep.

Where are the maps?

As the thought slides into my mind so do floor plans for Villa Thomassi. A blink and I'm looking at the map of an area west of Zabo Square; another blink and Farlight is spread out beneath me, flicking between an aerial photograph and what looks like a transparent overlay. The kyp is feeding me information faster than I can swallow it. Returning the map to close detail, I try to make sense of the house plans.

"What's down there?" I demand, pointing to a corridor. On the plans a chute can be seen. It seems to lead to a basement. The big advantage of that is it will take us through the rising flames into the coolness below.

"An old laundry."

"We go that way."

Aptitude looks like she's about to protest, which is good, because it means she's already thinking of us as a team. Short-term maybe, but Aptitude's no longer looking to escape from me at the first opportunity. "How old are you?"

"Why?"

"Just wondered."

For a second it looks as if she's going to refuse to tell me. Not that it matters really, I'm just interested.

"Fifteen."

I'd killed half a dozen men by then, gotten drunk, gotten laid, caught whore fever, and been whipped for the stupidity. But that was then and this is now and we're very different people, not just because she's a girl but also because our worlds are not worlds that are meant to collide.

"Sven," I tell her.

She looks at my outstretched hand, then good manners click in. "I'm Lady Aptitude Tezuka Wildeside," she says, shaking my bloodstained fingers.

See what I mean?

CHAPTER 23

DAWN FINDS us limping through the landing fields at Bosworth. A plume of black smoke rises into the sky behind us, newly visible now that the sun has begun to rise. No one seems in a hurry to put out the fire, although two copters hover overhead and fat cargo ships keep straying from their courses to take in the sight.

Aptitude's still furious because I threw her down the chute when she refused to jump, and her head still aches from where I put a slug along the side of her skull. It's been a long walk and her feet hurt, along with everything else. My shoulder's not good, but the pain is getting better. Sometimes I forget that other people don't automatically mend.

I'm looking for a small boy and a newly morphed spider bot. When I find him, he's sitting near the wing of a rusting drone while his spider chews the wing into something that looks like iron filings. These fall into a plastic bucket that the boy moves occasionally as his bot shifts position.

"How you doing?"

"Okay." He looks up, tries to work out if he knows me, then flicks his eyes to the bot and I know he has it. "Who's she?"

"A friend," I say. "Got hurt in a fall."

The kid cocks his head sideways, considering Aptitude's bloodied skull. "Looks like a bullet to me."

I laugh, and Aptitude glances between us.

"Your dad around?"

"Out the back," the boy says. "I'd show you, but I'm not supposed to leave here."

Per Olson is standing next to a broken Casmir coil, and every now and then he sucks his teeth and walks around the wreckage of a cargo cruiser's heart. It's a mass of precious metals and crystals. All he has to do is extract what's valuable without consigning himself and a five-hundred-yard circle around him to oblivion.

"Trouble?" I say.

He glances up from a hand slab, checks something on its screen, and then does a double take on Aptitude. "Looks like I should be asking you the same."

"We need a doctor."

"We?"

"She does."

Per nods, and when he sucks his teeth it's not over the Casmir coil. The directions he gives are precise. I'm to use his name. It would be best if I wrapped her head in something before walking her into the shadow of Calinda Gap. I'll need to pay gold.

He hesitates. "Have you got money?"

"Yeah." He doesn't ask me how much or where from, and I realize I like this man. He's the real thing. All I did was fix his spider bot but he's ready to sub Aptitude if I don't have enough for a doctor.

Reassured, he watches us walk away.

The doctor is young, nervous, and an addict. He gives his name as Josh3 and looks bemused when Aptitude tries to shake hands. His office is crude, full of medical lash-ups and naked chunks of memory crystal, with one fist-sized piece tied to a slab reader with glass wire. The widows are tar-papered and protected with freshly welded bars.

I give him a month at most before the gangs or the police force him out. Both will want protection money, and neither will be able to save him from the other. Farlight is beginning to look like Karbonne written extra large. But Josh3 is here now, and the gold coin I'm holding is enough to focus his attention.

"Bad wound," he says.

"Not that bad," I tell him.

Josh3 looks like he wants to disagree.

"Do what you can," says Aptitude. "But I want to stay conscious."

He looks like he wants to disagree with that as well.

She really is Debro's daughter. Her face is pale—more so than mine will ever be—her eyes are wide, and her mouth tightens with pain as Josh3 lifts the edges of her wound with a ceramic hook, but she doesn't flinch and she swallows her pain as he swabs grazed bone and stitches the edges tight.

"Your ma would be proud of you."

I mean it as a compliment. I certainly don't mean to make her cry.

SKULL STITCHED AND head scarf hiding where her hair's been cut away, Aptitude walks beside me through Calinda Gap's early morning. This is a weird city: Expensive yachts trawl lazily overhead, but most of the buildings around us are foamstone or fiberbloc, and a few are wood. Cheap motorbikes fill lanes with a thick fog of hydrocarbon. I've even seen a couple of donkeys, laden down with panniers.

Satellite dishes sprout like fungus from the sides of most of the houses. It's still early, but already the air stinks of warm dogshit and human sewage. There is a water shortage in this city, at least out here on the edges.

"God," says Aptitude.

"You didn't know places like this existed?"

She shakes her head, and then winces at the pain. Her eyes are glazed with analgesics, but Josh3 was good to his word and kept her conscious through the entire operation. My shoulder is also mended, not that it was bad to start with . . . a cracked bone, busily healing itself by the time Josh3 cut his way inside.

"Where are we going?"

"Safety . . ."

Aptitude stares at me, so I sit her on a low wall and tell her a few home truths, starting with the fact that a number of important people want her dead and will kill both of us if they ever discover that this is not already the case. The identity of these important people is left unspecified, and it says something for the state of Farlight politics that Aptitude never once doubts that what I tell her is true.

"And my mother's alive?"

"Yes," I say.

"You promise?"

"I promise."

She slides herself from the wall, ties the scarf tighter around her head, and links her arm through mine. "I suppose," she says, "we'd better go."

GOLDEN MEMORIES IS nearly empty, for which I'm grateful. Bacon is being fried in the kitchens and the stink of garbage comes from a bin outside. I'm beginning to recognize the signature scents of this city, at least the bits of it I know. And I like the smell of food I can recognize. While I was ruining Aptitude's wedding supper I could barely tell what was food from what was table decoration.

Lisa grins as I walk into the kitchen, then sees Aptitude behind me and begins to scowl. There's a good way to approach this and a bad way, and if I knew which was which I'd do it, but Lisa's still a stranger, for all that we've shared a bed.

So I settle on the truth.

"I need your help."

Both Aptitude and Lisa are looking at me. To make matters more complicated, Angelique comes out from a stockroom and walks over to join her cousin.

"Who's this?" she demands.

"The daughter of a friend—"

"A friend?"

I put my guns on the counter, one after another. It's not a threat; I just need them to know who I am. At the sight of the last weapon, Lisa's eyes widen.

"That's . . ."

"Yeah," I say, "illegal."

Angelique grins.

They could sell me to the police and probably get a good price. We're negotiating here. I've just told them they're going to get something that's worth more. At the moment they probably think it's one of the guns.

I take gold coins from my pocket.

Eyes widen.

"Ten Octo," I say, "you keep an eye on her . . . Another ten, you let her work behind the bar until I get back." I put a final twenty coins on the counter. We're talking much more than they make in a month, legally or otherwise.

"And that?" Lisa asks, looking at the final pile.

The kid gets my room. It's not as if Golden Memories has many real guests. And at a hundred credits to a single Octo, I've just bought Aptitude a lot of room time. The rules are clear: She works behind the bar, no one tries to make her work on her back, and she gets to eat with Lisa and Angelique.

"Learn to blend in," I say once we're alone in the room that's about to become hers. "Watch the others and do what they do."

She's a good kid, but I can see the worry in her eyes.

"This is your life now."

"My life?"

"Maybe forever . . ."

Calinda Gap is visible through the window, and the rocky edge of the caldera shows dark against the sun, with a skim of shantytown rising steeper than you'd think it possible to build. There are things I want to say. Things I wish the lieutenant had said to me, in the spaces between those things he did say.

Finding the right words comes hard.

And she's uneasy to be alone in a room with me, which is not surprising given I killed her husband, her bodyguard, and most of the hired muscle at her wedding; but it's a conversation we need to have. Even if Aptitude's part is mostly silence and my part is made up of words I find almost impossible to say.

"Your mother's not coming back."

It's probably the wrong way to begin.

"She's got a camp of her own in Paradise. Anton is with her. She's become someone."

"Someone?"

"A person who matters."

The girl wants to tell me that Debro Wildeside always mattered. Of course Debro did, but that's not what I'm saying. "People change in prison," I tell her. "More than they change most other places. They become someone else. Your ma's the exception. I really believe she's going to remain herself."

"And she's got Dad."

I nod.

"You really know them?"

"Yes," I say. "We landed on the same shuttle. Shared a camp. Fought a couple of battles against other camps. Well, your dad and I did. Setting the boundaries, so others would learn to leave us alone."

"Why were you let out?"

"To kill you . . ." I take a deep breath. "Only I'd already promised your ma that I'd look after you if I could, and I made that promise before I was given the assignment."

"Won't you get in trouble?"

Her question makes me smile. "Behave yourself," I tell her, "and no one will ever know. The senator is dead. His villa is in ruins. And you . . . well, you're already dead on the stairs, aren't you?"

Aptitude nods, doubtfully.

CHAPTER 24

OCTOV IS thirteen, his hair falls in waves over thin shoulders, and his eyes are clear and fixed on the future. He's been thirteen for my entire life and will probably still be thirteen when rust finally eats the cheap metal cross over my grave. Quite why he likes that age is hard to say.

No one has dared ask.

Maybe he believes a child emperor is intrinsically more heroic, or maybe he really does have no sense of human time. It's probably unwise to speculate.

Either way, this city is full of statues of a smartly uniformed child. He wears cavalry dress, frock coats, pilot's goggles, and sometimes carries a cane or a swagger stick. In the most famous statue of all he wears the shapeless uniform of an astronaut, from the days before Octovians rediscovered style.

It has to be intentional.

The poor touch his statues for luck, leaving OctoV's hands and feet worn smooth and bright, while the rest of him remains the strange green that bronze gets when it grows old. Farlight is a city of statues.

Senators in robes and generals in uniform, noble-looking gods and naked women, more naked women than you can possibly imagine.

All are made from bronze, all ridiculously beautiful, mostly with full breasts and wide hips . . . mothers washing their hair, feeding children, sitting contemplating or composing poetry, girls with bows and quivers, with wings, clutching bunches of flowers to their hearts.

The subject doesn't seem to matter so long as they are naked, which probably tells you more about the inhabitants of Farlight than a dozen slab guides do. I'm in a park beside a statue of a girl washing her feet in a bronze stream. The stream has ripples and the faintest suggestion of a current. The girl has curling hair, soft hips, and neatly crossed legs, so she can reach her ankles.

SERENITY, announces the label.

Maybe in Farlight. Anywhere else, and she'd need guards to fight off the crowds if she sat around on a riverbank like that.

Mr. deCharge is late.

At least I'm assuming the message is his. It gave a time—five minutes ago—and a place, here beside the *Serenity* statue. As I wait, an old woman comes to nod at the bronze girl and a boy leaves bread crumbs beside her feet, while a child half the age of Aptitude rips bougainvillea from a bush and tosses its blossoms into bronze water, as if she believes the stream is real.

Serenity has another name, obviously.

One known only to . . .

The poor, I think, as instinct kicks me off the bench and the air ripples. A carbon dart passes through the space where my head was, then splinters into fragments against the statue behind.

A twig breaking.

That's what I heard. Sixteen years of combat training overrides a handful of days in this strange and sloppy city. As I wait, flat on the ground, I try to work out if there are two attackers and if one of them is busy creeping around behind me, puff gun in his hand.

It's a strange choice of weapon, except that a pulse rifle might melt the bronze girl, and that would undoubtedly cause more trouble than one dead soldier in a public park, so maybe there's logic to the choice after all.

"You can stand up now."

The voice is familiar. Amused, positively pleased with itself.

Rolling over, I extract a throwing spike from its sheath and hurl it toward where I think the voice should be. Someone swears.

"Enough," says the voice.

I've got a gun in my hand now, and as the uniformed figure twists my spike from the fir tree behind which he's been hiding, I reach kneeling position and draw a bead on his head.

"Targeted," announces my SIG diabolo.

Major Silva blanches.

"Targeted . . ." The gun's getting impatient.

"You passed," says the major. "That was the final test."

"Wait," I tell the gun.

The major is the same dapper figure. His diffidence is as much an affectation as it ever was, and he seems to be alone, which impresses me.

"You can put that down," he says.

I look at the SIG, then shake my head. "Where's deCharge?"

"Dead."

"You killed him?"

Major Silva nods. "He supplied your kyp, which was faulty . . . The man breeds them," he says, amending it to "bred them."

"And I can't get the bloody thing out?"

He shakes his head.

Something interesting has just occurred to me. "So you can't get another one in?" He realizes the importance of this, or maybe he just sees the relief in my face. I've been shot, I've had bones broken and suffered beatings from Sergeant Fitz that left me barely able to crawl across a floor, but nothing comes close to my body's battle with the kyp.

"No," he says. "We can't."

During the course of this brief conversation, my gun gets lowered, although my trigger finger is still hooked through its guard, and the *shell-retained-in-chamber* diode on its handle remains red.

"Where did you get that?"

"Took it off Aptitude Wildeside's bodyguard."

"It shouldn't work for you."

"Well, it does," I say. "And I'm keeping it." I raise the muzzle slightly just in case I need to make the point.

The major sighs. "You can't go around threatening Death's Head officers."

"Yeah," I say. "I can."

"You're covered," he tells me. "I've got a dozen snipers out there."

"Bullshit."

"Are you prepared to take that risk?"

"Yes."

At this, the major grins. "You'll do," he says. "Colonel Nuevo said you would . . . I'm going to break this down, okay?"

After he's stripped his puff gun into a dozen pieces, he tosses the chassis, barrel, and air cylinder in a trash can and rips open a silver sachet of dark red powder, which he sprinkles over the top. Seconds later there's a flash and the gun goes up in a sheet of white flame. It takes the can with it, but casual vandalism obviously doesn't come high on Major Silva's list of worries.

"Usually," he tells me, "I'd put you through training. Six months in the academy and then a tour of duty, but at the colonel's suggestion we're going to skip the academy."

It takes me a second to realize what he's saying.

"You leave in three hours . . ." Major Silva catches my stare. "Report to the Death's Head HQ on Casaubon Square. They'll issue you a uniform. And if anyone asks, tell them you have my permission to carry that."

He's referring to the SIG diabolo.

We walk to the edge of the park together, a weird-enough couple to attract glances from those we pass, although the glances are discreet.

At the road, the major hesitates. As I said, it's an affectation. All that diffidence, the irony and dry humor exist because the uniform he wears allows them to exist. This man is a killer, just as I am, but he's a killer with manners and a good tailor, or whatever people like him use to make their uniforms.

"By the way," he says. "Well done."

I want to go back to Golden Memories, say my good-byes to Aptitude. Not to mention Lisa and Angelique, although it's a very different type of good-bye I have in mind for us. Instead I find a public video booth and feed it a credit, patching myself through to the public booth at Golden Memories. Someone answers after the thirty-eighth ring.

"What?"

"Yeah," I say. "Good to hear from you, too."

"Sven?" It's Lisa.

"Everything okay?"

She hears the worry in my voice. "Sure," she says. "All cool. My cousin from the country and Angelique have gone shopping. But I can take a message, if that's why you've called."

My cousin?

I'm grinning like an idiot into the screen, my reflection overlaying Lisa's face, like a ghost image. Maybe this is going to work out after all. "Say hi to the kid for me. Tell her I'll be back soon, and look after yourself, okay?"

"Back soon?"

"Got a job," I say.

"Off planet?"

"Sounds like it. Oh, and Lisa." I hesitate, watching her wait for me to find the right words. "Just, thank you, all right? For everything . . ."

She breaks the connection, but not before she flashes me her smile.

THE HQ ON Casaubon Square overlooks a dusty fountain and a small rectangle of tired grass. Wrought-iron railings surround the grass on all four sides, as if to protect it from those who might want to trample its beauty, but the beauty is missing and so are the hordes. The square is almost deserted, its only occupants two uniformed Death's Heads who stand on either side of a black-painted door.

Farlight is OctoV's largest city, his capital. It's bigger than any of the Uplifted cities, so we're told. Although obviously not as big as their orbital habitat, because nothing is as big as that—well, nothing that's impinged on my life.

Who knows what the U/Free have? Apart from genius, high art, and all the things we don't . . .

And yet being in Farlight is like being trapped in the center of a cluster of broken clockwork. It's strange, maybe more than strange. Looking at the deserted square and the ruined grass and the shabby buildings, it strikes me that this must be intentional.

OctoV is saying something. I just wonder if anyone but OctoV himself understands what it is.

"Halt."

It seems best to do what I'm told.

"I'm expected."

The guards on the door look at each other.

"Name?" one of them demands.

"Sven."

"Sven what?"

In my pocket the SIG gets itself ready. A quick shiver as the chassis unlocks and loads. The combat chip has tied itself to my emotions, which should worry the hell out of me, but actually makes me feel very happy.

"Well?"

A name comes unbidden. It's the one Debro mentioned, back when we were being inducted into Paradise. "Sven Tveskoeg," I tell them. "It's an old Earth name."

They wonder whether I'm taking the piss.

And then there's a creak, and a man I recognize is standing in the open doorway. Both guards snap to attention at the sight of Colonel Nuevo's uniform.

"Sven," he says. "What are you doing out here?"

"Trying to get in," I tell him. "Without killing your pet goons."

His smile is thin. "These are the regiment's finest."

I'm obviously expected to reply, but I let silence say it for me, and the colonel sighs. "The major told me to expect you."

"Really," I say. "Was that before or after he tried to put a carbon dart through my skull?"

Colonel Nuevo decides it's time to take our conversation inside.

MY REAL SURPRISE comes when I arrive to get my uniform. This comes last, after a medical, a second medical to check that the results of the first were correct, and a psychometric test, which is canceled halfway through when an intense-looking woman stands up from her desk, wanders over, and turns off my screen.

"It's better," she tells me, "we don't have this on record."

She says the same to Colonel Nuevo when he turns up at the end of our session.

"Right," he says. "We'd better get him geared up."

I expect a quartermaster, a rack of uniforms, a row of helmets, rifles piled in one corner. That's what you get in the legion. Instead I get an old man who tells me to strip and stand in the middle of the room.

Colonel Nuevo excuses himself for this bit.

Lasers play down my body from all four corners of the room. The lights come up and the old man comes out from behind his screen with a pair of trousers, a shirt, and a jacket hanging over his arm.

He smiles at my surprise. "Fabricators," he says. "Subvisual spiders."

As he holds the jacket out to me, I frown. "You've made a mistake," I say, handing back the garment. A silver collar bar on each side gives my rank as second lieutenant, and a silk ribbon tucked into one of the buttonholes proclaims me holder of the Obsidian Cross.

Third class, admittedly. But it's still the Obsidian Cross.

The old man checks his right wrist, skim-reading an implant. "No," he says. "No mistake. Second Lieutenant Sven Tveskoeg, Obsidian Cross third class." He shrugs, watches me climb slowly into the jacket, and invites me to choose a holster style for my gun.

PART 2

CHAPTER 25

COMBAT BATWINGS come in hard and fast over stunted trees, their guns blazing as they dip to just above ground level and try to kill everything in their path, which happens to include me.

These machines are fast, hellishly fast, maneuvering at g's that must take their pilots to the edge of unconsciousness with every twist and turn. A trooper next to me raises his pulse rifle and takes aim.

The batwing stays steady and the man is gone. As burning meat mixes with mud on my uniform, I roll into the nearest ditch and see the batwing bank tightly to come around again.

"Big man, small ditch," says the gun. "Go figure."

So I flip myself out and roll behind the wreckage of a fat-wheeled combat bot. We've a thousand of the bastards, and they're about as useless as a nun in a brothel.

As the batwing screams toward me, I raise my gun.

"Locked on," it says.

"Take it."

The SIG does what it's told.

In doing so it trashes 15 percent of its power pack. When this is over I'm going to find the wreckage, because I want to know what the

Enlightened have flying those things, and why shooting them makes my gun burn through its battery.

Batwings are small, much too small to take a human pilot. Rumor says they're flown by the heads of dead Uplift soldiers. But rumor is usually wrong. In the meantime I'm working out what to do next and wondering how the fuck I got here.

As if I could forget.

"MOUTHPIECE," a computer says.

A technician offers me a breathing tube. She offers it politely, with no indication that I'm holding up her launch. A glance at the trooper beside me tells me the tube really is what I think, so I stuff it into my mouth, closing my teeth around a ridge put there for the purpose.

"Doors," says the voice.

We're being prepped by machine, because it's more efficient than using humans—or so I've been told by the techie, who keeps her eyes lowered and turns away from my questions as soon as politeness allows.

It used to be me that made people nervous; now it's my wrapping as well. Black combat armor, black-visored helmet, black gloves . . . And that dinky little silver skull on the front of my helmet, just in case anyone's too stupid to realize the obvious.

Glass doors close over my head, and everyone around me shuts their eyes. Seconds later our pod fills with shock gel. From drop to landing we're going to be in free fall, and I mean free fall. We're also out of communication range, not that this matters. Once dropped, nothing can change a pod's trajectory.

Like every other pod in the drop we have landing legs to take the worst of the shock, with gel to cushion us from the rest.

I'm counting down in my head.

Three, two, one . . .

Half a minute is the time I've been given from gelling to drop, and it's accurate to the second. As my body rises, the gel cushions my shock and settles me back in my seat. Twenty men to a pod, five hundred pods to a ship, twenty ships to a fleet. That makes two hundred thousand men free-falling toward Ilseville, capital of Sxio province and second city on the newly re-Uplifted and -Enlightened planet of Maybe Here.

Our job is to re-UnEnlighten it fast.

Ilseville is a trading depot for fur, amber, and a rare and fabulously complex leather taken from cold-water alligators, which are actually something else altogether, but look enough like alligators for the name to stick.

I've been briefed on the city we're about to take.

It's little more than a small town protected by stonefoam walls. The outer areas are constructed mostly of fiberbloc, which is warm, cheap to manufacture, and utterly useless against artillery. The inner city, which is also walled, is stone-built, with two temples. We're to spare these, if we can.

"Steady yourselves."

A thud, hard enough to shake my teeth, a suck of vacuum as a pump sucks away the gel, and then my ears pop as air flows into the pod hard enough to blow open its doors.

"Up and out," a sergeant shouts, but he's talking to his squad.

I've just piggybacked a lift with them. My men don't exist; I'm a second lieutenant without a platoon, which strikes me as pretty odd.

Hitting the ground, I go facedown. A swift roll sees me covered from head to foot in mud and I'm happier. So I grab some wild grass and force it under the webbing on my helmet, then flip down my visor.

At least I'm camouflaged.

Fat-wheeled combats roll down a ramp behind me. A junior NCO sits on one, his hands gripping wide handlebars and his thumb already on the firing button.

"Moron," says my gun.

His vehicle bounces once and slaps wetly on landing. Wheels slip, mud sprays from one side, and his vehicle goes over. Its engine dies a second later. Other pods are having similar luck.

"Incoming."

A dozen conscripts do the meerkat search.

"Twelve o'clock," I shout, adding, "get down."

A batwing, coming in hard and fast. Rolling into a ditch, I see the driver of the dead fat-wheel raise his rifle and watch him become history. Another glorious martyr for the mother system, whatever the hell that might be.

"Locked on," says the SIG.

"Take it."

We kill the batwing without thinking about it. Somehow I've abandoned my ditch for the burning wreckage of a fat-wheeled combat bot. I'm still alive and so are roughly half the troopers around me, but that's not going to last.

A hostile cannon spits from a hill to our left, while the enemy have an old-fashioned belt-fed dug in the trees to our right. We need to attack the position in those trees or take the hill, because at the moment we're all in the cross fire. But the ground between here and both those places is marsh, with hillocks of grass surrounded by filthy water.

"Get the fuck down."

A couple of troopers hit the ground, but not at my shout. One of them is now minus his head; the other probably wishes he was. A batwing has taken his legs below the hip, clean-sealing the wounds as the pulses pass through.

He's screaming.

A helmetless grunt stands beside him, covering his own ears. Militia, by the look of his uniform. Out of two hundred thousand troops, a thousand of us are Death's Head, maybe another ten thousand are from the legions, and the rest are conscripts and recruits.

I put a knife through the injured man's heart.

He stops screaming.

"Get down," I tell the grunt. "Right down," I add, when he falls as far as his knees. "Where's your sergeant?"

The man looks at me blankly.

"Sergeant?" I say.

Another trooper points. What's left of their sergeant is staring blankly at a cold gray sky, and no one's even had sense enough to steal his plasma pistol.

"You're the new sergeant," I tell the trooper who pointed, giving him the pistol. As an afterthought, I get him to unbuckle his own helmet and cram the sergeant's helmet on his head in its place. Demands are flooding through the earpiece.

"Down," I hear the trooper say. "The new sergeant," he adds. And then he tosses his old helmet to the grunt who seems to be without.

He'll do.

"Cover me," I tell him.

Pulse cannon or belt-fed? Which to hit first . . . Spotting a group of troopers who've abandoned their fat-wheels and are dragging a mortar toward the hill, I decide to take the trees and the belt-fed for myself.

Behind me the new sergeant fires a burst from his pulse pistol, and I hug dirt as return fire skims over my head. A second burst, then another burst and another; he's got the rest of his troop firing now. If he lives long enough he's going to make a good NCO.

Grinning to myself, I roll into a sodden ditch and shake my head. *Good* and *NCO*—now, there are two words I never expected to hear in the same sentence. The channel is deep enough to let me crawl on my belly through marsh grass and cold water toward the sound of the belt-fed weapon.

The grunts are keeping pace with me and I'm officially impressed. To the man with the machine gun it must look like they're advancing on his gun camp. I just hope he doesn't get too many of them before I can reach the trees.

"Fucking chaos," says the gun when I wake it up again.

"Remind me to reset you."

There has to be a character button somewhere, because I can't believe this is its default personality. SIG GmbH would never make a profit.

"Distance," I demand.

"About fifty yards."

"I don't want *about.*"

"Forty-eight yards, eleven and a quarter inches, approximately. I can give you a more accurate measurement if you want."

"Can you get him from here?"

The SIG's sulking.

"Well?"

"Of course. It would help if you told me what rounds you want."

"Whatever does the least damage."

"Why?"

"Because I want that belt-fed in one piece. Not for me," I add quickly, in case it's the jealous type. "For the men behind me." I'm crawling through cold water as this goes on, the gun carefully giving me new distances every few seconds until I tell it to stop.

We're still thirty yards from the trees, and the soldier with the belt-fed is a couple of yards back from that. I'd try to go around him, but that would mean leaving my ditch, and the ditch is the sole reason I'm still alive.

"What are my options?" We're talking about rounds, obviously.

"Ceramic, fléchette, incendiary, explosive, overblast . . ."

"Overblast."

The gun unlocks and loads.

And I wait for a particularly heavy burst of fire from behind me. Something that's going to make the man in the trees want to keep his head down. When the burst comes, I wait it out and pop my head up in the split-second silence that follows, adding one shot of my own. It helps that overblasts don't need to be accurate; anything within about ten feet works fine.

I'm up and running the second my round explodes, splashing my way through a dozen yards of sour marsh and boggy ground. The gunman's on his side, hands tight to his ruptured ears. One of his eyes is pulped and blood oozes from his nose, but he's still conscious enough to try to crawl away from me.

He dies in silence.

Swiveling the belt-fed, I turn it toward the hill where the enemy pulse cannon is busy cutting down the troopers advancing toward it. A handful of our militia are trapped halfway up a slope; they're what remains of the brigade I saw earlier.

A blast of belt-fed ceramic concentrates the minds of the Ilsevillect troops opposite. One of them swivels the blast cannon toward me, igniting a tree several paces to my right, which is pretty good for a sighting shot. Unfortunately for him, it frees our militia trapped on the slope below. I keep firing, just to make life more interesting, and by the time he realizes it's time to swivel his cannon back to where it was, it's already too late.

The hill is overrun.

CHAPTER 26

"SIR . . ."

It's the man I made sergeant. He's out of breath, as are the four troopers who struggle out of the marsh behind him. Five men out of ten—not a bad rate of attrition for a battle this fierce.

"Sergeant?"

"What now, sir?"

"We attack."

He checks to see if I'm joking.

"*Fucking Death's Head,*" one of them mutters, but the voice is impressed despite itself.

"What's your name?"

"Neen, sir."

"And the others?"

"Troopers Will, Shil, Franc, and Haze."

Crop-haired and filthy, they salute, looking nervous. In name order they're runtish, scowling, white-faced, and overweight. Only Neen looks vaguely like a soldier, and that's probably just the way he carries his gun. At least he looks more likely to shoot someone else than shoot himself.

"Stick with me," I tell them. "Anyone asks, you're already obeying orders. Got it?"

They nod like the neat little row of cannon fodder they are. It's all I can do not to turn my back on the lot of them and walk away, leaving the group to fulfill their manifest destiny, which is get slaughtered for the greater good of OctoV. But being a lieutenant without men to command, that sucks.

So I order my new sergeant to choose himself a corporal.

"Franc," he says without hesitation. His choice looks young and nervous, but it's the sergeant's decision.

"Okay. Now hit some batwings."

Neen smiles, nods. Catching his mood, the others do the same.

"You're going to fire this," I tell Neen. "And I'm going to show you how."

The belt-fed is a new model. More complicated that any machine gun I've handled before, but the thing about belt-feds is that they all follow a basic pattern, and it's a pattern that is centuries old. A belt goes in, spent ceramic is ejected, somewhere down the line the block and barrel overheat and the firing mechanism jams. An experienced gunner can read the signs, letting his weapon cool between bursts for just long enough to keep it firing the rest of the time.

"Okay?"

He looks doubtful, so I run him again through the routine, doing my best to keep my temper, which is never good at the best of times. We touch on range and the fact that the gun has no brain at all, and why that can be an advantage when the Enlightened start letting off logic bombs.

We're all aware there's a battle going on around us.

"Got it this time?"

He takes one look at my face and nods.

"Good."

Batwings continue to cut swaths through our troops before they can muster. Half the time new drops don't even get clear of the pods. And our pods are still dropping, providing the batwings with a limitless supply of fresh meat.

We have twenty thousand dead already according to a readout on my visor. From habit, I double that for a true figure, and then double it again for what we'll have lost by nightfall. Eighty thousand out of two hundred thousand, pretty much what the high command must be expecting.

The fleet can be seen in low orbit; General Jaxx's mother ship is a black fleck in the sky above that. An early drop managed to set up an anti-aircraft gun. Most of their time is spent trying to take out high fighters before they can chase our pods to the ground. About one shot in ten hits its target. I've been in battles most of my life, but combat like this is outside my experience.

Dragging the belt-fed to the edge of the trees, we place it facing the city, because that's where the batwings are obviously based.

"Kill them all," I tell Neen.

Remembering his training, he snaps me a salute.

I smile.

Our belt-fed attracts attention, as we knew it would. As soon as the enemy realize we've moved it, a batwing peels off from the pod run and doubles back toward our small circle of trees. Bullets rip apart branches and then the batwing's behind us, banking tightly for another run.

"Anyone injured?"

"Me," says a voice.

Behind me lies a trooper. A sliver of branch protruding from his stomach. Out here that's a death wound, three days of blood poisoning and flesh rot. It takes me a moment to remember his name. It's Will, the smallest of the five.

"You," I say to Franc and Neen. "Keep firing." Franc feeds belt to the gun and Neen targets a batwing, making it swerve.

"That goes for you, too," I tell the others. So Haze and Shil drag their gaze from the injured grunt, sight along their pulse rifles, and start firing. Haze is a shit shot, but at least he's pointing in the right direction.

"You're Will, right?"

He nods. "It's bad, isn't it, sir?"

"Hell," I say. "It's nothing."

His eyes want to believe me. "You mean it?"

"Oh yeah, definitely."

The trooper smiles, and he's still smiling when I stab him through the heart. Flipping his jacket back into place, I close Will's eyes and make the soldier's sign over his body. Godspeed, and a better life next time.

"Dead," my gun tells his friends. "Never had a chance."

They're doing well, not yet hitting a batwing but definitely tying up several of the bastards and taking them out of the fight. And they keep doing well, right up to the point their belt-fed jams.

"Fuck," Neen says.

Franc grabs for the belt, burns his fingers, and swears.

"*Enough!*" I shout.

Both troopers freeze.

"Panic, and I'll shoot you myself."

The batwing is finishing its circle and readying itself for another run. My gun's power pack now holds less than 38 percent, so I'm not keen to waste shots, but needs must . . .

Coming out of sleep, it scans for local threats and finds plenty. "Don't tell me," it says. "We're up shit creek again."

"See that batwing?"

A diode on the gun lights for *locked on,* and then blinks out again. "Thing's shielded," it says.

"So deal with it."

The SIG diabolo whirs, a dozen diodes flicker, and it runs some routine to talk its current load through whatever needs doing.

"Done," it tells me.

The batwing comes apart like a cheap firework. We destroy a second in the same way, and the others peel off and climb out of our range.

"Out of here," I tell my new sergeant, grabbing his belt-fed by the barrel. He's about to help when I shove him away. He looks shocked and I have to remind myself how green this lot are.

"It's hot," I say. "Burn your flesh to the bone."

Flicking his gaze to my arm, Neen realizes the obvious. "Shit," he says, then, "Sorry, sir."

I almost ask him, *What for?*

We run back to our own lines, crouched low. And as we do, the first salvos of an enemy barrage reduce our previous position to splintered wood and an ugly black column of smoke and fire.

"How did you know, sir?"

It's Franc, the new corporal. No such thing as a stupid question, I remind myself; just several thousand that sound that way.

"Cost them two batwings," I say. "You think they're going to let that go?"

"No, sir."

A line of militia opens to let us through. Some of them are whistling their approval, although this stops the moment a fat young uniformed officer appears. He's from a later drop, obviously, and the only reason he's been able to keep his uniform clean is that we've pushed the enemy back the best part of five hundred yards.

That's us, the entire first drop, most of whom are now dead.

"What's your unit?" he asks Franc.

The grunt glances at Neen, who glances at me. And I'm standing there, dripping mud and clutching a red-hot belt-fed, my uniform splattered with blood and slivers of other people's flesh. The young man's gaze sweeps over me and returns to Franc, who's beginning to look nervous.

"I asked you a question."

The lieutenant has one of those voices. The kind I've always hated, right from my early days in the legion.

I tap him on the shoulder.

He swivels, mouth already opening in outrage. So I knee him, hard enough to lift him from the ground and drop him in a heap at my feet. When I roll him over his face is slack and his eyes have tipped back in his head.

"The name's Sven fucking Tveskoeg," I announce to no one in particular. "Lieutenant, Death's Head, Obsidian Cross, third fucking class . . . Let him know that when he wakes."

CHAPTER 27

TROOPERS MOVE out of my way as I make my way through the camp. Maybe they've heard about what just happened, or maybe it's just the way the SIG at my side keeps up a running commentary on their shortcomings.

"Crap tent."

"Bloody awful uniform."

"Call that a pulse rifle . . . ?"

The battle is over for the day and both sides are busy licking their wounds. I don't know about the Uplifted's forces, but ours taste pretty sour. We've taken heavy losses and the ragged militia through which I walk are sullen and afraid.

With the last of our pods landed, the enemy's high fighters have returned to their landing strip on the far side of Ilseville. Their batwings are also gone, leaving the sky empty except for strange stars.

"Over there," I say, pointing to a low hillock that looks slightly less sodden than those around it. A group of militia are doing their best to light a fire from damp twigs and strips ripped from someone's uniform. A foil tent is already erected with its flap facing where they hope the fire will be.

Their best is pitiful.

"Move," I tell them.

One of them stands and finds my gun under her chin.

They pack their possessions in silence. As they turn to go, Neen tosses them a fresh tent from his pack and I shrug. "Send someone along in a few minutes," I tell their leader.

She turns back.

"We'll have a fire going."

I'm speaking the truth. When she returns, flames dance against sodden logs, which hiss and spit with escaping steam. Mind you, setting a fire is easy when you have a holster full of incendiary rounds. Fixed properly, a single round can burn for hours, assuming it doesn't blow your hand off first.

"Frederica," she says. "Sergeant."

She's tall, dark-skinned, and dark-haired. Frederica looks as if she'd be good in bed and good in a fight. Life needs more women like her.

"Sven Tveskoeg," I tell her. "Lieutenant."

She feels better after that, because I outrank her and that makes losing the spot easier. "Which regiment?"

"Death's Head."

Her glance checks whether I'm joking.

"I'd better be going," she says.

I watch Frederica retrieve a burning brand from our fire. She's a good sergeant, and she's going back to tell her troopers how narrow an escape they just had, but it makes me wonder about the outfit I've joined.

In the legion we regarded officers in the Death's Head as mythic beings, the elite of an elite. Frederica's response is based on something other than respect, something much more primitive.

"See you around," I say.

She doesn't look back.

Being semi-chameleon, our tents have already adopted the dirty green of the ground beneath. Fooler loops will help dampen their thermal pattern should the Enlightened bother to overfly this site. Although given the fires and the smoke that curls up into the darkening sky, few people in Ilseville can have any doubt that we're here.

Behind our camp is a muddy-edged pond. It feeds from a narrow stream on our side and soaks away into marshland beyond. We're filthy, stink of smoke, and need a wash, plus I'm tired and need something to snap me awake.

Cold water should do it.

"Get ready for a swim," I tell Neen, stripping off my combat armor and tossing it into the pond.

My sergeant looks shocked.

There was an oasis behind Jebel Jebel, south of Karbonne. I remember the lieutenant making us wash away the memories of our first battle. Of course it was high summer back then, and we were filthy and the water was cool.

Unbuckling his boots, Neen discards his jacket, strips off his shirt, and climbs out of his trousers. He has the body of a farm laborer, rangy but lacking muscle. No implants, no augs. It makes me realize I don't know which world he came from. Somewhere backward, from the looks of things.

"And the rest of you."

Franc strips next, unbuckling heavy boots and fumbling with fastenings. When his shirt hits the ground to reveal breasts I realize the obvious. Franc's a she, and the troopers in my group are mixed. Franc has no augmentations, either, but she's been in battle before, because three knife scars cross her gut like claw marks.

"Seen enough, sir?"

"No," I say. "Come here."

She glares but obeys my order.

The scars are raised, stitched badly, and poorly healed. "Nasty," I say, though I've seen nastier. "How recent?"

"Six months ago."

"Combat?"

Franc's smile is sour. "Family argument," she says, and then waits for me to dismiss her.

I make her wait.

She's got broad shoulders, small breasts, and tight hips, with no body hair anywhere, not even on her head, which has been shaved or something.

"Do you have ferox on your planet?"

It's obvious from the bemused expression on her face that the answer is no.

Neen and Haze are male, Franc and Shil are not, although Haze has a body almost androgynous in its softness and whiteness. Shil is the eldest, at least that's my guess. She undresses with her back to us all and discards her shirt only when she's already in the water.

"Scrub your uniforms," I order. "The fire will dry them quickly enough."

The water is cold and fresh and tastes metallic. After a second even Shil is grinning and gasping as the coldness of the water takes her breath away. I make them stay in until their clothes are clean and the battle forgotten. And then I turn my mind to other things.

"We need food."

"But we've got . . ." Neen hesitates, uncertain if he's allowed to disagree.

"Go on."

"We've got our food packs, sir." He nods toward the tents. A cart has just been around, piled with extra battlefield rations. Vacuum-packed foil sachets of dried shit that just needs water to taste like dried shit with added water.

"Have you eaten that stuff?"

As one, they shake their heads.

"Keep it that way." Having wrung the worst of the water from my uniform, I dress and go check my gun.

"Call this a camp?" it says, coming out of sleep mode.

"You seen better?"

The SIG names three campaigns noted for their viciousness. And my respect for Aptitude's bodyguard reaches a new level.

To Shil I say, "Get your rifle."

She does as she's told, scowling furiously.

"Be back in an hour," I tell Neen. "Anyone asks, I'm on reconnaissance and your orders are to wait here."

He salutes, his eyes flicking to the woman beside me. And I wonder if there's anything between them. She's in her late twenties, scrawny as a skinned rabbit, and smiles when she sees him. The rest of the time she looks like thunder.

"SHIL," I SAY, when we're on our own. "A couple of questions . . . Have you known Sergeant Neen long?"

Our fat-wheeled combats cool on a hillock behind us. God knows the machines are hopeless in battle; they might as well be used for something, even if it's just a hunting trip into the marshes.

"He's my brother, sir."

Fucking great.

"And Franc and Haze?"

"My cousins, but Haze lives in a different village. So I don't know him that well."

"And your militia mixes sexes?"

Shil slicks me a sideways scowl. It asks, *How can he not know something that basic?* Only she swallows the comment and nods instead.

"Got a flash bang?"

She nods to that, too. "Good," I tell her. "Go around that way. Qu etly as you can. Toss it into a channel and come back, making as mu noise as possible."

"Where will you be, sir?"

"Waiting."

THERE IS A right time for things and a wrong time. I want to ex this to the SIG diabolo, but it's too busy turning off a row of diod listen, and it's all I can do not to hurl the useless machine into a and let it sit out the next fifty years underwater.

"Shutting down," it says.

"Wait . . ."

It doesn't, so I hurl it at the alligator instead.

The bastard is black and leathery, longer than Shil and probably four times her weight. Six legs power it through the mud toward me as it flees Shil's stun grenade. Its teeth are blunt, but its jaws are tough and when they close on my thigh I can feel bones crack.

Nothing shatters, which is good.

"No you fucking don't."

As the beast rolls, trying to drag me under the water, I grab my laser knife and twist the handle until the blade flares brightly enough to be seen a mile away. Startled by the light, the alligator freezes and a smell of freshly seared reptile suddenly fills the air.

"*Sir* . . ." It's Shil and she's shouting.

We'll need to talk about that.

"I'm fine."

She slams to a halt, scowling. "Thought you were dead."

"Well, I'm not. And, Shil . . ."

Shil looks at me.

"Don't shout," I tell her. "It unnerves people."

Her eyes flick to the empty wastes around us.

"In battle," I say. "It upsets people."

"That why you killed Corporal Haven?"

A memory of an NCO with his legs smashed enters my mind. *Only happened this morning,* I remind myself, although it feels much longer ago. Can't remember killing him, but that probably means nothing.

"Help me up."

She struggles with my weight but gets me standing. My hip is better than I deserve, although it hurts and blood has filled my boots. My uniform is shredded down one side. If I were still in the legion I'd be carrying thread, a needle, a knife, and wind-dried meat, our basic survival pack. As it is, I've got my laser blade, throwing spikes, cracked bones in my leg, and a gun I'm going to need to find.

Looking at Shil it's easy to understand my earlier mistake. She's not

bald like Franc, but her head's been cropped back to her skull and her uniform is a baggy mess of cheap cloth with too many pockets, patches, and fasteners, all guaranteed to fill with water every time it rains. She looks like any other grunt.

"Got a needle and cotton in one of those pockets?"

"Yes, sir."

"How are your nerves?"

"They're fine."

She's insulted, which is good, but she needs to learn not to let it show. *"They're fine, sir."*

"My nerves are fine, sir."

"Good, then fix my leg."

My injuries will heal faster if the wound's sewn shut, and it gives Shil something to do while my bones knit enough for me to go find my gun. And if that doesn't given me long enough, there's always the alligator for her to skin and joint.

"Not too bad," I say when the job's done.

In the end I skin the creature myself while Shil mends my trousers. The beast has no bones, though it possesses a leathery hide, strange teeth, and plates of something white and slimy where its skeleton should be. What look like feet turn out to be shrunken fins.

Throwing its innards, rudimentary lungs, and most of its skin into the marsh, I remove its head by cutting deeper into the wound I slashed across its throat, discard the last bit of its tail, and climb back into my newly mended uniform.

"Hold this."

The scrap of skin Shil takes is slimy enough to justify her disgust.

"Taste it," I say.

She stares at me, realizing that I'm serious and that things are going to get ugly if she doesn't do what she's told. So she does. She even manages not to wipe her lips afterward.

"Disgust gets you killed," I tell her. "Before this is over you'll be eating food that would now make you vomit. Understand me?"

I hold her gaze until she nods, then hold it some more.

"Yes, sir."

"Good. Now go find my gun."

WITH THE ALLIGATOR slung over my shoulder and the gun at my hip, I power up a fat-wheel and wait for Shil to do the same. We need to find the crashed batwing before we can head back. All I know is that the machine went down between where we killed the alligator and our camp. My best hope is that the bog hasn't taken it already.

Water splashes from our wheels and a sour stink fills the night air around me. Shil stays close and I realize she's frightened by the dancing flames of marsh gas around us.

"It's not magic," I tell her.

She makes a sign against the evil eye anyway.

CHAPTER 28

"PEOPLE WERE looking for you," says Neen before I've even had time to unload the creature's carcass. The trooper looks cowed and nervous, not the proud young sergeant I left behind.

"Which people?" I ask, tossing the alligator onto the fire. My plans to joint, hang, and wash the beast first have just been discarded.

"A lieutenant . . ."

"Death's Head?"

Neen nods, carefully not meeting my eyes.

"Not your problem," I tell him.

"He wants you to report immediately. There's an HQ set up toward the middle of the camp. You're expected."

No one else is meeting my eyes, either. Whatever has been said, they're upset. I take the square of skin from Shil and give it to Franc. "Got a knife?"

She nods.

"Cut four death's heads from this and sew them onto the sleeves of your uniforms. As of now, you're auxiliaries. And there's only one rule, *Whatever it takes, that's what we do* . . . Cut off all other badges. Any questions?"

"No, sir."

"And you."

Shil looks at me.

"Dump the batwing chip in water in case it's still alive, and then help Franc to sew the patches . . . Your sister's good with a needle," I add, glancing at Neen. "She fixed my leg."

"He got bitten," says Shil. "By a monster."

They all look from the fire to my leg and back again.

"Hack off the meat as it cooks," I tell them. "Offer it around. There's more on that thing than any of us can eat."

"We could save it," says Franc, adding, "sir."

"Yeah," I agree. "We could. Or I could just go kill something else tomorrow."

Since the kyp began taking its share of what I eat and drink everything tastes sour to me, but I leave Neen and his group by the fire feeling happier than when I found them. Anyway, armies fight better for being properly fed.

About twenty paces into the half darkness, in the shadow between two tents, I pass a tall and smartly dressed lieutenant coming in the other direction. He's marching toward our fire with something close to anger on his face.

"If you're looking for me, I'm here."

The lieutenant swings back, his eyes taking in the slime on my uniform and the fact that I'm limping, although less badly than five minutes earlier.

"You're Second Lieutenant Tveskoeg?"

"Got a problem with that?"

He stares at me from a great height, the only problem being he's shorter than me and not used to meeting men twice his width. "You should know," he tells me, "that I outrank you."

"And you should know I don't give a fuck."

Someone laughs, and we both realize that the tents on both sides of us are listening. His face tightens and he wheels around without another word. I leave it just long enough to make him nervous and then follow.

. . .

"TVESKOEG." The voice is warm, amused. "I'm Captain Roccaforte. Come in. We're all dying to meet you." The captain is immaculately dressed, and his feet rest on a leather stool. I double-check that his chair really is sitting on an ornate and probably priceless rug. It is.

"You look a mess."

"Been killing things," I tell him.

The others are watching with interest. All that telling Neen and Shil to use *sir,* and I've forgotten to do it myself.

"What things?"

"Long, ugly bastard. Eight feet long and a big mouth." I point to the newly mended rip in my uniform. "We're eating it at the moment. Well, my men are. I'm here, obviously."

The captain smiles. "Your men," he says, then nods to the lieutenant who came to collect me. "Miles mentioned them. I didn't think we gave you any men."

"I found them. Their sergeant got killed and then their corporal; they lost half their troop and needed commanding." I look at him. "I'd like to keep them. They've got the makings of a good unit."

Someone snorts, and I glare into the darkness.

"We took out a belt-fed," I say. "Used it to take down a plasma cannon. Killed a few batwings, too [illegible]."

"That was you?"

"Yes, sir," I say. "That was us. I'm co-opting them."

The captain looks interested and I'm glad he doesn't ask me what *co-opting* means, because I don't know. It's a word the legion use to describe the tribes who take guns and flags and silver in return for fighting the ferox.

"What does co-opting them involve?"

"I've told them to make Death's Head shoulder patches."

Someone protests, and the captain silences them. "From what?"

"Ugly bastard skin."

"Who's doing it?"

"Two of the women. One of them helped hunt the beast."

Captain Roccaforte starts. "You've co-opted women into the Death's Head?" He's looking at me slightly strangely.

"They're auxiliaries," I say, using another legion word. "I'm Death's Head; they just owe me their allegiance."

The captain nods, apparently satisfied. "This beast of yours, how big was it again?"

"About the same size as me. But a lot uglier."

Behind us someone laughs and comes out of a tent. It's Major Silva, who seems to have acquired a pair of spectacles, much like those worn by Colonel Nuevo. They're reflecting in the firelight.

"*Dylidae lagarto,*" he says. "Deadly creatures."

"This one was half asleep," I say, adding, "sir."

"I'm sure it was," says the major. "Probably dying of old age like that ferox you killed."

A couple of Death's Head officers glance at each other. The smartly dressed lieutenant gets slightly less arrogant. The major's telling them I might dress like shit but I also come with a health warning.

"We've got a job for you."

I wait.

"Something unexpected."

He wants me to ask, and it seems rude to refuse. "Unexpected, sir?"

"We've captured a ferox."

"Fuck," I say without thinking. "It must be half dead with cold." It's a weird metabolism the ferox have, one that needs heat and cold in equal measure. Without both the beasts die. "Where's it being held?"

"In a pod. We've glue-gunned the lid shut. I'll have Miles take you there."

"I need to go back to my tent first."

The major raises one eyebrow. He really does.

"You need me to question the beast, sir?"

"If you can . . ."

I knew of his doubts. Sergeant Hito, back on the mother ship, was open about the major's belief that I'd been hallucinating.

"Then I have to go back to my tent. There are things I need."

At the camp I collect up the others, already wearing their new shoulder patches, their fingers greasy with meat from what's left of the alligator, which is a lot less than I expect.

"We shared it," Franc says.

"Good," I tell her.

In the bottom of my roll are my Death's Head dagger and my throwing spikes, where I left them. I'm going to need both, although not in the way those watching think.

"Let's go," I say.

"My orders are to take *you*."

"And I'm going."

Lieutenant Uffingham doesn't like this answer. "No one said anything about my taking them."

"You're not," I say. "I am. If you don't like it, we can always wait while you take the problem to Major Silva." Now the lieutenant really hates me, which is too bad, because I'm not after his job or his seniority.

I don't even know what his job is.

He walks ahead, which is fine. The others trail behind me. We're moving into parts of the camp where only my presence and the smartness of the lieutenant gives them leave to enter. The fires are bigger, the tents more elaborate, and I can smell food that didn't come out of a foil pack or from the marshes. Someone clinks glasses in a tent behind us, toasting victory in a voice that sounds like it believes what it says.

"You," I say to Haze. "Find a generator and get this recharged."

He takes the SIG nervously, holding it between two fingers as I unbuckle my belt and hand him both belt and holster.

"What if they won't let me?"

"Then take my name in vain. If that doesn't work, take the major's name in vain. And if that still doesn't work, say it's on direct orders from the colonel."

Now he looks more nervous than ever.

"Just do it."

The trooper vanishes into the night, a slightly larger-than-average shadow trying not to trip over his own feet.

Guards halt us as we approach a pod ringed with razor wire.

"Lieutenant Miles Uffingham."

The men salute while failing to move out of the way.

"On Major Silva's orders," says the lieutenant.

Both guards stay where they are. I'm beginning to enjoy this. Also, I'm one step ahead of Lieutenant Uffingham. The only reason guards ever fail to acknowledge a rank is that they're already acting on the orders of one more senior. Maybe you need time as a bottom feeder to know how these things work.

Franc, Neen, and Shil understand. They look more nervous by the second, and if not for the walk back through the camp, I think they'd be fading into the darkness as discreetly as possible.

"Is Colonel Nuevo here?"

One of the guards rips his attention away from the smartly dressed lieutenant. He grins at the state of my uniform, and then remembers where he is. He nods, uncertain how to address me.

"Would you tell him that Second Lieutenant Sven Tveskoeg is ready when he is."

"Sven . . ." The colonel is dressed for combat, full body armor and a helmet, with its visor tipped up. A pulse pistol sits in a holster on his hip. "Any chance of this working?"

"Whatever it takes, sir," I say. "That's what we'll do."

"That bad, huh?"

"Where did you capture it, sir?"

"In the woods." He points toward a row of distant scrub. "One of our forward patrols . . ." He glances behind me and sees the others. "Who are these?"

"My unit."

His gaze skims across the three troopers and he sighs. "Are those Death's Head patches?"

"Yes, sir . . . These men are auxiliaries."

He stares at me, eyes almost mild. "I didn't know we had auxiliaries in this regiment, Sven. It must be new."

"Only in the section that talks to ferox, sir."

The colonel laughs. "Oh, fuck it," he says. "Keep them."

I try not to wonder what would have happened to the troopers if he'd disapproved.

I SEND SHIL and Franc for firewood, a case of incendiaries, and anything else that looks flammable. And then, as the guards step back, I show Neen how to pry the core from an incendiary shell and extract its ferric oxide, aluminum, and magnesium. As instructed, he shreds the mix over the sticks that the others are beginning to pile around the pod.

Shil and Franc bring broken boxes, half a thorn bush, a crate of military-issue fire lighters—something I didn't even know existed—and an old door complete with rusting handle, hinges, and wooden frame.

"Where did you find that?"

"A shack," Franc says. "Behind the trees."

"Tear it apart," I tell her.

It's not an order she likes. The farm is poor and badly positioned, working land that is obviously waterlogged for most of the year. Its shabbiness probably reminds Franc of home. All the same, she does what she's told and does it efficiently, and that's what matters.

Shil rips apart a straw mattress and spreads its contents as kindling. A table and three chairs she stacks on one side for later.

I'm not sure how long it's going to take to give the ferox back its body heat, but I want the beast vaguely content before anything else happens. Always assuming its need for heat isn't tied to a matching need for sunlight, because if it is the colonel's plans are fucked and I'm going to be the one to tell him.

"You," I tell Shil. "Light it."

She comes forward and sets a flame to the straw.

The powder from the incendiary flares brightly, and damp wood spits and hisses until it is dry enough to catch by itself. Another five minutes and I decide it must be getting warm inside the pod.

"Open it," I tell the guards.

A dozen men with pulse rifles stand around the pod as a technician tries to work out how to unglue the pod without being burned. In the end I take his cutting tool, step across the flames, and cut the glue myself.

"You ready?" I ask the riflemen.

Their sergeant nods. "Yes, sir."

"Right, then this is how it works . . . I'll hammer on the glass when I'm ready to leave. See me before that and the ferox is using me as a shield."

"They don't have the intelligence," says a voice. It's the first sign in half an hour that we haven't gotten rid of Lieutenant Uffingham.

I ignore him.

THE BEAST IS injured. A gash has been opened across its face, and blood is matted into the fur beneath its throat armor. Our fire has warmed the pod, but less than I've been expecting. Knocking several times on the wall, I lift the glass.

"More heat."

Neen nods.

As I duck back inside, Franc and Shil begin smashing up wooden chairs to throw onto the fire. A minute later the ferox turns its head and slowly focuses its eyes on my face.

Lips draw back and the beast opens its mouth to reveal yellowing canines. One of them is broken, and human hair hangs from the jagged stump.

"At least you've already eaten."

Dark eyes stare back.

So I twist the handle of my laser knife and sear the back of my hand, trying not to wince. And as the pain fades, I catch a burst of aimless fear, tied to crippling cold and a desire for death.

What? it asks.

"Sven."

What Sven?

"Sven lived with ferox."

The beast opens its eyes in disbelief, so I send it a memory of the caves and Youngster.

The fire outside is raising the temperature in here close to desert heat. This wakes the ferox even further, although it also sets the animal's wounds bleeding as warmth draws blood back to the surface. The pain, when it reaches me, practically knocks me back on my heels.

Almost gone, it says.

Remembering this isn't Youngster, I resist the urge to nod and think *Yes* instead. The beast, indeed, is almost gone.

Snakeskull did this.

"What?"

Got sick.

"You got sick?" I ask.

But it's locked itself into a loop involving a tunnel and cold water, remembering intensely and repeatedly the same twenty or thirty footsteps. There's something unsettling about sharing an alien's final moments, not least because bits of the beast's memory are bleeding into my own thoughts as it prepares to die.

"Wait," I tell it. "Who got sick?"

Snakeskull, it says. *Had to guard . . . Hurt us.*

There are too many gaps between its thoughts, too much pain. All the beast can still remember is walking through a tunnel, and it was dying even then.

Death, it demands.

"Deep rest, and a better life next time."

My dagger takes it through armor plating and skewers the heart beneath. I feel the beast's death and it locks my throat. So either I'm getting soft, or it's one of those glitches I get before adjusting to a new set of rules.

I make a soldier sign over his body from habit, and then hammer several times on the side of the pod. Just to make sure there are no mistakes, I hammer again, and, even after that, the guards still keep their pulse rifles pointed at me as I clamber over the edge, letting the glass lid bang shut behind me.

"Fuck," someone says.

Which is when I realize I'm covered in blood.

"You okay?"

It's Colonel Nuevo.

"Yes, sir," I say. "Unfortunately the ferox is dead."

"Unfortunately?"

"It didn't finish answering my questions."

"But you definitely questioned it?"

I ask his permission to talk in private.

His guards fall back and so do my four troopers. The fire around the pod is now just ashes, and the moon has shifted across the sky. It makes me realize just how long I've been inside.

"Snakeskull," I say. "Does that mean anything to you?"

The colonel begins to shake his head, and then hesitates midshake. "Could be," he says, but he's talking to himself. "Braids and snakes. Sounds possible . . . You ever seen a silverhead?"

I'm back in the conversation. "No, sir."

"Metal braids for hair. Might look like snakes to a ferox." He hesitates. "We're talking about something the ferox said, right?"

"Demanded guarding."

"The Enlightened are psychic," says the colonel. "If you can talk to ferox, maybe they can talk to ferox."

The Uplifted number fewer than us, but their technology is good enough to trade with the U/Free, who let us fight each other, probably hoping we'll destroy each other and solve the problem that way.

The United Free administer 85 percent of the known galaxy. If you believe their propaganda, the U/Free live in a state of crime-free bliss, spared the trauma of illness and hunger, able to reach their true potential over the span of a dozen lives. As they keep telling us, they're really disappointed we won't join them.

Someday the U/Free will choose between the Enlightened and the

Octovians. At the moment they sit it out, proclaiming their sadness at our childish inability to make peace with each other. And in between expressing their sadness, they buy steppewolf furs, wild-side implants, and obscenely sized diamonds from long-dead star systems. Anything exotic, anything natural. Amber, comet ice to mix with cocktails, trinket boxes made from ferox shell.

I've just left a fortune in raw materials behind me.

"You're scowling."

The colonel is right, I am.

"Okay," says Colonel Nuevo. "Snakeheads. What else did you discover?"

"It escaped from the Enlightened through a tunnel under the city's defenses. It looked to me like a sewer."

The colonel's staring at me. "You could see into its mind?"

"I saw its memories."

"So," says Colonel Nuevo. "There's a sewer." Even in the half-light of the dying fire I can see the calculation in his eyes. "Tell me," he says. "Just how good is that little group of yours?"

CHAPTER 29

SHIL WON'T meet my eyes, Franc gives a strained salute and excuses herself, and Haze hands me the SIG diabolo and turns away, before making himself turn back.

"It woke up." He sounds upset and scared . . . and he's staring everywhere but at the blood splattering my uniform.

"Woke up?"

"Yes, sir . . . So I reset it."

"Reset what?"

"Its scan parameters."

"You played with the settings on my gun?"

My voice is quiet, which scares him even more, and he's right, because unless he comes up with a really good reason for messing with the SIG, I'm going to hurt him very badly indeed. I've seen soldiers get killed for less.

Taking a deep breath, Haze says, "I just stopped it draining quite so much power. I can restore the earlier settings, if that's what you want."

He's bought himself a reprieve.

"Go on."

"The combat chip was set to real time plus."

"Which means what?"

Haze thinks I'm testing him. Actually, he might as well be talking another language.

"Five seconds absolute, fifteen high probable, two minutes high likely, and fifteen high possible; that's a huge demand for any AI to carry. It looks like you were worried about . . ."

Haze hesitates, realizing what he's just said.

"Don't stop now," I tell him.

"I mean," he says, "you obviously expected a high-probability, high-impact event, set the AI accordingly, and then forgot to . . ."

Yeah, Haze just dug himself another hole.

NEEN IS THE only one who remains with me as I strip off my combat armor, stuff handfuls of cold *Dylidae lagarto* meat into my mouth, and motion him to follow me down to the water's edge.

"Keep guard," I tell him.

Neen salutes. What's worse, it looks like he means it.

The water is colder than earlier, and the mud is sticky beneath my feet; tiny predators nip at my legs and pond weed drags at my ankles like fingers. I'm not superstitious. Well, no more than the next soldier, but this night is leaving a sour taste in my mouth.

Unless that's the kyp.

Idiot, I tell myself. All battles end with this feeling.

A scar on my knee is aching, as it does when it gets cold. The cut was into bone, a saber slash so powerful it embedded a blade in my leg that had to be wrenched free. Weirdly, the very viciousness of the blow saved my life. While the tribesman was still struggling to retrieve his sword, I put a knife through his heart.

Karbonne feels a long way from here.

Adapt or die, adapt and die . . . the options aren't great, but one is definitely better than the other. As I climb from the water, the thoughts crowding my head are gone. The ferox is just a beast, its memories of death washed clean. I toss Neen my armor to scrub, struggle into the sodden trousers, and return to our fire. A minute or so later steam is rising off me like a saucepan on the boil.

"Right," I say. "Tell me."

"What, sir?"

"Where the others are. What's troubling them?"

My sergeant's face goes blank.

"Neen. *That's an order.*"

He looks at me, at the gun I've just drawn from its holster, and at the Death's Head dagger driven into the dirt by my feet.

"Permission to speak freely, sir?"

My laugh surprises him. I can't remember the last time anyone used that phrase and actually meant it. "Speak away."

"You tortured a ferox to death, sir. You tortured it so badly you made it talk."

"Fuckers can't talk."

"Everyone says this one did."

"Everyone?"

He gestures at the camp around us. It is quiet, at least where we are. All the goodwill gained by sharing the alligator meat is gone in a single rumor.

"You're a Death's Head auxiliary," I tell him. "You don't worry what other people think. You worry what I think. Do you understand?"

He nods.

"Good," I say. "Now, the ferox was injured, frozen, and half starving. It was trapped on the wrong planet in someone else's war."

The others are creeping back to listen. I'll be teaching them to move more quietly.

"Join us," I say.

As Neen's eyes flick to the darkness, he smiles and I realize he just spotted his sister. She's skinny as a rat and wears her scowl like a uniform, but I'll forgive her for now, because she held up well enough when we were hunting the alligator, and besides she looks good naked.

"The ferox wanted to die," I tell them. "I offered it death in return for information. The beast was grateful."

"Sir," says Franc, sliding herself between Neen and me. "That's not what most people are saying."

So I explain to her why that's also good.

A MOON CLIMBS high in the sky and sets a silvery sheen across the marshland around us. The river glistens like a cheap ribbon, and my pond becomes a mirror. Lights can be seen in the distance, the city of Ilseville. We should be fighting. If this were the legion, we would be fighting. Instead we're waiting for the peace talks to fail. Apparently the U/Free want to broker a clean surrender of the city.

We don't want that. The Enlightened don't want that. But we're going through the motions because the United Free demand that we do, their need to interfere being almost as strong as their hunger for news and their obsession with anything exotic. Which, bizarrely enough, apparently includes us.

In the meantime we're watching the Uplift city with our hiSats, and they're watching this camp with their equivalent, and we're both busy planning our next attacks come tomorrow noon.

An hour or so after my troop settle, Franc wanders out of the tent she's sharing with Shil and I hear the noise as she pisses in the darkness. On her way back, she stops and takes a slow look around her, but doesn't see me where I sit in the shadow of a broken fat wheel. Neen wakes two hours before dawn and disappears toward the center of camp; when he comes back it's with an armful of someone else's wood to feed our fire.

"Sit," I tell him.

He does what he's told.

"How old are you?"

The trooper debates lying. "Eighteen," he says at last.

It's all I can do not to swear. "And the others?"

"Franc's twenty-one. I don't know about Haze."

"And Shil?"

"Twenty-eight," he says. "You know how it goes. She got drafted because I'm the only boy and we had to provide two soldiers, everyone did."

"Describe your training."

Neen looks at me, wondering how to answer. "We only got our uniform and rifles the day before yesterday," he says. "And we didn't really have training, as such. We're from the next planet along."

"But that's . . ." I think it through. I only skimmed my briefing, since most briefings are bollocks; but this system has three planets, and all of them belonged to the enemy until recently.

"You were Enlightened?"

"No, sir. Not us. Only important people were that."

WE LEAVE FOR the sewer and the city at dawn. Everything we own except our uniforms and weapons is left behind: our tents, food supplies, rucksacks, and fat-wheel combat. We're going to do this on foot, because we stand a better chance of success that way.

As we move out, a trooper wishes us luck, and another makes the sign against evil. He bolts when he sees me notice.

"You enjoy it, don't you, sir?"

Shil catches my stare, begins to look away, and then makes herself look back. Maybe she's seen the way I look at her, or maybe she's just enough like me to know that rank means nothing.

It's what you do with the rank that counts.

"I'm used to it," I tell her. "And you'd better get used to it, too."

"You know, sir," she says, "people around here say you're not human." Shil raises her chin, and I know she's wondering if she's gone too far.

"Do you think the Enlightened are human?"

"But that's the point," says Shil. "They don't want to be."

"Whereas I was born like this?"

Shil glances away, and the next few minutes pass in awkward silence. "I'm sorry, sir," she says finally. "I didn't mean to speak out of turn."

"You didn't. Believe me; you'd know if you had."

The others are listening in, so I address the next comment to all of them. "Within reason, you can say anything. But question or disobey an order and I'll kill you on the spot."

They grin when I grin, but we all know it's not a joke.

"What's within reason?" asks Haze.

"No blasphemy. No treason. No saying we're going to lose."

"Are we?" Shil asks.

My smile is sour. "Not if I can help it."

Our own tents come to an end shortly after this and we string out in a line, heading for a distant row of trees. I take point and Neen brings up the rear; the rest of them walk fifteen paces apart, trying to tread only in the footsteps of the person in front.

As we get closer to those trees the ground grows firmer underfoot and our boots stop being sucked by mud. The thorns are stunted, ripe with berries that are probably poisonous. A dragonfly the size of my fist hovers over sullen water; its wings in the early-morning half-light are as iridescent as its body is drab.

I stop, feeling the others stop behind me.

The way looks clear. So far I've been relying on flickers of memory taken from the ferox, but it was in pain and sometimes close to unconscious . . . Tracks are what I really need.

My troop wait.

A cold wind from behind us carries the faintest traces of our distant fires. We're out of sight of our own camp. What I need to know is whether anyone is watching us from up ahead. My kyp is useless; it hasn't been able to pick up anything in days. And I'm not certain it could recognize the Enlightened anyway.

Communicated, freely tied, willingly of one accord. A dozen different phrases pretend to tell the UnEnlightened what it's like to make the change. I suspect few of them come close to the reality.

A quick flick of my hand and the others begin to move forward. Roots catch at our boots and low loops of thorn act like trip wires, but we keep moving until the trees thin and we hit a plowed field. It's the first such field any of us have seen since landing. Huge footprints lead toward the gate where I stand. A twist of fur is caught in the hinge, and dry blood on wood indicates where the ferox halted to gather breath.

I've got what I need.

We find bodies an hour later. A woman missing half her skull, and a man ripped from abdomen to shoulder, despite his body armor. Both have fired their weapons from the smell of the barrels.

Behind me I hear Franc and Haze vomit.

Another three corpses wait for us half an hour after that. One is clean-killed, head twisted so far his vertebrae have simply shattered. The others are messy, but still cleaner than the first two.

"Strip the bodies," I order.

Haze shakes his head, and then staggers back, clutching his jaw. It's not hard as punches go, but I've still not forgiven him for messing with my gun, even if he did make it better.

"Want to join them?" I ask, nodding at the bodies.

The others go very still.

"I'm sorry, sir," Haze says.

He gets to strip the three bodies on his own, as punishment. The boy's overweight and clumsy and it takes him twice as long as it should, but he manages it eventually.

Two women, one man . . . all very dead.

Shil, Haze, and Franc swap uniforms. Although I allow them to scrub clean their new outfits first. The ditch they use is muddy, and I'm not sure that washing the uniforms makes that much difference, but it seems to matter.

About ten minutes after this we reach the sewer.

It sounds simple. First two bodies, then three bodies, a change of clothing for the junior troopers, and a quick march to the entrance of a tunnel. But my ankles are rubbed raw by my boots, and if I feel like that, then God knows how the others must feel. We've just marched for two hours across marshland and mud, enough to exhaust even hardened troopers.

I've ordered them to swap weapons, too. So now they're armed with pulse rifles belonging to the enemy. It's Shil who asks me why. After she makes absolutely sure I understand she's after information only, and she's in no way questioning my judgment. Her voice as she explains this is just deadpan enough to avoid outright insolence.

We stop. I stare at her. "You tell me," I say.

Shil chews her lip, the first sign of weakness she's displayed since we hunted alligator together, and she stops the moment she realizes I've noticed. Neen and the others are watching us.

"If you get captured," Shil says finally. "We simply say we're Ilsevillect militia and you captured us. And we're really glad to be rescued."

"And . . . ?"

"If necessary, we can pretend that we captured Neen and you."

"Well done."

Shil's brother looks so shocked it makes me want to laugh. So I sit everyone down in the entrance to the tunnel and tell them what's going to happen, why it's going to happen, and exactly what I expect of them.

I don't bother explaining what's going to happen if they fuck up. They're not stupid; they can work that out for themselves.

In the center of Ilseville is a Trade Hall. Old and decrepit, it's impressive on first viewing but poorly defended with too many ways in. These are the colonel's words to me and he'd better be telling the truth. Inside the hall is an Uplifted; our job is to capture it.

"You mean an Enlightened," says Haze without thinking. He's backing away from me before I've even turned to face him.

"No," I say. "I mean Uplifted."

"It'll be guarded," says Neen.

"Well guarded," Shil adds.

And I realize something: These people know about this. "You've seen an Uplifted?"

Everyone glances at everyone else. If it wasn't so funny, I'd be angry.

"Haze has," says Franc. "Once, in passing."

The way she says this sounds like she's giving Haze his story, a story to which she's expecting him to keep, and from the way the boy's refusing to meet my eyes, whatever the real story is . . . It's way more complex than Franc's simple outline makes it sound.

"Haze," I say, "this Uplifted you saw *once,* describe it . . ."

He hesitates, but only because he's struggling for the right words. "It's like a machine," he says finally. "Pyramid-shaped and full of lights, almost pretty. But very dangerous."

That's it, the sum total of his description.

It doesn't matter how much I demand clarification, all my anger does is lock the truth tight in his throat. We go into the darkness in silence and no one looks in my direction for a very long time.

CHAPTER 30

"LIKE THE guts of an ice worm," I say when we're twenty minutes into the tunnel. Some round-mawed machine has bored its way through compacted mud, shitting concrete onto the walls as it goes, only the concrete is crumbling, and fractures reveal dark earth beyond.

Neen bites. "What's an ice worm?"

"Bit like this," I say, "only natural. Eats its way through ice, obviously enough. People live inside them."

"Where?" demands Shil.

"On Paradise."

"You were a guard?" She's reassessing.

"A prisoner."

"And now you're a Death's Head officer?" says Haze, finally turning to look at me.

"Things change."

He glances away, and then looks back when he thinks I'm not watching. So I hold my laser blade higher and light a little more of the tunnel through which we walk. Everyone has secrets, but I'm pretty certain that boy has more than most.

"How much do you trust Haze?" I ask Neen a few minutes later.

"With my life."

"You understand," I tell him, "I'll be holding you to that?"

Slime slicks under our feet and guano streaks the walls. A quick flick of my blade toward the roof reveals endless bats, hanging silently. Tiny sullen eyes watching us as we pass. The only good thing that can be said about their ammonia stench is that it takes our minds off what is to come next.

"How do you know which tunnel to take?" Shil asks.

Increasing the intensity of my blade, I sweep it along a wall. When it dims, Shil is still puzzled so I step behind her and take her shoulders, feeling her freeze beneath my grip.

Now would be a really good time to let go. But I don't, because that would mean admitting I've noticed. Instead I angle Shil until she's looking toward the wall, pass her the laser blade, and take her arm at the wrist, bringing the brightness closer to the crumbling concrete.

"All of you," I say.

A scuff in the bat shit stands out, where the ferox stumbled and its fur left traces of feathering. A shift of her wrist lets the brightness highlight a much larger scrape, just above the waterline.

It's the heel mark of a ferox.

Instinct makes me take the last half a mile in silence. This is the way the beast came, and it was held at the Trade Hall. So I already know it is possible to get from the sewer to the hall; the question is, where did the ferox enter the system?

Water is rolling out of small pipes jutting into the tunnel, and it's also beginning to rush through sluice gates on either side of us. In the city above our heads it has just begun raining, and gutters are channeling the runoff into this sewer.

We can cope with the water rising, because if it comes to it, we'll just swim. But I'm anxious not to lose the tracks of the ferox.

"Over there, sir," says Haze.

I flick my blade toward that wall.

He's right: There's a scuff mark at shoulder height.

Another scuff a hundred yards later shows the beast kept to that side of the tunnel for a while. The current is harder over there, because the tunnel curves away from us, and a rusting ladder has been bent away from the wall of an access shaft by the weight of something heavy.

"Take a look," I tell Neen.

Shil shakes her head, the action utterly instinctive. So far she's done everything Neen tells her, younger brother or not, but I refuse to have things unravel between them if the situation gets serious, and it's going to get serious.

All five of us need to understand that.

"Neen goes," I tell them.

He climbs swiftly and vanishes from sight. We wait for five minutes and then ten. I'm about to call Shil on her simmering anger when we hear footsteps on the ladder above.

"Difficult climb," says Neen.

"How far?"

"A hundred rungs or so, but the ladder finishes at a ledge halfway up. After that there's only wall." His voice is matter-of-fact, despite grazes to his hands and a nasty gash on one side of his head.

"Fell," he says, seeing my glance.

"Do we need ropes?"

"No, sir." Neen shakes his head. "I've worked out a route . . ."

THE STREETS AROUND the Trade Hall are almost empty. A truck that spits smoke, a couple of electric three-wheelers piled high with furs, business still going on as normal, despite an army camping beyond the gates.

Few people bother to look as Neen and Franc saunter under a broken arch and find themselves in a narrow alley. Militia uniforms are much the same everywhere: combats and boots, cheap helmets and web belts. Haze hurries out behind them, then makes himself slow down.

Shil goes next. She still looks like a boy at first glance, and probably second glance as well. Had it been just the four of them everything would be fine. But I'm there as well, and it's hard to mistake me for anything but what I am.

A professional killer.

A woman turns, nudges another. A man on a gyro bike stops to see what they're looking at and finds himself looking straight into my eyes.

Idiot, I want to say.

He opens his mouth to shout and I cross the street in a blur, wrap one arm around his thick neck, and twist savagely. The crack echoes off a nearby wall. Neen kills one of the old women and Franc kills the other. She does it cleanly and savagely, a single stab to the heart, then a swipe across the throat.

I'm speechless. Also impressed.

Grinning, Franc wipes her knife on her trousers and thrusts it back into its sheath. Her eyes catch Haze's glance, and he nods. When I look at Franc again she's humming to herself.

My sergeant, meanwhile, is looking at his sister, who is anything but happy. After a second, he goes back to lowering his victim to the ground. Quite how a man that thin manages to support a woman that fat beats me.

"Right," I say. "Drag them into the tunnel."

Franc reaches for her victim, and Haze moves forward to help.

"Shil," I say. "A word . . ."

The others pretend not to hear.

"Franc and Neen just saved your life," I tell her. "They saved my life, and they saved Haze's life, too. If that happens again, I expect you to act faster."

"They were women," she says.

"So are you and Franc."

"Old women," says Shil, close to crying. Although I suspect it's more with frustration than anything else.

"Was that going to stop them raising an alarm?"

I wait for her answer and, after a few seconds, she shakes her head.

"No," I say. "It was not."

On my orders Shil and Franc take the dead women's scarves and wrap them around their own heads. After a moment's thought, I take a shawl from one of the women and make Haze wear this as a scarf. All that puppy fat makes him look like a girl anyway. When they're done, I discard my own jacket and struggle into the trench coat of the man I've just killed.

Now we're two men and three women, all militia.

"Walk on," I tell them. "Eyes down, talking quietly. Step aside, be polite, and salute anything that looks like it needs saluting."

"And you, sir?" asks Haze.

"I'll be a hundred paces behind you. If you hear a disturbance keep walking."

THE SILVERHEAD WHO begins to follow Neen made the change decades before the trooper was born. He's tall, swathed with a mess of tubes that loop from his ribs to his legs. The virus has strung steel plaits from his skull, which ripple as he walks. He's a five-braid, and he's an arrogant bastard, far too sure of himself to worry about covering his back.

"Hey," says my gun. "Take a look at ugly."

A full battery pack and settings that only require it to forecast a handful of seconds into the future have made the SIG hyperactive, happy, and talkative. I preferred the thing in *fuck-off* mode.

"You know," the gun says, "that silverheads used to be human? Some of them quite recently . . ."

Just as I think the SIG's about to riff off silverhead history, it stops and half a dozen diodes beginning to flick through a rapid sequence.

"Phasing," it announces.

"What the fuck does—"

And then I find out, because the silverhead walks confidently toward a wall and disappears in a shimmer of light.

"Move," says the SIG.

I move.

We find the silverhead two streets later, entering a road Neen is already on, although the silverhead enters it from a doorway on the opposite side. A clever trick, one I'd always believed a myth until then.

"Oh shit," says the gun.

The silverhead has stopped, almost as if listening intently. And my gun's gone very quiet indeed, to the point of stopping its lights exactly where they are.

If one myth is true, how about another? Ripping a throwing spike from its sheath on my wrist, I waste a fraction of a second finding its sweet point and flick it free from my fingers.

"*Got you,*" says the silverhead, turning.

He becomes aware of my throw as the spike hits his shoulder. *Injury locks the Enlightened into now.*

"Can I suggest subsonic?"

My gun sounds happy to be back in the game.

Two shots take the silverhead to his shattered knees. And then, extracting my dagger, I simply walk up to the whimpering creature and drag my blade hard across his throat.

He flickers from view, but the damage is too serious. For a second he's almost transparent, and then he reappears, just in time to let my knife finish taking the head from his body.

Self-proclaimed god or not, he drops like a wall collapsing.

"Good riddance," says the gun.

A sweep of my dagger and most of the silverhead's scalp comes free. There's flesh beneath the shell, so I scrape it clean and cram the mass of steel braids onto my own head. It's a tight fit.

What am I going to do about those tubes?

Discarding the jacket I stole earlier, I slash open my shoulder and stab my hip . . . It hurts like fuck, but I do it anyway, and then I force the fattest of the tubes into the open wounds and watch flesh begin to seal itself around them. Black's not really an Enlightenment color, but my prosthetic arm is definitely not normal and that's good. And my gun, that's definitely not normal, either.

"Flash faster," I tell it.

"What?"

"Make like winter-tree lights."

The SIG does so, with very bad grace.

"Neen?"

The boy turns, catches sight of me, and swears. I'd grin, but silver-heads take themselves far too seriously for humor.

"Fall in," I say. "All of you. We're going to visit the Uplifted."

No one stops us as we cross a square; no one even glances our way. A child almost does and is slapped into silence by her father, who bows nervously without ever meeting my face. If this is the response the Enlightened elicit, I'm not sure I like them much, either.

Neen stalks ahead, his rifle ported across his chest. The three girls, who are actually two girls and an increasingly sulky Haze, walk behind like a shadow, stopping when I stop and keeping their eyes on the ground.

Up ahead is a steel gate cut into a foamstone wall. A guard stands on either side. These are real soldiers, not militia. We're being watched, scanned by some kind of lenz above the door, and one of the guards is already unporting his gun.

He'd kill Neen as soon as look at him, but my braids and the gun, which is now chanting Uplift prayers, give the man pause.

"Open," demands my gun, taking a break from its chanting.

The guard falls back before us.

He wants to stop me but can't bring himself to touch someone he believes Enlightened. The mistake costs him his life, as Franc jabs a blade under his jaw and up into his brain.

Neen kills the other guard, a savage swipe of hardened steel across his jugular. It leaves Neen soaked in blood, but I understand this well enough. The trooper's washing away the memory of his earlier kill, giving himself something legitimate. From the grin on Franc's face, it doesn't look like she's too bothered about stuff like that.

"Stand back."

Neen blows the gate out of its arch with a belt mine and we're inside, guns held combat-style and our eyes scanning an inner courtyard. It's not what I expect. Someone's roofed the entire area in spun glass, which shifts through a thousand patterns so swiftly that it makes my eyes ache.

"Don't look," Haze tells Franc.

She drags her gaze away from the ceiling.

The floor beneath our boots is a thin skim of water over huge squares of marble. Colors drift in the water like opalescent clouds, not mixing but passing through each other in fingers of pure purples and blues.

A door ahead begins to open and Franc raises her pulse rifle.

"May I?" she asks.

I nod, and a soldier goes down with most of his skull missing. It's a clean shot and Franc's grin is wider than ever. She lived under Uplift occupation, I remind myself; she's bound to have issues.

We hit the corridor beyond and kill everything we see. A NewlyMade, skull still soft and first braid still growing. A full-blown two-braid, too shocked at being attacked to phase out in time. A handful of guards, who die before they realize what's happening.

A girl sees us and begins to scream. It's Franc who takes her aside and quiets her down, talking intently. She's the daughter of the two-braid, hunting for her father. We all know what she doesn't, that her father is already dead.

As the slaughter ends, a couple of women appear, utterly human and crippled with fear. Neen pointedly indicates the door behind us and tells them to get the fuck out of here.

I nod. Shil smiles. The earlier incident is forgiven.

"What now, sir?" Neen asks.

"We find the Uplifted."

Everything I've heard says Uplifted are vast pyramids of diamond and silicon, able to protect themselves from anything. When I told Colonel Nuevo my Aux could take one, I was boasting; he must have known that.

"It's up those stairs," says Franc. "The girl told me."

"Why?"

"I told her we were here to protect it."

"It's here, sir," says Haze. It's the first thing he's said to me since I made him wear a woman's shawl half an hour before. "I think it's sick."

He's right.

A small metal pyramid hangs from an intricate web that spreads across most of the ceiling. A fist-sized diamond hangs from filaments at the pyramid's center. Lights run the length of every strand in the web and within the pyramid itself. They run unevenly, in a stuttering motion that lacks the fluidity this object deserves.

A dim light pulses at the diamond's center. Only Haze could equate an Uplifted to a machine. And yet . . .

"What's wrong with it?"

Dropping to his knees in front of a tangle of filaments, Haze takes a closer look. "Burnout," he says. "You want me to fix it?"

"Can you?"

"I can try."

That's good enough for me. The Uplifted comes apart in a burst of flame and static. As I drop my pistol back into its holster, Haze is staring. "Fuckwit was flying the batwings," my gun tells him. "You want to face those again?"

CHAPTER 31

THERE ARE some simple rules to occupying a city. Rule one says grab yourself a good base. That doesn't mean somewhere secure, because if you lock a city down properly even the ghettos are secure. It means find somewhere warm, dry, and comfortable, preferably with its own stock of food and a cellar full of alcohol.

Hotels are good, as are clubs, glitzy bars, and posh houses. But we're in Ilseville, where the first three of those are rarer than hen's teeth.

I order the Aux to head uphill, because hills usually equal expensive—unless they're absurdly steep, like in Farlight. Of course, finding a hill in Ilseville isn't easy. The city's mostly flat, being built on a floodplain. The few hills that do exist are artificial, made from silt dredged from the Ilseville River back when the wharves and landing stages were built.

All this I discover in the time it takes the Aux to walk from the Trade Hall to a residential district overlooking the river. I've ditched my dreads and removed the silver body hose, losing both once Colonel Nuevo's troops begin pouring through the recently opened gates.

"How about that one, sir?" asks Franc, indicating a huge house on the shady side of a square.

"Or that?" Shil says, pointing to something even grander.

"Too flash," I tell Shil. "We'd lose it to the colonel. We'll take the first."

It's still large, faced with sheets of solidified foam cut to look like sandstone. The high windows that stare at us are barred and reinforced with toughened glass, which suggests Ilseville isn't quite the haven of tranquillity the Enlightened have been suggesting. As I suspect, the front door is cored with mesh and its lock is semi-smart.

"Hello," says my gun.

And then it explains, using very simple language, exactly what is going to happen to the lock if it doesn't cooperate. Three seconds later, five bolts click back and the door begins to open as we watch. A maid in full uniform is waiting on the other side.

"Welcome," she says.

If she's shocked to be greeted with a faceful of drawn weapons she does a good job of keeping it hidden. The maid is young, in her early twenties probably, and bright enough to know she stands a better chance of getting through this alive if she makes herself visible and useful rather than hiding behind a locked door to be hunted down.

"Whose house?"

"Lord Filipacchi, of Filipacchi Trading."

The name means nothing to me.

"It's mine now," I say. "Mine, and theirs . . . Understand?"

She does.

Her name is Maria, and she walks me around the house as if I really am the new owner. There are five floors, not including an attic, which makes this the tallest house I've ever seen. A turret on the top floor overlooks the city, and I claim this for my own. The room is filthy and full of old furniture.

"Are there any other servants?"

Maria shakes her head.

"Hire some," I tell her. "Have them prepare this room."

Neen selects Lord Filipacchi's own bedroom, complete with silk hangings and a huge bed that labors under the weight of a vast fur.

From the glances he's been giving Maria, it's obvious who he wants to crawl under the fur with him.

Shil and Franc decide to share a much smaller room on the floor below. As for Haze, he drags a mattress into a ground-floor office stacked with computers and hits the larder and kitchens for all the carbohydrate he can find. When I check, he's flicking his fingers across a slab, pulling up real-time pictures of the city.

"How did you do that?"

He jerks his thumb toward the ceiling. "HiSats, sir," he says, "self-focusing. They'll stay in orbit until the U/Free tell them to come down or their packs run out of fuel. Thought I might as well take a look."

THE KNOCK ON our door comes ten minutes later. It's heavy, someone hammering their fist against solid wood. We're meant to be impressed, so I let them wait.

"Soldiers," says Maria. She's looking nervous.

"How do you know?"

"Lenz," she says.

So Haze flicks his fingers over the slab, replacing his satellite pictures with a shot of a Death's Head officer and two corporals.

"Sir."

He's accessed the house system and cut to tight focus so I can see the flaring nostrils of the smartly dressed lieutenant. Needless it say, it's Miles Uffingham, the idiot who collected me from the tent when Colonel Nuevo wanted someone to talk to his ferox.

"Let them in," I tell Maria. "Say we'll be down in a moment."

Haze gets Neen, and I drag Shil and Franc out of their room. We're a mess, uniforms torn and faces filthy.

"Arm yourselves," I tell them.

"You don't think—"

"Obviously not," I say. "But we should look like we mean business."

"We do, sir," says Neen.

. . .

"AHH . . . TVESKOEG. Here you are."

I'm meant to remember Uffingham's name, return the compliment. I can't be bothered. There are few staff officers who couldn't be improved by a hollow-point implant to the back of their neck, and Miles Uffingham isn't one of them.

"The colonel wants to see you."

"Okay . . ."

"You might want to change."

"Into what?"

Turning on his heels seems to be a habit with this man. So we follow the lieutenant out of our own front door and into the square in silence, and I'm glad to see my group are scanning the roofline, behaving like proper soldiers. The man we're following just marches straight ahead as if snipers don't exist.

"Visitors for the colonel."

The guards let their eyes drift across us. At least two of them are doing their best not to grin.

"You hear me?"

"Yes, sir." Their immaculately dressed sergeant snaps to attention, and I wonder if Uffingham has any idea how much contempt is in that salute. As we follow him through the door Colonel Nuevo's staff stop talking.

Maybe it's the girls, still in their head scarves and both clutching enemy pulse rifles, or maybe it's the bloodstains down Neen's uniform. Or maybe it's just me, with my missing sleeve and prosthetic arm.

"In here . . ."

The room to which we're shown is huge and hung with pictures so old the paint's cracked. Since the Enlightened don't believe in pictures, this house has to belong to someone important enough to be left alone. And it has that pragmatic mix of old and new, wooden furniture and intelligent doors, china plates and drexie boxes to pull food out of nothing.

"Expensive," says the gun when I wake it from sleep mode. "Tasteful, quietly understated, obviously the home of a connoisseur . . ."

You can tell it hates the place.

"Just scan the bloody room."

It does, and tells me we're being targeted by 205 different weapons, which it considers overkill. I'm saved from arguing by the entrance of an orderly.

"The colonel will see you."

"Keep quiet," I tell the others. "Answer only if asked a direct question, don't stare at anyone, and let me do the talking. Understand?"

"Sven."

My salute is smart enough to make Colonel Nuevo smile.

"You look like shit."

"Yes, sir."

A dozen officers stand near his desk, almost half of them militia officers or legion; some don't even look like regulars at all. It makes me wonder what they're doing here.

"You want to tell me what's in your hair?"

It takes me a moment to remember. "Dead Enlightened," I say. "Used his braids to disguise myself, haven't had time to wash him off." This is not strictly true. It simply hadn't occurred to me.

"You scalped an Enlightened?"

"Yes, sir . . . though I killed him first."

"Glad to hear it." The colonel is smiling. "And his scalp was enough to disguise you?"

"Used one of his tubes as well. Across my chest and into my hip."

"Tricky to glue?"

"No need, sir. I cut holes."

"In yourself?"

I nod, lift my shirt so he can see the scar.

"And what were your auxiliaries doing?"

"Killing Uplift guards, sir. Plus a NewlyMade and a two-braid. We saved the Uplifted until last."

"You killed the Uplifted?"

"Yes, sir." I'm nervous for the first time since entering this room. Some very strange emotions are messing with the colonel's face.

"How?"

"I shot it."

Colonel Nuevo shuts his eyes.

"It was dying, sir. Already senile. Probably long beyond questioning. Any routines it ran were from habit. The equivalent of remembering to breathe." The voice isn't mine and it certainly isn't anyone who is meant to be speaking. Haze has gone bright red, as if he's just remembered what I said about silence.

"You are—?"

He's about to blow everything, I just know it.

Instead, Haze salutes. "One of the team, sir. My name is Haze. I took the Uplifted apart, what was left of it."

I don't remember giving him permission to do that.

"What did you find?"

"Anemone optic, diamond memory, couple of teraflips of quantum processor, the usual . . ."

The colonel is looking at him very strangely. "Usual for what?"

"A machine, sir." Haze looks around him, goes red again. He knows he's the center of attention; his thoughts are just too much on the question in hand to realize why. If Haze did, he'd be white and it would be with fear. What he's said is close enough to blasphemy to make no difference.

"It was dying," I say. "Maybe already dead."

"And your man is describing its body?" The colonel considers that. "Machinery is to a dead Uplifted what meat is to a dead human—say, to the dead body of Trooper Haze himself?"

I nod, trying not to hold my breath.

A second later the colonel nods. "That would be it," he says. His gaze flicks over the room, challenging them to disagree. No one does.

"Line up."

We do as ordered, coming to attention. At which point Major Silva appears carrying a black silk cushion. Both officers stop in front of me.

"For being first into the city I promote Sven Tveskoeg to full lieutenant, awarding him the Obsidian Cross, second class . . ."

I salute, because I can't think of anything else to do.

Major Silva offers Colonel Nuevo the cushion and the colonel hangs the medal around my neck and everyone salutes again. As the colonel steps back a sergeant appears. He's carrying an armful of filthy clothes. They're the uniforms I made Franc, Shil, and Haze abandon before we entered the tunnel.

"Draw new clothes," orders the colonel. "Retain your patches."

The sergeant follows us from the room. He wants to make sure we collect the uniforms we've just been promised.

CHAPTER 32

ILSEVILLE SQUARE stinks of vomit, smoke, sex, and piss. A Death's Head sergeant is taking a woman against a tree while a queue of junior NCOs wait their turn. Her child sits in the dirt, happily oblivious to what's going on above. An Uplift temple is in flames, and one of the corporals waiting his turn is wearing the tasseled cap of a high priest.

Bars and brothels are hastily reopening in the streets behind us, making the best of what is going to happen anyway.

A trooper feeds hungry flames with broken furniture outside our house, and a beast turns on a spit above his fire. With its four horns and narrow shoulders, the animal looks rare and exotic, as if stolen from a zoo.

Heat has blackened its skin, and the drunken trooper who carves a fist-sized chunk from the beast manages to end up with a meal that is both burned and bleeding. If he doesn't end up on his knees vomiting from alcohol, he'll probably go down with food poisoning instead.

"Is it always like this, sir?" Shil's voice is quiet.

"Always," I say.

A trooper stumbles into me and I put him into a wall, angry not at his drunkenness but by knowing I was once him, half cut and impatient, waiting my turn for a skirt in a town that had just fallen.

"Lock the doors," I order Maria.

She nods.

To the others, I say, "You can go back out, or you can stay in. Either way, your choice is made for the night. This door remains locked until morning."

Neen opts for a night in the city.

Shil would object, but he outranks her and I'm watching.

Franc glances at Haze, who shakes his head. And so the decisions are made. Neen slips back through the door and everyone else stays inside.

"Let me know when you've locked up," I tell Maria.

"Yes, sir."

"I'll be in my room."

She's twenty-three, with a birthday in two weeks' time, silken body hair between her legs, and nipples that look strangely pale in the candlelight. Her hips are full and so are her buttocks, too full really for my tastes, but her breasts are high and hard and she sits astride me with no shame, rocking herself into an orgasm that looks convincing.

"What's your other name?"

"I don't have one, sir."

"No," I tell her. "Nor do I, not really."

She leaves my bed with a couple of red handprints on her buttocks and a bite below one breast. I have no doubt that, if ordered, she'd come to my room again.

"See you later."

Maria giggles.

Midnight comes and goes, darkness deepening as clouds take the moon, and the blackness of the sky only serves to make the fires in the streets outside look brighter. Some are simple bonfires, others more serious. From a window on a landing two floors above the front door, I can see at least five burning houses, and something larger also in flames. Another temple maybe, or a brothel where the alcohol was too expensive or the whores insufficiently willing.

Steps creak and I spin.

A dot dances across the wall and finds my chest, remaining there. "Who is it?" demands Shil, her voice steady. She's clutching a pulse rifle.

"It's me."

"Sir?"

"Yeah," I say. "Me."

"Do we have a problem, sir?"

"No. I'm just watching idiots burn the city. It's fine, go back to bed."

She hesitates.

" 'Night, Shil . . ."

Five minutes later, when I get to the top of some stairs, I find her at a window watching the flames, her rifle forgotten. She's quite obviously worrying about her brother.

"Trust him," I say.

"It's easy for—" she begins, then stops. "Sorry, sir."

"He's your sergeant," I say.

"Your choice."

"Yes," I agree. "My choice." There's something in my tone that makes her turn. We're very close to an argument, and it's not one she can win.

"Franc might make a good sergeant," she says finally.

I smile. "Franc's a hairbreadth from insanity. Don't get me wrong, I really like that in a woman, but as a replacement for Neen?" I shake my head. "It's never going to happen."

"What about me, sir?"

"You're volunteering?"

Shil nods.

She says nothing when I stand behind her, and even less when I grip her shoulders, feeling them tremble. Her arm muscles are tight, and her shoulder blades hard-edged beneath the cloth of her borrowed nightgown. I can count off every rib as my fingers drop to her side, and her hip is sharp beneath my hand for the second it takes her to twist away from me.

"Is that your price?" she demands.

"Why? Is that what you're offering?"

Her slap almost connects and then she's against the wall, one hand twisted high behind her back.

When I step away, her fingers drop toward a knife on her hip that isn't there. The action is entirely instinctive, and says more about her previous life than I've discovered in days.

"Neen's a natural," I tell her. "Deal with the fact he's your brother or I'll transfer you."

CHAPTER 33

A KNOCKING WAKES me, and a trooper announces that one quarter of the city has risen. He's not looking for me in particular; his orders are to rouse every house in the square. Other soldiers are working the streets behind us.

Neen is behind the soldier, slouched on our doorstep. He has a black eye to match the graze he got climbing from the sewer, but he's awake and mostly sober and looking very pleased with himself.

"Good night?"

Scrambling to his feet, he snaps out a salute.

"Yes, sir. Very good, sir." If he notices Shil's sourness he brushes it off, assuming it has more to do with him than me.

"Helmets," I tell everyone.

Neen has to go upstairs.

Pulse rifles at the ready, we hit the street. At which point something becomes obvious. My team are militia and I'm Death's Head, but many of the soldiers out here are neither.

We're outnumbered by mercenaries. Not legion-type mercenaries: *Sign on, get paid shit, and die to order.* These are the other kind, free-lance looters, people discharged from militias for being too vicious or damaged to take orders, ex-penal-battalion officers, the sweepings of half a dozen prison planets, people like the person I might have been.

"What?" demands Shil, seeing me stop.

I wait.

"Sir."

"Mercenaries."

"Came in on the final drop," says Haze, and then blushes.

He's been up all night, patching himself into the data feeds. We have quite an audience, apparently. Propaganda is one of this war's greatest weapons. It's why OctoV complains about U/Free observers, Greater Council monitors, and freelance data collectors, but lets them in anyway.

"Take point," I tell Neen. "We'll be right behind."

He leads us between dying bonfires and drunken troopers being kicked back to sobriety. Gunfire comes from a low-lying district ahead, which explains the column of black smoke rising in front of us.

The batwings are back.

"That's not possible." Haze is staring up at the sky.

Rolling as languidly as a fish surfacing, a tiny plane twists itself around its own axis and drops like a supercharged stone. It keeps dropping and a second column of smoke joins the first.

"Someone's controlling them," I say.

He nods, and Franc points beyond distant walls to where another batwing is dropping from the clouds.

"What does it mean?" asks Franc.

It means we're fucked.

But I don't say that, because that's one of the things you just don't say. "Insurgents," I tell her. "Must have a few left over from yesterday. Not sure how they're controlling them."

There's another Uplifted, obviously.

A gap stands like a broken tooth in a row of houses ahead. The buildings on both sides are cheap, fiber-made, and already rotting. Past the gap, the ground dips and we can see even cheaper buildings beyond. In the middle of these stands a metal turret, black with age and ringed by shacks that huddle below what look like flying buttresses. After a second, I realize they're fins.

"What happened to the house?"

The trooper stops, registers my rank, and salutes. "Control post, sir. Got hit just before dawn. Killed a captain."

I let the man go, and he scurries away with obvious relief. The next person I see is Major Silva, still looking neat as always and still wearing his tiny spectacles. He greets me with a smile, which tells me all I need to know about how serious this situation is.

"The colonel's waiting."

We follow the man through a roadblock, under a bridge that supports a broken railroad, and into the rubble of the ruined building.

"Sven . . ."

"Sir."

"They had a belt-fed in the turret and snipers everywhere . . ." He steps closer. "Lieutenant Uffingham volunteered to clean them out."

"What happened?"

"You're the new senior lieutenant."

Apparently my Obsidian Cross automatically gives me five years' seniority. I can take a wild guess how the other lieutenants feel about that, not that I care.

"We've got rockets," I say. "Why not just blow the thing to fuck?"

Colonel Nuevo's eyes flick sideways, and I see a girl wearing the uniform of a recognized U/Free observer.

"Meet Paper Osamu," he says. "She has plenipotentiary status."

Plenipo . . . what? "He's ex legion," my gun tells her. "Up through the ranks. He doesn't understand stuff like that."

"There are civilians down there."

"And up here," says the gun tartly. "Doesn't stop the machine heads crashing their planes on us."

"They're not *machine heads,*" Ms. Osamu says, pronouncing the words with distaste.

"Well, they're sure as fuck not human."

At this point I take Colonel Nuevo's unspoken advice and put my gun back into sleep mode. The next few seconds are wasted as Neen and I go into a huddle. It's obvious from the shock on the faces of my fellow officers that they think this outrageous. But too many battles have been lost because officers were too grand to take advice from their NCOs.

"Anyone else have an opinion?"

Franc wants to attack from the front; Haze wants to hack into the batwings and corrupt them, preferably from the safety of a cellar several miles away. Neen's already had his say, and Shil keeps glancing toward the tower.

"Say it."

She shrugs.

"That's an order."

Tight-lipped, she scoops away a handful of dirt, and then carves a line next to it with her dagger. She's looking at me as she does this.

"Okay," she says. "That's the river . . . and this is their tower." She stabs her dagger hard into the depression. Taking Neen's dagger, she cuts a much shorter line from her river to the edge of the dip. "That's our canal."

Standing up, she fills her hands with water from a puddle and tips the water slowly into the tiny river, letting it run through the canal into the depression.

"Welcome to my world," she says. "Where if you're not trying to find water, you're trying to get rid of it."

The others nod.

If we had a combat satellite we could burn the ditch with that. Of course, if we had a high-orbit laser we wouldn't need to cut a ditch, because we could obliterate the tower without damaging the ghetto around it. This makes me wonder where General Jaxx's mother ship has gone.

All the same, it's a neat answer to a difficult question and it should keep the U/Free observer happy.

So I go find Major Silva. "Can you give me troops?"

The major looks slightly shocked. When he comes back it's with Colonel Nuevo. The U/Free observer is following along behind.

"I hear you want more men."

"Yes, sir."

"How many?"

"About five hundred."

Colonel Nuevo's eyes widen. He doesn't like being surprised in front of Paper Osamu. "You want to attack the tower with five hundred men?"

"No, sir. I want them to dig a ditch and flood it."

I can tell he's disappointed. We're his suicide squad, afraid of nothing. We exist to irritate his other officers, keep them unsettled. Safe options and engineered solutions are not welcome.

"Haze," I say. "Explain to the colonel why this makes sense."

The boy looks stricken. He's fumbling for a reason when he stumbles over the real one. "There's an Uplifted inside, sir."

Haze thinks about it some more and realizes the obvious. "The Uplifted is controlling the batwings. So it's still fully functioning."

"If we destroy the tower," I say, "we risk killing the thing."

The colonel gets his smile back.

Five hundred men dig for the best part of a day. Being militia, they expect the shitty jobs. I want the mercenaries to do it, but it isn't my choice and Major Silva insists they're being saved for later. The grim satisfaction in his voice when he says this is reassuring.

Warnings are broadcast and transport is arranged. And when everything is ready, the women, children, and old men are evacuated under the suspicious gaze of Paper Osamu, licensed witness and plenipotentiary for the U/Free. We begin to flood the tower just before nightfall.

BACK AT THE house, Neen retires to his room, while Haze goes to play with his slabs. Franc excuses herself, and about an hour later the smell of baking fills the house.

"Didn't know we had a drexler."

"We don't," says Maria. "She's making it by hand."

"Really?"

"Yeah, really."

She grins at the look on my face. "You want coffee?"

"Sure," I say. "I'll be in the study."

The coffee is hot and strong and Maria makes enough for two. Realizing Lord Filipacchi's ornate desk is buried under my open maps, she places her tray carefully on the floor. The maps are printouts showing Ilseville as it used to be, which is pretty much the same as it is now except for the newly flooded area and old warehouses where temples now stand.

"What are you doing?"

"Checking a few things."

"I'll be downstairs," she says, picking up her mug. "If, you know . . ."

"If what?"

"You want me."

Taking the mug from her hand, I put it on top of a map and turn Maria toward me, raising her face with one hand. "What's to doubt?" Reaching for her dress, I undo the first two buttons.

"Not here, sir," she says.

"Where then?"

I should be studying the map and working out my best route into that tower, but the truth is I'll probably riff it anyway, because planning and I never got on that well to start with. Most battles are simple: The fastest and the nastiest group wins. Anyone tells you different probably has red tabs under his or her insignia and issues orders from several miles behind the front line.

Maria and I go to her room together.

Her body is as full as it was last time, and her nipples are still pale enough to be almost invisible, but I see things I didn't notice then, like the neatly sewn track of a bullet scar above one hip. She'd been shot from behind, then given medical treatment by an outfit who obviously knew what they were doing.

"Long story," she says.

I have enough sense not to ask.

We sleep and fuck and sleep some more, and dawn finds us in the bath, Maria behind me scrubbing my back with what seems to be the

dried skin of a local slug. After a while I decide that I'm clean enough and we swap positions, although not much back scrubbing is done once I'm behind her.

I've just picked Maria up by the hips when there's a tentative knock at the door.

"Sir . . ." It's Neen.

Yesterday he'd have come straight into the bathroom; today he knows Maria's in here with me. So does Shil, because her eyes refuse to catch mine when we meet on the stairs, both struggling into our jackets.

"Lieutenant Tveskoeg?"

The boy's young, little older than Neen, but his uniform is immaculate and silver braid waterfalls from his left shoulder. The poor little shit's even wearing a dress dagger, hung from a chain on his hip.

"You're a new staff officer?"

"Yes, sir."

"Hope you last longer than the last one."

He chews his lip. "The colonel requires you."

"Be with you in a moment."

"Sir . . ." He hesitates, not yet secure in Death's Head arrogance and unused to borrowing the power of whomever sent the message. "He requires you now."

"And I'll be with you in a moment."

My group dress in their new uniforms, which are Death's Head issue with all the distinguishing marks cut away and skin patches sewn in their place. The boy blinks, opens his mouth, and shuts it again.

"What's your name?"

"Benj . . ."

"Your other name."

"Flypast, sir. Second Lieutenant Benj Flypast."

I shake his hand, which he doesn't expect, then introduce him to the group, which he expects even less. "And this is Haze," I say. "Our expert on Uplifted and Enlightened."

Both boys blush.

The colonel is waiting impatiently near the tower. Having flooded the area, the militia are now busy pumping the water out again. Apparently a number of enemy soldiers tried to escape on a homemade raft in the night, but they didn't make it. A row of bodies provides evidence.

Our side has experts, real experts. Officers who trained on Death's Head scholarships and intelligence analysts who've spent their entire lives studying the enemy. I'm not even sure why my group is here.

Pretty soon I find out.

"Enter the tower," orders Colonel Nuevo. "Kill anything you like, except the Uplifted."

WATER HAS STAINED each room. Sometimes the water has risen to the ceiling; other times the positioning of windows means layers of air got trapped. This is made obvious by tide marks high up on a couple of walls. I begin to see why the colonel wants my groups to check the building first.

Just to make the job interesting, he's landed me with Lieutenant Flypast, who needs bloodying. So now the boy hangs back and holds his pulse rifle as if it's about to turn around and bite him.

"Report," I tell Neen.

"Clear, sir."

"Very good. Carry on."

So far we've swept eleven floors, with only one kill. An old man huddled over a crude fire. He'd obviously hidden himself rather than be evacuated, not one of life's better decisions.

It looks like there's one, maybe two more floors to go, and logic tells me this is where anyone waiting to attack us will be.

"Right," I tell Neen. "Take us up a level."

He hits the stairs, rifle ported across his front. Shil follows, with Haze and Franc behind her. Benj trails after them and I bring up the rear. Neen is good at this, but he's angry with me about Maria and it shows in the way he carries himself. His shoulders are locked and his movements overrapid.

Bollocking someone for not staying chilled is counterproductive, so I swallow my irritation.

"Hold it." Neen's instruction filters down the line.

A creak comes from overhead. It could be metal warming in what passes for this planet's sunlight; alternatively, it could be someone with a gun. It's Neen's call and he has to be allowed to make it.

Our galaxy is rumored to be full of planets able to adjust their own weather, but most of these reside in the center and are owned by the United Free. The Enlightened have their Dyson habitat, also climate-controlled and endlessly enjoyable, but they keep that for themselves. As for our beloved leader . . . OctoV believes in traditional values, which is just as well, because he certainly can't afford any new ones.

"Back . . ." Neen drops to a crouch, signaling for everyone to retreat. Shil hesitates and I grab her ankle, pulling her down a handful of stairs. She manages to take the bumps in silence.

"Wait," Neen orders.

Edging forward, he vanishes almost from sight.

Neen's call, I remind myself.

But that doesn't stop me from getting impatient.

So I make myself listen to the noises inside and out while trying not to notice Shil's hips, which are next to my face. Part of my irritation is at not being able to use my gun. Apparently the Uplifted are worse than the Enlightened for being able to read data patterns. Use my gun in here and I might as well climb the stairs shouting, *Hi, it's Sven, anyone home?*

That the SIG's version anyway. Of course, it might simply be sulking about Paper Osamu. Shifting pipes disturb the air around me. From outside comes the noise of a pump as engineers drain the last of the floodwater, and the five hundred militia who dug yesterday's canal prepare to fill it in again. The air through an open window smells sour, because the flood has opened sewers and made latrines overspill their banks.

"Not yet," I whisper when Shil starts to shift forward.

The sniper hiding in the room above gets bored before we do. A handle creaks and a face peers through a gap. He's looking straight ahead when he should be looking down, and Neen's shot takes him under the chin, painting the ceiling behind him with blood, skull, and brains.

"*Move . . .*"

Another two Uplifted go down as Neen sweeps the room. They're already dead by the time I hit the door.

"Good call."

"Thank you, sir." Neen looks at me, then looks at his sister, and makes a decision. "Permission to . . ."

I nod.

"Please don't send Shil to another unit."

"Why would I?"

"Shil said she asked you to make Franc sergeant instead of me, and now you're angry with her."

"Forget it," I tell him. "I already have."

The Uplifted sits in one corner. Wherever the thing originally sat it wasn't here, because a bundle of filaments have been slashed in a hurry. A huge diamond nestles in anemone optic, a jumble of teraflips are tied into the matrix memory, and the thing is pulsing like festival lights.

Something tells me the colonel is going to be pleased.

CHAPTER 34

WHO'S RUNNING the water?"

"Haze, sir," says Franc, slicing dried fruit onto a wooden board. I can't help but notice she's using the blade she used to stab the old woman and the guard outside the Trade Hall.

We're in the kitchen, and pipes are hammering in the corner. The last time anyone but Haze went into Lord Filipacchi's bathroom, it was so damp that tiles had begun to fall from the walls.

"I'll talk to him."

She shakes her head.

"Something you want to tell me?"

Franc shakes her head at that, too. "Please, sir," she says. "Leave it." Something about the way she says this is almost desperate. She's put the knife down and is facing me full-on, completely defenseless. Sometimes it's how people behave without realizing it that matters.

"He's not what he seems, is he?"

That gets her attention. "In what way, sir?" Franc asks.

I think about it. "He's a girl after all."

Franc laughs. "Oh," she says. "He's definitely male." And then her face goes red and it's obvious she's wondering how to approach something.

I'm her boss, her commanding officer, but something is worrying her at a much deeper level.

"Tell me."

"Please," she says. "Let it go, sir."

That's not the way the army works.

But she's already moved on. "He trusts you," she says. "And there's something else, sir." Franc hesitates. "Your gun told Haze he required a role model. You're it."

"Franc . . ."

"It did, sir. I'm serious."

So am I. "He's a soldier," I tell her. "An auxiliary. He obeys my orders. That's all there is to it. And tell him to stay away from my gun."

BY THE END of the week a routine is established. Maria buys food and Franc cooks it; Neen spends his nights on the town, or he does for the first three nights then stops when he realizes Maria is no longer coming to my bed.

She's sweet, more than willing.

But I'm restless and know myself well enough to know when I need to sleep alone. There's a taste like static in my mouth and an ache behind my eyes that I only ever get in the last few days before a battle.

As for Haze, he takes baths, plays with his machines, and comes out only when he feels like it. And then one morning, toward the end of the week, there's no heat in the house and no hot water and I find Haze in the kitchen, swaddled in towels, being comforted by Franc.

"Coffee," I demand.

Franc makes it, which involves lighting a fire in a bucket, using broken bits of kitchen chair, a handful of wooden cooking utensils, and sparks from a tinder stick, which she carries on her belt.

"Bring it to my study."

She nods, but it's Haze who arrives at my door with coffee and news. Insurgents have killed our electricity. Instead of doing the obvious and hitting the power core, they chose to blow up the pumping station next door. Without water the power station has had to shut down. "Thought you might want this, sir."

He hands me a power pack.

"For my gun?"

Haze nods, looking guilty.

"I've told you . . ."

Now he's scared as well. "We only chat, sir. That's all."

"About what?"

"Azimuth and angle, how to trig building heights. Really basic stuff. It's just, sometimes I need to talk tech."

He's serious.

Tossing him the SIG diabolo, I say, "Clean it, check the power, and fill any clips that need filling, but remember who owns it. Understand?"

"Yes, sir."

"Good, because otherwise I'll put you up against a wall myself."

The night after the attack on the pumping station, a suicide squad targets Colonel Nuevo's HQ, and the most beautiful house on Ilseville Square becomes rubble. The colonel is dining at a restaurant nearby; Major Silva and Benj Flypast are asleep in rooms on the third and fourth floors, respectively.

I wake to find sappers still sorting through the rubble, and smoke from the explosion still drifting across the square. And a knock on my door tells me it's going to be one of those mornings.

"Sir . . ."

It's Maria, which means she's had to roll out of Neen's fur-covered bed, dress herself half decently, and climb two flights of stairs to my turret. She's out of breath, but that's not necessarily from climbing the stairs.

"I know."

We're seeing a pattern here. A pattern familiar from any occupied city. Maria's moved from sharing my bed to sharing Neen's. In the scheme of things it's probably a wise move. And who knows, maybe she actually likes him.

Shuffling on my uniform, I head downstairs and answer the front door myself. Passing messages back and forth simply wastes time. A boy, even younger than the last one, stands on my doorstep. His chest looks too thin for its waterfall of silver braid.

"Sir, the colonel, sir, he wants—"

"To see me."

The new second lieutenant nods.

"We'll be there."

"No, sir. He just wants to see *you.*"

I take my team anyway.

"Sven . . ."

The colonel is standing by a window; two serious-looking men sit at a table behind him. They look anxious, tired, and rather afraid. Engineers, I think, still failing to give us back our power. The house to which I've been led is large, just not as large as the one that lies in ruins three streets away.

"Good," he says. "You came alone."

"They're waiting out there," I tell him, nodding toward his office door.

Colonel Nuevo sighs.

The two men at the table might as well not exist for all the attention he's paying them. Taking two glasses from a silver tray, the colonel pours me something clear and bitter. I get the feeling he's really pouring one for himself. "I need a new ADC . . ." He raises his glass. "You're it."

"Me?"

"I have my reasons," he says. A wave of his hands dismisses the two men, who scrape their chairs against the floor in their haste to escape. "Wait outside," he tells them, to their obvious disappointment.

"Engineers?"

"No." The colonel shakes his head. "Experts on the Uplifted, completely fucking useless, both of them. I'm going to shoot one of them. I just haven't decided which. It died, you know."

"The thing?"

"Simply shut itself down. But we've got bigger problems." He flicks up a screen, touches his finger to a slab, and the city spreads out below me, seen from a great height.

"View from the mother ship?"

"I wish . . . high-orbit satellite. Still, at least the general left us that."

So General Indigo Jaxx is gone. Do I dare ask where? Somehow in my thoughts his mother ship is still riding shotgun up there in high orbit, our final defense and weapon of attack.

"Concentrate," orders the colonel.

Ilseville is smaller than it seems from the ground. Our river is a tributary of a larger river that splits on the plain and loses itself in vast marshes beyond; the waterlogged terrain across which we attacked is simply a small corner of this. Clouds scuttle below us, obscuring the view. I'm not sure what I'm meant to be watching, because the city looks peaceful and the marshes are empty.

"Here," he says, losing patience.

Black insects skim the surface of a tiny stream. Only the stream is the larger of the rivers and the insects are boats and we're about a day away from the insects reaching the coin-sized circle that is Ilseville.

"Hex-Sevens," he says.

I count fifty, and then give up. No sooner do I count than more fill the edge of the screen. It's like kicking an ants' nest and then trying to make sense of the reaction. "How many soldiers to a boat?"

"A hundred," he says. "Maybe more."

"You want me to go out there and see if I can stop them, sir?"

He stares at me, then smiles. "You're insane," he says. "That's probably why I like you." He dips his hand into a desk drawer and retrieves a handful of silver braid. "Fix this on," he tells me. "And consider yourself promoted to staff officer."

The colonel laughs, and I realize my face probably says it all.

"What do you know about politics?"

"Nothing."

"Good," he says. "And bad."

It seems OctoV likes to cover his bets, so he spread-bets against himself and then covers the long odds with small sums that occasionally pay out and cost little if they're lost. We're one of those small sums. This is not the way Colonel Nuevo puts it, but it's what he means.

This battle, which I thought key to OctoV's planning, is a diversion for a diversion. And there are other layers that make our situation even more complicated. The late Lieutenant Uffingham was nephew to EmpireMinister Othman, who is currently in disgrace. Major Silva owed his position to General Jaxx, who has the ear of OctoV, making him dangerous as a patron and doubly dangerous as an enemy.

Colonel Nuevo asks if I follow so far.

It seems best to say yes, although I consider asking what an empireminister might be but decide I can work that out for myself. It's someone important enough to be mentioned in the same breath as General Jaxx.

"We're a sideshow," the colonel says.

Looking from the screen to the river beyond his window, I consider asking if the sideshow is about to close early and decide I know the answer to that as well.

"Where's the real battle, sir?"

The star system he names registers vaguely. All that can be said is that it is a very, very long way away. About halfway across the outer spiral if my memory is right.

"Attrition," says Colonel Nuevo. "That's what this comes down to. How many brigades can we tie up? How many of us can they kill . . . ? Who can do it fastest?"

Pouring himself another drink, the colonel raises his glass.

"Make your choice," he tells me. "Death or glory."

I can't work out if he's joking.

Although his next comment answers that for me. "We're ringed with ball busters. You know why they're there?" The obvious answer is to destroy Enlightened ships. Only if the answer is that obvious, why ask the question?

"Mercenaries," I say, "are sometimes known to abandon battles."

The colonel laughs mirthlessly.

"So if I was the general, I might circle this planet with sats designed to kill unexpected traffic. Say for the next six weeks."

"Try six months," he says. "And it's all traffic, unexpected or not."

"Do the mercenaries know that, sir?"

"No," he says. "But you're going to tell them."

CHAPTER 35

THERE'S A Hot Bar Wild in every city on every planet at this end of the spiral. It might be illegal; it might advertise openly; it might be called something else . . . but it's there. All you have to do is find it.

In Ilseville it's down on the river dock, squatting in a patch of wasteland between two crumbling warehouses. IMPERIAL TRADING, reads one board, IMPORT/EXPORT.

The board is rotten, and the warehouse it advertises is empty.

Maybe such bars find scuzzy areas or maybe they blight the areas in which they're set. Someone knows, but it's not me.

Pushing my way through the door, I make for an empty table, beating a huge man with luminous tattoos, who swings his dreads from side to side and scowls. He's meant to look like an Enlightened but it's not even a good likeness.

"Mine," he says.

I put my gun to his head.

The man leaves, still scowling and muttering threats.

"Bring it on," says the SIG. "We'll be waiting."

I have to admit that I'm quietly impressed by Hot Bar Wild . . .

Shil, on the other hand, is anything but. Two rather young gymnasts are performing on a low wooden stage, and they're wearing nothing, not even body hair.

One of them is bent so far backward that her head protrudes from between her legs. As we watch, she uncoils faster than a spring, does the splits, and picks up a gold coin with her vulva.

Not to be outdone, her companion drops to the floor, rolls her legs over her head, and tucks them behind her arms. The next coin lands exactly where its owner intends it to land; a second later it vanishes.

A group of men by the bar begin to cheer. "Remind me why we're here," Shil says.

"You're covering my back." Turning to Haze, I raise my eyebrows.

"Nothing even comes close," he tells me, checking his slab. And my gun preens itself in a run of flashing diodes. These guys have money, and when mercenaries aren't spending their cash on alcohol, implants, or drugs, they're buying weapons, the flashier and smarter the better. So it's as well to know what we're facing.

"Here," I say, tossing Neen a money roll.

Neen catches it easily, breaks out twenty gold coins, and heads for the bar. I'm aiming to come out of here ahead of the money Colonel Nuevo staked us, but we need to spend some cash to get things rolling.

He pays with gold, because that's what mercenaries use, and some customs are too ingrained for even OctoV to change. Neen must look convincing in his new uniform, because its lack of insignia is exciting interest.

I'm wearing something very similar: All my usual braid is gone from my chest and the lieutenant's bars are missing from my collar. Pretty soon one of these guys is going to ask Neen or me which unit we're with.

We've planned how this is going to go.

Someone is about to be taken down hard. It's unfair, but it's necessary, and *fair* isn't a word that has much of a place in a bar like this.

Neen tells the bar girl to keep the change. And then, picking up the bottle he's just bought and five shot glasses, he begins to return to our table. When it comes, his stumble is convincing. No alcohol is spilled, no one's uniform gets wet, but someone's chair gets joggled and respect needs reestablishing. At least, that's what the squat man with the scarred face decides.

He taps Neen on the shoulder.

And goes down as Neen smashes the bottle into the side of his head. A kick to the gut lifts the man half off the floor and Neen follows up by stamping hard on the man's wrist.

The whole bar hears bones break.

A friend of the injured man launches himself at Neen just as I put a shot through the ceiling, dropping plaster onto the crowd below. A woman screams from a cubicle above, but it's fear, not injury. And the two contortionists freeze midmaneuver, giving their punters a prime-time view of all those sinuous moves previously denied them.

"Enough," I say.

"Or what?" It's the squat man's friend.

His ear vanishes with just enough chopped meat decorating the table behind to make one of the contortionists projectile-vomit. She makes a nasty mess of herself.

"Good shot," says my gun.

No one's quite sure which event it means.

"Give my sergeant another bottle," I tell the barkeeper.

The man does what he's told. No one suggests we might want to pay.

At the table we toast one another, our unit, and the stupid fucking war. And then Haze produces a pack of cards and we begin to play. About ten minutes later a man in a leather coat with a pistol stuffed in his waistband saunters over. He's thin, gray-haired, and wearing one of those really obvious cerebral implants. His T-shirt reads HAPPINESS IS A WARM BELT-FED WEAPON.

Removing a glove that is weighted across the knuckles and armored around the wrist, he thrusts out his hand. "Ion," he says.

We shake.

He nods at a spare stool.

"It's an open game," says Haze.

So the man pulls up the chair and Haze deals him in, taking five gold coins from him in the first three rounds. Understandably enough, Ion's not happy. Round four sees him win two coins back, round five sees him win another two, and the round after that gives him two more, meaning he's one ahead.

The man folds his hand, excusing himself from the game.

"Have a drink," I say.

Ion fetches himself a glass from the bar. We've made him happier than if he won ten coins straight. It's weird, but then what makes people happy often is.

"You think this is a bad gig?" asks Ion. It's the opening we've been waiting for.

"Yeah," I say. "Real bad."

Ion empties his glass, pours himself another one, and toasts the fresh-washed gymnast who's just come back on, to a mix of catcalls and rapturous applause.

"You know," says Neen, "I'd be surprised if even a quarter of us get out alive."

Listening in, a woman asks, "Why?"

Haze drains his glass; his hand is steady, but his elbow misses the table. You wouldn't know it's the first alcohol any of us have had all day.

"General's fucked off," says Haze, and a couple of mercenaries at the next table exchange glances with each other.

"Gone," says Neen. "Pissed off to Farlight."

"Yeah." Franc's voice is hard. "Apparently he's gone home to a warm bed."

Ion looks interested, although that's probably because he's just realized Franc is a girl; with her shaven head and baggy uniform it can get hard to tell.

"And then," says Haze, "there's that flotilla of Uplift landing craft crawling up the river. Thousands of the fuckers."

"Landing craft?"

"X-Seven-i's," says the SIG, refusing to be left out. The designation means nothing to me, but the colonel was pretty sure it would mean something to them.

"Hex-Sevens?" says Ion.

"Yeah," says Haze. "And then just to really screw things . . . Jaxx's seeded the entire fucking upper atmosphere. No one gets in or out for six months."

"You sure?" It's a man from a table two down.

When Haze dips under the table, half a dozen men reach for their guns. But all he's after is his slab, which wakes as he flicks his finger across its surface.

Everyone waits.

"Here," says Haze, pushing his toy across the table to Ion, who glances at the screen and then takes a long hard look. A weapons set is clearly visible. Behind it sits another, with another behind that and another in the distance. If you look carefully and check their alignment you'll see they form part of a pattern.

"How the fuck did you do that?" demands Ion.

And Haze flinches.

We've lost him. He's out of the loop and back to being the pudgy kid in the corner no one wants in their game. Franc touches his arm, almost diffidently, and I watch Haze tense and then relax.

"Ball busters," says Ion, he's talking to a mercenary at the next table. "Fucking thousands of them."

The man pulls up a stool without being invited.

We'd make a deal of it, but this routine is running itself, and we have the attention of half the bar. The music's dead and the contortionists have gone back to sulking, probably because they can't find anyone to buy them a drink.

"How do you know about this?" the uninvited man asks.

Neen glares at him, a real thousand-klick stare. That flat-eyed-snake routine Colonel Nuevo runs without even thinking about it. Neen's hardened in the brief time he's been on this planet.

"We're Death's Head auxiliaries."

A lot of people go very quiet.

"What, the fuck," Ion says finally, "is a Death's Head auxiliary?"

"Like mercenaries," says Shil. "Only we get paid less, we do nastier jobs, and we get to work for men like him." Shil is looking at me as she says this, and I'm not entirely sure she's joking.

I smile anyway. "Sven," I say, introducing myself. "Lieutenant Sven Tveskoeg, Obsidian Cross second class."

"Bullshit," says a woman. You can say one thing for mercenaries, they speak their mind.

"You don't look like an officer," adds Ion, staring at my arm.

"Lost it killing a ferox."

"Yeah, right . . ."

Anything else the uninvited man is likely to say gets lost as Neen palms a gun and puts it to the man's head. "Now's a good time to say, *Fuck, that's really impressive.*"

The man does as he's told.

Ion's looking at me. He's grinning. "You're the maniac who gutted a lagarto, then cooked it and started handing bits of alligator around?" He looks really pleased to see me. "Always wanted to hunt one. What was it like?"

"Big," I say. "Ugly."

"What did you use to kill it?"

I tap my pocket. "Laser blade, seriously useful. Used it on Paradise to cut tunnels in the ice. That blade can do pretty much anything."

"*Paradise?*"

"Yeah. I got sent there by accident."

A man I don't recognize suddenly grabs a spare stool from another table and places it very close to mine. He looks like he's working out whether he can take me. We both reach the same conclusion: He can't.

It's one of those you-and-whose-army moments. Given my army is sitting at my back and most of the drunks in this place don't look as if they're about to volunteer to be any part of his, the man's not very happy.

He is, however, seriously angry. "You were a guard on Paradise?"

"Not a guard," I say. "A prisoner."

The man blinks. *That's impossible,* he wants to say. *No one gets out.*

Ion is laughing. "Don't tell me," he says. "They made you an offer you couldn't refuse?"

"Yeah," I say. "Swap all that for all this." I gesture around Hot Bar Wild, with its vomit-stained floor, sulking strippers, and metal-grilled windows. As I said, we could be in any strip club, in a thousand different cities, on a hundred different planets, we just happen to be here.

"And now," I tell Ion, "I'm going to make you a similar offer. You and a hundred close friends can swap all this for anywhere within ten star systems of here. Onetime-only offer. You get to leave three days from now, in the only ship with a key code for getting through the ball busters."

I've got his total attention. "What's the catch?"

"You have to live that long."

Someone swears, and Ion holds up one hand, silencing them. "Lay it out for us," he says.

CHAPTER 36

IN THE early hours of the morning, with most of the city still ignorant of the horrors about to happen, I hear clattering downstairs and find Haze crouched over a bucket in the kitchen, vomiting.

"Alcohol," he says.

He doesn't want me to think it's fear.

A towel is wrapped around his head, and when Haze comes down to breakfast he's wearing his Death's Head cap. He eats almost nothing, yet still looks bulkier than he did a week before. Also, he's sweating.

"Hangover," says Franc when she sees me watching.

Bread, cheese, and a cold chunk of goat are set out on the table. A coffeepot is bubbling over a fire built on what was meant to be an ornamental hearth. The engineers never did get the city's power back.

"Eat," says Maria. "And take food with you." Her eyes are red; her fingers when she leaves the table brush Neen's shoulder. When she returns with another jug of coffee, his hand covers hers as she pours him a second cup.

She follows us to the door to say good-bye.

"Lock it once we're gone," says Shil. She hugs the other girl, which comes as a surprise to all of us.

Dawn is a slash of pink on the far horizon when we meet Ion at the river gates. The militia are already gathered and shock is their dominant expression, because they've been ordered to hold the gates until sunset. Against the enemy, obviously, but also against us, should we try to retreat to the safety of the city.

Even Ion is rattled.

"Volunteers only," I tell him. "Anyone who wants to stay on this side of the gates can. The rest of us hold until sunset or we die."

"And anyone left alive gets to go off planet."

"The first hundred," I say.

He snorts; we both know the final figure is unlikely to be that high. Ion's bought five hundred men, the ugliest, nastiest collection of money-grubbing mercenaries you've ever seen, and I'm glad to see every one of them. All are armed to the teeth, mostly with pulse rifles. A couple of groups lug belt-feds between them, while a man built like a tank is dragging an eight-barreled rocket launcher by hand.

A slightly more sophisticated rocket launcher—well, one sophisticated enough to roll along under its own power—is being maneuvered through the gates by two women who seem identical from their cropped hair to their uniforms. When they meet our stare, it's obvious their faces are identical as well.

"Twins?" Haze asks Ion.

"Vals 9 and 11," he says. "Copies."

"Of what?"

"Each other." He says it as if it should be obvious.

"Does the original still exist?" I ask.

Ion shakes his head.

"So they're copies of copies?" says Shil.

"Aren't we all," Ion says, turning his back on us. When I next see him, we're through the gates and he's telling Vals 9 and 11 where to place their rocket launcher. The glare all three shoot at Shil is undisguised contempt.

"Rules differ," I tell her.

"Yes," says Haze. "The U/Free use soldier bots to do this shit." He nods at a group of militia who are delivering ammunition to the trenches they dug earlier. Mercenaries fight, but they don't dig ditches.

"The Free have no army," I tell him.

Haze looks like he wants to disagree.

"Believe me," I say. "They don't need one."

"Why doesn't OctoV have machines?" demands Shil.

"Because he doesn't have Free technology and people are cheaper."

CHAPTER 37

ON THE one day of the year we could do with fog, sleet, or something to make the landing parties even more miserable, the planet decides to give us blue skies and high-feathered clouds.

We're dug into a foxhole. Imagine a broad arrow pointing downward; we're its point. Ion is ahead of us, to one side; Vals 9 and 11 in a matching foxhole on the other side. We have people dug in right up both sides of the arrowhead, almost to the riverbank.

Most of us are still alive. A handful are already dead.

"Incoming," says my gun.

The batwings are back, screaming over the marshes, their banshee howls enough to unnerve almost everyone. Me, I'm just irritated.

"Come on," says my gun. "Just one."

I shake my head. We're saving ammunition until the Hex-Sevens get closer. The SIG diabolo already knows that.

"In a minute," I promise.

There's a fallback position behind us. A single trench slashed into the dirt and covered with brush and thermal net to hide it from heat-reading satellites overhead, although I've always doubted if such netting actually works.

"Ready?"

Everyone gives the affirmative except Haze, who sits hunched over his slab, his rifle untouched beside him.

"Haze."

When he answers, his voice is little more than a fevered whisper. "They're coming around again." Sweat is running down his face and every now and then he scratches furiously at his skull.

"We need to talk," I say.

He shakes his head, flinching as I reach for his cap. "Please, sir," he says, and then, "I'm on your side."

"Okay. We'll talk later."

I'm finally beginning to realize the obvious . . . Haze is a Newly-Made. The virus isn't catching, but that wouldn't stop a dozen of the nearest mercenaries from ripping him apart on the spot, just in case. I'm not sure if he's an odd or an even, a soldier or a thinker. We'll know that when his scalp sheds its hair and he grows buds for either one or two braids.

"Pretty please," says my gun.

I have Haze check his slab and decide the Hex-Sevens are close enough for me to put the SIG out of its misery.

"If you must," I say.

Less than a second later the SIG's locked on to a batwing and is torturing it through a fast twist of spirals and crash dives as the tiny plane fights to break free. When the batwing does, the SIG regrips, releases the batwing, and catches it again.

"This is fun."

"Just kill the bloody thing," I tell the gun, and the batwing blows apart in a fireball that drops sizzling metal into the marsh.

"That was vicious."

"Brutal," agrees Franc, grinning wildly.

"And for my next trick," the gun announces, as a second batwing begins to stagger its way across the sky.

Vals 9 and 11 are also busy. A flash, a single rocket, and a third batwing hits the dirt with a satisfying *crump.* Someone jeers. Between us and our five other launchers, we account for eighteen batwings in the next seven minutes, at a cost of thirty-one rockets. We know this because Haze is keeping count, or at least his slab is. We have 172 rockets left.

"Shil," I say, "how long have you known about Haze?"

She goes very still. "You share a room with Franc," I say. "How can you not know?"

"Franc told me a while back, sir."

"And is Haze really her cousin?"

Shil wants to lie, but honesty makes her hesitate. It's Ion who saves her from having to choose. "Incoming," he warns us.

A high fighter is rolling itself out of position and looping in a slow circle over the marshes. As we watch, it drops low and fire begins to fall from the rear edge of its wings.

Vals 9 and 11 are winding a handle on the side of their machine. I understand that mechanical gearing protects rocket launchers from logic bombs, but it also makes aiming dangerously slow. And the plane is using a force field, because every rocket they fire explodes before it gets close.

"Take it," I tell the SIG.

Diodes blaze, flicking through a rapid sequence that slows and then falters. A second attempt fails in the same way.

"Double fuck," says my gun, launching a third attempt.

But it's too late for that. *"Get down."*

We hit the dirt, followed by most of the troops around us. You can't face rainfire or try to fight it. You just live through it, if you're lucky. A dozen people aren't. The liquid ignites as it hits and eats their uniform to reveal blistering flesh; the flesh strips back to ribs, shoulder bones, and spines, with the bone incinerating itself only seconds later.

"Fléchette," I order, and my gun switches clips.

I shoot the first five human candles I see, nodding as other soldiers begin to do the same. The lucky ones are killed by their companions; the unlucky die screaming as their friends watch in frozen horror. The Uplifted have us killing our own side, a good trick if you can pull it off.

"What?" I demand.

Shil looks away.

"Sir . . ." Haze wants to say something.

I nod to a patch of earth next to me.

"Please," he says. "Not here."

My shrug says it all. *Where then?* All hell is ready to break loose and this is the spot we have to hold for at least an hour, until we fall back to a trench we need to hold for eight times longer. Neither foxhole nor trench has the slightest real value; their worth in lives is completely arbitrary, utterly artificial.

Where exactly does he want me to go?

Maybe over there, sir? says Haze.

And in my gullet the kyp spasms for the first time in weeks, and I'm on my knees vomiting before I've even realized his voice was in my head. Ion is staring across from his foxhole, as are the Vals.

"Implant malfunction." My voice is little more than a croak.

The Vals look sympathetic. "Want us to cut it out?"

I touch my throat, indicating the kyp's position. "Better not," I say, trying for a grin.

Ion is looking at me strangely. "I scanned you yesterday," he says. "In the bar. I only got the arm and some weirdshit at the base of your spine."

Base of my spine?

"Soft implant," I tell him.

Now I've got Franc and the others looking at me weirdly as well. Soft implants are illegal, punishable by death. Real death, the kind that wipes out all copies. Assuming you're rich enough to make copies in the first place, which I'm not and probably never will be.

"It's a long story."

And it's a story I'm not going to tell. The three days in Farlight while the kyp bedded in are still real enough to mess with my dreams.

You can hear me?

Yes. I can hear you . . .

I can take down that high fighter. The boy is podgy, fevered, and nervous. With his sweat-stained uniform and Death's Head patch he looks like a kid caught dressing up; the others are starting to look like soldiers.

You know, he says. *Don't you?*

I nod. *How did you get involved with Franc?*

My family owned her. Haze looks embarrassed, and I realize how little I understand about his world. *We played together as children . . .*

All of this is wrong, he adds. *The war, people starving, people owning each other or paying others to fight for them. People like you and me.* Haze wonders if he can say it, decides he can.

We shouldn't exist.

Oh fuck . . .

I have a rebel NewlyMade, camped out in a foxhole a hundred yards from a landing jetty, with a battle about to begin. I wonder to myself how I'd explain it to the Aux if I just shot him here and now.

You don't need to, says Haze. *Order me, and I'll do it myself.*

Whose side are you really on?

His gaze flicks to Franc, Neen, and Shil. There's no hesitation in his voice whatsoever. *Theirs,* he says.

"Go talk to the Vals," I tell him.

"About what?" he asks, answering aloud.

"The high fighters." I stare pointedly at the slab he carries. "Tell them how your slab can help overcome the shield."

Vaulting from the foxhole, Haze sprints across sodden grass, throwing himself into the ditch behind the rocket launcher. Both Vals look surprised.

"What do you want?"

Can I really hear their words from where I squat? Or does Val 9's question filter into my head through the kyp? It's impossible to say.

"The high fighter's going to attack again."

"Obviously."

"I can stop it."

"You can stop it from attacking?"

Haze shakes his head. "I can unlock the codes," he says. "Then you can shoot it down." He'd say more but Val 9's got him by the throat and she's looking at Val 11, her eyes calculating the odds of this being likely.

"You'd better not be lying."

"I'm not," insists Haze.

He hunkers down with his slab, fingers flicking over the screen as his gaze dances among the high fighter, the rocket launcher in front of him, and the two Vals, who are watching, hard-eyed and suspicious.

"It's about to roll," he says.

The plane does.

"Take it before it reaches the river," says Haze.

"We decide when to fire."

"No." Haze shakes his head. "You have to take it before it reaches the river. Unless that's too hard a shot?"

Both Vals look like they want to get their hands back around his neck. Climbing out of their foxhole, they start to ratchet the wheel, raising the barrels; everyone can see it's going to be a long shot.

A second later Haze climbs out of the foxhole after them.

"What's he doing?" asks Shil, sounding worried.

Franc looks at me and smiles strangely. "Helping the Vals."

"The Vals take help from no one," says Ion. So I shrug and point and he shrugs in his turn. Stranger things in love and war, and we're seeing the side effects of both of those.

The high fighter is closer now, a delta wing so thin it's near invisible when seen from the front. A dot and the slash of a line, fire waterfalling behind it.

"Now," Haze says. "Now."

He's almost shouting.

The two Vals hesitate for a second, and then one of them yanks a lever and all eight rockets fire at once. It's wasteful and they've depleted a tenth of their weapons in one go, but it's probably our best chance of making this work.

Smoke trails zip toward the incoming plane. It's right around now our rockets should self-destruct, leaving the high fighter to fly unharmed through smoke and shrapnel. Only our rockets are still closing.

"Fuck," says Ion, sounding genuinely impressed.

"Five, four, three, two, one . . ." The Vals are counting aloud. When the explosion comes, they hug each other and then punch Haze in the shoulder, which seems to be about as close to affection as either one is likely to get.

"Watch," Haze says.

What's left of the plane is hurtling toward the jetties on the far side of the river. An area used for mooring if the city gate quays are already jammed with incoming cargo. It hits smack-on, exploding in a ball of flame, then expands into black smoke and an even bigger ball of fire as the fuel it carries ignites.

Vals 9 and 11, and Haze, are almost blown off their feet.

"Fuck, fuck, fuck . . ." Ion's saying it like a mantra. Like he doesn't believe what just happened, which make two of us, or thirty, or three hundred, or however many there are still crouched in foxholes in front of the city gates. Haze would know, but he's busy scraping mud from his face and turning bright red as the Vals forget the prejudices of a lifetime and try to hug him . . .

"Haze," I shout. "Get yourself back here."

He shoots me a grateful glance.

We've taken down their batwings and we've knocked out a high fighter, something that just shouldn't be possible. In the afterglow I'm pretty sure that Ion, at least, is aware the best has just been.

All the same, he's laughing and joking with his men. Passing obscene comments up and down the line, so jokes and insults run from the point of the arrow up one side, back down again, and up the other side. We're in a gap between the softening-up and the real attack, and a silence settles across the line as everyone finally begins to realize that.

The earpiece Ion is wearing crackles.

"Sure," he says. "Understood."

"Outpost?"

"Yeah. They've reached the last bend in the river." He lowers his voice. "We're facing Silver Fist."

A lot of mercenaries think the entire Death's Head should be out here with us, but the Death's Head are kept for when they're really needed, and the mercenaries are the ones who've been offered passage off planet, should they live. All the same, Silver Fist isn't good; they're elite. The Uplift's answer to OctoV's Death's Head, unless it's the other way around.

"Belt-feds," I suggest as the first landing craft comes into sight.

Ion nods. My suggestions are allowed. Control rests with Ion—that's been agreed in advance. He expects an argument and is initially suspicious that I agree to his demands. So I explain the obvious. My job is not controlling mercenaries, who already have their own command.

We're here to kill enemy officers. It's that simple.

"Fire," shouts Ion.

A dozen mortars lob their loads toward the river.

"Again."

Water explodes around the first five landers in steady thuds, but nothing we throw at them makes a difference, and the Hex-Seven has been specially adapted for river work.

One side on each is preparing to drop.

A junior officer will be first ashore and die within seconds. Somewhere in the craft behind will be an officer the Enlightened are reluctant to lose. And somewhere in the craft behind that will be a collection of majors and colonels and maybe even a general . . . killing or capturing them is our first duty.

"Rifles," I say.

Midbarreled and easy to carry, but not so lightweight they can't be steadied, the Ursula 12e fires a single pulse that can melt combat armor and kill a trooper five back from the original victim. The pulse doesn't spread; it barely dissipates.

Each weapon costs more than a legion sergeant earns in a year, and we have four of them: one for Franc, Shil, Haze, and Neen. I've seen the way those around us look at the guns and have no doubt there'll be a fight over who gets the weapon if one of us drops.

I could stop this by tying the guns to our individual DNA, but a dead gun next to a dead soldier is a criminal waste, so I've left the codes open. Ion knows this, but only Ion. Genuine friendly-fire incidents are common enough without adding temptation to the mix . . .

CHAPTER 38

WE SLAUGHTER a hundred Silver Fist in a handful of seconds as a landing craft drops its side. Their second lieutenant goes down, his skull half gone. The burn through his heart is Neen, my own shot cuts his brain stem, and he's technically dead before a mercenary even lobs a mortar, but no one's arguing.

We're all too busy killing.

As ramps fall from another four craft, a wave of uniformed elite rolls over the wooden quayside like silver smoke, hiding what was there before. As their front row goes down, the troopers behind march straight over the top, boots crushing their own wounded.

"Fuck," says Franc, sounding impressed.

They're less than a hundred paces away now, and every single step has got to cost. "Take the officers," I tell my crew.

A lieutenant twists as Shil hits his shoulder, then goes down when her next shot explodes vertebrae from his neck.

"Good shot."

She shrugs.

I put a hole through a knot of braid and see the major behind sink to his knees, then become one with the mud as three men clamber over

him. One of them is a corporal with a rocket launcher on his hip. It's a near-impossible weight to carry, but he's doing it anyway.

Shooting him is like shooting myself.

The soldier behind grabs the launcher and swears as red-hot steel burns his hands, but he still has time to fire off a rocket before shrapnel opens his stomach and he stumbles, torn between reloading and the need to repack his own guts.

As the five landing craft empty, another five take their place. The ramp releases are better coordinated this time, steel sides hitting the riverbank in unison.

I take a major; at least I think he's a major. The man behind him dies, and the man behind that, and my next shot rips open the face of a corporal who steps into the gap. She goes down, ground to pulp as those behind her scrabble to reach solid ground.

Vals 9 and 11 have their rocket launcher cranked as low as it will go, which is still not low enough. In desperation they spin the handle in the other direction, raising the barrels until it points almost vertically. Eight rockets hit the sky together, arc high, and fall toward the next wave of Hex-Sevens. Unfortunately the ramps go down seconds before the rockets can hit.

And most of the rockets miss anyway.

Mortars are being lobbed from inside the city. And the Silver Fist are retaliating with rockets from batteries on the far side of the river. There's a whole other battle going on above our heads, but one thing I know for sure: Both sides are extracting a heavy cost in enemy lives.

"Fall back," orders Ion.

"Not yet . . ." My words are drowned under gunfire, and it's too late anyway: The mercenaries are abandoning their foxholes and moving toward the trench behind us. Crouched over their weapons, they walk backward, never once taking their eyes off Silver Fist.

Both Vals die, and a woman darts forward, drops to a crouch behind them, and slices into the backs of their necks with her dagger. The implants are still twitching as she stuffs wires, broken nerves, and core into her pocket. At least their memories will be going home.

"We need to hold," I scream at Neen.

"Zero minus ten," says my gun. "Timing's okay."

Seventy minutes have gone, ten longer than we needed to hold. It seems impossible, but then I realize fifteen Hex-Sevens have disgorged their troops, the floodplain in front of us is slick with blood, and I'm almost out of ammunition. I have to retreat, if only because the trench is where my next arms cache is waiting.

"Sir," says Neen. "Please." He looks worried that I might want the Aux to stick it out on their own.

"Fall back," I tell him.

The next few hours take our numbers below a hundred. Anyone who makes it through to the end of the battle is guaranteed a way out of here. Apart from us, obviously . . .

It shows in a change of tactics. Driven by his determination not to be overrun, Ion sets up a row of belt fed machine guns and fills the gaps with snipers, half a dozen marksmen he's been holding in reserve. Most are female, which is interesting. I'm not sure I knew women made the best shots. At my suggestion, the Aux join them.

Occasionally suicide squads set out from the Silver Fist side, and that's when we really come into our own, picking off the teams one by one and leaving the last out in the mud, badly wounded and usually screaming.

We've hit them hard, certainly hard enough to ensure that the final run of Hex-Sevens begins to unload its cargo on the far side of the river where Silver Fist sappers are busy constructing a camp.

Night is creeping across this world, and a cold wind is rising from the marshes around us. An alligator booms its challenge, unless it's something else. I used to know the sound of every animal in the desert. Where I am now, its animals and plants are strange, its winds unexpected, and its weather patterns unclear.

We can fight in the dark, of course, and so can they. Night goggles are piled in boxes behind me. Ion wears a helmet with a visor that achieves daylight clarity with minimal weight. My own helmet does

much the same. At this point I'm wishing I insisted on similar helmets for the Aux.

"You okay?" Ion asks.

Turning, I find him beside me. "Yeah."

He nods. "Good. I'm pulling back to the gates. You guys intend to stay?"

Neen is watching me, his glance nervous, then resigned. A couple of seconds and he's already adjusted to the idea—pretty impressive, if unnecessary.

"No," I say. "We'll be coming with you."

Sixty-eight people out of 505 make it back to the city. When you knock me, Neen, Haze, Shil, and Franc out of that figure, you get sixty-three and that's not even going to fill the available seats on the last ship out of here.

But the colonel's rules are clear. If you weren't beyond the gate when the Silver Fist attacked you're not eligible for one of those places. They'll go begging and the ship will take off with thirty-seven seats still empty.

CHAPTER 39

MAYBE IT'S their backstory, but Franc, the shaven-headed woman with the evil grin and a belt full of knives, turns anxious every time Haze speaks to her.

It would be funny, if it wasn't sad.

We're sitting in the kitchen of our house. Maria is boiling water for coffee, for washing, and to dress the wounds we didn't even realize we had until we made it back to warmth and safety.

Neen has taken a slug through his shoulder, just below his left arm. It's a clean shot that shows daylight on both sides. I'm not sure he realizes how lucky he is. Maria's fussing, Shil's doing her best not to be jealous, and Haze has just told Franc that he'll protect her.

"From what?" I ask. "What are you expecting to happen?"

"Nightmares."

Maria and Shil both flash the sign against the evil eye. Maria, I can understand, but Shil . . .

"What, sir?" she demands, seeing me look at her.

"How can you believe that stuff?"

"Sir, how can you not?"

She's got using *sir* as an insult down to a fine art. It doesn't help my temper that she probably learned it from me.

"Tonight," says Haze, "is going to be grim."

"You know what they're planning?" asks Neen. The speed with which he asks this reveals his desire for a rapid change of subject.

"Yes," says Haze. "I believe so."

"A psychic attack?" asks Maria.

He shakes his head, not bothering to hide his smile. "That's a myth," he says. "They'll use gas. The wind is from the marshes. The Enlightened won't want to waste that."

"I should tell the colonel."

"Tell him now," says Haze, glancing at his slab.

COLONEL NUEVO IS drunk. One of the great advantages of being the most senior officer in an occupied city is that no one is going to point this out, at least not to your face. The other is that when you decide to go walkabout, because you're bored and have nothing better to do, half a dozen officers and bodyguards are going to ride shotgun like fancy shadows behind you.

"Thought I'd find you here," he says when I open the door. "Was going to send for you, but . . ."

But what never materializes. Instead Colonel Nuevo wanders into my house and hesitates in the hall. "Where is everybody?"

"We're in the kitchen."

He follows me down a corridor, the sound of his cavalry boots echoing off the walls, his posse of silver braid following along behind.

"Bread," he exclaims, and Franc freezes, a freshly baked loaf in her hands. Everyone else jumps to their feet, although Neen is marginally slower than the rest of us.

"You're wounded."

Neen shrugs, realizes this isn't polite, and says, "Minor, sir. Pretty clean, went straight through."

It's the right answer.

Without being asked, Maria puts a fat slice of freshly baked bread in front of the colonel, then adds a saucer of oil and watches him demolish the lot.

"How did it go?" asks the colonel. He's talking to me. A major and two captains are waiting to see what I'll reply.

"No worse than I'd expect."

He smiles. "I'm letting the mercenaries go."

"So I would imagine, sir."

"You want to go with them?"

I shake my head.

Something ghostly crosses his face. "Sleep well," he says. "Come and see me in the morning . . ."

THE SHIP CARRYING Ion and his crew explodes when it passes the first ball buster. Haze, my gun, and I see this as a fireball high in the night sky, like a new star burning over Ilseville. As ash and metal fragments rain down on the city, the SIG says, "Glad we're not on that."

I can only agree. "Silver Fist?"

"No," says Haze. "Us."

We're both wearing full combat armor and breathing a mix from canisters fixed to our belts. The city is spread out beneath us, a jumble of streets and squares, all poisoned by the psychotropic gas that has been carried in on the night wind.

People howl like animals, and marsh foxes scream like murdered children. I've got the Aux locked indoors, in the house below. All have injected themselves with battlefield opiates in an attempt to hold their nightmares at bay.

Except for Haze, obviously. He's on the roof with me, and we're talking about how to handle what comes next. He's going to be an even, a thinker. Two buds have already broken through his scalp and most of his hair is gone, probably still tangled into the drain of the shower where I found him an hour ago.

Somehow I'm going to have to find a way to tell Colonel Nuevo about this that makes it sound good. And I'm worried about the colonel's own capacity to deal with the dreams.

Although, as it turns out, I needn't have bothered.

When I reach his HQ next morning Colonel Nuevo is washing vomit from his naked chest and shouting at his orderly for a clean uniform. The orderly looks the way his superior deserves to feel, but obviously doesn't. It seems Colonel Nuevo drank himself into such a stupor that no dreams had the strength to infest his sleep.

"Bloody useless man," the colonel tells me. So I repeat what I originally told him about the gas.

"Jacket," shouts the colonel, ignoring me.

Bringing him a dress jacket, the orderly lays it out on the bed. Before the colonel can object, he says, "It's all you have left."

This is a Colonel Nuevo I haven't seen before.

"You know what's going to happen today?" asks the colonel when his sleeves are straight and he's managed the braid fastenings on his own.

I shake my head.

"Probably just as well. Take your auxiliaries and establish a new base by the cathedral. Inside the second wall . . ." He hesitates. "Who was that girl who gave me the bread?"

"Maria," I tell him. "Our maid."

He snorts. "Take Maria with you," he says, and then he tells me why

MARIA AND NEEN are in bed, their faces hollow and eyes unable to meet mine. Enough of the nightmares crept past the opiates to ruin their sleep, though ruined sleep is cheap compared with the price the gas extracted from some in this city.

Walking back from the colonel's HQ produced open windows and broken bodies on the streets below.

"Get up," I tell Neen. "Pack only what you need, plus your weapons, and be downstairs in two minutes. That goes for Maria as well."

I give Franc the same message and go looking for Shil. She's in the bathroom half naked, washing under her arms with cold water from a basin.

Her body is as good as I remember.

"Get out," she says. When I don't, she hurls a glass mug.

"We leave in two minutes," I tell her. "If you're not ready, we go without you."

"What?"

"Two minutes. Get your weapons, get dressed, carry some food."

"Wait," she demands. "Are you okay?"

Punching a hole through her door is probably the wrong answer, and I don't mean to do it. Well, maybe I do . . .

"No," I say. "I'm not fucking okay. The ship carrying Ion and his friends exploded last night."

Shil gets it instantly, her brain as quick as her tongue. If Ion's ship was taken out by Uplifted guns I'd be upset, but not like this. And since it probably wasn't an accident, that leaves only one other option. No code was carried to unlock the ball busters. The mercenaries were betrayed.

"Colonel Nuevo?"

"More like General Jaxx. Probably planned it before we even landed . . . And now we're falling back to the inner city."

"All of us?"

"Very much doubt it."

I pack my weapons in a cold anger that blows through the house like an arctic wind. Even Neen stays out of my way. They're waiting in line when I hit the hall a minute or so later.

"Move out," I tell them.

Shil has packed all the food in the kitchen. When she tells Maria to carry it, Maria adds the bag to her own without complaint. Two rifles are slung across Shil's back, another three rest against her hip; she's tucked pistols into her belt, five of them that I can see.

No one needs that many weapons, not even me.

Only Shil is giving them away the moment we leave the house. "Take this," she says, and such is the determination on her face that the boy does what he's told. "You'll need it," Shil tells him.

He looks puzzled.

A couple of minutes from our door and she's down to one pulse rifle and a knife tucked into the side of her boot. She keeps these two weapons and her silence for the rest of the journey.

"What's going on, sir?" asks Neen. He's carrying the bag his sister gave to Maria.

I shrug, not daring to put it into words.

CHAPTER 40

THE BATTLE for Ilseville's outer ring lasts thirteen days. This is how long it takes the Silver Fist to destroy the river gates, swamp the outer city with their soldiers, and fight street to street and house to house until a circle of flame swallows the entire area. Sixty thousand of OctoV's troops remain outside the inner walls when those gates get locked.

Mostly they're militia.

All will die.

We know that, the enemy knows that, it takes those trapped a while to catch up. Group after group falls back toward the inner gates expecting to be let in. Some swear and others just accept their fate. Mainly it's the mercenaries who go down fighting. Given how the Enlightened feel about those who fight for money rather than belief, it's not a surprising choice.

Their slaughter is viewed by neutral observers and watched with horrified fascination across the known galaxy. Haze patches us between Uplift and U/Free but there's small difference between their data feeds. Our troops are killed in running fights and bitter last stands; little is added by way of commentary because little is needed.

And the Enlightened are clever. They wait until the afternoon of the second day, when a group of our militia captures and beheads two Silver Fist officers, before launching their most vicious attack.

Over the course of three and a half hours, a single high flier seeds and reseeds the offending section of ghetto with flamefire until the buildings eat themselves and those inside become fragments and ash.

"Do something," Franc begs Haze.

We have rockets targeting the high fighter, but most of our batteries are busy protecting the inner city, and anyway nothing we own can eat its way past the fighter's defenses. As if to prove this, a rocket explodes impotently, and the high fighter casually flies through the explosion, fire dripping from the rear edge of each wing.

"Please," she begs.

Hunched over his slab, Haze shakes his head. Tears are rolling down his face, which is thinner and older than when the slaughter started. "I can't," he says. "I don't have that level of power."

"Power?" says Neen.

"Control," he says, amending his words hastily. I leave them to it.

HAVE YOU EVER stayed drunk for six weeks? Believe me, it takes real effort. Hot Bar Wild is gone, obviously enough. It's that black patch of ash down near the river's edge, between those two patches of ash that used to be warehouses.

I can go down there if I want, in theory at least, because a new truce has just been announced, and it's going to last just long enough to take us all to the edge of deep winter.

That's probably called strategy by the U/Free.

As I said, there's a Hot Bar Wild in every city, and if you get really lucky or the city is really scuzzy, you'll probably find two, or three, or four . . .

The SIG and I go hunting for alcohol.

We find it first at a cellar bar behind the cathedral, inhabited by Ilseville's lowlife. They glower and glare, but once I put my gun on the table and my gold behind the bar they decide it would be simpler to leave me alone. And I'm impressed: No one even gets hurt while we're reaching this decision.

I'd share the colonel's supplies, but that offer he made me of a place on Ion's ship nags at the back of my mind. So much so that I waste some days in the bar just wondering whether or not to kill him.

His offer and the explosion could have been a coincidence. But then as the gun reminds me, I could have been a career sergeant in the legion with a long and impressive record behind me, Franc could have kept her knife use for the kitchen, Haze could have been born virus-free, and Shil could have fallen for my sophisticated charms.

We leave Maria out of it, because she's normal. In fact, we can't really work out what she's doing with us in the first place.

"She opened the door," says the SIG. "Remember?"

Thinking about it, I do . . .

On the third day Neen tracks me down.

"Sir?"

If I really concentrate, I can see only one of him. "Sergeant."

He wants me to return to the house. I tell him it got burned and he tells me he means the new one. I send him away anyhow.

The gun and I move bars. Frederico's is above a machine shop, backs onto a laundry, and is approached through a particularly unsavory railway arch. It takes Neen five days to find me and he comes back every day for weeks. He even tries staying to drink with me, but I tell him drunks are boring and he'd be better off staying at home to fuck Maria.

We're now halfway through the new truce. Forty-two days of enforced stalemate while trained negotiators shuttle between Colonel Nuevo and the Enlightened general.

It's going to fail. Everyone in the bar nods when I tell Neen this. It's going to fail, because these things always fail. You'd think the U/Free would have learned to stop trying by now. Everyone nods at that, too . . .

The final bar is built into the city's inner walls. You have to know someone in the previous bar to discover that this bar exists, which is fine, because by now I know pretty much everyone in the previous bar. They're survivors, like me.

A pimp called Vice—which may or may not be his real name—introduces me to the madam. An old ex–militia sergeant, given to wearing silk dresses and too much rouge.

LEAVE YOUR GUN AT THE DOOR, reads a notice. Apparently it was put up as a joke. A lot of strange things go on at Madame Jess's. There are racks, whips and chains, and a room with a plunge tub so cold it freezes around you if you sit inside it for too long.

This isn't surprising, since snow now hides the blackened ruins beyond our windows and helps keep the corpses from stinking. Ice has closed the Ilseville River, and the Silver Fist are using the truce to build better camps and reinforce their positions. Enough of the customers at Madame Jess's think the U/Free favor the Enlightened for me not to bother to disagree.

The madam even has a pair of nude contortionists to entertain her customers. I think they're the two from Hot Bar Wild, but that could just be the alcohol, or maybe nude contortionists are a type. And it's weird: You always think you want to meet a woman who can get her knees behind her ears, but when you do, it's like having sex with a sea anemone.

"Visitors," announces my gun.

So I help the contortionist untangle herself and struggle back into my trousers. She leaves with a gold coin and a smile that lasts almost as long as it takes her to reach my door. I don't know what she says, but Franc is grinning sourly as she comes into my chamber.

"Nice," she says, taking a look at the rack and chains. I'm looking for the irony, but she seems to mean it, and that makes me wonder a bit about home life with the Hazes of this world, or her world, or whichever world is appropriate.

"Drunk as a skunk," the gun says.

"Join me," I suggest.

Franc shakes her head. "The truce is about to end."

It seems I'm a week out, not that it matters. My metabolism means staying drunk takes real effort and sobriety comes all too soon. Only that's still not quick enough for Franc.

"You're needed."

"The colonel?"

She spits with great accuracy, hitting dead center on a floor tile. Her opinion of Colonel Nuevo made clear, she helps me to my feet.

"There's a cold tub next door," says the SIG.

I go in, trousers and all. I must help somehow, because looking at Franc it doesn't seem possible she could maneuver me over the edge on her own. The water is freezing, and feels even colder when she ducks my head under and holds me down for a couple of seconds.

"You stink," she says.

"You stink, sir."

"Ignore him," says my gun.

HAZE HAS LOCKED himself in the cellar with long loops of copper wires nailed to our side of the door. The wire begins and ends at a fat-wheel battery, which sits on bricks below one hinge.

When Franc finally persuades Haze to release the door, I discover he's nailed similar loops of wire to the walls on both sides of the stairs. My arm brushes one of the wires, and sparks flare in the blackness. It's dark, but I don't need light to know he's crying.

I strike a match all the same.

Hollow eyes stare at me. It's like looking into the face of death.

"We need to talk."

He shakes his head, closes his eyes. I want to shake Haze or slap him, but that's just my hangover arriving. Anyway, I'm scared of driving him deeper, and I've just realized something else.

"You've lost your ability to read my mind?"

Whatever he says is below the edge of my hearing, and my hearing is good. He points to a candle, so I light it with my last match. Then he points to a scrap of paper and an old-fashioned pencil. A design for the wires on the wall is scratched on one side. It's been drawn and redrawn half a dozen times.

Haze holds out his hand.

I give him the paper, then the pencil.

They're looking for me. His writing is shaky, far worse than the writing next to his drawings of the wires, and that is shaky enough.

"Who is?"

Everyone . . .

I take a deep breath. This boy saved our lives when he downed a high fighter before it could flame our trenches for a second time. And with that thought I have my answer. "The Enlightened?"

Yes, writes Haze.

"In here?" I tap my head.

He nods, but I already knew the answer.

"WE'RE GOING HUNTING," I tell my gun.

"About time." The SIG is sulking because I've been drunk and it's been bored, but it forgives me when I let it select its own ammunition.

"Ceramic hollow point."

I load a clip with the right shells.

"Fléchette."

The gun doesn't really like fléchette, but we both know they're useful and anyway the tiny carbon darts take up so little room.

"Overblast, explosive, incendiary . . ."

I alternate the shells in a single clip, four of each, and slam the final clip into the SIG's handle. And then, wrapping myself in my coat, I sling a pulse rifle across my back, stuff the SIG diabolo into my belt, and check that I'm carrying a dagger, throwing spikes, and my laser blade.

No one tries to stop me as I make my way across the inner city . . . My face is known to most Death's Head officers, and the others take one look at my scowl and decide I must have official business.

"Sven." Colonel Nuevo stares at me through the bottom of a glass. "I've been wondering where you were."

"Sir . . ."

We're in his bunker, because this isn't an official meeting. So I finally get to see his famous blast walls after all. More blocks of gold than you can imagine. Utterly useless, providing an illusion of protection. We both know that a direct rocket strike would wipe Ilseville Bank off the map, strong room or not.

"I've got to get out."

"Haven't we all." He smiles. "Not going to happen, though. Is it?"

"I mean . . . I've got to be allowed into the outer city."

The colonel pours himself another glass. On his table are a bottle, a glass, a pistol, and a map of the inner city with dozens of pencil lines dividing it into small squares. It looks like he's been playing one of those games where you block out every hit and put a cross for every miss. No one can have any doubt about who is winning.

"Want to know how many buildings we have left?"

I shake my head.

"Very wise," says Colonel Nuevo. "No point depressing yourself. Now tell me why I should give you permission to leave."

"Don't want to leave," I tell him. "Just go into the outer city."

"You don't want to leave?" He shrugs. "You're weirder than I thought. Everybody else is desperate to get out of here."

This is going to be more difficult than I thought.

"The enemy have food," I say. "And weapons. Okay, not as many as they'd like, but more than us. I want to hit a couple of their dumps, cause some damage before they have a chance to get stuck into us again. And I'm sick of being cooped up in here. I want to kill some Enlightened."

His eyebrows rise.

"As many Enlightened as I find." For a second I consider telling the colonel about Haze being NewlyMade, then decide not to complicate the issue.

"The Silver Fist are preparing an attack," he says.

"Soon," I agree. "While the ice still means they can cross the river without needing pontoons or bridges."

"Did I say that?"

I shake my head. "Worked it out for myself."

Colonel Nuevo raises his glass. "We'll make a proper officer of you yet."

"God forbid."

He smiles sourly. "Let's pretend I didn't hear that." Pulling a sheet of paper from a drawer, the colonel hunts for his official seal and finds it where he found the paper. He scrawls his signature across the bottom and seals it.

"Write your own orders," he says. "Get killed, see if I care. I can always find another ADC."

I salute, smartly enough to be insulting.

His comments about my parentage, manners, and lack of anything resembling breeding follow me from his bunker, leaving the captain and lieutenant in the next room wondering what is funny enough about this to make me grin.

BY THE TIME night arrives, I'm as sober as the silver moon that hides behind scudding clouds above my head, and my hangover is little more than a faint echo. On the dot of 2100 a dozen mortars arrive from across the river to celebrate the end of the truce, but they explode where mortars have already exploded and the rubble they destroy is worth nothing anyway.

The streets beyond my house are silent as I stamp my way through freshly fallen snow. A militia patrol catch me in their torches, see my uniform, and apologize. We salute each other and I walk on, moving toward a pump station with a heavy lock on its doors.

I've been watching a sector beyond our wall all evening. The houses are expensive, used by senior Silver Fist and members of the Enlightened. A house two streets back has a three-braid, while a house on a square behind has another. They'll do for a start.

According to the map in Colonel Nuevo's office, a tunnel runs from the pump house to a substation in the outer city. I'm about five minutes away from finding out if that's true. Slashing away the lock, I take a deep breath and steady myself. When I walk out of the substation only one thing must be on my mind . . .

Killing Enlightened, plus anything else that gets in my way.

Silver Fist engineers have welded a grid across their end of the tunnel, so I wrap fire string around the bars, debate stepping back, and decide a falling grid will make too much noise for me to take the risk.

Molten metal splashes my face like tears.

On the other side is a long ladder rising into darkness. It leads where I need it to lead.

CHAPTER 41

THE STREETS that the Silver Fist own are as quiet as ours are, equally deserted. I'm tempted just to knock at the first door I reach . . . Knock at the door, kill whoever answers, and riff this thing from there, but I have no idea how many guards the average three-braid keeps on call.

So I do it the difficult way.

A pipe runs up the front of the house. My Death's Head uniform is black, it's nighttime, and few lights show in the outer city. Even the campfires across the river are fewer than last week, but the silver moon insists on slipping from behind its clouds, and I find myself frozen beside a second-floor window as a five-man patrol passes underneath.

No one looks up.

Sliding my dagger between the window and frame, I catch the lock and hear it break with a slight crack. The room is dark, and I'm almost inside when I see a middle-aged woman alone in bed. She sits up and opens her mouth, but closes it again when I put a finger to my lips. It's probably my gun that concentrates her mind so quickly.

We're lit by moonlight.

"Shut it," says the SIG.

She does.

If there's a discarded uniform on the floor then she's dead anyway. But it's okay: A dress hangs over a chair in one corner. The dress is expensive but filthy, the shoes worn at the heel and trodden down at the back.

"Ilsevillect?"

She nods, begins gabbling at me in Ishvelict, so I put my finger to my lips again, switch to common tongue, and tell her to keep quiet, go back to sleep, and tell no one she was awake when I came through.

"They'll kill you," I tell her.

"And if they don't," says the gun. "We will."

The look on her face says she knows that already.

Outside the door I wait, wondering if she'll scream. When she doesn't, I take a peep through the door and find her already feigning sleep, her head buried firmly under the covers.

The room opposite contains a major, plus a blonde young enough to be daughter to the woman across the landing. They're asleep in each other's arms, blankets pulled up tightly.

"Subsonic ceramic," suggests the SIG, "quarter charge, hollow point, preset fracture lines." It's just showing off.

The man's a Silver Fist.

At least he was.

My shot passes cleanly through his ear canal, cuts his brain stem, and ricochets off the inside of his skull, splintering into fragments that pulp his cerebellum as surely as if I'd just dropped his brain in a food mixer.

"Now who's showing off?" asks the gun.

The girl will wake to find a dead man in her bed, but at least she'll wake, and given he's three times her age and she's got a split lip I think she'll cope.

"Scan warning," says the gun, and before I can ask *Scanned by what?* the bloody thing kills its laser sights and turns itself off. So I tuck the SIG diabolo into my belt and talk to myself instead.

A floor below this I find two guards standing outside an ornate door.

They die quickly.

Wiping my dagger, I slide it back into its neoprene sheath and pull out my laser knife, tuning its blade to invisible. It's a wasted effort, because the three-braid is sitting up in bed and his eyes are fixed firmly on the blade in my hand. Should have known the Enlightened could see across a wider spectrum, just as I should have known who was scanning for weapons.

"You won't get away with this," he says.

"Want to bet?" says the gun, snapping out of sleep mode. And then to me it says, "More guards heading this way."

"He call them?"

No one's clear what power braids have. Certainly not on our side, and probably not theirs. The Enlightened have a lot to gain from keeping everyone ignorant.

The three-braid's still smiling smugly when he realizes I'm not where I was. That's because I'm behind him, one hand reaching over his skull to hook my fingers into his nose and yank back his head. He does that flicker thing, but it's too late. Meat sears as his throat opens, and my blade seals every artery except the last.

"Steps on the stairs."

Another silverhead, junior enough to have only one braid, but still a silverhead . . . I kill him fast, and then shoot both his NCOs through the head, hearing brains slop against a wall.

"And again," says the gun as another two soldiers burst into the room.

It's chosen subsonic, or maybe I chose that myself. A pull of the trigger and both men go down. I burn out the three-braid's implant and grind his memories under my heel. That, as much as his death, is what will upset everyone in the morning.

Shutting the door behind me, I hesitate.

A booby trap is what I need.

Gumming a belt mine to the inside of the door, I set it for two movements and use up the first shutting the door behind me.

. . .

A LIGHT SHOWS in a top window.

Darkness stretches out for five floors beneath. It's a rich house, almost ornate for this city; built by a foreign fur trader, perhaps. People will travel a long way to make themselves rich, even to Ilseville.

The front door is bolted, the windows have locks, and an alarm system winks from above the rear door. There is undoubtedly an alarm system on the front as well, probably made less obvious by a blanket of snow. Three floors up a window is open and a tiny red dot flares and vanishes, flares and vanishes.

A soldier is smoking.

I try to remember what rules the Enlightened have about such things and fail. Most of their rules seem more concerned with what you may or may not eat, wear, or sleep with. All the same, the man obviously doesn't want to be caught.

"Fléchette or regular?"

The gun practically snorts. "What do you think?"

Setting itself for fléchette, the gun signals ready and I wait for my victim to take another drag. That tiny red dot makes the perfect target. By my reckoning the shot takes him under an eye socket and blows out the top of his skull, missing his brain stem entirely but trashing his frontal lobe.

Spiraling like a dying firefly, his cigarette extinguishes itself at my feet.

The wall is rough, handholds easy to find. All it takes for me to climb in through the window is pushing his body out of my way first.

A flight of stairs gives way to another, and I climb both in silence. The house is cold, my breath visible in a slash of light coming under one door. It seems I've arrived at the right place. Killing the person most likely to raise an alarm is pretty basic really, and in a house full of sleeping people, anyone awake has got to be the obvious target.

I'm hoping it's the Enlightened, but it's a man very like me. Young, but old enough to have seen something of life. A soldier, who reaches automatically for a gun, because instinct is already running ahead of his thoughts. Our eyes meet and outrage flicks to resignation, without passing through fear.

He dies cleanly, on his feet and facing me.

Silently I say a prayer for a similar death when my time comes, then touch stone to keep that time away.

The other guards die less well.

A shot to the chest, a shot to the throat. A kick to the balls, a twist of someone's head, and a snap loud enough to wake a silverhead in the room beyond. He gets his shot in first and I find myself hitting a wall, my face flattened by an expensive wall hanging as the blow spins me around. That's my blood, splatter-patterning antique cloth.

It's bad, almost as bad as when the ferox took my arm. Reeling that thought in, I check my status . . . My prosthetic arm is in place, my legs are unbroken, and my head turns, though it hurts like fuck, which is good, because not hurting at all would be far worse. All that's wrong is a hole in my chest. He's missed my heart, but that's probably not difficult. Half a dozen women will tell you I don't have one.

He stands over me.

He's as tall as I am, probably taller. Seven braids stream back from his skull. He's the most senior silverhead I've yet seen.

"That's illegal technology," he says, kicking my gun across the floor.

"And you can fuck off, too," says the gun, then goes dark as all its diodes switch off at once.

The silverhead smiles. "This is where you die."

And in the back of my mind, a skull grins.

"Not here," I say. "And not yet."

His reply is a steel-capped boot to my guts. Another kick like that and something will rupture. So I curl myself tight, trying to make it look like instinct while fighting the very instinct that makes me want to curl up into a ball in the first place. It's a tough trick.

The next kick catches me in the ribs, breaking a couple. The seven-braid smiles at the crack and draws back his boot for a final go. It's the moment for which I've been waiting. Another rib breaks, and my gut muscles barely survive the blow, but I reach right around his ankle and grip the toe of his boot, then pull . . .

A single twist locks him into the present.

His foot dislocates before his knee, but it's a close call, and his knee only gives to stop his hip from dislocating entirely. The seven-braid falls, because there's nothing else he can do, and I slam my elbow hard into his throat. I'm not sure what all those silver torso tubes do but I rip them out of his body anyway.

And then I remove his head without bothering to check if he's dead first. It hangs from my fingers by all seven braids and leaves a trail of blood as I make my way downstairs and out into the street.

"Wow," says the gun when we're clear of the house. "Five broken ribs, a smashed shoulder, and a ruptured spleen. Cheap at half the price."

I get the feeling it's just being kind.

My feet are heavy as lead, it's cold, and the temptation to lie down in the snow for a few minutes is overwhelming. So overwhelming that the gun curses me from one side of a deserted square to the other.

And I'm back at the pumping station before an explosion two blocks away tells me someone has just opened a bedroom door they should have left closed.

"Kaboom," says the gun.

I have to agree.

CHAPTER 42

I'M GRINNING, also bleeding and trying to climb a rusty metal ladder while holding the head of a self-elected god, not necessarily a good mix. It takes me longer than I'd like, but I manage it anyway, and then make my way home.

The head goes in a bucket, because I'm fed up with the mess. The food, taken from the kitchen of the first house, goes into the larder, leaving me with what I've been putting off.

Seeing how bad my wound really is.

My uniform is half glued to my side with dried blood, and my jacket peels back reluctantly, although water helps the cloth to pull free. I can see splintered ribs and torn muscle, a pulsing artery, and sinew that looks like it should go somewhere. Straightening the ribs makes me wince.

"Leave it." Shil's voice is fierce. "Just fucking leave it." She steps up beside me and turns me toward her flashlight. "What happened?"

"Someone shot me."

She sighs. "Obviously. Who?"

"A silverhead . . ."

My answer stops her in her tracks. "Where was he?"

"Into the outer city. I killed three Enlightened, plus several humans. One of them could have been me."

"Believe me, sir," says Shil. "No one could be you."

"I'm fine."

"No," she says. "You're not." Without being asked, she banks a fire, finds me a chair, and pours me a glass of brandy. A moment later she has a second glass of brandy mixed with two glasses of water, and she's heating the whole lot in a saucepan over the fire.

"I can do that myself."

She stops midstride, then squats in front of me. Her face is hard, and something unforgiving has fixed itself behind her eyes. "You don't want me in this group, do you?"

I shrug. It hurts.

"What did I do?" she demands. "To make you hate me?"

Twist away from my caress, offer yourself as the price for demoting your brother, hate me yourself . . . There are a dozen things I could say and all of them would be half true, and none of them would be honest.

I know the real answer.

It goes back to those locked gates, the high fighter seeding the ghetto with fire, and how Shil and Franc feel about our militia's slaughter by the Silver Fist. Franc's better at keeping her disgust hidden, but then she's been a possession most of her life and that has to be good training.

"Listen," I say. "There was nothing I could do."

"Yes there was, sir. You could have stayed here. Not gone into the outer city." She thinks I'm ignoring her question.

"I mean the gates . . ."

"Sir, now's not the time."

"Yes," I say, "it fucking is. So I'll say it, and you'll listen."

She waits.

"The code to lock the gate was broadcast by a hiSat. A hiSat dumped up there by General Jaxx's mother ship. I could no more break its coding than could Haze. Even the colonel was powerless to stop what happened next."

"Why, sir?" says Shil.

She's asking why the general had the gates locked in the first place. Shil already understands why none of us could break it open, even if we'd dared try to disobey General Jaxx's orders.

"To save food, maybe to save ammunition. Because he knew the mercs would fight to the end once they knew they were trapped. God knows I'm not the general . . ."

"You could be," she says. "One day. Everyone's afraid of you. No one ever knows what you're going to do next."

"You're not afraid of me."

"Me?" she says. "I'm fucking terrified."

The water is hot and the alcohol stings. Shil keeps her mixture just below boiling, which is ninety-six degrees Centigrade on this planet. And when she's dressed the wound, she pulls the saucepan from the fire.

"This is going to hurt," she tells me, not sounding as upset as she should be by the idea.

She's right, it does. Although she tries not to wince as I grip her hand. "What were you doing anyway?" she demands, folding her injured fingers into the crook of her arm when she finally gets them back.

"Killing silverheads."

"Yeah," she says. "You said. The question is why?"

It's a night for the truth.

"Wake Haze," I say. "Ask him how he feels."

Shil does. She wakes the others as well, sending Neen for a doctor. He goes without question, despite the fact that he outranks her and she's his sister. Franc comes down, takes one look at the bread and cheese I stole from the three-braid's kitchen, and smiles.

"Thank you," she says.

The house still has furniture to burn and we can always hack up doors when that's gone, so I tell Franc to bank up the fire and make some toast. I'm hungry; hunting does that to me.

And then I wait, second-guessing whether Neen will return before Haze can be coaxed up from his cellar. My coffee goes cold and the griddle gets hot enough for Franc to make toast for everyone. Our kitchen smells of bread and wood smoke when its door finally bangs open and Neen comes in, leading a tired-looking old woman.

She halts, smells the air. Envy is obvious in her eyes.

"How the other half live."

"He stole it." Shil's voice is fierce. "Got half killed doing it." She speaks in an accent the old woman recognizes. If not from this city, then from this system.

"Took it from a *silverhead,*" says a voice in the doorway. The final word is laden with scorn, although mostly that's bravado. Haze looks like shit—his face is haggard, a bloody sheet is wrapped around his skull, and sweat drips from his jaw—but his eyes are clear.

"How do you feel?" I ask.

"Looks like I should be asking you, sir," says Haze, glancing at my shoulder.

"Like shit," I say. "And you?"

"Also, shitlike, but better . . ." He hesitates. "Do I want to know how you did it?"

"What has seven braids and takes a long time to kill?"

It sounds like a riddle, but my question is straight. I've seen three-braids and five-braids, but the last of my kills was taller, harder, and faster than anything I've faced since the ferox. And a bit of my mind is burned, as if something cold seared it along the edge. When I look up, Haze is frozen about three steps into the room.

"Seven?"

"Yeah," I say. "Ugly bugger."

He doesn't even break a smile. "A general," he says. "How many chest tubes?" Haze mimes pipes going in and out of his own chest.

"Three, maybe four," I tell him. "Fat as my arm."

"And he was tough?"

I touch my chest, watched by the doctor, who is undoing what looks like a tiny jewelry roll made from black leather. "Very tough, also very reluctant to die. Until I cut off his head."

Haze vomits.

He makes it out of the room and into the night, but we can all hear him spew onto the cobbled courtyard. On the way out he passes the silverhead, staring from its bucket. I'm not sure that helps.

"Lazlo," says Haze, when he returns to the room. "General Lazlo . . . He was leading their troops."

"How do you know?"

He shrugs. "I hear things."

The boy might mean rumors, but somehow I think he means exactly what he says. Haze hears things, and that's fine, because I hear things, too. Not recently, and not since Haze decided to stay out of my thoughts, but I hear things all the same.

"It's okay."

"No," he says. "It's not. They're going to slaughter you."

WHEN I WAKE the doctor is gone, my shoulder is bandaged, and I'm tied to a chair in the kitchen. The towels beneath my chair are blood-soaked, and some of them have been ripped apart for rags. Franc is emptying a bucket of pink-tinged water and Haze is ashen, clutching his stomach as if someone has just kicked him in the guts.

"What's with him?"

"So," says Shil. "You're back."

She drops to a crouch in front of me and everyone suddenly decides they want to be someplace else. One after another the Aux traipse from the kitchen, until only Haze is left.

"Thank you," he says, then shuts the door behind him.

"You know," says Shil, "I'm really tempted to leave you there." But she doesn't; she cuts the ropes on my chair, helps me upstairs, and puts me to bed, then takes off half her clothes and climbs in beside me.

"Molest me," she says, "and you're dead."

These are the last words I hear before sleep takes me. She's still there when I wake, next to me when I sleep again, and still there the morning after, although my sense of time is screwed and three weeks have gone before I reach for Shil, and it's for more than the simple comfort of knowing someone is there.

She slaps away my hand hard enough to mean it.

"We need to talk."

"Later."

"No. We want to know who you really are."

"Sven," I tell her. "Sven Tveskoeg, lieutenant, Obsidian Cross second class."

For a second Shil looks as if she's about to punch me.

"Don't even think about it," I say, then grab her wrist before she can launch herself off the bed. She's fully dressed, which must mean I've been getting noticeably better.

"All right." My voice is resigned. "What do you want to know?"

When she turns it's her thinness I really notice. Her arms are shrunken and her wrist is sticklike beneath my grip; as for her face, it's made mostly from hollows.

"Have you been ill?"

She looks at me, and there's something dark in her eyes. "You've been gone for three weeks," she says. "It was a good choice. We've begun walling our dead into cellars to stop the living from eating them."

I remember soups and stale bread, softened in water.

"You gave me your food?"

"Everyone did," says Shil.

She pushes me back when I try to sit up. There's enough strength in my body to get past her, but I stay where I am and let Shil sit next to me. "No one had to give you their food," she says. "We chose. And we understand about the gate. It's just . . ."

"Say it."

"Haze says you're like him. NewlyMade."

"Bullshit."

"And Colonel Nuevo's been sending some kid hourly to see if you're awake and everyone says the Silver Fist will attack any day."

"The colonel?"

She nods, scowling.

"How's the weather?"

Shil looks puzzled by my change of topic, but something's been worrying away at the edges of my thoughts since I killed the seven-braid and I've just remembered what it is. Any attack on us is going to come before the river melts.

"It's getting warmer," she says.

"Get me my uniform and my gun."

My jacket's been washed and patched. Someone's pinned an enamel star onto my sleeve. Serious wound—I don't need a badge to remind me of that. Just putting my feet on the floor and trying to stand reminds me.

"About fucking time," says the gun as it swallows a battery pack. "Next time you go walkabout inside your own head, try feeding me first."

CHAPTER 43

FOUR OFFICERS I don't know guard the door to the old bank. They've all been awarded the Obsidian Cross third class. And I'm pretty sure that at least one of them was a corporal the last time our paths crossed.

Not good. In fact, so not good that I understand before I'm even through the door that we're into the end days, and Colonel Nuevo expects to lose. So do I, but it's the colonel's job not to let it show.

The officers salute.

I salute.

My gun snorts.

I start to give my name and rank, but the four know it already. The youngest knocks on the door, three raps, followed by two, followed by another three. As a piece of code or security mechanism it's worthless.

"The colonel will see you now."

A girl stands at the top of the stairs. She's beautiful; she's also roughly the same age as Franc and speaks the local patois. The kid should be keeping her distance from us because most of the inner city will soon discover that their lives depend on swearing they hate us, have always hated us, and have never collaborated in any way. Even that may not be enough to save them.

"Pretty," says my gun.

"The girl?" I ask, surprised.

"Her rig."

Looking closely, I can see she's wearing a neat little holster beneath her left arm; it obviously carries a very slim gun, because I'd missed it.

"Local?"

"Doubt it," my gun says. "Not built like that. Way too foxy."

It's still talking about the weapon.

"Come in," says a voice when I hammer on the colonel's bunker door.

Colonel Nuevo wears full military uniform. A silver stripe runs down the side of his dress trousers. Medals hang in an imposing row across his heart, and braid cascades down his chest; chain-mail epaulets protect each shoulder.

His rank is declared by his collar badges, while his Obsidian Cross first class hangs on a black ribbon around his neck.

"Join me," he says.

His first bottle is already empty, so the colonel pulls another from his desk. Someone's used my glass before me—maybe two or three people, judging by the overlapping fingerprints. The spirit is bitter, clear as ice, and so strong that inhaling its fumes makes my throat tighten.

"Got a room full of this stuff," he says. "I can spare you a few if you'd like. I mean"—Colonel Nuevo smiles almost happily—"it's not as if I'm likely to have time to drink it all."

On his desk is the same map as last time. Only it has significantly more glass stains and several more rows of crude blocking to indicate enemy rocket damage. We're surrounded. That is, enemy reserves have crossed the river. The colonel is carefully shading in enemy mortar positions; there are dozens of the bastards.

"Silver Fist hacked my slab," he says. "So now I use only this. Got to keep my plans secret."

I wonder about the girl, how much she sees and hears, where she lives, and who, if anyone, she tells . . . Not that it's going to make much difference. We're obviously fucked anyway, mere hours from a full-on attack.

"You stirred up a real hornets' nest," he says, "slotting that seven-braid. I'd award you a first-class Obsidian, but we're right out of those and you've already got a second."

Putting down my glass, I wait for whatever it is Colonel Nuevo really wants to say. The man's been sending messengers to my house for the best part of three weeks; there has to be more to this conversation than his current twittering.

"You kept me waiting."

"Sorry, sir. I was injured, sir."

Must be my tone that makes him look up. "Self-inflicted," he says. "You know the penalty for self-inflicted wounds." Pulling his pistol from its holster, he jacks the slide and checks the safety. Which is already off, or he wouldn't be able to jack the slide in the first place.

Colonel Nuevo really is very drunk.

"Going up against a seven-braid," he says, "sounds like a suicide attempt to me. Nothing brave about committing suicide."

"Except," I say, picking up my glass, "the seven-braid's dead. And I'm here, enjoying a drink with my commanding officer." The glass is cheap, which is good. It looks like it would break easily. Say, against the side of a desk or directly into an enemy's face.

And then there's my gun, which has unlocked without being asked and is doing its own version of a discreet vibrate against my hip. It sounds like a cheap tractor.

"Oh, for fuck's sake," says Colonel Nuevo. "Put down that glass and tell your bloody toy to go back to sleep. I haven't got enough officers left to kill any more of you."

We're headed for the heart of his bitterness.

"You know what my orders are?"

"Death or glory?"

"Of course . . ." Putting down his pistol, he pulls a small cylinder from his pocket and flips up its lid. The button is red. I'd always thought that was just a rumor. "Unfortunately," he says. "We're right out of glory. Which just leaves this."

Colonel Nuevo's thumb hovers over DESTRUCT.

"That's illegal technology," I say.

He nods. "Pretty, isn't it? Also effective . . . I can take the whole fucking city. Inside and outside, houses and temples, streets, boulevards, the lot."

He puts a mocking stress on *boulevards,* as if Ilseville is too poor, insignificant, and out of the way to have streets that qualify for a label so grand. He's right, of course. Maybe in a hundred or two hundred years it will have impressive buildings and smoked-glass palaces, but not yet.

"You want to do the job for me?"

I shake my head.

"Too bad," he says. "Because you're going to. That's a direct order." He puts the cylinder on his desk, reaches into a drawer, and pulls out an envelope. LAST DAYS, it says. I'm expecting code, something complicated that needs translating, but General Jaxx's instructions are uncoded.

"See," says Colonel Nuevo. "Hold the city or die."

And then he says something that makes me realize this man hates me and has probably always hated me; all that shit about liking me was lies. "You could do it," he says. "No problem. After all, you murdered Debro Wildeside's daughter."

I look at him.

"It was a test," he says. "You passed."

"Sir?"

The colonel shrugs. "If you can do that," he says, tossing me the DESTRUCT button, "I'm sure you can use this."

"Sven," says my gun.

But it's too late.

Opening his mouth, the colonel jams his own gun against its roof and yanks the trigger. Colonel Nuevo, leader of Octovian troops in Ilseville, has just shot himself rather than take it to the wire. He's also just broken the arm of a chair and knocked over his vodka bottle on the way down.

"Idiot," says the SIG.

Flicking my gun to fléchette, I target the door and catch the first of the running guards in my sights.

"Explosive," I tell him. "Burn you to a cinder."

He stays exactly where he is.

"Come in," I say. The three boys behind him enter without being told. All four line up against a wall on my order.

"We have a situation."

Shock keeps their faces slack. These are meant to be Death's Head officers, but I've seen better raw recruits.

"While drunk," I tell them, "the colonel slipped and shot himself."

"Fatally," adds my gun.

"This information is confidential. Understand? You will behave exactly as if Colonel Nuevo is alive. I want you standing guard at his door. Anyone wants to see the colonel, you come in, ask if he wants to see them, and then tell whoever is waiting that the colonel says come back tomorrow."

Four pairs of eyes watch me.

"You understand?"

All four boys nod.

"Good," I say.

Sitting at the colonel's desk, I fire up his slab and see that its power reserve is almost gone. So I keep the order brief. Each officer will prepare for the final attack, food is no longer to be hoarded, ammunition is to be shared, and all missing officers are to be replaced by NCOs. All missing NCOs will be replaced by promotion from the ranks. The battle for Ilseville's heart will be bloody. Whatever happens, we will go down fighting to the last man.

I certainly hope the colonel's pad has been hacked, because I want that order read by the Silver Head as much as I want it read by our own side.

CHAPTER 44

EVERY BELT-FED we own is up here on the city walls, with a thousand ammo belts waiting in open boxes. We have pulse rifles, pistols, and a handful of hunting crossbows. We even have fifteen rockets, although we'll probably fire those in the first ten minutes.

The attack comes at dawn, and I'm right about the rockets.

"Hostiles, two o clock . . ."

Behind me someone coughs. It's a gunnery officer, a second lieutenant twice my age and with probably three times my experience. Most of the Death's Head officers treat him as an irritating fool.

"Sir, is your man ready?"

"He'd better be," I say, casting a glance at Haze.

The boy nods, his head wrapped in a bloody towel. We've told everyone he's taken a head wound that won't stop bleeding; it's easier than trying to explain about the new-grown braids.

"Target and fire," the gunnery officer shouts.

A high fighter goes down, flames billowing as it hits marshland, and its fuel tanks burn up in one go. Two of our rockets miss other planes, and their targets withdraw.

"You okay?"

"Yes, sir." Haze wipes his mouth with the back of his hand and sips sugar water. He's pale as paper, and his eyes are washed-out ghosts of what they used to be. Shil, Neen, and Franc stand guard around him, which works for me and is better than having them trail me as I set off along the wall to check how things are going.

I'm Colonel Nuevo's eyes and ears, that's the official story. So far most officers seem to accept it. And the high fighter we've just downed goes a long way toward explaining the determination I find on most faces. A handful of women wait up on the walls, ready to be deployed as necessary.

"You know your orders?"

The snipers glance at one another.

"Yeah," I say. "Of course you fucking do. Now repeat them back to me."

"Kill anything that looks like it's wearing too much silver."

"Then go do it," I say, watching them lope away, rifles slung across their backs or carried cradled in their arms.

"A good sniper's worth ten generals," I say, repeating the old mantra.

"And a SIG diabolo's worth fifteen snipers," says a voice from my hip. "So I guess you just got lucky."

"Incoming," someone shouts behind me.

A batwing is headed in low.

"Mine," yells a blond kid with a pulse rifle. It's an impossible shot, only he's too inexperienced to realize this and takes it out first go. I'd like to say that was me once, turning red and shaking off the praise of his friends, but I'd be lying. I never had that many friends.

Yanking the Obsidian Cross from my neck, I toss it to the boy. "Now do it again."

He grins.

I'm walking down a run of steps when I see a sour-faced officer heading toward me. Captain Mye takes my salute as his due. "You've relayed my message?" he says.

"Yes, sir. The colonel notes your doubts about his strategy." Obviously untrue, but worrying enough to make any officer pause. Captain Mye wants to hold some of our ammunition in reserve.

"I'm thinking about tomorrow," he says.

"And if tomorrow never comes?"

He looks at me, so I stare back and my gun takes time out to remind us both there's a war on.

We hold the Silver Fist until dusk, and then half our troops rest while the other half stand guard. Those who can't sleep huddle in the shadow of the walls, warmed by fires made from old blankets, dead men's shoes, and broken ammo boxes. Our food is gone and we're reduced to scraping snow from the walls for water.

"Come on," says Shil when she tracks me down.

"Where?"

"Out of the wind."

I don't realize how cold I am until she herds me toward a small fire and Neen puts a cup of black coffee into my hands.

"Where did this come from?"

"Been saving it," says Franc. "Thought now might be a good time." She nods toward a pot balanced precariously in the ashes. At her side rests a whetstone, plus a collection of blades. She's been sharpening everyone's knives for them.

That's when I realize the Aux, at least, know what's coming.

"Grind me an edge," I tell her, extracting my Death's Head dagger from its sheath.

She takes the blade, flipping it over in her hand approvingly. "Sweet," she says.

"If I fall," I say, "it's yours . . ." And then, catching something in her eyes, I add, "But only if it's the enemy that kills me."

Franc smiles.

The days might be getting warmer but the nights are as cold as they ever were. A silver moon hangs above us, and thin clouds scud across a dark sky. Snipers on both sides break the silence, the crack of their shots more unnerving than the familiar bursts of automatic fire.

"Spy sat," Haze says suddenly.

My eyes open with a start. "Where?"

"Up there," he says, pointing to a purple speck overhead. It crosses the night sky like a windblown ember.

"Ours or theirs?"

"Neither," says Haze. "It's U/Free." He checks his slab. "Guess they want to make sure we die according to the rules."

THE SOUR-FACED CAPTAIN arrives at dawn, dragging two senior lieutenants behind him, and it looks to me like the delegation it is.

"Captain," I say, rising to my feet.

"Lieutenant," he says, then cuts to what matters. "Please tell Colonel Nuevo that we need to see him as soon as possible. All I can get from his staff is, *Come back tomorrow.*"

I'm still wondering how to handle this when a redheaded sniper rushes up, her hair blowing like banners in the wind. "Five-braid," she says. "Under a flag of truce. Demands to speak to you, sir."

Captain Mye's eyes narrow. "Did it ask for Lieutenant Tveskoeg by name?"

It seems the five-braid did.

She's old and simple in her augmentations. Her braids are less ornate and look more functional than those of any other silverhead I've seen. Also, she wears a uniform, which is unusual.

The silverhead is as tall as I am, and her boots are planted firmly on the dirt below her feet. The gate behind me is locked; a pulse rifle is trained on her head, its laser dot just visible in the early-morning light.

A dozen similar dots speckle my jacket; this is not a surprise. The surprise stands on either side of her. Two ferox, who watch me with sour grins. Their stink reminds me of the caves and tells me something about the silverhead. Either she's not as fastidious as most of her kind, or she's been around these beasts for long enough to be inured to their smell.

"That's a prohibited weapon," she says, nodding at the gun on my hip.

"So's that," I say, jerking my head toward the nearer ferox.

She smiles. "Five-braid Ison," says the woman, introducing herself.

"Sven," I say. "Lieutenant Sven Tveskoeg, Obsidian Cross second class."

Her eyes look for the medal, fail to find it, and flick to the ribbon tucked into my second buttonhole. That's interesting in itself.

"You killed General Lazlo?"

I nod. "Tough bastard," I tell her. "Died well."

Again that smile. "You can surrender to me," she says. "And I'll let the city stand. The alternative is I burn Ilseville to the ground."

"Everyone else goes free?"

Perhaps it was impolitic to sound so surprised, but I needn't be worried. The enemy general is laughing, and not pretend laughter, it's real. As if what I've just said is the funniest thing she's heard in a long time.

"No," she says, drawing breath. "The others do not go free."

"Then what do we gain?"

"We spare the city."

I shrug, wondering why she thinks rubble and broken houses worth saving. It's not even our planet, when you get down to it.

"The city stands and its people live . . ." Her eyes hold mine. "Perhaps I didn't make myself clear. Reject my offer and we will slaughter every living person in Ilseville. Soldiers, civilians, children, even the animals. All this you can prevent."

"And me?"

"You will die."

That much is obvious. "Where," I ask, "when, and how?" Not that it makes a difference.

"In the arena at Bhose. Before the eleven-braid."

I blink and catch one of the ferox watching me; his eyes are as dark as pits, his teeth yellow, and his armor cracked across the front.

An eleven-braid.

"General Lazlo was her brother," says the silverhead.

"I need three hours," I say. "While I talk to the colonel and he talks to his other officers."

"Our intelligence says Colonel Nuevo is dead."

"Then your intelligence is wrong." I look for some sign of doubt in the silverhead's face, but she's smiling again.

"You have thirty minutes," she says.

We compromise on an hour.

CAPTAIN MYE IS waiting on the other side of the gate, and I can sense the exact second the prickle of laser sights on my back is replaced by an identical prickle on my chest as half a dozen snipers check no one has come through with me.

"Well?" the captain demands.

Flicking my gaze toward the two officers behind him, I shake my head. He's meant to understand that what I have to say is not for them. Only they're his officers and he's unwilling to lose his audience.

"Tell me."

"We lay down our arms," I say. "Or face total annihilation. The Uplifted will burn this entire city, civilians and all. No one escapes."

"The colonel will never accept it."

"Let's ask him," I suggest.

At the captain's side one of his lieutenants nods.

CHAPTER 45

TAKING A demand for surrender to a ranking officer can be regarded as a bad career move for anyone hoping for a long-term military career. Such a point obviously occurs to Captain Mye, because he stops just before we reach the colonel's HQ and turns to me, his face serious.

"As his ADC," says the captain, "it's your job to tell Colonel Nuevo. Particularly since you were the one to negotiate with the silverhead."

So now it's a *negotiation.* I smile to show my understanding. "You'll be coming in with me, of course?"

Captain Mye decides this is acceptable.

The four guards on the door to the old bank are down to three. I consider asking what happened to the other one but let it go.

"Is the colonel busy?"

All three nod. The guards look scared and tired and so far out of their depth that they're drowning without even knowing it in a cesspit of betrayal and politics.

"You're relieved," I tell them.

It takes a moment for my words to sink in.

"Lose your medals and badges of rank, find a pulse rifle, and get yourself up to the walls. Mix with the others; go back to being ordinary soldiers. Steal a militia uniform if you can. That's an order."

"Yes, sir. Thank you, sir."

Their relief is obvious.

Inside Colonel Nuevo's HQ the pretty blond girl is gone and so are the colonel's cook, his maid, and all the food in his kitchen. Someone's let the fire go out in the boilers. So the captain and I go down to the strong room alone.

"Colonel?"

Pretending to hear an answer, I nod to myself and slide my way through a half-open door. "Shouldn't take long," I tell Captain Mye.

The stink inside is appalling. Shit stains the colonel's trousers, and what is left of his brains has liquefied and glued itself to the carpet. His watch cuts into a bloated wrist, and a rat has been chewing at his fingers.

I'd vomit, but I'm used to it.

On the table lies the canister with its lid still open and its red button waiting for my finger. I can return to five-braid Ison and blow her, the ferox, and most of her bloody army into small pieces. Of course, doing so will kill the Aux, what's left of our army, and every family still left in Ilseville, but that's war . . .

Or maybe it's politics.

As if one isn't just the flip side of the other.

Shutting the top, I twist a band that locks the lid into place and unscrew the base. A needle-thin hydrogen trigger drops onto the desk. I pocket it and reach deeper into the cylinder, hooking out the core with my bare fingers, and then I sit at the table, pull a piece of folded paper from my jacket, and write my own orders. After that there's only one more thing I need to do.

The single bullet I put into the ceiling ricochets off the strong room's underlying steel and damn near kills me.

"That was intelligent," says my gun.

What I say isn't for repeating.

"We surrender," I tell Captain Mye, showing him the paper.

"I heard . . ."

"A shot, yes. Colonel Nuevo has taken his own life." I shrug, as callously as possible. "Only to be expected in the circumstances."

"General Jaxx will require a second witness," says the captain, reaching around me for the door handle.

"Sir," I say.

He's halfway into the vault when he realizes what he sees. Captain Mye tries to turn back, but I'm one step ahead.

It takes death to wipe the shock from his face.

After wrapping the captain's hand around the grip of Colonel Nuevo's gun, I thread his finger through the trigger guard.

It looks like suicide to me.

ON HEARING COLONEL Nuevo's decision, Five-braid Ison gives us until the following dawn to prepare our surrender. I reckon she needs that long to round up a decent collection of lenz, observers, and U/Free data collectors.

Her demands are simple: We will surrender. All weapons will be given up. Any shot fired in anger will be regarded as having been fired by all. The Death's Head are to abandon Ilseville as individuals. No marching and no massed ranks. The galaxy will see a shambling defeated mass, stumbling gratefully toward captivity.

In the hours that remain I disband the Aux and give each a handful of coins taken from Colonel Nuevo's strong room. My final order is simple: They will destroy their alligator-skin patches.

They are local militia, pressed into service by me. Their gratitude at being rescued by the Enlightened knows no bounds.

A hundred scores are settled that night. A group of militia trap three Death's Head in an alley, kicking two of them to death. If they'd killed all three they might have gotten away with it. But five Death's Head walk into the militia camp less than an hour later and gun down a dozen soldiers in revenge.

The first night in a month that the enemy aren't trying to kill us, and we're busy killing ourselves. Tomorrow we surrender, without honor, without being allowed to retain our weapons, and with helmets held in our hands as we leave the city.

News grabs of Ilseville's fall will spread everywhere.

The U/Free already know. Their observer general left the inner city this afternoon, given safe passage and an honor guard by the Enlightened. They're playing it safe, the Uplifted; showing how civilized they can be. All those rumors of mass slaughter and cities burned are lies, obviously. *Look at us,* their actions say. *How can you compare us to the Death's Head? In what way are we like OctoV?*

In the meantime we are destroying ourselves in a frenzy of fear, hatred, and retribution, and you can bet the U/Free know that, too.

When the time comes, I go join the defeated.

I give Franc my dagger. My gun I leave with Haze.

CHAPTER 46

FIVE-BRAID ISON flies out half an hour after we surrender. Before she goes, Ison makes a speech for the gathered lenz about inviolable borders, territorial integrity, and what happens to people who underestimate the Uplifted. The speech is addressed to OctoV; at least that's what she says, although it sounds more like it is addressed to the U/Free to me.

And then, with Ison gone, we're herded into a column and told we're to march south, toward the harbor at Mica and waiting transport. This is where we've been heading ever since.

Anger keeps me from stumbling. Anger and common sense, self-preservation and pride. Our column's been on the road for five days now, marching into sleet and a poor pretense for snow, as if chasing the last echoes of winter. The sick and the wounded, the starving and the weak fall daily, shot through the head or trampled under the unthinking boots of those behind.

"*Move,*" I snarl at the woman beside me.

Dragging my boots, I force one foot in front of the other and keep walking through the mud, despite the fact I'm supporting the red-headed sniper, although *almost carrying* probably describes it better.

Who knows what her name is? She fell fifteen minutes ago. So a Silver Fist officer upended her, raised her buttocks into the air, and took her at the roadside, putting his pistol to the back of her skull before he'd even withdrawn.

And then he caught me watching.

"You going to carry her?"

Stupidity made me say, "Yes."

So now I'm carrying a sobbing woman who wants to know why I didn't just let the bastard kill her.

We sleep beside a ditch, tentless and without food, while our Silver Fist friend inflates a bubble tent and eats self-heating ration packs. Uplift rations are probably as vile as our own, but hunger gnaws at my guts like a fox and I'd eat pretty much anything.

"Fuck off," says the sniper.

So I do, all of ten paces.

This takes me to the very edge of the laser fencing. There's no real reason for the corral the Silver Fist construct, because we're too shattered to think about escaping, and there's nowhere for us to go anyway.

The silence is what gets me.

Guns and rockets, mortar rounds and snatches of small-arms fire have become so much a soundtrack to my life that their absence shocks me more than any noise. Only when some guard shoots a straggler does my day feel vaguely normal. When I mention this to the sniper she stares at me strangely. This may be why she won't look at me anymore.

We stink, all of us.

Shit, sweat, death, and defeat, who knew they smelled so similar?

I miss my gun and its arrogance. We do what we do, we do it well, and no one else comes close. Maybe its arrogance merely matches my own.

The next day the sniper walks for an hour almost unaided, and then tries to sit. Hooking my arm under hers, I drag her to her feet and make her keep walking. Her punches are so weak they don't even bruise me. Around this time I remember to ask her name. Rachel.

"Well, fucking walk," I tell Rachel.

Anger's good. It gets her through to the evening.

Mornings turn to afternoons and get swallowed by the night. But the successive nights do little to dampen Rachel's misery. One time, a couple of guards come by with flashlights in their hands and rape on their minds. A single look at the state of her is enough to make them go elsewhere.

Come dawn, there's another woman crying and a man dead, his head smashed and blood crusting his mouth. A boy offers to help bury him, but we move off before the job is done.

Anyone else would have dropped Rachel by now, and I know the Silver Fist are placing bets on how long I can keep going. Most of them have already lost, which probably explains the viciousness of their passing kicks.

Night comes around again, the eighth . . . at least I think it's the eighth. Tents go up and the enemy eat, leaving only a handful of guards to erect the laser fencing that keeps us secure. Our hunger makes their job easier by the day.

"Get up," I tell Rachel when dawn arrives.

"Piss off."

I slap her so hard I have to carry her for the rest of that day, although she regains consciousness around noon. The Silver Fist who are still in on the bet think it's hilarious.

Personally, I hope to see them all dead.

The next morning is much the same. I want Rachel to get up; she wants me to fuck off and die . . . Sheer obstinacy stops me from leaving her. Rachel's alive and she's bloody well going to stay that way.

"Stand," I say, twisting my fingers into her hair.

Shadows shift behind me, and I turn expecting to see a guard. Only it's someone else entirely.

"Hi," says Shil. "Still relying on your charm?"

Having sworn loudly enough to make a Silver Fist look around, I stamp my anger into silence and take a deep breath, then another.

"All right," says Shil. "You've made your point. You're really fucking pleased to see me."

"I told you to stay behind."

"No. You said I wasn't Aux, remember?"

"Yeah."

"So," she says. "Who the fuck are you to tell me what to do anyway?" She glares past me to where Rachel sits. "Do you want help with her or not?"

Around us the defeated are picking up their packs, struggling into sodden boots and forcing themselves to their feet. A few are glaring in undisguised hatred at the Silver Fist, but most are too hollow-eyed to care.

"As long as it doesn't void their bet," I say.

Shil looks at me strangely. "You've been close to dropping her," she says, "for a couple of days now."

"What's that got to do with it?"

Hoisting Rachel between us, we set off in silence along a track that barely qualifies as a road, and as the sun reaches the high point of its journey—roughly as high as a tree on the horizon, had any trees been able to grow in this wilderness—right around then Neen and Franc appear behind us, position themselves on either side of Rachel, and release us from her burden.

"Fantastic," I say. "Don't tell me . . ."

"Yeah," says Neen. "Good to see you, too."

He's taller than I remember, even thinner. His shaggy mop has been cropped to the skull and he's back in uniform, complete with Death's Head patch made from alligator skin. So are the others, I realize, even Maria. Only Haze wears militia uniform, with a fat cap pulled down tight over his ears.

"How are you handling the . . ."

He glares at me, almost tripping over his feet as he turns his attention from the road. "By not thinking about it."

Our column is now a third of the length it was when it set out from Ilseville. No lenz line this road to record us. Our surrender was news; our march to the coast at Mica is a given. At most a few families turn out from their farms to watch us pass. They look like everyone else on this planet: badly dressed, damp, and cold.

A woman gives Franc soup and is sworn at by a guard.

She swears back and three men from her village suddenly appear behind her, which is interesting. The Uplifted might hold this planet, but it seems they still have hearts and minds to gather in.

Sipping from the cup, Franc smiles her thanks. When I look again, she's given the cup to Haze.

That night we make a fire from scraps of wood and huddle around it while Rachel tells her story. It's depressingly familiar. A daughter when she should have been a son, she fills a quota for conscripts that her brother is still too young to fill for himself. Her biggest mistake is having proved useful with a gun.

"Only," says Rachel, "I'm not going to swap sides again." It takes me a moment to realize what she means.

"You were . . . ?"

"Uplift militia, before I joined this lot."

"So were we all," says Franc. I'm still considering this casual revelation of treason, when Franc adds, "And we're not going to keep swapping until we're dead. We plan to escape."

Rachel looks interested. "How are you intending to do that?"

"No idea," says Franc. "Shil thought Sven might know."

Laughing is probably the wrong response, but since the alternative is swearing at them for a bunch of idiots it's the best I can offer.

CHAPTER 47

SEVEN CARGO ships lie at anchor in Mica Harbor. They're old, badly maintained, and rusting. Oxide inhibitor has been spray-gunned across their sides and left unpainted, a tattered flag flaps from each stern, and ropes run from high on deck to rusting bollards on the jetty below.

From where we stand to the headland opposite is five miles. Marching around the fjord's edge would mean navigating a shoreline twisty enough to be almost fractal. We might walk it in a week if we were lucky. So we're about to make an eight-hundred-mile journey in those ships, down the coast from here to Bhose.

There's only one problem.

Six of these ships are not going to arrive.

It's looking at the last of them that tells me this. Whoever spray-gunned the *Winter Wind* with oxide inhibitor was wasting his time, because it's obvious that the steel was already fine. In fact, the vessel is newer than the other six by several years, if not decades. We're meant to look at these and see seven rust buckets. And from the swearing of the prisoners around me that's exactly what most of them are seeing.

"What's wrong?" asks Shil.

"I'm not sure yet, but something's badly wrong. We're going to need weapons."

Haze and Franc glance at each other, then look away.

"What?" I demand, calling them on it.

Franc goes red, but Haze stares back with eyes that are almost hollow. I've no idea where he is, but it's obviously not anywhere that the rest of us would recognize.

"I'm a weapon," he says finally. "And so are you."

I sigh. "Anyone got a knife? Anything useful at all?"

"What do you want?" asks Rachel.

"A gun," I tell her. "But I'll settle for a blade."

She walks away without another word. Her red hair is simplicity itself to follow through the crowd as she heads toward a pair of Silver Fist. One of them turns to see who it is and smiles a particularly nasty smile. His arm reaches out to catch her, and Rachel allows herself to be caught.

"That's the bastard who . . ."

"Yes," says Shil, cutting short my outrage. "We know."

AMBER AND ARTIFACTS announces a sign above the men. As we watch, one of them tries a door behind him, finds it locked, and leads Rachel around to the side of the warehouse, although *drags her* might be a better description. The second Silver Fist stands watch, leaning against a wall.

About five minutes later he turns in response to something unseen and vanishes around the corner. When Rachel returns it's from a different direction and her mouth is bleeding, but not enough to keep a smile from her lips.

"You okay?" asks Haze.

"Sure."

"What happened?" he says, and then blushes.

"Nothing like that," she replies.

Franc's laugh is sour. "Don't tell me. They got more than they expected?"

"Yeah," says Rachel. "If rather less than they hoped." Tucked under her jacket are a pistol, two knives, and an ID card made out in the name of Sergeant Zil Lanlyr.

There's blood on the blade of one of the knives. I don't know what the glance that passes between Shil and Rachel actually means, and I don't want to. At the moment I'm just glad they're both on my side.

GUARDS JOSTLE PRISONERS up the gangway onto the first ship. When the lower levels have filled and even the deck is crowded, the gangplank is dragged along the jetty to the next ship, which fills just as swiftly.

And then the gangplank is dragged to the third and fourth ships. A group of Silver Fist begin cutting prisoners out of the crowd for the fifth ship and one of them reaches for me, only to be slapped down by his sergeant.

"Leave him."

The trooper is that much rougher with the next few prisoners he cuts out of our dwindling crowd. When the fifth ship is full, the gangplank is moved again and most of what remains of the defeated is herded onto the ship after that. A corporal grabs at Rachel, who backs away as Haze steps between them.

The corporal looks shocked, obviously unsure which of the two to deal with first. Reaching around me, he chooses Rachel. So I grip his wrist, swing him around, and put him into the side of a crane. Only I keep hold of his wrist, so his shoulder dislocates with a wet sucking sound.

He howls.

One of the other guards is reaching for his own holster when an officer appears, his fists already clenched. His punch flattens the injured corporal, dropping him into the dirt, and then a pistol is in his hand and its muzzle is touching my forehead.

"Come on," I tell him. "Pull the fucking trigger."

Neen is moving forward but freezes at the shake of my head. This is a test and I'd better be right, because otherwise I'm dead.

"Well?" I say. "You got the guts?"

The lieutenant backs away, pistol still raised and pure hatred in his eyes. This man would kill me if he hadn't been told that was somebody else's job.

"These are the Aux, they're with me, okay?" My gesture takes in Neen and the others, including Rachel, who looks terrified.

"Okay?"

He nods, not quite meeting my eyes.

"So we're back in business?" says Franc.

"Yeah," I tell her. "My own personal supply of cannon fodder."

She grins, knowing it's not a joke.

WE'RE ABOUT TO be loaded onto the only ship out of the seven that is actually seaworthy. Haze and I are standing near the gangway, staring out at an oily swell of Mica Harbor with its local boats and old steamers and fishermen keeping well away from whatever the hell is going on along their quayside.

Storm clouds are gathering on the horizon, the sea swell is higher than when we first arrived, and waves are beginning to fray in the wind. It might be coincidence that brings us to this place tonight, or it might be perfect planning. Either way the Enlightened have what they need: A storm is about to roll right over us.

All soldiers believe in luck, which is just skill used wisely. And there are things I can and will do without even thinking about them to put luck back on our side, vicious and bloody things.

Only they're not going to be enough on their own.

"Haze," I say. "A question."

His eyes go wide, and then his mouth goes tight. He knows he's not going to like what I'm about to ask.

"How good are you really?"

He wants to pretend he doesn't understand. Failing that, he wants to lie . . . Instead he changes the subject. "You still haven't told the others what's going to happen to you in Bhose."

"Haven't told you, either."

A scowl crosses his face. "The arena," Haze says. "Facing two ferox."

"You can see the future?"

"Dreams," he says, adding, "not mine . . ." And then Haze hesitates, wondering how to say what comes next. "There's a three-braid around here somewhere. He's been thinking about little else."

"Fuck."

Haze nods. "One other thing. The three-braid is scared. I couldn't get away with staying shielded if he wasn't. It's that soft tech in your throat; he's worried it's going to reboot."

"Doubt it," I tell Haze. "My body fucks with implants."

"It's not your body that's the problem."

"What is it then?"

"Your mind," Haze says. "Fix that and you won't need my help."

CHAPTER 48

DEEP IN the belly of our ship the engines start, and the deck beneath our feet begins to shudder. One of the vessels ahead of us is having trouble. A dull thud announces that its engine is turning over but refuses to fire.

One of their officers says something to an NCO. We hear the engine start about three minutes later, and when the NCO returns he's rubbing his fist.

"Belowdecks," an enemy corporal tell us.

The others look at me.

"Do what he says."

Behind me someone laughs, so I turn to face him. It's a Death's Head captain I don't recognize, wearing full combat ribbons.

"Got a problem?"

"I outrank you," he says.

"So fucking what?" asks Neen, and the others laugh.

Part of me is appalled; part of me knows it's exactly the sort of thing I'd have said at Neen's age, although my insubordination was confined to sergeants. Mind you, back then I still believed lieutenants were godlike.

Belowdecks the bulkhead is clean and the grating over which we're led is freshly scrubbed. Inset lights indicate routes for escape and entry, and the crew move from job to job with cold efficiency. This is a military vessel. Probably armed to the teeth and undoubtedly crewed by professionals.

"In there," orders the guard.

Seven clicks follow as electronic locks engage. It's time to ask if anyone else has a weapon, and if the enemy are listening in on us, then that's just too bad.

Blank faces greet my question.

"Come on," I say. "Who's carrying?"

At a nod from Neen, first Shil and then Franc put up their hands. He's learning fast. As I told Shil way back, the boy's a natural.

"What have you got?"

Shil produces a dagger and Franc reaches into her top, palming a blade. It's only when Rachel produces another dagger that I realize Franc has been carrying her weapon all along.

"Let me see."

It's my Death's Head dagger, still oiled and razor-sharp.

Turning her back, one of the younger women reaches under her skirt and produces a blade. It's crude and cut from cheap steel, but she's ground the edge as fine as it can go and the point is vicious enough to pierce everything but body armor.

Four knives.

"Anyone else?"

"I've got this." It's one of the militia sergeants with a flip-out cosh. "But it's not going to be enough. We need a gun, at least."

His eyes widen as my hand dips into a pocket and I produce the pistol Rachel stole from the Silver Fist on the quayside.

"Very pretty," says the captain. "But we've still got a locked door. And why would they follow you anyway? If you hadn't killed the seven-braid, Colonel Nuevo could have negotiated a proper withdrawal."

"OctoV kills people who retreat." My voice is matter-of-fact.

"Our dear emperor is three crystals short of an Uplift."

The captain is upset, that much is obvious. Too upset, it seems to me.

And how the fuck does he know it was a seven-braid anyway? It's not like Colonel Nuevo advertised the fact widely. And then there are those medals. You can't have ribbons for two battles fought the same week on opposite sides of the spiral arm, it's just not possible . . .

"Traitor," I say, stepping forward.

His neck snaps so easily that I'm lowering his body to the ground before most people have come to grips with the fact that I've moved.

"God bless OctoV," I tell the room.

Whatever Haze sees on my face is not what everyone else sees, because he smiles. "We need to talk," he suggests.

MY CONVERSATION WITH Haze is brief and to the point. The kyp in my throat is dying, but because symbionts are hard to kill, its death is eating up my body's resources and leaching power where it can. I can embrace the soft tech or die myself: Those are the only two choices open to me.

"Why didn't you tell me before?"

"Didn't know you well enough," says Haze, and I realize how private a person he really is.

It seems my metabolism is at war with something that has already tuned itself to my mental frequency and grown suckers that now reach into my brain and wrap my spinal cord like ivy.

Haze doesn't call them suckers, he calls them dendritic spurs, but they sound like suckers to me. "These things," I say. "How are they captured?"

"Sven," he says.

Haze shouldn't be calling me *Sven,* but I let it go.

"They're grown. Kyps combine a viral matrix with a gene-spliced leech. They're not alive in any sense you'd understand."

"It sounds like Uplifted technology."

"Yes," says Haze. "It is."

A dozen people are watching our intense, half-whispered conversation, so I wait while Haze takes a deep breath to steady himself. "OctoV," he says. "You know what he is?"

I give our beloved leader his titles, rolling the words off my tongue as newscasts always give them, a long list of grandiose phrases stripped of meaning by overuse. Haze checks to see if I'm serious.

"OctoV is an Uplifted," he says.

It comes as less of a surprise than it should.

"We're soldiers in a war fought by machines," says Haze. "Well, augmented hive mind composites." Seeing from my face that he's lost me, he simplifies. "OctoV is the rebel; the Uplifted are original. They began as machines for the Enlightened, but things changed."

I should have known this from the fleeting visit OctoV paid my mind in Farlight. So cold, so distant, so obviously not the heroic child emperor of his own homespun legend.

My decision makes itself.

We're here; we need to be somewhere else. OctoV or the Uplifted, it's not much of a choice, but it's the only choice we have, because the great and the good of the U/Free are not about to take us in. And since we're already on OctoV's side, we might as well stay there.

"The kyp," I say. "What do I need to do?"

"Stop trying to kill it."

"That's my body," I tell him.

Haze shakes his head. "It's your mind." His smile is sour, and in his gaze I can see the man behind the boy; the power he will become if he lives that long. Haze is no more human than I am . . .

And as I stumble over that thought, light floods through my skull and Haze locks me down so hard and so fast that I stumble, both hands clutching my head. Shil is moving toward me before I can wave her away, but Haze does it for me.

"Leave him," Haze says.

My mind is a circular wall collapsing under the waves that suddenly hit it: readouts from my own body, levels of tiredness, stamina, and battle damage. Apparently I'm in a lot better shape than I thought, and half my danger levels haven't even been approached, ever.

And then, as my thoughts stabilize, the wall fades and there's another in its place, only this time the wall is mine, and the wall Haze originally erected tightens to enclose only him, and then it's gone. Although Haze still stands in front of me, his hand under my elbow as I struggle to stand.

"Lock it down," says Haze.

So I do. It's odd taking orders from someone who takes orders from me, but he's right and I need to be invisible to anybody searching for wave echoes in whatever dimension it is I now inhabit.

"What the fuck just happened?" Shil demands.

"He became a god," Haze tells her. The boy's only half joking.

I shake my head, realizing something. "Angel, maybe . . . demon, possibly. But we're not gods; none of us comes close to that level."

"You became an angel?" says Rachel.

"Not really," I say. "I just became a better fighting machine."

"Speaking of which," says Haze. "I've got a present for you." Turning his back on the room, he undoes his jacket and shirt, then untapes a package wrapped in strange silver cloth from his chest.

"This is yours," he says, untying it.

"Too right," says my gun. "Try not to lose me again."

CHAPTER 49

SINCE A crowd is now gathered around me, I tell them the truth. That the six ships with which we travel will never arrive and nothing we can do will save them.

As if on cue, sound waves shake the bulkhead and I understand instantly that this is not coincidence. I just read the signature of a rocket nearing its target half a mile away.

A second explosion follows, and then a third. The fourth explosion comes as a flat inevitability, and it's not only the militia who are upset by the time the fifth and sixth vessels explode. Most of us had friends or colleagues on those boats.

"Why?" someone demands.

"Because everyone the Uplifted want is already here," I say.

"That's true," says Haze. "The rest was just window dressing." Anger shows in his eyes, a bitter hatred toward those who created him.

We're twenty-five people at the most. A hundred thousand made that drop, back in the days before I created the Aux, when my future was a simple case of *Hit the ground, shoot anything that isn't us, and keep shooting until I'm dead or there's only us left.*

"Listen." I tell them. "You think you're going to be left alive if you behave yourself? You're wrong. If they don't kill you, I will . . . We're going to fight, all of us. And we're going to win."

I'm manipulating them, obviously. But I'm also manipulating myself, and trying to find my old anger. Only it's gone, replaced by a cold clarity that terrifies me.

"Haze," I say. "Take the perimeter."

Whatever he's about to say is swallowed when he sees me glare.

"Just do it," I tell him.

To the others, I say, "I'm going to unlock the door."

Shil's staring at me as if I'm mad, and Neen can't work out why I've replaced him with Haze, and I don't have time to explain that I haven't.

Turning from Haze, I face the entire room.

"Shut up and listen."

We're in semi-darkness. The locker room is large, steel-floored, and lit from the ceiling by flat sheets of luminex, which release something close to twilight. Maybe their psy-ops experts think this will make us less likely to resist. If so, we're about to prove them wrong.

"We fight now, or we all die later anyway." They're listening; the threat of death usually does that to people.

"Haze, tell them why."

"Mostly you know something the Uplifted think is useful," says Haze. "Get lucky and they'll rip your minds. Unlucky, they'll rip your bodies first, because it's a quicker way to extract information."

"Either way," I tell them. "You're fucked."

"Believe it," says my gun.

People are shaking their heads and sucking at their teeth, the things crowds do when hearing truths they'd rather ignore. "Anybody here think that's a lie?" My gaze sweeps the room.

No one does.

"So," I say. "This is what's going to happen . . . I'm going to get us out of here, and this man is going to protect me while I do it."

Being close to the dead bolts has nothing to do with what's about to happen, but all the same I walk across to the door and put my hands on either side of the lock plate.

"Ready?" I ask Haze.

A wall of silence enfolds my mind almost before he nods.

I can see the inside of the door, examine how it fits together: The sheet ceramic is bonded to a honeycomb of high-tensile carbon fullerenes. The lock operates electronically, with a manual override set into the wall on the far side of the door.

Schematics lay themselves over everything that falls under my gaze, and I'm giving myself a headache until I blink a map away and realize the overlays can be summoned and dismissed at will.

Seven bolts click, snapping themselves back into the frame around the door.

"Impressive," says Haze. "You check the corridor outside?"

When I shake my head his face blanks momentarily.

"Clear," he says.

The steps on this ship are steep, like someone forced stairs and ladders to breed, then welded their bastard offspring to the walls. There's a sailor at the top of the first set of steps, but he's facing away from us.

He's alone, says Haze.

Hooking my hands around the man's ankles, I jump backward, landing cleanly fifteen feet below. His own landing is much messier. Somewhere in the drop, his head clips the edge of a step and renders the knife in my hand redundant.

Neen carries the man back to the locker room. In his pockets are a knife, a pistol, a cosh, and a half-finished bar of chocolate. Around his neck is a medal of Legba Uploaded. Finding it upsets Neen, who wears one very similar.

"*Many names,*" Haze says. "*Many faces.*"

Neen repeats the mantra, and somehow that makes it all right. Although letting Maria have the chocolate probably helps.

"You want to go fishing again?" asks Haze.

"No." I shake my head. "That's enough for now. Find me the armory."

By now I'm getting used to seeing his face blank. It's not something I want to start doing myself. That level of disengagement could get you killed in battle. Also, my party trick with the door has left me feeling as if I've just run five miles straight up the side of a mountain, carrying a rucksack full of rocks.

"One level down," says Haze.

"Let's go."

I take point, Shil goes second. We're armed; I have two knives and my gun stuck in my belt. Its combat chip is shut down for the moment, so Haze and I don't have to waste energy shielding it.

The SIG's not amused.

But then it doesn't see why we need additional weapons anyway, given we already possess the smartest gun ever made . . .

"Modest, too," says Shil.

Haze and Maria follow behind Neen, with Franc bringing up the rear and Rachel walking just ahead of her.

The rest remain exactly where they are. There are two things interesting about this. One, the Aux still operate as a tightly knit group. And two, the others do what we tell them, outranked by us or not.

We're Death's Head. Worse than that, we're running some juju shit routine obviously stolen straight from the Enlightened.

"Cover me," I tell Haze.

He locks down the ceiling cameras so they replay the same endless loop of safe nothing as we head down a level. And as I touch my fingers to the armory door, Haze spins a wall around my mind that's cold and white and hard-edged, like ice or frosted glass. The door is semi-sentient. I'm still considering this when I realize that I can simply kill the door at a local level while leaving fail-safes and complicity algorithms in place.

Complicity what?

Except I'm inside the armory and no longer care. Wall-to-wall pulse rifles, maritime issue; a couple of belt-feds, although they're too heavy for anyone but me to hoist, and anyway a belt-fed without a tray is an invitation to trip over your own feet and shoot the ceiling.

And then I see something really interesting.

"What?" demands the gun.

"Over there."

It scans the armory, its humor worsening as it sees what I do.

A permanent-fire pulse gun, aka *the cinder maker.*

The cinder maker is slate gray, with a small red dot for a sight and laser optics and aimer slung in an elegant tube under the barrel. The power pack is a fat disk hung just in front of the trigger. The barrel is midlength, the muzzle narrow. The handle can rotate three clips in case permanent pulse is inappropriate. It has to be the most beautiful weapon I've ever seen.

"Cheap shit," says my SIG. "Vulgar design. Probably jam on you first time out. Can't imagine why anyone would want one."

"But with a real fuck-off power pack."

"Worthless."

"So you don't want to transfer?" says Haze.

"Can't be done," my gun says. "Utterly incompatible."

"But if it could?"

Haze knits code to make the cinder maker accept the SIG's character base while I lash up a physical fix. Given my newfound knowledge and some of the shit I had to mend back in the legion, making a Colt SW 37-12 accept the diabolo's combat chip is practically child's play. I add a fold-down wire stock almost without thinking, checking that it flips down easily and folds up again without a problem.

We've just created the SW SIG-37 diabolo, the galaxy's first fully intelligent machine pistol, with added stock and cinder gun capability. Although that's nothing like as impressive as the other thing we've done, which is reduce my gun to silence.

"You're grinning," Shil says.

We leave the armory with enough weapons slung around our necks to start a small war—which is the plan. Haze does his trick with the cameras and we're back at the locker room within minutes.

"Here," says Neen. "Take a weapon."

Everyone wants a pulse rifle, even those who've never been near one. I make them all take knives as well, for hand-to-hand. And then the Aux stick half a dozen knives in our belts and lanyard a couple of pistols around our necks. We don't need them, but we're already living up to our own myth.

"I'll go first . . ."

Neen's words are half boast and half plea. He requires telling about Haze, because so far Neen thinks we just got lucky in the corridor. And though he knows Haze is different, he has no idea how different. Also, I don't have time for this.

"Stand back while I talk to my sergeant."

People do as they're told.

"If I go down," I tell Neen. "You're fucked."

My own sergeant glares at me.

"But if that does happen," I say, "you lead the Aux. Because you're the best combat grunt in this room. Not that you have much competition. Apart from Franc, and she's a basket case."

A grin lifts his face.

"You take command and you take my rank." I explain about the cameras, about how my trick with the lock is sleight of hand compared with the power Haze displays every time he throws up a mental wall.

"We're going to win this," I tell him.

"You really think so?"

"Too fucking right," I say. "Even if we all get killed doing it."

Neen laughs.

CHAPTER 50

EVERYONE LISTENS as I tell them about Neen taking my place if I go down, and though a scowl flicks across the face of a couple of militia officers no one objects. We've given these guys guns and jacked the door to what was their cell. And more to the point, we represent hope for them.

A stinking, badly dressed, and forlorn hope, but hope all the same.

"This is Haze," I say, introducing him. "He's got more shit in his head than you've got in your guts and he's my intelligence officer. If you haven't heard about people like him that's because you're a bunch of ignorant grunts.

"Haze," I say. "Find out where we need to be."

His face blanks for a second.

"This side," he says. "Three levels up, a hundred paces forward. The ship's on automatic." He hesitates, and then he's back. "There are thirteen people between here and the control center."

"You heard the man," I tell the Aux. "That's where we're going."

"How many on the ship altogether?" asks Neen.

"Fifty-eight," Haze says without vanishing. He obviously found this figure earlier. Glancing at me, he asks, "Do we do this noisy or silent?"

"Both."

A knife takes the first guard in the back. It's a clean kill as Neen rams his blade neatly between two ribs and shocks a man's heart into silence. He kills two more in quick succession, both silently.

All's going well, much too well. It doesn't last.

We're one level above where we were, and our next target is the set of steps when a three-braid suddenly appears.

"Fuck," says Haze, sounding really upset with himself.

The braid shouts. He also hits a panic button, and Shil and Franc both fire, fingers hard on their triggers as they fry the braid back to a greasy shadow on the steps behind.

Unfortunately the siren keeps yowling.

Boots slapping, Neen reaches the steps first, firing from the hip. I want to be ahead of him, but things are unraveling too fast for me to get there in time. Five enemies down leaves eight out of thirteen. Except other doors are now opening and a Silver Fist is screaming orders somewhere nearby.

A hand grips my arm.

I punch Haze without thinking. I'm not angry with him, I don't think he should have protected me better, I'm just ramped on violence and my reflexes are way ahead of my thoughts. It's all I can do to pull the second blow.

"My mistake," I say.

Climbing to his feet, Haze grabs me again. Tears mix with blood from his broken mouth, while his eyes flick in and out of focus as he tries to explain.

"I'm sorry," he says.

"Leave it."

"She uncloaked. I wasn't ready."

Grabbing him in my turn, I flip him around and realize he's afraid of me. That's fine, I'm afraid of me. He's also afraid of where he finds himself, of whatever the fuck is going on inside his head and whoever just uncloaked. But he's holding it. I mean, he's unraveling in front of me, but he's holding the wall.

"Who uncloaked?"

"She's here," says Haze. "On this ship."

"Who is here?"

"Duza, the eleven-braid."

I let Haze go and lean him against the bulkhead. There's a firefight on the level above, but this needs saying. "Listen," I tell him. "No one else could do what you've done."

Without even realizing it Haze wipes blood from his mouth with the back of his hand and something toughens in his voice. "Whatever it takes."

Yeah. He's got that right. "Get me to the control room."

"If I do," he says, "I'll have to drop the shields on everybody else. Duza will know how many there are . . . and where they are."

"Just do it."

Pulse fire rages on the level above. Shil and the others have vanished; only a handful of militia remain at the foot of the steps. They're armed but scared, and now that I've noticed them they're more scared still.

"Get up there and die," I tell them.

They do what they're told.

When I hit the top of the stairs, I realize that the only thing we have in our favor is the sheer bloody-mindedness of Shil and Neen, who are flat on the floor, ripping pulse shots into any Silver Fist stupid enough to stick his head around a corner in the corridor.

Against us we've got numbers, training, and better armor.

At least we've got these against us right up to the point I unholster my pistol and tell it to max out its combat potential.

"You're on."

"About fucking time." Scanning the corridor, the newly uprated SW SIG-37 runs through a dozen loading options in a split second, although my money's on it choosing cinder maker.

I mean, why else would I be lugging three power packs?

One pack lasts seventy-six hours under normal combat conditions, or so it says on the label. My bet is we can burn our way through all three before this is over.

"Stay down."

Fire sweeps the corridor above Neen's head.

When I glance back, Rachel and Maria are kneeling behind me to fill in the gaps, only there aren't any gaps because the SW SIG-37 spits a single line of plasma that melts metal and cuts ceramic as cleanly as a hot wire through butter.

The SW SIG-37 is practically singing to itself as it burns a hole in an armored steel wall for the hell of it, then rips out a section of ceiling.

"Move," it tells me.

But I'm doing that already.

We hit the corner at a run, roll sideways, and burn the passage ahead, incinerating five or six guards. Luck is on our side, or maybe it's simple insanity. Lenz above us are swiveling frantically and I take them out, then burn the luminex panels, throwing the area ahead into darkness.

"Fuck," Shil says.

"Follow me."

The SW SIG-37 lights our way. It also gives the Silver Fist something to aim at, but none of them comes close to getting off a shot.

"Five o'clock . . ."

"Four o'clock, low . . ."

"Twelve o'clock . . ."

My reactions are so fast I'm tearing my own muscles, though I've long since ceased to care. I'm happy to sacrifice every single person this side of the line, including myself, to take out an eleven-braid.

"Sniper on the roof," someone shouts.

There is no roof, but old phrases die hard and a shot zaps from an air duct in the corridor beyond.

"Mine," says the gun.

A burst of plasma drops a cindered body to the deck below. Molten ceiling sets in a splatter pattern around it.

"Maria's down, sir." The voice belongs to Shil.

"How bad?"

Her eyes flick to where Neen crouches beside his lover. He's draped his jacket over Maria's lower half, not a good sign. He has one of Maria's hands folded into his own; in his other hand is a dagger.

"Cover me," I tell Shil.

To Neen, I say, "You want me to do it?"

He shakes his head. "My job."

As I turn back, Neen jabs the blade under her ribs and takes Maria through the heart. When he looks up there's a blackness in his eyes.

"Clean kill," I tell him, clapping him on the shoulder. "No one can ask for more." The darkness stays where it is, so I go find Haze.

"How far to go?"

Haze glitches and comes back frowning. "Up a floor, along a corridor." He hesitates. "They're setting up a belt-fed. You want me to help Neen take it?" The boy is shaking, really shaking. Whatever Haze is doing inside his head is obviously killing him.

It's time we changed the rules.

"No," I say. "Leave that to the others. I want you to jack their hiSat system and fix me an off-planet broadcast."

"Who do you want to call, sir?"

"Everyone . . ."

He looks at me, puzzled.

"I want to spam the fucking galaxy," I tell him. "It's got to reach the U/Free. It's got to reach OctoV. It's sure as hell got to reach the Uplifted."

Haze runs with the problem, his thoughts almost visible as he juggles his options and reaches a conclusion he doesn't like. "It's possible," he says. "But I'll have to uncloak you as well."

"Works for me."

"General Duza will be able to see you."

"That's the idea." I grip his shoulders, focusing his attention. Something has just occurred to me. "You know when the Enlightened flick dimensions. How do they do it?"

He feeds the answer straight into my mind. Which fucks me over, because I don't understand a single one of the concepts, until they begin to unravel and my mind scrabbles to keep up with what my unconscious now knows.

I've got levels to my abilities I didn't even realize existed, and I hate this voodoo shit, always have. Give me a gun and give me an enemy and I'll take it to the wire and beyond every time. This Uplift stuff hurts my head, literally.

"Is he okay?"

It's Neen, standing next to me. We seem to be in a different bit of corridor and his rate of fire has slowed to the point that a Silver Fist sticks his rifle around a corner, begins firing, and decides to follow his weapon to see what's happening.

Five different people burn him back to nothing.

"What about that belt-fed?"

Neen looks puzzled. "We killed it." *A while ago* goes unstated.

"Okay," I tell Haze. "Do it in five."

Haze nods.

To Neen I say, "The command is yours."

Neen wants to say something, only Haze is counting seconds down with his fingers and we hit zero before Neen can object. Angel or demon, I'm about to find out which . . .

CHAPTER 51

"THIS IS SVEN TVESKOEG, lieutenant with the Death's Head, Obsidian Cross second class. Half an hour ago a ship commanded by General Duza sank six sister vessels carrying Octovian prisoners on their way to Bhose. I am a soldier, an ex-legionnaire; we expect death. But this was not an act of war, it was not even judicial execution, it was the murder of five thousand disarmed men and women."

I double the figure on instinct.

"A simple check of overhead hiSats will reveal the truth. Unless, of course, these have mysteriously malfunctioned . . . I want to add something else. With me are fifteen survivors, the last living witnesses to this atrocity. We've broken out and armed ourselves. And this bit of the message is for the crew of the *Winter Wind.* Arm yourselves, because we're going to kill every last one of you. And the least you gutless bastards can do is die with a weapon in your hands. Something you didn't allow the bulk of your prisoners . . ."

Neen is staring at me wide-eyed; Shil has her hand over her mouth. Neither is concentrating on the corridor ahead.

"Do your fucking jobs," I tell the two of them.

Their nods are the last thing I see before I vanish.

White light and static, molecules dance like smoke, and colors collapse into each other until all I've got is darkness. This was never going to be easy. Haze is like an echo in my mind and I realize he's shielding me again.

You're there, he says.

"I'm here," I say.

The eleven-braid turns, her jaw dropping with shock. She's tall, older than I expected, with flesh like weathered oak. This woman radiates power, and she's fast.

She's gone before I realize it, a blow from the side knocking me into a wall. She should have used a knife, not her fist, and the wall is gone, somewhere behind me, because I'm outside for the split second it takes me to be somewhere else.

Duza spins, glares at me.

Pulling the trigger, I unleash a blast that rips a wall out of the command center, revealing night winds and rain. As I turn, my SW SIG-37 clears the room of anything that might be human. It's not even intentional.

I'm looking for Duza.

"Behind you," says my gun.

A blast incinerates where I was standing. Only I'm not there, either, because I'm behind Duza nursing a burned hip.

Too slow, I hear my gun say.

Move faster.

As Duza turns at the voice I grab the first of her eleven braids. Electricity sears flesh and glistening bone is revealed where the skin of my palm should be. Swapping hands makes me drop the SW SIG-37, which swears viciously as it hits the floor. But changing hands is instinctive and so is wrapping Duza's braid around my fingers. In the end she simply reaches up and rips the steel plait from her own head.

White light and static.

She's waiting for me when I step through a wall, her pistol already raised. Several things happen simultaneously.

Duza says, "It finishes here." But that's the least of them.

When her finger tightens on the trigger, I hurl my dagger as hard as possible, straight into her face, and she really is as good a shot as people say. I know this because she vaporizes the blade midthrow. *Carbon, chromium, cobalt, manganese, molybdenum, silicon, and vanadium.*

I taste it happen.

And I see it also, only I see it from behind her, which is where I'm now standing. And Duza is right: This is where the thing ends. Wrapping my fingers into a handful of braids, I yank back her head and feel the general flicker frantically as she tries to switch dimensions. Fear, pain, and my grip lock her into place for the few seconds it takes me to hack off her head with her own blade.

And it's true: Her flesh really is hard as old oak.

"This thing you've got for knives," says the gun when I pick it up again. "We need to talk about it sometime."

"SIR?" THE SHOUT comes from Neen.

"Yeah," I say. "It's me."

"You can stop firing, sir," he says. "We've done it."

The Aux take one look at the severed head hanging from my hand and glance at one another. "You might want to lose that, sir," says Neen.

I'm expecting a battle report, numbers lost and injured, what the Aux are doing to lock down any remaining guards or crew, but it's obvious Neen's mind is on other things. As are all their minds.

"Why?" I demand.

"Because," says Haze, "we're about to have visitors."

Shil begins to straighten my uniform, then takes a look at my face and decides to leave it as it is. "Take the gun," she suggests. "Although I'd keep it pointed at the floor."

By now I know who is out there.

"How do I look?"

"Like shit."

"That's *Like shit, sir . . .*"

She snaps a half-mocking salute, then lets her gaze flick to my burned hip. "You want me to battle-dress that first?"

"No," I say. "It'll keep."

We go out together. Not just me and the Aux, but the whole crowd of us, right down to the girls originally chosen to keep the crew amused on their journey to Bhose. We carry a motley collection of daggers, pulse rifles, and pistols, although everyone is careful to keep their blades sheathed and their fingers well away from any firing buttons or triggers.

THE ONE THING you can say for the United Free is that their stick is so unbelievably big, they can afford to speak very softly indeed. You don't need to raise your voice when you can swat whole planets as easily as children can brush away a fly.

Lights illuminate the decks of the *Winter Wind,* although none of us can pinpoint their origin. Some form of force shield is holding back the storm so that rain trickles down invisible walls in the distance. Above the slow waves hovers a vast black oval that shifts slightly until it hangs unsupported next to our ruined deck.

"Attention," shouts Neen.

And as we watch, a sliver of the oval disappears. It doesn't open or slide back or nictitate, it simply vanishes, and a young woman steps onto our deck. She's wearing a simple jacket, ordinary black trousers, and light-colored shoes; somehow the effect is far more elegant than she has the right to expect.

I recognize her immediately.

"Paper Osamu," she says, introducing herself.

We all know that citizens in the Free can replace their bodies and hold back the years, so there's a chance Ms. Osamu is really older than we are, perhaps by centuries. But she looks about Neen's age, which I find disconcerting in someone who goes on to announce herself as newly promoted U/Free ambassador to this section of the outer spiral.

"Which one of you is Sven Tveskoeg?"

I step forward, aware that my injured hip makes me limp.

Readouts in my head tell me we'll be on lenz from the moment the ship arrives until the moment it leaves. So I try to keep my shoulders straight and my chin up, but tiredness makes me stumble and when Paper Osamu shakes my hand it's impossible for me not to wince.

She turns my ruined hand in hers so the burned flesh is visible against the black leather of her glove. "You're injured."

"There's been a battle."

Her mouth twists, which could be the beginnings of a smile. "We heard," she says. "We also piggybacked the local spy sats and you're right, all appear to have suffered the same simultaneous malfunction. However . . ." She pauses, like someone used to public speaking, and that's when I know she's older than she looks.

"We have identified wreckage, also bodies. A U/Free team is collecting evidence as I speak and if what you say is true . . ." She hesitates, for real this time. "And I tend to believe it is, then I will be filing a galactic crime report. Third-degree genocide. You may be called to give evidence."

"You got here fast."

The words leave my mouth before I can catch them.

Paper Osamu smiles. "We have fast ships."

What she means is, *We have ships that rip holes in space and post themselves through nonexistent slots.* Her tone is smug, and her gaze as it scans the deck in front of her is a little too neutral. Any minute now she's going to offer us all the U/Free equivalent of beads and I'm going to lose my temper.

This is not a good idea.

"We've got injured," I say. "Can you spare medical supplies?"

"Are you asking for help?"

Something about Paper Osamu's tone worries me. It's formal. We've entered a negotiation to which only she, and half a trillion others, knows the rules. Unfortunately, we're not among that number.

"Yes," I say, not giving myself a chance to change my mind. "I'm asking for your help."

Slots open in the side of her craft and what exits is dust. Only this is dust that moves under its own power and folds itself around my hand and hip before I can object. Others behind me are also enveloped.

"Stand still," says Paper Osamu. "You'll find it makes things easier."

We're being treated to a full-on presentation of U/Free power. That's when I realize this little scene is being relayed to the Uplifted as well as to Farlight and OctoV's other cities. At the gates of Ilseville, the Enlightened issued a challenge to the Free while making it sound as if the challenge was to OctoV.

This is the reply.

And there's an elegant symmetry in the U/Free using us to warn the Uplifted, just as the Uplifted used us to challenge the U/Free. Something else about politics falls into place for me: Presentation matters.

"Thank you," I say, holding up my newly healed hand. "That's really very impressive."

Paper Osamu's mouth twitches. "Glad you like it," she says. "Is there any other way in which we can help?"

My glance takes in the others, the ruined ship on which we all stand, and the dark swell of a sullen ocean around us. I've had enough of this world. My guess is that we all have.

"If it's okay with you," I say, "we'd quite like a lift off planet."

CHAPTER 52

SIX WEEKS pass before we are released by the United Free. At no time do they suggest we are prisoners or hostages of any kind. We're treated with respect, fed well, given additional medical treatment, and allowed access to a gym and a weight room. Of course we're also kept in isolation and only allowed to see outsiders when we go for medical treatment or questioning.

What I do is dangerous, Paper Osamu tells me.

At first I think she means being a soldier.

She doesn't. She means all that glitching dimensions with the kyp, reading events ahead of them happening, and stealing information from all available sources. It's dangerous, quite possibly illegal. And apparently there's a really good chance that it will kill me.

I'm not to do it while I'm aboard her ship.

All in all I'm interviewed five times. Always by Paper Osamu, although the audience changes. Her ship is somewhere unspecified, but obviously out of our own system.

Everything is so quiet I begin to believe we've slipped through one of those rips in space Haze talks about. When I suggest this to Ms. Osamu, she smiles kindly and talks about self-canceling sound and acoustic engineering. This is the point I decide not to try any of my other theories out on her.

She gives Haze access to the library.

After a few days, at his suggestion, I'm also offered access.

There are ten to the power of twenty-four living stars, beyond counting in any real sense. Dead stars can be the size of small cities or five times bigger than Fort Karbonne's sun. The energy from a single photon released at the center of a star takes a million years to reach that star's surface. A number of stars are actually older than the universe, which suggests levels of complexity not yet understood.

Haze loves it, but then he's rapidly developing into a two-braid. At the end of the day I'm still a fighting machine. All the same, some of the things I learn are interesting, and a few are even useful.

Enlightened technology is illegal within areas claimed by the U/Free, but only because the U/Free regard it as crude and unstable. Personality uploading is perfectly legal for U/Free citizens, as is melding with a hive mind, provided such melding is consensual. Bodily augmentation, either viral or surgical, is commonplace. But nonregulated technology is to be regarded as inherently unsafe, hence the ban.

On instinct, I look up OctoV.

Renegade hive mind, now self-assimilated, reads the entry. OctoV was Uplifted but is now separate. The *Id* to their *Ego*. The entry makes it clear that the Free regard this as a bad thing.

That evening I'm visited by Paper Osamu. She's neatly dressed and intensely professional. If I would like to ask for asylum from the Free she feels certain it would be granted.

I am, apparently, *more than I appear.* Also, *greater than the sum of my parts.* Just listening to this adds to my headache. The idea of exile becomes less attractive when I ask about the Aux.

"Define *aux.*"

"My fighting group . . . Shil, Haze, Neen, Franc, and Rachel. We come as a unit."

Something tells me Paper Osamu is wondering whether offering me asylum is a good idea. Not that she need worry; I refuse as soon as I realize asylum means leaving the others behind.

I ask to see them.

Ms. Osamu tells me this is not possible.

All of us, what remains of the army . . . we're kept separate by rank, corps, and gender, apparently because Paper Osamu believes our social and sexual models of interpersonal relationships are unfair, and does not wish to implicate herself by encouraging hierarchical models while we remain in her care.

Haze says she's a prude, and her announcement that postsexuality is an ideal just means she's so bored by fucking she doesn't want anyone else to enjoy themselves, either. The blush as Haze says this tells me things have gone further between him and Rachel than any of us guessed.

The morning after I'm offered asylum, Paper Osamu wakes me at dawn to tell me to collect my belongings; all of us are being returned to Octovian care. Almost inevitably we're arrested for treason, desertion, and cowardice the moment we step aboard General Jaxx's mother ship.

CHAPTER 53

MY TRIAL is simple and quick, its verdict obvious. A lieutenant I've never met represents me. He barely bothers to see me beforehand.

A colonel sits behind a desk.

He's wearing full uniform, complete with battle ribbons and an Obsidian Cross first class. Braid drips down his chest, because braid always does, and his eyes are as cold as glass. His mouth has a permanent twist, as if he can't stand the stench of treason in that tiny room.

I'm the first to be tried.

The verdict passed on me will apply to all others. This is Death's Head logic and legal precedent: I led the group that took the silverhead ship.

The colonel asks if I understand.

"Yes," I say. "I understand perfectly."

"Read the charge."

The charge is simple. Although Octovian soldiers are expected to fight to the last, we obeyed an order from Colonel Nuevo to surrender. Because our duty to OctoV outweighed all other duties of obedience, this was an act of treason.

"How do you plead?"

"Guilty."

The colonel looks up from his slab, his hand poised over whatever task he was actually doing while the charge was read out. Maybe he was expecting me to plead not guilty.

"Except Colonel Nuevo didn't send the order."

The officer for my defense leans forward. I will be allowed time to make a brief statement, but that comes later. Until then I'm to keep quiet.

Only the colonel has other ideas and it's his courtroom, and he outranks everyone, so when the man decides to question me directly my defense officer sits back in his own chair and keeps his face carefully neutral.

"How do you know he didn't?"

"Because I was there."

The colonel glares at me. "You will address me as *sir.*"

"Why?"

It's worth saying just to see the man's face. Although to his credit, the colonel's lecture on rank, respect, and hierarchy is delivered in a voice that is almost conversational. And when I say *interesting* . . . he carefully ignores the fact that I don't add *sir* to the end of that, either.

"And where was this?"

"Our HQ at Ilseville."

The man checks something on his slab. "You were delivering a message?"

"I was Colonel Nuevo's ADC."

He controls his surprise well. We can go on like this for another five minutes, maybe even half an hour, but I can't see the point. So I decide to simplify things, because that's how life should be lived.

"I sent that order."

The courtroom is quiet. I have their total attention. Admittedly, the officer for the prosecution is almost purple with rage, but since the colonel is silent, he makes himself stay silent, too.

"It was part of a bigger plan."

Officers glance at one another. The colonel checks his slab, and then checks it again. Whatever he's hoping to find isn't on there.

"You are under oath," he reminds me.

My intention was to plead mercy for the Aux and accept all the responsibility myself. Only that stopped being an option when I discovered a judgment on me was a judgment on them. I need a stronger plan.

Putting my fist over my heart, in the old legion sign of respect, I sail dangerously close to the truth, with a few vital changes. "Having signed the order paper, Colonel Nuevo shot himself; Captain Myc followed his example . . . This left us to carry out his original orders."

"Us?" the colonel demands.

"The Aux. Myself, Sergeant Neen, Corporal Shil, and Troopers Rachel and Franc, plus Trooper Maria, who was killed in combat."

He checks his slab. "Your group has one other."

"Haze," I say. "Our intelligence officer."

The colonel leans forward, interested despite himself. Prejudice is a wonderful thing. He's got us down as a bunch of militia led by a renegade officer. Only we took down a silverhead ship and called in the U/Free. And militia groups don't usually worry too much about gathering intelligence.

"You were a lieutenant," he says. "Surrounded by majors and captains. Why would you know this plan?"

"I can't answer that."

"Why not?"

"Because you don't have sufficient security clearance."

Punch the right buttons, use the right words, and even the wildest lies sound real. So real, in fact, that I'm beginning to believe them myself. Something that obviously shows in my face, because the colonel is talking intently to a major who sits just behind him.

"Who can confirm this?"

The entire court, all five officers, know what I'm going to say before I even open my mouth. Just as they know the judgment is no longer theirs.

. . .

SERGEANT HITO ARRIVES to escort me from my cell. I'm not sure which irritates me more, trying to work out what to say to General Jaxx or the sergeant's refusal to answer a single one of my questions.

In the five minutes it takes us to walk from the cell to the elevator, drop fifteen floors, and make our way to the general's office, Hito keeps his silence. He doesn't tell me to shut up or even shake his head; he simply ignores me right up to the point that he knocks on a heavy steel door.

"Enter . . ."

The command is loud enough to be heard clearly in the corridor.

A major I don't recognize looks up, skims his gaze across me, and dismisses Sergeant Hito with a nod. The major is young and rather too aware of his own elegance and I see the sergeant's lips tighten, but he simply salutes, spins on his heel, and leaves me standing in the outer office.

"What's that?" demands the major, staring at the silver sack in my hand.

"A present for the general."

"I'll take it."

"No you won't."

He stares at me, openmouthed at my insubordination. And finally I begin to enjoy myself for the first time in several days. The problem with being boss is there's no one above you to insult.

"Give it to me."

I shake my head.

So he does something very stupid indeed: He draws his gun. Now, I know he's not going to shoot me because that would make General Jaxx very cross, and even this man isn't that dumb. And there's a basic law in combat: Never draw a weapon if you're not prepared to use it.

"Hand it over," he says, holding out his other hand.

I shake my head again.

"I'm warning you."

Laughing isn't my best move, nor is punching the man in the stomach when he tries to club me with his pistol, but having hit him once it seems a pity not to finish the move.

"That will do." The voice is mild, but only a fool would miss the edge of steel that runs beneath it. "Hitting a senior officer is a serious offense."

"Worse than treason?"

General Jaxx looks at me before turning his attention to the major. "You may go," he tells the man. As we both watch, the man holsters his gun and limps from the outer office, being careful to salute the general before he leaves.

"Treason," says the general, "is a nasty thing."

"Yes," I say. "The worst."

"Apparently you killed a Death's Head captain for treason."

Which is how I know he's questioned at least one other survivor before me.

"No one's hurt," says the general, as if reading my mind. "I talked briefly to one of the militia generals."

He smiles, seeing my confusion. "The man disguised himself as a common soldier. Not impressive in my opinion. Although he's very pleased with himself . . . Apparently you killed the captain for insulting OctoV. What did the man say?"

"That our beloved leader is a simple machine."

"And what do you think?"

"Me?" My shrug is careless. "I refuse to believe it."

"That he's a machine?"

"That there's anything simple about OctoV."

The general laughs and pours himself a glass of whiskey from a decanter on a side table. He doesn't offer me one. "Go on," he says.

"Who knows if OctoV is a machine?" I say, pouring a glass of my own. "Or if it matters? I don't do big questions. I do small ones."

"Such as?"

"Can we take that hill? Yes, probably . . . Are the Aux good? Yes, we're fucking excellent . . . Did we win at Ilseville? You bet we did . . . That's my level. I leave the difficult stuff to people like you."

General Jaxx is watching me, very carefully.

And that's fine with me, because every minute he's watching me is a minute he's not ordering my execution. When he reaches the end of his whiskey, I pour him another, and the fact that he lets me get that close makes me feel a tiny bit more confident. Although it may just be that I'm covered by several hundred hidden weapons systems.

To check, I put down my own drink and say, "I'm going to put my hand in my jacket pocket. Is that okay?"

His smile answers my question about those defenses. Part of me wants to scan the room to see what he's got, but I'm not sure that's such a good idea. Haze has suggested I limit my use of the kyp, and his reasons are as convincing as Paper Osamu's. We're deep enough in the shit as it is.

Reaching into my jacket, I find what I want. The folded scrap of paper is authentically filthy, crinkled with sweat, rain, and blood. "This is why we surrendered," I say, putting it on the table between us.

The general unfolds it carefully, reads it once, and then reads it again. A click of his fingers brings an orderly running.

"Verify this," he says.

We wait in silence until the corporal returns. He's looking nervous, which is understandable in the circumstances. "The paper is authentic, the signature genuine. The writing is not Colonel Nuevo's . . ."

"It's mine."

General Jaxx is surprised. "You can write?"

"My old lieutenant taught me."

A wave dismisses the orderly. "So," says the general. "You expect me to believe that Colonel Nuevo lost Ilseville intentionally . . . as part of a greater plan. But that you were the only officer he told?"

I nod.

The general laughs. "I imagine," he says, "this is the point I'm meant to ask what's in your pretty little silver sack."

"Except you already know."

He shakes his head. "Free technology," he says. "Beyond our scanners."

"Then how do you know it's not a bomb?"

General Jaxx looks at me as if I'm an idiot. "Because Paper Osamu gave her word you'd be returned to me unharmed and unarmed. She also gave me a gun, which she insisted belongs to you."

"It does."

"Yes," says the general. "That's what the gun says."

He nods at the sack in my hand. "We'll be taking that bag later, as I'm sure our friend Colonel Madeleine will want to play." He names the old woman who made me my new arm.

"How is she?"

"Same as she's been for the last two hundred years. Annoying, but brilliant." Cool eyes examine me. "She likes you. I doubt you realize how unusual that is."

And I remember this man is supposed to like me, too. Someone said that months back, Sergeant Hito possibly. "Sir . . . the Free offered me asylum."

I thought that would get his attention.

"And you refused?"

"Yes, sir."

"Already knowing the penalty for surrender?" The man's sigh is deep, almost irritated.

"I killed a three-braid."

Blue eyes turn to watch me.

"Then I killed a seven, only I had to leave his head in a bucket, because it seemed stupid to bring it with me on the march. So there goes my proof."

"Asylum and two dead braids . . . You know," says the general, "I almost believe you."

"But I did bring this."

He takes my bag and winces at the stink as he loosens its drawstring. "Another one?" There's no need for me to answer, because he's already extracting the contents, holding the rotting skull by the braids.

"Shit," he says. "Xantro . . . Tamdell?" The general looks puzzled. "Where did you get this?"

"Killed it, just before the U/Free arrived."

"This is a ten-braid," he says. "What was a high political doing aboard that ship?"

"Used to have eleven snakes, sir," I tell the general. "One of them got torn off during the fight."

"Duza?"

I nod, watching glee flood his eyes.

Politics is a weirdshit thing. The implications have escaped me, but I've got them now. The surrender at Ilseville hurts the general as much as it does us. Of course, he's not actually dead like most of the drop, but he's damaged in the eyes of OctoV, and damaged in the eyes of OctoV is not a good place to be.

"Let me get this clear. You killed General Duza?"

"Yes."

"How?"

"Cut off her head."

"*Sir,*" he says. "That's *Yes, sir . . . Cut off her head, sir.*"

Then Jaxx is laughing loud enough to startle me. "Ah, Tveskoeg," he says. "What will we do without you?"

Without me?

"You'll find someone else . . . sir."

"Indeed I will," he says.

EPILOGUE

GOLDEN MEMORIES is almost empty when we walk through the door. A handful of half-dressed girls sit in one corner chatting. Per Olson, the man from the breaking yard, is at a table with his son, who's dismantling a spider bot with the single-minded intensity that only small boys can bring to such tasks.

Lisa sees me first.

And then Lisa sees the Aux behind me. Maybe it's the sight of us all; maybe something in Shil's eyes warns her that things have changed. Whichever, Lisa's both a survivor and a quick learner. She walks across the barroom and kisses me carefully on both cheeks.

"It's been a while."

"Yeah," I say. "Longer than I expected. How's my niece doing?"

Niece . . . ? Shil's eyes flick to my face. The others are content just to listen.

"Helping Angelique."

A memory of Lisa and her cousin floods my mind . . . they're naked and slightly drunk and very very willing. I try to shake it away.

"What, sir?" Franc demands.

"Old memories," I tell her.

"It gets better," says Haze, and I'm grateful for his interruption. "Like the headaches. You'll lose the feedback soon."

Shil scowls, because we've agreed not to talk about this stuff in public. Only Golden Memories isn't *in public,* and I probably need to let Lisa know that. The Aux know already, though they're puzzled by my reasons. Mind you, as I'm beginning to learn, that's not always a bad thing.

"Lisa . . ."

"Yeah?"

Gesturing at the group around me, I say, "These are the Aux. As of now, they own this bar."

"He owns it," says Shil firmly.

"Ignore her," I say, to Neen's obvious amusement. "We own it among us, also the café next door and the lodging house beyond. You will be running this bar."

Lisa looks like she wants to hug me.

Shil, on the other hand, looks cross. There's something I'm missing about Shil's unhappiness, but I can't work out what it is. We got a bounty for killing Duza; this is what I'm spending it on. She ought to be pleased to have a base and somewhere to call home.

"Lisa . . . ?" Someone calls from the street outside, and two girls come tumbling through the door, clutching a basket between them. It's hot and damp out there, and Farlight's heat has glued tendrils of hair to their faces and left their skin shiny with exhaustion.

"Sven," says Angelique.

Sticky arms wrap themselves around me, and her kiss only just misses my mouth. And then she sees Shil's scowl and disengages, although I suspect it's too late. But I'll deal with that later, because my eyes are on the girl standing frozen in the doorway.

"Won't be a moment," I tell the others.

Aptitude has grown up. It would be wrong to say she belongs here, but she's no longer the spoiled child I dragged from a burning building, having just killed her entire family. Well, the bits of it that weren't locked down on a prison planet.

"I didn't think you were coming back."

Her voice is quiet, so quiet that I have to strain to hear it myself, and I'm standing almost directly opposite.

She puts out a hand to shake.

I put out my own.

Her fingers are sticky with sweat and callused from hard work. A twist of gold circles one finger; her ring is cheap but pretty, something she bought for herself from a local market. "Sven," she says.

"Aptitude."

We look at each other.

"I will always come back," I say. "I promised Debro and Anton that I'd look after you, and I will."

And suddenly she's crying in my arms, childlike sobs that shake her shoulders and rasp in her throat. *"I didn't think you were coming back."*

"And I've told you."

"I know, *but I didn't think . . .*" She wipes her nose with the back of her hand, then sees the mess she's made of my jacket and looks as if she's about to burst into tears all over again.

It's Shil who walks over to give the girl a tissue. "I'm Shil," she says. "I take it you know this lunatic?"

Aptitude smiles despite herself.

Shil glances at the bar, at the dampness on my shoulder, and then at Aptitude. She's putting things together. "That's what the fuck this is about?"

I nod.

She sighs. "Why didn't you tell me?"

SHIL AND I kill a bottle of cachaca that night, sitting under a pine tree in the yard out back. She asks if I've fucked Angelique and I admit I have. So she asks if I intend to do it again and I tell her that's not the way I work, which ends up with me having to tell her how I do work. Something that is trickier than I thought, since I hadn't put it into words before.

She doesn't ask about Lisa, so I leave that confession well alone.

Shil's so drunk I get to know more than I want about what happened to the boy she was meant to marry. Death in battle sounds a lot better to me by the end of it.

And then we talk about Aptitude.

Shil has her head on my shoulder, although that's probably just the drink. The fan in the bar is chugging in a lazy swirl and the night noises of this strange city are distant enough to sound less threatening than they should.

"You haven't . . ."

Turning, I look at her. "Aptitude's a kid."

"I know men who would."

"Yeah, but that's not the point."

"You want to tell me what the point is?"

And so I end up telling Shil about being locked down on Paradise. I don't tell her whose child Aptitude is, because she doesn't need to know. But I make it clear that she's the daughter of two people who matter to me and I've promised to protect her.

"This isn't where she grew up, is it?"

My gaze takes in the darkened yard, the broken hover bike in the corner, and the bundle of fur and bone watching us from the top of the wall. Apparently Aptitude's adopted a stray cat.

"No," I say. "Where she grew up is a million miles from here."

"Thought so."

Before we finally fall asleep where we sit, Shil asks me one last question. It's about my meeting with General Jaxx, which happened three days earlier.

"What did he want?"

"He wants us to take it easy and enjoy our vacation."

She scowls at me.

"I'm serious," I tell her.

"Maybe, but what does he actually want?"

This isn't a conversation I've been planning to have, at least not until the end of next month, which is when we're due to present ourselves at an elegant building in an area of Farlight that really is a million miles distant in every way that matters from the clapboard boardinghouse in which we now live. But I'm drunk and Shil's leaning against my shoulder and I still can't get over the answer myself.

"The Free want to borrow us."

"They what?"

"You heard me. Apparently, Paper Osamu asked for us by name. We'll be told why when we present ourselves at their embassy in five weeks' time."

"We're working for the U/Free?"

"Yeah," I say. "That's the plan . . ." A request from the U/Free is as good as a command from anyone else. And they're rich, filthy rich. Seems to me it won't hurt if some of that wealth rolls in this direction. Taking another gulp of cachaca, I swallow the fiery spirit before passing Shil the bottle.

"Drink up," I say.

She does as ordered.

ABOUT THE AUTHOR

Smartly dressed, resourceful, and discreet, DAVID GUNN has undertaken assignments in Central America, the Middle East, and Russia (among numerous other places). Coming from a service family, he is happiest when on the move and tends not to stay in one town or city for very long. Gunn lives in the United Kingdom, and this is his first novel.